Worst Case Scenario...

Stunned by the body-blow, Deena clutched the envelope of evidence to her chest.

Stunned as well by the face peering down—a face she remembered too darn well.

Dark hair verging on black that failed to show any tell-tale grey. Thick and tousled from running his fingers through it—she remembered that signature action all too well, just as she remembered wanting to run her fingers through it.

Heck, she wanted to now.

Eyes, searing blue and right now narrowing in suspicion above high cheek bones that looked just a little too drawn with fatigue.

Hands found her shoulders, steadied her. Tall as she remembered. Broad shouldered. He hadn't gone soft around the middle like so many men of—my god—he must be almost forty-five to her forty. And still with that mouth that always seemed to slide into a slightly mocking grin to hide what he really felt. Right at the moment it wasn't doing that too well.

He looked almost speechless.

"Is this some kind of joke?" Deena snapped, pulling back and fighting the frisson of excitement that Rich Webster's presence had always evoked in her.

"No," the low growl of his voice sent a sensual shiver up her spine. "No joke. *You're* the D. Hunter on the last incident report. Well I'll be damned."

BOOKS BY THE AUTHOR

Romance
Ashes and Light
Shades of Moonlight
Judas Kiss
Second Spring
A Different Nightmusic
Shadow Play
Mutable Things
Surviving Safe Harbor
Coming Down Christmas

Fantasy
The Cartographer Universe series:
The Cartographer's Daughter

Afterburn
Aftershock
Aftermath
Afterimage

Terra Incognita
Terra Infirma
Terra Nueva

Also by the Author
Emberstone
Ice Dragon
The Crystal Courtesan

JUDAS KISS

Karen L. Abrahamson

Dedicated to the women in policing and corrections.

Acknowledgements:

Well-deserved thanks to the writers of the Oregon Writer's network and to all the co-workers in Corrections who taught me so much.

Chapter 1

THE TWO-STORY, WHITE metal ceiling of the living unit echoed the sound of running feet as Senior Correctional Officer Deena Hunter swiftly climbed the stairs to the second level tier of cells. Below her, in the main living unit area, were the pool table and vacant plastic couch and chairs that were the daytime habitat of the inmates. At night they were locked in their cells, or holes—as the guards called them. Inmate faces pressed up against the small door windows, their palms beat a tattoo on their doors as she passed towards her destination.

The stench of sweat and death met Deena at the cell door and she knew the story even before she saw the inmate inside. It was a small room, a single bunk against the far wall, a desk and tiny cupboard to the right of the door and a sink and toilet to her left. That was the inmate's life was reduced to. Two Correctional Officers working the prone figure on the narrow bunk kept up the CPR like a well-oiled machine. They'd deserve a commendation for this, because the EMTs were taking way too long to get here and that left her men doing exhausting duty over the body way too long.

"You want relief? Heywood can take over." She nodded at the big redhead behind her. The cream-colored concrete walls echoed with the two men's efforts.

Chad Preston, young and good looking in a body-builder kind of way, looked at her as he air-bagged the inmate. Amarjit Sandhu, slim, but athletic, straddled the body administering chest compressions.

"We'll manage."

"Good man." She turned to the big redhead who had been on staff at this center far longer than her. He'd responded to the call for backup from Sandhu. Beyond him, along the tier, inmate faces pressed against the narrow plexi-glass panels in the other cell doors. "Heywood, get the camera, would you?"

With a nod he shifted along the concrete upper walkway back to the stairs in that smooth, silent, ground-eating way that made him such a great 'prowl' man—conducting bed-checks during staff coffee breaks, checking perimeter. She wanted this recorded. The whole scene before the Emergency Medical Technicians arrived.

Behind her she heard the newbie she'd assigned to scene preservation urging the corrections staff who had gathered in the living unit to get back to their units and get the day underway. The kid had solid potential even if she had that thousand yard stare after seeing her first suicide. Damn good potential given how she'd put herself back together. Something familiar about her, Deena realized.

She glanced at the cell number and back at the figure on the bed, tangled in bedclothes. Cell 22. She didn't recall anyone assigned to cell 22 and usually she knew where all the inmates were assigned. Must be a new admission.

"Who is it?"

"Stickley. Jim." Sandhu brought her attention back to the cell as he grunted into another compression. The airbag hissed. Sandhu eased his shoulders before leaning in again. Chad kept up the air bagging, counting off the numbers.

The name caught Deena off-guard. Jim Stickley. A low-rent conman who'd been picked up for running a bank card scam at one of the local gas stations. He'd been caught with a little electronic device that read pin numbers and copied card data at a frequently used bank machine. He'd been picked up before he could use the data, but other material found at his home had shown how long he'd been working the scam at various machines around the Vancouver area. You could almost admire his staying power.

He'd been one of Deena's best snitches, even if he was a bit of a bug to the other inmates. And he'd been on her appointment list for today. That caused an uneasy stir in her belly. She looked back at the body, the tangle of bedding.

"How?"

Chad looked up from the airbag. "Sandhu here found him when he first came on the unit. Had his shoelaces caught around his throat. He must have been pretty determined."

Sandhu nodded. "He must have tied them off tight himself and then just laid there and died."

Deena looked back at the bedding. It could have been torn up like that, she supposed—if he had second thoughts after he'd begun to choke. But then surely to god he'd have been able to get the knots undone or to have called for help. And there was something about the room she just didn't like.

Stickley, for all he was a con, was a good con with neat habits even if his cell smelled like every other inhabited, enclosed space. He always had his hair combed, his prison uniform neat and he was meticulous in his cleanliness. She'd expect that tidiness to transfer to his cell as well, but instead the small space was a bit of a disaster with clothing falling on the floor from his half-open cupboard, and his desk covered in a cascade of papers. She bent down, peered under the bed.

Photos torn from the wall, tape still attached. Maybe bad news from home? Her gaze locked on Stickley's runners neatly under the head of the bed. Velcro closures and her skin went cold.

They'd been a special request, she remembered, because he needed a shoe that would fit his prescription orthotic insoles.

Her gaze traveled back to the bed as the two Corrections staff kept working the body. Heywood returned, hefting the video camera. She stepped aside to let him film.

"Control, we got an ETA on the Ambulance? I've got two staff here who are gonna need life support themselves pretty soon," she said into her radio.

"Checking." A moment of silence and then: "They're just pulling into Sentence Management Unit. I'm cracking the doors."

Click-buzz below her and she knew a long string of doors across the breadth of cross-shaped Hatzic Regional Correctional Center—The Hat to those who worked here - were sitting open and staff were escorting the ambulance gurney through at a run.

She turned back to Heywood. "Get everything, the condition of the locker, the desk and his shoes on the floor." She scanned the bed. "Chad, those the laces?" She motioned at a tangled pile near the head of the bed.

Chad nodded. "I cut 'em off when I got here and we cracked the door."

She grabbed the laces off the floor and tucked them into an envelope she always kept in her breast pocket for just such occasions. The police would want to take a look, as would the coroner. "What were you doing here, Chad? You were in my office and then you were here. You're assigned to E2, aren't you?"

Chad nodded and glanced at Amarjit. "Sandhu had just checked the unit. When he called it in, I was just heading into E2. I responded."

Deena looked him up and down. It was prowl's responsibility to respond, not another living unit officer's, but it was pretty typical that the guys would back each other up.

"Good man."

A crash and cursing behind her interrupted. Deena stepped back on the walkway. Half way up to the stairs, where the risers turned back on themselves, the ambulance gurney had caught between the walls and wasn't budging. The EMT staff were swearing and trying to get their equipment back down the stairs. Finally they gave up, climbed over the gurney and dragged equipment up to the cell.

"Name's Stickley, Jim. Found at approximately zero six ten. CPR underway since that time." She stepped out of the way and the two EMT's tested vitals. One took over from Sandhu and he, his partner and Chad hefted Stickley onto a stretcher one of the unit staff had passed over the still-stuck gurney. It gave Deena a chance to see Stickley's face.

She didn't like what she saw. His eyes, even dead, held the shocked look of fear—as if he hadn't planned this, as if he'd been surprised. Sure, death always surprised, but this was something more, as if it was the means of his death he couldn't believe. She stepped back as the EMT's started to move.

"Hey, get that gurney out of there," she yelled down to the newbie and McGuin—a long-time officer. McGuin handed the evidence and personnel log to the newbie and went to lend his strength to the fight to get the gurney free. Another damned design flaw in the Center—after seven years of operation they were still finding them. No way in hell it should have been build in a way that didn't allow emergency access.

The gurney came loose with a squeal of metal and the EMTs and Chad hauled Stickley down and placed him onto the rolling stretcher. The one EMT rode to continue the compressions on the race to the

Ambulance. The living unit was suddenly quiet except for the shouts of the other inmates still in their cells.

Deena blew her blonde hair back from her face. She took the camera from Heywood. "You get it all?"

"Think so."

"Including that flippin' mess on the stairs?"

He nodded. She hefted the camera and filmed a couple more frames of the cell now that it was empty. The bedding was wadded strangely at the head of the bed, but the things that were the most strange were under the bed.

She crouched down to film the shoes and the photos torn from the walls. Stickley's wife, who'd stuck with him while he was doing his deuce less a day, her photo laid on the floor under the edge of the bed with a clear footprint across her face.

Not something Stickley would have done. Not unless things had changed between he and his wife. She picked the photo up by its edges and showed it to Heywood. "What'd'you think?"

Heywood shrugged. "Maybe he got some bad news from home. It happens."

The big man was right. It happened way too often. But Stickley was going to be released in less than a month. He'd told her about his plans when he'd last had an opportunity to talk to her alone. In fact, he'd been caging for some money in exchange for his information because he was hoping to take his wife for a little holiday in Reno. Or so he'd said.

She looked back at the room and felt someone come up behind her.

"Watcha got?" Mitch Digneault, Deputy Warden of Operations, short, round and cherubic.

Deena shook her head.

"Something's not fitting." And being an orderly person she didn't like it when that happened. Liked it even less when it happened on her shift and when her shift hadn't been running the way it should have been. She closed her eyes at the disastrous morning. Running late because of her very sick kitty. Car covered with toilet paper as a gag for her birthday. And then the party her staff had thrown when she arrived. It had all conspired to make her late in getting her crew out to the units.

She hated messy and this was messy with a capital M.

She motioned to the photo, the shoes, held up the laces. "See what I mean?"

"Something." A slow nod of concern as she thunked the cell door shut. Digneault got it. He was her ally in her demand for excellence.

"Control, Hunter. Lock down E1 22 for police evidence collection."

"Roger that, Hunter." She listened for the shudder and click as bolts slid into place and walked with Digneault and Heywood down to the main floor.

"Hell of a thing," the big man muttered. "I hate hangers."

"And I hate the impact it has on everyone. Briefing notes all round for me," Digneault said. "Morning's shot."

He went to leave.

"Boss?" He stopped at the door. "Just so you know. Chad Preston and Amarjit Sandhu—they did a fine job of CPR this morning."

A single nod and she knew it was duly noted. That was the thing she admired about Mitch Digneault. He practiced management-by-walking-around; it gave him a chance to know his staff and to recognize a job well done. He would remember, too. Like an elephant, Mitch Digneault.

Then he was gone, leaving Deena to accept custody of the personnel and evidence log from McGuin. She glanced at the newbie again. Underhill. The familiarity clicked in. Still small framed, and with the size of the bun on the back of her head, still with that enviable Rapunzel hair.

"Anita Underhill, have I got it right?"

The newbie looked her straight on, her gaze clear and determined and Deena remembered that look far to well, then suddenly the gaze softened and recognition and remembrance flooded in.

"Dee? Dee Hunter?"

"In the flesh."

"But you went into the RCMP..."

Deena shrugged. "Ancient history, now." Out of the corner of her eye she saw McGuin and Heywood look at each other. Her history in the RCMP was well known and still a matter of some resentment amongst some of the career Correctional Officers, because she'd risen so fast in the Correctional Service ranks. "I've been here what—seven years. Since the Center opened."

She could see that Anita was getting all ready to have a fluttery reunion and Deena just didn't have the time or the tolerance to join in, in the midst of her correctional center. Deena slapped her on the shoulder and hoped the kid would get the hint.

"Good to see you again, Little Sister. And good job today." She nodded at Heywood. "She hold together okay?"

"Pretty good, actually."

Deena grinned. "This old galoot don't show it, but he knows this jail better than anyone. Been around since Hector was a pup and he's the one as showed me the ropes, too. If he says you're doing pretty good, you can say you had a good day."

Then time demanded she get back to business. "McGuin, I want you to hold the fort here in E1 so Sandhu can go get debriefed and get his report written. I'll call in another auxiliary to backfill programs for you until the auxiliary arrives. Heywood, you get back on prowl so we don't get too behind with break and lunch relief. Take Underhill with you, but make sure she gets time to get her report on the incident written up while it's still fresh. Got it?"

"'Course."

He headed out, Underhill in his wake. Deena blew a sigh up through the spray of her bangs. She'd hang around here a few minutes before heading back to her office.

"Control, Hunter."

"Got you Hunter."

"You can open unit E1 for the day."

"Roger that. E1 opening."

Buzz-click and the cell doors unlocked and twenty three pissed-off inmates in various states of undress pushed out of their rooms for the showers.

Their grumbling was nothing unusual—actually it wasn't bad at all given their day had been delayed by about—she checked her watch—a half an hour.

A half an hour and a man was dead on her watch. She nodded at McGuin and waved her card at the hip-high electric scanner to get through the door. Buzz-click and she stepped through the heavy metal door into the wide concrete hall replete with the scent of man-sweat no air-con could ever completely wipe away. She headed back to her office making sure she looked confident. You had to, when you never knew when you were picked up on the cameras that saw most of what went on in the Center.

The trouble was, they didn't film what went on in the living units or the inmate cells, and she was pretty sure whatever had happened to Jim Stickley hadn't been something he planned.

Nope. Today was a day of surprises and someone had sure'nuff surprised Jim Stickley. She just had to figure out who.

Hell of a way to celebrate her fortieth birthday.

Chapter 2

CORPORAL RICH WEBSTER pulled his unmarked police cruiser into the curb and looked up at the sun-lit, white-trimmed, blue-stained house. His house—or what used to be his house before he separated from Ivy.

Looking at the fine stonework around the patio at the front of the two–story structure, and the white fence that surrounded the acreage and the matching sky-blue barn, made him clench his fists on the steering wheel. He was the one that laid that stone, that built that barn, that hand-dug the post holes and built and painted that fence with skills his Dad had taught him.

Not that it mattered a damn bit when it came to the separation of family assets.

Ivy had been so hell-bent on self destruction and so damn heartbroken at the thought of leaving the marital home, he'd given in and if not legally, he'd at least mentally signed away the farm. He'd caused her enough pain so it was her home now.

Showed it, too. The lawn was overgrown and filled with platter-sized dandelions, the paint was peeling from the fence posts—it should have been repainted last summer—would have been if he'd still owned the place. Boards were down around the barn and the in the unforgiving sunlight, the house looked like wood needed re-staining. Hell, he'd even been tempted to offer to do the work, because Ivy just wasn't capable of taking care of the place. She never had been, he realized now, and the thought saddened him.

Once he'd thought she really would do what she'd said and keep house, be his wife, and train that big galoot of a horse he'd bought her well enough to compete in the Western Canadian Dressage Competition.

Instead, she'd crawled into her bottle and the expensive piece of horseflesh stood out in the middle of a well-gnawed pasture. The truth about Ivy McCloud, Rich had learned far too late. She couldn't take care of herself, let alone a husband, let alone a marriage or a horse or a cat. Hell, the woman could kill a cactus—had almost killed something deep inside him.

Rich swung his long frame out of the car holding onto that thought because every time he dealt with Ivy he was left with a profound sense of grief. For the mistake of his marriage, for what might have been, but most of all for the bright, shiny woman he had married after the right one got away. The Ivy he married wasn't ever coming back and he'd realized five years ago he had to move on.

He had, he kept telling himself, but he still felt responsibility for the small-town nurse he'd married and the fact that she seemed to know she hadn't been 'the right one' even though he'd gone through with the marriage. That knowledge had sent her over the edge.

At the front door he knocked, then ran his hands through his heavy black hair. Hadn't even combed it. Finally he used his key to let himself in.

"Ivy?" Ivy had called thirty minutes ago, half in her cups, and it was pretty likely she wasn't going to be in any better state now.

No answer.

"Ivy? It's me. You wanted me to come over." Just what he was doing here was the million dollar question and the one his partner Chuck Kozloff asked with his eyes every time he heard that Rich got a call from his ex. 'She's your ex, for god's sake,' he'd always say. But after eight years of marriage Rich had gotten used to rescuing Ivy all the time.

Even now, it was a habit he hadn't been able to break. Ivy needed him and, well, who else did she have?

Who else did he have?

The darkened house smelled of old kitchen garbage. He checked the living room with its oversized sofa they'd chosen together—because it seated lovers comfortably. Stained now. The huge stone fireplace Rich had installed himself yawned empty as the he felt beyond the once cream-colored carpet.

No sign of her in the dining room or kitchen either, though there was a broken glass and wine spatter on the white tile floor. Not a good sign.

Steeling himself, Rich headed for the stairs. When he had to go up it meant that Ivy had either not gotten out of bed, or had gone back to it. Either way she was falling into one of her heavy depressions.

What had once been their master bedroom complete with sitting area stood disheveled and empty of Ivy and reeking of over-sweet booze, but the light was on in the bathroom beyond. Rich stood there, tallying the bottles on dresser and bedside table, the clothing heaped in the corners and asking himself—again - just what he was doing here.

Sure he was responding to Ivy's frantic call. But why not the crisis center? Why not her friends?

He was trained to do this.

At least that was what he told himself. He crossed filthy carpet and shoved at the bathroom door. It barely budged, but vomit-stench assaulted his nose.

"Ivy?" Still nothing, and now his skin prickled in cop-sign that something was even more wrong than usual.

He pushed the door and something gave behind it, allowing him to see long, bare legs tangled in a faded blue bathrobe on the floor. Stay cop-cool.

"Shit, Ivy, what have you done now?"

He shoved the door harder and pushed into the large bathroom.

Ivy Webster—once Ivy McCloud - was a lovely woman when Rich met her. Petite and dark with flowing black hair and blood-red lips in a pale face; he'd been drawn to her haunted eyes from the first time they met in a Lethbridge, Alberta emergency room. She'd capably sewed up a knife wound he'd received taking down a crystal meth dealer on a local Indian Reserve.

The woman half-braced against the door wasn't that Ivy. Long hair was a tangled mat around her flaccid face, her lips pale as the rest of her, and her eyes closed, lost behind weirdly caked lashes. There was none of the vibrancy that attracted him. None of the life, either. Just vomit down her front. If she'd been prone she'd have asphyxiated. He went cop-cold, but he was on his knees in an instant.

"Ivy?" He caught her wrist. Found a thready pulse. "Ivy, wake up."

He tapped her cheeks and she frowned and pulled away.

"Damn it, Ivy." Seriously concerned, now, he scanned the bathroom, his gaze catching on an open pill bottle. She'd been depressed, but she'd never tried suicide before, even if she had a penchant for the dramatic. He grabbed the bottle, scanned the label: Seconal.

"Damn, Ivy, what did you go and do this for?"

He dialed 911 on his cell phone, telling dispatch his location and to get the Emergency Med Techs out here ASAP. He should be headed to work himself. The quiet of the shift change was when he got most of his paperwork done, but that wasn't going to happen today. Already he could hear the ambulance sirens in the distance; the EMT Hall wasn't far away.

"Hang on there, Ivy. Help's on its way." He hauled her up with her arm over his shoulder then began to half-drag, half-walk her around the room. Christ, she was thin, too thin. Her flesh had almost melted from her bones as if she hadn't eaten in far too long. Her robe fell open, revealing jutting hipbones and ribs and desiccated breasts. One handed he tugged her robe decently closed.

The walking didn't have much effect. Whatever she'd taken had had time to take hold. Hell, maybe she'd taken it before she called him. Or maybe after he'd been pissed off at the early morning phone call and told her he no longer was at her beck and call.

That shook the cop-cool, even though he knew he couldn't own Ivy's illness. Even though he'd learned he couldn't rescue her. She had to want to quit the drinking and the drugs—just as she had to learn she was a worthwhile person in her own right. It didn't take a man in her life to give her a reason to live. Or it shouldn't.

At least that was what he'd told her.

"Come on, Ivy. Stay with me." At least her limbs were moving.

"Rich." It came out as a whisper from the battered face she turned to him. "You came. You always come."

She faded away again as the sirens switched off at the front of the property. He heard the thump of the ambulance doors, the clatter of the stretcher and the heavy footsteps as the EMTs pushed in the front door.

Rich half-carried Ivy to the bedroom door. "Upstairs. Second door on your right."

The footsteps came closer and Jack Collins, long time Fraser Valley EMT pushed in the bedroom door. He was a big man, solid, with a set of blazing blue eyes under a shock of almost white hair. His gaze widened when he saw Rich. The world of emergencies was pretty small in this part of Greater Vancouver and all the EMTs and cops knew each other and went to the same parties. Following him came a slight-framed, thirty-something, brunette named Erin Acted, who'd been Collins partner for the past five years.

Rich handed Ivy off to them, then held out the empty pill bottle. "My ex. Seconal. Overdose, probably."

"Shit man, I'm sorry." Collins shook his head as they lowered Ivy onto the gurney and began checking vitals—airways, breathing, cardiovascular.

"Don't be. It's been a long time coming. Surprised she didn't try it before." He sagged down on the edge of the disheveled bed as Collins and Acted went through their routine.

Why hadn't he come right over when Ivy called? He knew she was depressed. Hell, she called when she *needed* him.

Trouble was, she needed him all the time these days—to the point where her incessant calls were getting in the way of his work and his life. He'd actually been with someone when she called and that just made this whole thing worse. But he needed his own life, damn it.

"How bad is it?"

"Not great," Acted said as she made sure the IV tubes were clear and began dragging the gurney toward the door.

"She'll pull through, Rich. We'll get her to the hospital in time." Collins gave Rich's shoulder a reassuring pat on the way past and Rich trailed after them down the stairs, held the front door for them and watched them trundle Ivy aboard and take off under lights and siren. It wasn't a relief.

"More like purgatory," he mumbled as the wail faded.

Grasshoppers hummed in the field, sparrows and chickadees chattered in tall cedar hedge by the driveway, and Majority Report gave a snort and blow from the field where he stood next to the water tough.

Rich stepped out into the heating, late-August morning and looked at the horse. White blaze, dark brown with two white hind socks that Ivy had told him made the animal's movements look more dynamic and flashy.

Looked like a horse to him.

Majority Report—stupid name for a horse—snorted again and tossed his head and Rich recognized the horse's problem. Ivy hadn't filled the water trough - in how many days?

Rich trudged across the overgrown lawn, kicking at the dandelions and scattering grasshoppers in front of him. Barn looked downright dilapidated even though Ivy had told him she'd leased it out a while back, and that expensive horse had too many ribs showing through that shiny hide of his.

The big metal basin had rust flaking the dry bottom. He tried brushing them out with his palm because he might not know horses, but he knew clean water was what he'd prefer. Finished, he twisted the knob for the water and it came off in his hand.

Water geysered into the sky, soaking Rich. The hard blast of water spooked Majority Report. He squealed, leapt away, snorted. Then thirst overcame caution and the horse dove his nose into the surging water in the trough and drank.

Rich stood there dripping and turning the faucet knob over in his hand and trying to see the ridiculousness of his situation. It helped diffuse the helpless fury.

Typical. Try to help someone and look what it got you—they got they wanted and he got hosed.

He really needed to focus on his own needs for a change.

Chapter 3

THE SENIOR CORRECTIONAL Officer's office was an eight by ten square and filled to the brim with the single desk shared by the three shift commanders, the well-worn wooden SCO chair behind the desk and the lone chair on the wrong side of the desk for staff who had, shall we say, a problem. No windows, recycled air and bulletin boards covered with job postings, union advisories and too many operational orders made Deena sometimes wonder just what the heck she was doing with her life. Sometimes it felt like *she* was the one in prison.

Today the feeling was worse. Taking bad news to the Warden was not something any Correction staff liked to do, but taking bad news to Ravi Sandhar was something Deena avoided like the plague. Taking bad news with no more than suspicions to support it was even worse. Let her take the bad stuff to Mitch who, regardless of his hard-assed attitude to staff, she could face down with clear eyes and clear conscience.

Sandhar, on the other hand, was a constant reminder of Deena's one inglorious failure. Well, maybe one of her two failures, her marriage being the other one.

She leaned back in her creaking office chair, and looked down at the stack of reports on her scarred oak desk. All were pretty darn good because her staff knew she wouldn't accept anything less. Even Chad Preston's.

Nope, this time around it was Deena who'd screwed up—by allowing her crew to linger in the shift change. She shouldn't have allowed the birthday party—not when she was barely on time for work as it was. Not even when the party was a sign of her crew's respect for her. Heck, some of Matt Jaeger's night shift crew had almost smirked at the fact she'd come in so late.

She grimaced remembering the comment about wanting to see if she was a superwoman—could ADW Hunter fly here if her car was out of commission? That had been Chad with his movie-star dimples—her own crew.

Well, in a Correctional Center rife with undercurrents, innuendo and back-stabbing, respect—even grudging—was as good as it got. And even with respect there were those who liked to test the limits.

But she refused to have a shift of officers who completed logs with the oft-used refrain of 'good shift, no problems'. Give her details, specifics. After ten years as a cop, generalities weren't good enough. She'd trained up her shift crew as she'd been trained up, and they were good damn it. But one of the reports was outstanding—almost as good as Deena's own.

A soft knock came at her door and her chair complained as she strightened. "Come in."

Anita Underhill cautiously stepped inside. She was a tidy little thing, with her long blonde hair coiled behind her head, her neat features with the button nose Deena recalled, but right now there was a little uncertainty in her eyes.

"You wanted to see me?"

"Yeah." She nodded at the chair facing her. "Have a seat."

The wide eyes said Anita was just as likely to bolt, but then she seemed to make up her mind and seated herself, her legs crossed at the ankles, her hands lightly clasped in her lap, just like the little church-going girl Deena remembered. God, it seemed like only yesterday.

"So how long's it been?" Deena rested her hands on top of the stack of reports as she studied Anita.

"About fifteen years." Anita said it with the sweet grin she'd always had a kid and Deena felt herself soften towards the woman, and then caught herself.

"I thought it was closer to eighteen. A lot of water under the bridge since then." It made Deena feel old and a little bit proud. The little kid she'd been a Big Sister to, who she'd hooked up to volunteer at the local vet clinic, now all grown up. Maybe she'd had a little influence on the girl, given where they were sitting. "How's your Dad?"

"Pretty good. Still ornery and set in his ways, but he's getting close to retirement and is thinking about buying an RV and seeing the country like he always wanted to. I keep telling him to go, but he's hanging around because he doesn't want to leave me on my own. He's gonna flip when I tell I'm working for you."

A grin managed to quirk Deena's lips. "Still trying to protect you, huh. He always did wonder if I was a good influence."

Anita shook her head in a charming look of frustration that all kids seemed to have about their parents. "He still thinks I'm a kid." Then a kid's grin lit her face. "Remember that rainy weekend when we went camping at Alouette Lake? There was no one there so you and I were prancing around in our bathing suits in the pouring rain and that was when Dad found us. 'Worshipping nature,' you called it. And 'being in the moment'. He never got over it, but I think it was the shock of realizing he had a half-naked goddess as a Big Sister to his daughter."

Deena frowned, remembering that uninhibited time of her life when she was in university and for a moment regretted its loss. What had happened to that young woman? Life, she supposed, and taking a walk down memory lane wasn't what she'd intended for this meeting.

"A goddess, I'm not. We both could have caught our death of cold—as I recall, I did. Your Dad had a right to be concerned. I think concern is in the parent genes. My Mom was that way right up until she died." Deena shook her head, her blonde pony tail bumping against her shoulders and irritating her—again - that this morning she hadn't had time to put it up in her usual tight French roll.

Anita paled a little.

"I'm sorry. I didn't know. That must have been hard. I remember how you were so close. She was like a surrogate grandma when you were my Big Sister—at least that was how I felt."

For a moment the memory of her mother brought Deena a wave of sorrow, quickly locked away.

"She was everyone's surrogate mother and grandma. I swear the whole town came to her funeral." It came out sadder than she'd intended, and this little meander through the past wasn't appropriate either.

"Listen, Anita, it's a nice surprise seeing you, but I asked you to come in to talk about the job." She had to set the tone here, one of professionalism, because professionalism was the base of top performance.

A little frisson of fear spasmed the younger woman's face, her knuckles whitening on the arms of the chair. "Heywood told you I sort of fell apart at the sight of the body. I'm sorry. Really sorry. I'll do better next time. I really want to get this right."

The concern in Anita's voice, the way her lips had gone white and two high points of embarrassed color formed in her cheeks, were not what Deena had intended.

"Not what I wanted to talk about."

"But I almost fainted..."

"You didn't. You got the job done. Heywood said you did good."

Anita's jaw clamped shut, her gaze wary, waiting and Deena saw a defiant strength there that reminded her of herself when she was just starting out with the RCMP. The kid would get along pretty good if given a chance. That was what Deena was going to do for her. Give her a chance.

"Listen," she pushed herself back from the desk and stood. "I know we go way back, but here, in this Center, that's ancient history—as a matter of fact it never happened. The fact we know each other—well that can't impact how I run the shift or how I treat you. Understand?"

"Deena, I wouldn't..."

Deena stopped her with a raised hand. "Let me finish. This is a lesson I'm going to teach you. My shift runs like the military. There can be no familiarity between us, given our ranks. The fact you feel comfortable interrupting me is bad. This place runs on nepotism and who and what you know and on friendships—but I don't. Here they only get in the way and make people use each other. For you—at work we're professionals who respect each other. You'll most likely be friends with your co-workers. You all work for me and you damn well better give me your very best or as an aux—an auxiliary—you'll never work my shift again. You got it?"

Those big blue eyes had gone round and serious. Anita nodded. It brought a little smile to Deena's lips.

"Good. We've got that settled." She closed her eyes and took a deep breath, for a moment resisting what she really wanted to do. But it had been so long since she'd seen a face at work that was friendly—just because—not sucking up because she was someone's supervisor. She looked back at Anita.

"Now, for this moment in time, this is not my cruddy little office and we are not at work. Now come here and give me a hug, little buddy."

It was what she had called her Little Sister so many years before and it felt so damn good to have Anita bound up from the chair, throw her arms around her and whisper in her ear.

"It's so great to see you."

"You, too." It was. From the smell of Anita's herbal shampoo to the warmth of her friendship it had been too long. She should have looked the kid up when she moved back to town, but she'd been too busy. Her life was too driven—her mother had told her that—and so did her tenant and best friend, Suz Miller, but there were just too many things to get done and to prove. Of course her mother had also said Deena had nothing to prove; that she couldn't keep herself busy enough to avoid the sense of failure the end of her marriage had brought. But what did her mother know?

She separated herself from Anita.

"What the heck are you doing here? I thought you were going to be a veterinarian?"

Anita flushed and wrinkled her nose. "I thought so, too. But when I got into college I sort of got swept away in political science and so on. I'm in Criminology now. I want to be a lawyer. I figured this was a good way to get some experience and pay the bills."

Deena gave her an assessing look. "Then look out B.C. Bar." Grinned, and pulled herself back to the matter at hand. "Okay, enough of the mushy stuff. We're in my lovely office again. I imagine Heywood is waiting to get back on prowl so you better get out of here."

Anita turned to the door.

"By the way, nice work today. Good job on the logs and your report is A1. You got potential, Underhill."

Anita just pressed her lips together to avoid a smile. "Thanks… Ma'am." Then she slipped out the door.

Still a quick study. Deena sighed as she picked up the stacked reports. Nice to find a friend again when so many had been lost. Those she'd grown up with had mostly moved on, and those she'd met along the way had mostly been left behind. Sometimes it felt kind of lonely at night, but then she had Sly who cuddled in with his big-ass purr that could actually wake her up.

Too bad the friendship with Anita couldn't blossom again. Bad to have a friendship with an individual on your shift because it eroded the equality of the team and that eroded morale which detracted from performance and she was all about performance.

She would not place that at risk. At work, Anita Underhill was just another tool to be used to run the jail. Besides, old friendships were notorious for not being able to be rekindled. She'd let this one go, too.

She tapped the stack of reports on the desk and, with them in hand, headed for the door. It clicked locked behind her and she buzz-clicked her way through the door into the Center reception area and the glass-windowed Administration and office wing that filled the front wing of the center. She'd already sent copies of her report out to the RCMP so they could conduct their investigation. Hopefully her report would raise enough questions they'd do more than their usual quick review.

And that was another reason why meeting with Ravi Sandhar was not going to be fun.

Through the glass doors into Administration, where the windows gave onto the green-clad mountainsides that surrounded the small valley where the cross-shaped institution sat. Here there was none of the institutional scent of recycled air and man-sweat. Instead, starburst lilies leaked heady perfume from their place on the counter. From Ravi no doubt. He had instituted a secretary appreciation policy that required he or his Deputy Wardens buy flowers every week.

These blooms almost reeked sensuality, which wasn't exactly what you'd expect in a workplace, especially not here. Yup, definitely a Ravi purchase. Mitch Digneault and the other managers would have bought geraniums or chrysanthemums.

"He in?" she asked Caroline Prevost, the pretty native woman who had recently taken over the office manager job. Not that Ravi would really let her manage anything.

Caroline's nod sent Deena past with the reports. She raised her chin 'hello' at Mitchell Digneault and stopped just outside Ravi's office.

The Warden of Hatzic Regional Correctional Center was on the phone. When he saw Deena, he motioned her into the cave of his office and mimed closing the door. That motion she pretended she didn't see, just as she 'didn't see' him motion her to a chair. Better to just get in, give him the bad news and get the hell out of Dodge.

"Alright, Sir. Thanks. I knew you'd want to know. We're doing everything necessary at this end. Hunter's just bringing in the reports now and Digneault is completing the briefing note. It should be to you in the next half hour. I'll let you know if there's anything, but I'm sure it's just another suicide. And I'll take care of that other thing as well."

He hung up and his gaze raked over her, making her skin prickle just like it always had and for a moment she wondered what the hell she'd ever been thinking to get involved with this man. But then, Ravi Sandhar had golden skin and dark liquid eyes with a fire in them that she thought must have given rise to the Hindu tales of Krishna as a love god.

Ravi's gaze could melt a woman's knees. She knew it from personal experience—she personally thought he'd managed to melt her knees and her spine right the hell out of her once upon a time. But no longer.

"The reports, Sir." She saw his gaze flicker briefly at her use of Sir. He liked to present himself as a 'man of the people'—and didn't appreciate being kept at arm's length. Well that was just too darn bad, because she knew firsthand what happened to a woman if she let Ravi Sandhar get any closer. "I just finished reviewing them. They're decent."

She set them on his desk, then stepped back, ready to leave.

"Hold on a moment there. We need to talk." He motioned to the door again. "Close it, would you?"

She couldn't avoid a direct order. She closed it and turned, waiting.

"Sit down."

She sat and the full impact of the man hit her—something she supposed he'd intended with the way he'd arranged his office.

The desk sat in the center of the corner, window office. The chair she sat in purposely—it had to be on purpose because Ravi Sandhar never left things to chance—was about six inches lower than his own. A large split-leaf philodendron sat at the corner in front of his desk, its sweeping branches and reaching taproots like a bodyguard—or a pimp that kept grabbing for you.

The cream window blinds, he kept half closed, allowed in only slanted shafts of light that illuminated Ravi in bands of light that never seemed to find his eyes. They gleamed with their own luminosity from the shadows across his handsome face.

He was the first Indo-Canadian Warden and that was a point of pride for him. He'd even had an article written about him back in India. A copy was framed and hung on the wall beside him, complete with a photo of him and Indian dignitaries from the last time he'd visited the family village in Punjab. He was proud of his Center and expected it to run smoothly enough that his eventual promotion to Provincial Director would be assured.

He was also a lying bastard and a womanizer.

Deena sat rigid as Ravi held her gaze. He smiled and it was a nice smile, a charming smile, even.

"How have you been, Deena?"

"Fine. A hundred percent." Since we broke up. Since I realized what an idiot I was and how I'd broken every rule I kept for myself.

"I miss you," he said, leaning forward in his chair as if he wanted her to help him, reach out to him and lead him past that expanse of wood between them.

"You wanted to speak to me about something?" She was not going to get into a discussion of their brief affair—the one he'd been trying to rekindle since she found out he *hadn't* left his wife, he *hadn't* been living on his own—and the apartment *had* been loaned to him as a place he could bring his various women.

She lifted her chin at the stack of papers she'd placed on his desk. "The reports. You should take a look, because I'm not convinced this was a suicide. Observations of some of the officers first on the scene and myself don't jive a 100% with a self-inflicted death."

Ravi sat back, his handsome 'lover's face' smoothing into that of a concerned Warden of one of the larger Correctional Centers in the province. "What are you suggesting?"

"Just what it sounds like. I don't think Stickley killed himself. I think he had help."

"Murder?"

"Could be. I think you should be encouraging an RCMP investigation."

His long finger tapped on the papers as he considered. Then he shook his head. "That wouldn't be good right now."

"Really? Well I think a murder doesn't really have a good time, Sir. It needs to be investigated."

"You're telling me that the scene, the evidence can't be explained in any other way."

That stopped her for a moment and she felt the surge of anger she'd been fighting to control ever since she saw Stickley's body. This jerk was just out to make his own career—not to do anything that was right.

"*You* might be able to explain it away, but *I* can't. It's suspicious. It needs to be looked at more than I can do in this role."

"That right?" He steepled his fingers in the considered way he always had just before he ran them over her body. She did an internal shake to rid herself of the memory. It might have been a long while since she'd been with anyone, but Ravi Sandhar was not her type.

He looked down at the reports. "I suppose you've said as much in your report."

"Of course."

"And knowing you, you've already sent copies off to the police." A small tremor of anger came through even his liquid voice.

"What else?" She crossed her arms across her chest, allowing herself a slight sense of satisfaction. She'd checkmated him this time. He had to do something, admit not everything was perfect in the Hat.

He nodded, glanced at her report on top of the others, flipped the page and she watched his brow raise, his lips firm into a hard line. Then he looked back at her.

"I don't agree that the evidence points to anything more than suicide, but the damage is already done." He leaned back in his chair, scanned the ceiling as if looking for a plan, then his gaze latched onto hers. His seriousness surprised her. She'd expected a fight. A big one.

"That was the Provincial Director on the phone. He was telling me about something they've instituted at South Fraser Regional Correctional Center. Apparently they've created a special team they're calling the Internal Security Initiative—ISI. That team works more or less undercover to investigate allegations like drugs in the Center, harassment, that sort of thing. Apparently they've got their drug problem down to nothing and the staff morale is way up. The provincial director has pointed out that there have been a few more drug overdoses in the Hat over the past year. I can't account for that, and frankly I don't believe him, but it will look good if we climb on the band wagon, so to speak. I want an ISI at the Hat and I want you to lead it. The first thing you can do is investigate your own allegations."

Deena tried to wrap her head around what he was telling her, even as his satisfaction told her he thought he'd just dealt with a major pain in the butt—namely her.

"So am I relieved of my ADW duties, because I don't want that? My shift is my shift." She was ready to argue her case, but he stopped her with a raised hand.

"I have no intention of taking you off day shift. You'll run the ISI off the side of your desk. Run it well and get some results, and I might make the position full time, but not yet. Definitely not yet."

She wanted to swear; had to remind herself of her resolution not to. Hadn't her mother always told her to be careful about what she wished for, because it might come true? And now her wish had landed right in her lap because hadn't she always said there were things like drugs happening at the Center that no one else would even acknowledge. She'd come to Ravi not too long ago with an inmate overdose and he told her not to investigate.

"So I do this and my job."

"Is there a problem? You'll be liaising with the police—something you should be good at." He ran his gaze up and down her again, leaving her uncertain whether he was referring to her RCMP background, or something less savory.

"Fine." She stood and the damn philodendron brushed her breast. "I'll keep you posted."

"Not by e-mail—in person. There's too much chance of computer hackers."

That stopped her for a moment because it meant he was taking her a little more seriously than she'd thought. She nodded, swung to the door, pulled it open and was about to leave.

"Hunter."

She stopped, half-turned.

Ravi Sandhar was smiling his full-toothed best. "Sometimes I wish I was that plant."

She choked back her retort. *No you don't*, she thought and gave a saccharine smile. *Because if you were, I'd snip you right off at the root.*

Chapter 4

T HE SMALL WOMEN'S LOCKER room had lockers on two
walls, showers on a third and a sink and mirrors and the exit
door on the fourth. It was overheated with shower steam and just four
women in the room and it reeked of too much perfume and some kind
of fruit-scented shampoo and baby powder. The former was the product
of Lucy Seger spraying herself with White Shoulders after her shower,
and the latter was Anita's contribution to the room. Anita liked the feel of
talc against her body, but seated on the wooden bench that ran under the
lockers, the closeness of the space was almost enough to make her gag.

Like the cell had been.

She paused in dressing and closed her eyes, fighting back the
fear spasm. She'd thought the scariest thing about working in Hatzic
Correctional Center would be all the men.

Nope.

The scary thing about corrections was all the locked doors and
knowing *you* were locked in. With something that had been a live person once.

She toed her bare feet into white runners, all the while telling herself
that regardless of what her Dad had said, she could do this job. Then she
stood to tuck her navy shirt into her white walking shorts and moved over
to the mirror to apply a little makeup and uncoil her damp hair. For work
she had braided it and then looped it at the back of her head, unbraided
it was a long fall of rich honey-gold that covered her bottom and that her
Dad had always called her crowning glory. In truth the hair was heavy on
her head, but it had become her 'signature' through high school and she
couldn't imagine not having long hair.

Just like she couldn't have imagined what she saw today. It had been a nightmare from the moment she'd had had to pound after Heywood responding to the call on the squealing from the portable radio. Cameras whirred and doors buzz-clicked ahead and then they'd run headlong into Unit E1, the two story unit that smelled of men and old socks. She'd scarcely been aware of the empty unit officer station, the plastic chairs and couch before she'd been drawn up the stairs to the cell…

"That is one hell of a mane," Lucy said, stepping back from reapplying eyeliner to scan the long, curled mass. "How the hell do you grow it that long? Mine gets thin the moment it gets to my shoulders."

Anita shrugged and brushed out the curls until the gold gleamed even in the florescent lights. *Two correctional officers looked up from a man on the bed. The air was ripe with a stench she'd never smelled before.* She yanked herself back.

"Family talent, I guess. In pictures my mom had long hair like this, too."

Lucy quirked her brows in an 'is that so' look. She was a pretty enough girl of average height and build with high breasts she emphasized with one of those push-up-push-out bras with extra padding. She wore close-fitting jeans and a clingy sleeveless shirt with sequins outlining a cheetah on the front. Shoulder length brown hair framed a heart-shaped face with large eyes and a cupid mouth that had just a tad of disgruntled downturn at the corners.

"So—how'd you like your first shift in the Hat?"

Anita grinned trying to push back the memory.

"How's she doing?" the dishy looking guy working over the prone inmate had asked. Then he turned to her. "Ever seen a dead body, kid?" He was treating her like a child. She shuddered a little, still feeling resentment.

"People have been asking me that all day. I don't think it has all sunk in yet, but so far, okay."

"Inmates go easy on you?"

"Well… I wasn't on the units alone, but they seemed alright. They did like they were told."

Lucy fluffed her hair and applied her lipstick. She was a full head taller than Anita. When she was done she looked down at her. "Probably were shocked at a little bit of a thing like you thinking you could order them around. It'll wear off."

And there it was. The bias she'd had to deal with all her life. Anita's spine stiffened, and she knew if she was a cat she'd be up on her toes, all fur on end.

"I might be small but I'm wiry. I manage to boss around a seventeen-hand horse and that's big. I've taken enough self-defense classes I could probably teach them. So don't underestimate me and don't call me small, little or a kid, because it just plain pisses me off."

"No, I haven't seen a dead body before, but there has to be a first time."

"Far be it from me to keep a girl from her first D.B."

Stiffly she stepped into the cell, the stench increasing. The figure on bed was flaccid and white. The good looking guy—Chad—had pulled the bag off the guy's face so she could see the mouth sagged open, the blue tongue, the eyes that looked right through her. Bile rose in the back of her throat.

"Smell the urine and shit? They do that when they die. Body voids. Gee, you're looking a little green, babe."

Anita came back to the locker room as Lucy's hands came up to ward off Anita's pique. "Whoa there, girl. I didn't mean to offend. You hear her ladies? She's got teeth in her."

Rosetta Charlie, a solid-built, soft-voiced Sto:lo Nation Indian woman, with short-cropped, black hair and surprising green-brown eyes, looked up sympathetically from buckling her sandals.

"Maybe you should listen to what she says. She doesn't like people talking about her size, just like I don't like people talking about my weight."

Anita tipped her head in thanks. At least someone understood. She'd get over today. She would. Her Dad didn't understand that this job was just a stepping stone to better things, but she was going to prove it to him. The buzzing that had filled her head at the sight of the body had almost faded back to nothing.

"Yeah, but being small could make you a bit of a target."

"And we're supposed to have her back, aren't we?"

'A target'? 'Have her back'? Both unknown phrases caught Anita's attention. She placed them under advisement and, given she didn't want to look like a dolt, waited to find out what they meant.

"Hear you're friends with the boss," Rosetta said quietly. The room suddenly went still as if all the feminine shrugging into jeans, pursing of lips, juggling of makeup, suddenly stopped.

"The boss? Oh! You mean Dee...na Hunter," Anita caught herself and hoped her stumble wasn't too obvious. She glanced at Rosetta and found those quiet eyes waiting. Anita shrugged. "Actually, yeah. I knew her when I was a kid."

She hoped that would be enough and hinted it was a subject she didn't want to discuss. She leaned in to focus on rubbing off the mascara that had smudged under her eyes. No such luck - Lucy grabbed her hand and turned her back to the others in the room.

"So? What's the scoop? What was the perfect ADW Hunter like in her younger years? Please say she wasn't as perfect back then. No one should be that responsible from birth."

Anita looked from face to face. This had to be why Dee—ADW Hunter wanted to keep things professional, but she'd already blown it when she'd let out that squeal on the unit when she realized her old friend was her boss.

"She was my Big Sister—sort of a mentor when I was young. She had energy. She was—fun." She shrugged again.

"Fun how?"

Lucy's face said she wasn't going to let this go, and darn it Anita needed to fit in. She grinned, hoping what she was about to give out wasn't going to cause trouble, but it was so long ago, how could it? Besides, Dee hadn't said she couldn't talk about their old dealings.

"We did stuff. Went camping. Went skinny dipping in the rain— that sort of stuff. Girl stuff. Stuff that showed me a woman could do anything she darn well wanted and that women could be strong. Now I don't want to talk about it anymore, okay."

Lucy licked her lips thoughtfully, like a cat with cream. Rosetta went back to her sandals.

"You coming out for a beer?" That was the fourth woman in the room—Janet Lefevre—a tall, buxom redhead who was a little older and a long time more senior on the job. She wore the years like a badge, but Anita had discovered she had a quick sense of humor. When Janet stood, Anita felt diminished. "We'll have your back there, too. Promise."

Rosetta and Lucy just looked at her, leaving Anita to try to interpret the glances passing between the three other women.

Anita checked her watch. "A beer now? It's barely 2:30."

"Come on kid, the sun's over the yardarm and it's important to show solidarity with the shift, you know? Get to know us all."

Lucy and Rosetta were still silent as Janet swept a muscled arm around Anita's shoulders.

"Just because she's cute you don't have to think of her as competition." The two other women still didn't respond and finally Janet rolled her blue eyes heavenward. "Lord, give me strength. These two are as bad as the guys. Worried you'll take the attention off of them. You going to do that?"

Anita shook her head, still trying to take in what was happening. That her female co-workers felt threatened by her.

"I'm not looking to hone in on anyone's territory. I'm not looking for a guy."

Lucy finally shook her head. "Don't worry—the guys'll be all over *you.*"

"Guess she deserves a chance to ease in." Rosetta tugged her hockey jersey down over her tight jeans.

Janet eased Anita to the door in a way that made her feel like she was being pushed onto a stage, or like a trap door was going to fall out from under her at any moment. She was being stupid, she knew. She'd dealt with men before and hadn't Dee said that she'd be part of the crew?

Janet must have read her hesitation. She stopped and Anita felt just a little bit stupid and a lot like she had as a kid—always being taken care of.

"So you're going to have a beer with us, right? We're the tightest shift in the place, so it'll be a little easier. You're going to have to get to know the other shifts, too, but we'll be your training wheels for this one. We'll have your back."

Anita nodded thanks and moved to the door, but Janet stopped her with a hand on her arm. Rosetta and Lucy flanked her.

"One thing you gotta realize kid." Janet said, her humor suddenly gone from her gaze. "After this you're on your own."

Chapter 5

MONDAY MORNING CARRIED the first chill of the end of summer, and out over the Fraser River and the corn field flats of Matsqui Prairie a thin mist hung in the hay-scented air. Mount Baker's sunrise flush was just fading out, leaving the volcano's snow-covered flanks still, cold and blue against the pale sky. Rich wished he could just stick his aching head into all that cool. Instead he took a deep drink of coffee from the Starbucks mug he held. Didn't help a damn bit.

It had been a long night, what with spending time at the hospital for Ivy and then picking up that brunette at the bar. The woman had come home with him, but the combination, followed by his alarm, had left him grumpy as a bear disturbed from hibernation. Damn it, if he had just gone home last night, instead of sitting with Ivy.

But he'd helped put her in hospital, and he was damn well going to see her out of there.

"Guilt isn't going to make her get better," Chuck Kozloff, Rich's Ukrainian partner came up behind him. Rich stood at the back of the bluff that held the Mission Royal Canadian Mounted Police detachment parking lot, trying to get rid of the bear inside and ready for a day of work. The folds of the hills and the gentle drone of the tug engines working the log booms along the river had always soothed the savage beast before.

"How'd you know I was out here?" Rich didn't bother asking how Chuck knew Ivy was in the hospital again. Chuck's wife, Greta, worked in admissions at MSA Hospital.

"Ya always are when there's a problem with Ivy. Like I said, guilt isn't going to help her and it's dragging you down bud. She has to be responsible for herself and she can't be as long as you keep rescuing her."

Chuck picked up a stone and heaved it off the bluff so it disappeared in the cottonwoods below. He was an unusual man, tall, thin—spider armed, Rich had heard it described—with a thoughtful way about him that he could disguise in a Barney Fife routine that seemed to work miracles in getting the truth out of suspects. He'd been Rich's partner since he came to Mission detachment six months ago from Maple Ridge, about twenty miles west. They'd known each other before Rich's transfer, but now they'd bonded as only partners could. Rich couldn't meet Chuck's gaze.

"You know, I never should have married her. That's the hard part. If I'd broken her heart at the time, she'd probably be happily married to some other guy right now. But I had to go through with a marriage that was a sham from the start. I should have broken it off as soon as I realized I was interested in someone else."

"That's old news, in the past, over. You can't take it back, so now you need to move on."

Rich shook his head. "You think I don't I know it?" So then what was the problem, why did he keep doing the exact things that kept Ivy and him circling in a downward spiral that had started before the marriage and had ended up here?

"You gotta get another girl, partner." The Barney Fife voice choked a little guffaw from Rich.

"That's the trouble, isn't it? Girls come pretty easy, but not the one I need."

"Maybe the trouble is you need. Maybe you should just quit looking so hard and the right one'll land in your lap."

Rich turned from the morning scene to his partner. The right one. There'd been an old song about how hard it was to belong to someone else when the right one comes along. It still played on repeat in his head at the worst times.

"You going all new age on me now, because I don't think I can take it."

Chuck shrugged his boney shoulders. "Nah. Just pulling out the old psych lessons from college." He caught Rich's doubtful look. "Okay, okay, Greta's started reading about Buddhism and letting go of desires so you can enjoy this life. She keeps making me read the stuff."

Rich rolled his eyes. "She really does have you under her thumb."

"Hell someone has to take responsibility for making the marriage work."

But Rich knew that wasn't the truth. Chuck and Greta both appeared to have what Rich had always wanted in his marriage—a deep abiding respect and a passion that showed every time they looked at each other—even after seventeen years of marriage. He should be so lucky to find even half that in his life.

He turned back to the low-slung brick police detachment.

"Come on. Must be some crime and/or evil out there to keep my mind off how my life's a shambles."

"Must be," Chuck said and followed him across the parking lot.

The General Investigation Section, comprised of Rich and Chuck, was what passed for a detective unit in the small detachment of twenty-five. It was housed at the rear of the building in an office with a glass brick wall to the outside. There, they were away from the noise of the day-to-day operations of the detachment. Only problem was, they were next door to the OIC of the Detachment who was waiting for them when Rich slouched into the office, hung his keys on the wall and collapsed. Damn his head hurt.

Inspector Martin Reeves was a tall Prairie drink of water, who hadn't been citified by working in urban Greater Vancouver. He still wore his old dog-man trousers with his uniform shirt as if it was a badge of honor. He seemed to think they brought him closer to his men, but Rich personally thought it was just because Reeves was too cheap to buy new issue.

Reeves sat on the edge of the two pushed-together desks, holding a file in his hands. "Bout time you made it in. I saw you standing outside fifteen minutes ago."

"Rich here had some thinking to do. Beside, you didn't want to have to deal with him any sooner." Chuck cast him a dour glance and Rich rolled his eyes again. Great. Now his OIC was going to think he was a prima-donna.

"Not quite how it seems, Sir. I was trying to clear my head."

Reeves flipped open the file. "This'll keep you busy and you'll need a clear head. Hatzic Regional Correctional Center. Apparently a suspicious death. Talked to the Warden this morning and he's betting on suicide, but says some of his staff suspect otherwise. Seems to me he's not too happy about it, but he's playing the game. Says he's got staff lined up to interview today if one of you is available."

Chuck groaned and Rich knew a long day at the correctional center loomed ahead. So much for clearing his head. He'd done interviews at a correctional center before, covering off incidents at Fraser Regional Correctional Center. It usually meant talking to a bunch of guys who didn't want to be talked to—and that was just the staff.

"How many we talking about?" he asked.

"Sounds like there's about ten or twelve."

"Shit. Nobody closes ranks like Correctional Officers. They're worse than the cons."

"You're talking about fellow Peace Officers."

"I'm talking about screws." They were mostly cop wannabees with all of the issues and none of the good sense.

He tossed his half-finished cup in the garbage and held his hand out for the file, knowing the day had just gone a long way downhill. He'd hoped to coast a bit, but this would require him to do more than go through the motions.

"What time's the first interview?"

"Seven." Reeves checked his watch "If you hurry you might just be on time."

"Shit." But he was grabbing his briefcase, a notepad and regretting tossing his coffee. He could imagine the swill at the Correctional Center.

"Look at it this way, partner, you'll get to meet our fellow peace officers so just..."

Rich held up his hand. "I know. I know. Just be in the moment and all will be better. Bunch of crap. Someone has to do *something!*"

He heard Reeves asking what the hell that was all about, but Rich was already grabbing keys off the wall and heading for the parking lot, wishing he had time to at least review the file.

§

The Boardroom at Hatzic Correctional Centre had to double as a police interview room when staff were involved. It was typical government space—too small a room for too grandiose a table and too little room for the number of executive chairs they had purchased. Institutional clock on the wall and crowd of furniture all conspired to leave Rich feeling like he was trapped in an Escher-esque furniture storeroom that would eventually consume him.

After eleven interviews in the crowded space Rich thought he must have really done something awful for Reeves to have sent him here. Eleven statements from staff who made it very clear that they liked cops about as much as he liked them. Well, maybe not eleven. There'd been the little cutie, Underhill who had sat there fidgeting nervously throughout the interview and who finally admitted that this was only her second day on the job. Whatever the hell would make a woman choose to work in this place was beyond him.

And there'd been that more than slightly embarrassing moment when Lucy, the brunette from last night, strolled in to be interviewed. What the hell had he been thinking—she'd told him she worked in a jail—his male mind had just automatically thought she was a secretary or something. At least in the interview he'd kept it professional even though she'd tossed none-too-veiled invitations at him the whole time.

He leaned back from the walnut table and the high-backed conference room chair squealed as he stretched his arms overhead. Almost four o-clock, and a vending machine food lunch, and too many pots of coffee later. No wonder he was feeling like he'd been dragged through a knot-hole backwards. He felt like he'd been sentenced here.

Hatzic Regional Correctional Center sat like a blight on the mountain side, the lush west coast rainforest clear-cut to provide space for the building, parking lot and its barren grounds. The tall fences, all barbed wire topped with well-spaced video cameras mounted strategically hadn't given Rich any more sense of security about the center. Far too many men escaped from the Federal and Provincial correctional centers in the Fraser River Valley.

He'd tried to leave those misgivings in the car, but the admin wing stank of too-sweet lilies, and the coffee had been just as bad as he feared. They both contributed to the headache throbbing behind his eyes.

The tick, tick, tick of the wall clock filled the room, while beyond the door everything had gone quiet. With his luck he'd been forgotten and locked in.

He was tempted to throw his feet up on the table and catch a few zzzs before his last interview, but instead he heaved himself up and stretched out his back. A few trapezium stretches and he felt a little better, but he needed to move to stay awake. Another cup of coffee and the top of his head might just blow off. For a moment he wondered how Ivy was doing.

Damn. Just let her go. Just move.

Get out of this room and get the blood circulating. He rounded the conference table, opened the door and almost bull-dozed over a tall blonde in a blue Corrections uniform.

Then she met his gaze and the world disappeared.

Chapter 6

STUNNED BY THE BODY-BLOW, Deena clutched the envelope of evidence to her chest.

Stunned, as well, by the face peering down—a face she remembered too damn well, she felt like she couldn't breathe.

Dark hair verging on black that failed to show any tell-tale grey. Thick and tousled from running his fingers through it—she remembered that signature action all too well, just as she remembered wanting to run her fingers through it.

Heck, she wanted to now.

Eyes, searing blue and right now narrowing in suspicion above high cheek bones that looked just a little too drawn with fatigue.

Hands found her shoulders, steadied her. Tall as she remembered. Broad shouldered. He hadn't gone soft around the middle like so many men of—my god—he must be almost forty-five to her forty. And still with that mouth that always seemed to slide into a slightly mocking grin to hide what he really felt. Right at the moment it wasn't doing that too well.

He looked almost speechless.

"Is this some kind of joke?" Deena snapped, pulling back and fighting the frisson of excitement that Rich Webster's presence had always evoked in her. It was too weird—too many blasts from the past over the last two days. Had someone set this up? But who knew?

Her thoughts went immediately to Underhill, but Underhill hadn't been around when Deena was in the RCMP.

"No," the low growl of his voice sent a sensual shiver up her spine. "No joke. You're the D. Hunter on the last report. Well I'll be damned."

Damn, was right. He recovered fast. That mocking grin had smoothed into place and his hands had felt just a little too intimate on her arms. She stepped back.

"You're the investigating officer?" She raked her gaze down the jeans and green golf shirt he wore. It set off his eyes, but didn't look anything like a uniform. "Let me guess. GIS. They gave you a friggin' promotion."

He shrugged in that way that used to drive her mad because it hid so much, but his gaze was still locked with hers and it brought too many old feelings rocketing through her—feelings that had just caused too many problems when she hadn't controlled them.

"Deena Hunter. Who would have thought?" Softer-voiced. He looked around the Administration wing as if checking for listeners, and then back to her. Raised his hands as if to catch her again, and then stuck them in his pockets. "What the hell are you doing working here?"

"Apparently being interviewed by you. I'm glad the Inspector decided to send someone up for interviews rather than just file the reports. That was why I called him."

Keep it official, Deena. Keep it official and keep your distance, because the first time around it was just too damn hard and she didn't need trouble any more than she had needed it then. She'd been the responsible one then, she had to be now, too.

"Aah. I was just stretching my legs, maybe going to get myself another cup of your wonderful coffee. I've been at this a while." He scanned the empty office again. "Guess coffee's out of the question."

He looked back at her and his eyes were almost amethyst as if something precious waited there. Something that was desperately trying to deal with this way-weird situation and not having much luck. She could almost feel sorry for him. Stupid thought.

"Come on in. Let's get this done."

"There's—there's coffee in the staff room," she capitulated. "I could get you a cup." Why was she offering? When had she ever fetched a cup of coffee for anyone but her parents? She was the ADW of the Center, for goodness sake. Not some fetch-carry-bring boy. Damnation, next thing she'd be checking his fingers for rings.

The slope of his brows said he knew just how out of character that offer was, and thankfully he didn't take her up on it.

"Nah. You're probably doing me a bigger favor keeping the stuff away from me. Institutional swill."

"Hey, you're talking about the coffee I love." And just that easy it was back to the banter they used to have, even if she couldn't quite relax as she had when he was her RCMP training officer so many years ago in Morinville, Alberta.

"You call that coffee? Shit, the Fraser River has a higher caffeine content."

"Like you need caffeine. Way I remember it your energy was legend."

He slid into his chair and motioned to one across from him—typical male and typical RCMP—establish a barrier between to show his authority. But instead of looking authoritarian, all he did was look wary and tired. There were deep shadows under his eyes and, narrowed as they were, lines deepened by years in the sun ran out to his hairline.

She wondered if he could see the years on her as clearly, and she had to fight back a need to smooth her hair as she settled in her seat and placed the envelope on the table.

"Guess the years have taken the edge off that energy. I guess."

She quirked her own smile. "What, the Webster certainty get broken somewhere? I seem to recall you had the answer for everything."

"Guess the years have taken the edge off that, too. You get to see the gray beyond the black and white."

Damn it, her hands went to her hair unbidden. She hauled them back to her lap. Was he seeing the gray in her hair? Don't be stupid. The woman who cut her hair said the few silver strands just made her hair fairer. She looked down at her lap and fought to settle herself. Business, Deena. Focus on business.

"So you've read my report?"

"Actually, no. I thought I'd let you run me through the events and then we'd review the report."

Not exactly by the book, but then when had Rich Webster ever been strictly by the book. When she'd met him, he was a hard drinking, hard partying cop who seemed to be trying to fit all that drinking and partying in before his wedding, and yet he was always top form when in uniform.

He'd been a trainer like every young cop should get—had made sure she learned the job right. But when the hours in the car together had led to a friendship she knew had potential to be far more, she'd asked for a transfer to a different trainer. It had been the hardest thing she ever did—next to burying her parents.

§

Her presence left him stunned, immobilized as a Taser shot would have left him. Rich felt unarmed and unready to deal with all the turmoil Deena Hunter raised in him, because damn it, she was the one. The one he'd let get away. The right one, even though he'd never even kissed her and that was the stupidest thing of all.

She looked almost the same, a little more seasoned perhaps, but on her the years only added interest. What had caused that small scar beside her upper lip? Was she still doing the archery that had caused her to scrunch up her dark secretive eyes?

That would have helped create the fine lines at their outer corners. Even though she wasn't smiling right now, she must have smiled a lot over the years because there were slight lines there, too, around the curve of her very kissable mouth. That hadn't changed either.

Nor the way she filled out a uniform—high breasts still, slim figure that spoke of care and activity and attention to self. She even still wore those damned silver earrings that he'd noticed the first time he saw her striding into the Morinville Detachment. He'd felt something light up in him, like a homing device. He felt like that now.

"I just can't get over how little you've changed."

She looked away, obviously uncomfortable. "I think we should focus on business, don't you? We've both had long days. I have—responsibilities—at home."

His gaze flicked to her fingers. No ring. But he'd heard she'd gotten married. He'd kept track of her as much as he could without calling attention to it. But he'd lost track of her when she suddenly quit the force—except for news of her marriage. By then he hadn't dared try to find her because things were already tanking with Ivy and he didn't need any more rumors flying around the Morinville detachment.

Business Webster. You can have old home week after this is done. Maybe go for coffee.

"So walk me through what happened. I'll be taking notes, of course."

"Of course." Dry humor there, as she folded her hands on the envelope in front of her, just as she'd always done when giving court testimony. It gave her an almost Madonna-like quality. Well, maybe not Madonna—more goddess-like because he'd spent too many nights imagining what it would be like to run his hands through that silken hair, and down that lithe body.

She told him everything. About the birthday party and the delay in getting staff to the units. Just like her to accept ultimate responsibility for the trouble. She always had high ethical standards.

About arriving on scene and the CPR administered by the two corrections staff. About setting up perimeter, collecting evidence, and the difficulties with the ambulance gurney. Her story was smooth, practiced, complete in its details.

"That's all good, but my understanding is that you think this wasn't a suicide and you haven't described anything that wouldn't fit with a suicide."

"Then you weren't listening." She looked at him, her gaze impatient. "The cell wasn't like it should be—not based on Stickley's type. I know we never got to know suspects that well as cops, but we always picked up on their type. Tidy about themselves, disorganized, someone who commits crimes of opportunity. Modus operundi, Rich. Well in here, those types run true. The bully, the slob, the neat freak. Stickley wasn't a neat freak but he was damn tidy. About his person, and I'd expect in his cell."

He went to interrupt her, but she waved him away so authoritatively that he waited. That was one of the things the years had given her—a greater sense of power. It sat well on her. Controlled and purring like an idling engine.

"He always wore a prison uniform that looked pressed so he must have kept his things hung up. He always had neat hair, parted cleanly and it stayed that way—as if all the hairs on his head were regimented and on parade. Hell, his nails were clean and clipped, and if runners were able to be shone, I swear his would have been. That kind of guy. But when I go into his cell, it's a disaster. Clothes on the floor, photos torn off the wall, desk a mess." She fumbled with the envelope a moment, then pulled out a sheaf of photos. "Take a look."

She shoved them across to him and he shuffled through them. She was right about the mess. "How much of this could have been caused in the response to finding him?"

He liked the way she didn't immediately answer. Consideration filled her face, just as it had so long ago when he'd asked her why the hell she wanted to become a cop. She had answered thoughtfully and truthfully that she thought the only way to change a system was to work from within. It had been an impressive answer when most new recruits came out with the same pat answer—they wanted to help people.

That thoughtfulness had always encouraged him to think twice instead of immediately reacting—which in most instances had been a good thing. She'd always been good with people, had actually taught him something about the responsibility of the uniform—that sometimes just a little humanity instead of throwing around the weight of his authority and size, could de-escalate a situation.

"Some could have been, but these photos were taken before the EMT guys arrived, so the photos reflect the scene as I saw it. The two attending officers were on the bed, so I don't think they disturbed the rest of the cell. So someone else did."

He looked back at the photos. Made sense. But not a strong enough foundation to build a case on. "Anything else?"

She still had that thoughtful look to her, her eyes narrowed, lips pressed together. Then she shook her head.

"Something I just can't put my finger on...And there's this. She went to the envelope again, pulled out a smaller envelope all neatly sealed and initialed, and shoved it to him.

Breaking the seal, tangled, knotted shoelaces fell into Rich's palm. He looked from them to Deena, not comprehending. She must have seen it because she nodded at the photos.

"Don't you see it?"

He glanced at the shoelaces and back at the photos. Obviously he was missing something.

She half-stood, leaned across the table and for a moment through the open collar of her shirt he caught a glimpse of the tops of her breasts. Smooth flesh that made him swallow. A scent of something like spice came from her as she tapped a spot on one of the photos. He had to pull his gaze from the white column of her neck to see where she had pointed.

He didn't want to. Nope, not at all.

Runners in the photo. He peered down at them. "So?"

"Look again, dammit. Those are Velcro closures."

He did and she was right. "Shit. I should have caught that."

"Yes."

Her gaze was on him, a small smile on her face as she sat relaxed across from him. She had relaxed talking about the case. But when he answered her smile, the curve tightened into a line, as if she wasn't used to smiling much anymore and the effort of it was too much. He wanted to see more of them.

"Okay, so I missed a detail. I'd have caught it. I'm not superwoman like you."

She jerked at that comment and the relaxation totally disappeared. She was rigid in her chair, her blue gaze edged with steel.

"The laces weren't part of Stickley's issue. He'd received special permission to use orthotics and needed special shoes to fit them. The laces don't fit. Neither does the suicide. Stickley was due for parole. He had a wife and a daughter. And he was a snitch for me and had asked to meet with me yesterday. He died before we could."

That was interesting. But if he was laying concrete foundations, there weren't enough forms. He closed his eyes a moment. Deena had good instincts, he knew. At least she had as a cop and judging by what he was seeing, she hadn't lost the talent. But there was a problem here. A problem he needed to point out. One big one.

He looked back at her.

"Let me see if I've got this straight. Stickley was last seen alive for certain before—what did you call it—lockdown at 10 p.m. last night? He was in a locked cell all night and checked at fifteen minute intervals—at least that's what the unit logs say. You came on shift at 6 a.m. and your staff were a little late getting on the units. You were just pushing them out the door when the code blue came in. Right so far?"

"That's when everyone responded."

Sitting here was like when they'd sat together working on a case in the old days. Then he'd had to keep reminding himself she was a co-worker and a cop, because he'd been mesmerized by how the light caught in the small hairs along her neck, and how she managed to stay so overtly feminine even in the god-awful man-cut uniform.

"Okay, so your guy, Sandhu, goes to the unit and he spots something's not right with Stickley. He calls for backup and your other guy, Preston, responds and they crack the cell. But it's already like it's been tossed and he's already dead. Right?"

She nodded slowly. "So you're wondering how the heck someone could have gotten in the cell to kill him."

"You got it. You got an answer?"

"Nope. Only options—and some of them I don't want to go to. I'm thinking maybe one of the other inmates did this just at lockdown. Someone moving fast—like one of the neighboring inmates—might have gone in, strangled him, and then left him on the bed looking like he was sleeping. Staff might not have noticed in the dim light after lights out. That's my best theory at this juncture because any of the others don't make sense."

"Like what?"

"I'm not going there without evidence."

"You're thinking about the staff. One of them might have done it."

She was shaking her head, but he could see the concern in her gaze that said she had gone there. "Not possible, I'm afraid. There are too many controls. The cell doors are opened electronically and any opening is noted in the computer log. No one but Senior Management can get to them. There are cameras in the Center as well. At night the Center runs a skeleton crew, so the prowl officer has to keep moving, he's on a tight schedule and there's no way he'd have time to kill someone and keep the time checks on schedule. There's just no way staff would have done this or could have."

"Okay, let's take that as a given for now." Her gaze said she knew he wasn't and that ticked her off some. Loyalty to co-workers had been another quality of hers. She refused to think the worst when things could be interpreted in a positive light. After 23 years of being a cop, it wasn't a quality he cultivated.

"You got any idea what Stickley wanted to talk to you about?"

"Unfortunately, no. He was a bit of a bug in the Center—always trying to hang with the big boys and they didn't take it too well. He'd been feeding me information trying to get on my good side so I'd put in a good word for him at his Parole hearing. Mostly it was about contraband—more smokes, chocolate, the occasional still making home-made raisin hooch. That sort of thing. Small stuff. But I'd asked him to keep an eye out for drugs, because I'd heard rumors things were getting into Fraser Valley Centers."

He looked down at his notes. That pretty much covered it, but he didn't want the interview to end. He didn't want her to leave. He set his pen down.

"So what got you here?"

She looked at him guardedly and he wondered what had happened to her that she didn't trust anymore.

"I moved back home—I'm from Mission, remember."

And he did. Some of the other young guys in Morinville had gotten a real charge out of asking her if they only used the Missionary position in Mission. Of course she'd had the quick comeback that Missionites won awards for the Missionary position, and the name only commemorated how good they all were in bed. Shut the guys down pretty well.

"You had a pretty good career going with the RCMP. Why'd you leave?"

She met his gaze squarely, crossed her arms. "Are we done with the interview? Because I have things I need to do and it has been one hell of a long day."

Damn it, he didn't want to let her go. He wanted to look at her, find out about her and how her marriage was going, if she was happy, how many kids she had. Hell all the things that had gone on in her life that he might have shared if he'd made different choices. Shit, how the hell could he miss someone he'd only known for such a short time? How could he feel obsessed with this woman when Ivy was in the hospital?

"We're done. I was just sort of hoping we could talk about old times."

"All water under the bridge, Corporal. All long gone." She said it as she stood, pushed her chair back in and reached across the table to shake his hand. He didn't take it.

"Before you go, I need your contact information. Phone number. Address. For the file. In case I need to follow-up."

Her look leveled at him. Held as if she knew damn well he was fishing not for the file, but for himself. She pulled her hand back.

"You can contact me through the Center. I'm usually here or they'll know how to get in touch with me."

Then, with a nod she was gone and he really wished he'd caught her hand. Caught it and not let her go.

Chapter 7

LATE AFTERNOON AND THE DAY had gone misty and golden with the sunlight slanting across the valley. Deena's old fashioned three-story house stood on the steep slope that made up the town of Mission, running down from the mountains to the sawmills and light industrial businesses along the river. When she'd inherited the house she'd moved upstairs because she didn't need much space and she'd rented the main part of the house, below. Normally she didn't mind climbing up and down the steep flight of red-painted stairs to her door, but today her head felt like it was going to explode as she clattered down the rickety, red stairs at the side of the gingerbread-style house her father had built.

There was too much going on. The death at the Center, meetings to start up the new ISI, and seeing Rich Webster again. Then there was trying to get her uniform business off the ground so that eventually she could quit Corrections and work from home. And Sly's illness.

In her car, she turned downhill into town, headed to the vet clinic. There had been so much going on in her life she hadn't even been for a run in the past week, let alone to the gym. She had to rectify that. Get some exercise and work off the tension or else she was going to go nuts.

It hadn't helped seeing Rich Webster again, because just seeing him evoked such a sense of loss and failure and old desire it made driving down the damn mountain from the Hat difficult and navigating through town hard. She just wanted to go home, pull on shorts and running shoes and set out. Problem was, if she started running, she wasn't sure whether she'd stop. And running away wasn't something Deena Hunter ever did.

In a world of people who mostly ran away from danger, she was the kind who ran towards it.

Rich Webster. Who woulda thought? Just thinking his name sent a small shiver of excitement through her. Get a grip. Rich Webster would only complicate her life even more, but even though her mind told her to run, all her instincts were to run right towards him.

Stupid thought. All she needed from him was an investigation as good as those he'd done in the past.

Stop thinking of Rich, and get on with your life. Funny, she hadn't had that thought for a very long time.

But now was the time to face her veterinarian. After Sly's accident yesterday she'd had to recognize there was something wrong, she'd had her tenant, Suz Turner, take her cat into the vet for tests. She'd left everything written out for Suz and the vet, and she knew five-year-old Lana could spot Sly like radar, so they should be able to find him, no matter where the old guy tried to hide. That was, if Suz remembered, because for all her charm, the woman could be a bit addled from time to time.

Deena pulled up in the small clinic parking lot and sat a moment, took a deep breath and set aside the tension that had ridden her since the interview. She could tell by Rich's face he wasn't sure about her theory Stickley had been murdered. It was likely going to fall to her to investigate, whether she wanted to or not.

In her jeans and an ancient Moody Blues t-shirt, she pushed into the vet clinic. It smelled not unlike parts of the jail: a little antiseptic overlaid on fear and ammonia. Sly would be happy to get home, not that the little guy hated it here.

Mary-Beth, the vet-tech and receptionist looked up at the ding of the bell. "Deena." A little smile of pleasure. "We've all been enjoying your friend today. He's been busy purring at everyone."

That, at least boded well. Sly had been in her life for fifteen years. The little, black, vagabond kitten had found her when she arrived in Morinville. He'd marched right up to her outside the small house she'd rented and demanded attention. He'd got it and he'd been demanding attention ever since.

Mary-Beth went around back and reappeared in one of the examining rooms. Sly sat on the table behind her, his buzz-saw purr filling the small room. "Doctor Brar will be right with you."

The old cat chirruped as Deena waited beside him, head-butting her hand for pats.

"Yes, your majesty. More pats." She stroked the fur kept soft and gleaming by daily brushings.

Julie Brar, a slight, mousy-blonde who somehow still managed to wrangle horses and cattle, had opened her practice in Mission at about the time Deena was leaving town. They'd met way back then and Julie had arranged a volunteer position for Anita at the clinic. When Deena had come back to town, Julie had been her first choice as vet for Sly. Julie had a good way with animals: no baby talk, but no roughness either. Just a calm, smooth, way about her that demanded respect.

"Hey."

Julie nodded her hello and ran a hand down Sly's back. The cat shoved his head at her for more.

"You know what you want, don't you old man?"

Sly chirruped his agreement.

"God, he's a good old cat." The comment set little hairs on end on Deena's arms, because the slight emphasis on old hinted at something.

"What's going on?"

Julie looked up from Sly, and the look in her eyes told Deena everything she needed to know.

"Tell me straight."

Julie stroked Sly again and he flopped down on the metal table to expose his belly for a rub. Obliging him, Julie sighed.

"What happens to a lot of old cats. His body is starting to fail. I've got a bunch of blood work out being checked and so far I know he's got diabetes. But there's something else going on here, Deena. Right now I don't know what."

Oh shit, but she didn't say it. Not knowing was the worst—had heard similar words once before. She fought back the concern that wanted to bring tears to her eyes, but Julie must have seen. She grabbed Deena's hand.

"It'll be alright."

Deena yanked back. She wasn't one of those owners who fell apart at the slightest hint of bad news. She wasn't. She'd been strong before and she would be again. He was her cat—not her mother. She scratched her neck.

"You'll find out what it is, right? And then we'll fix it. Right? Cause I'll do whatever it takes."

Julie's gaze was full. Deena knew she hated these talks with owners. A long time ago she'd said helping owners hope was the worst part of her job, next to putting down perfectly healthy animals.

"You have to remember, he's not young anymore, Dee. He's fifteen. Things like this are harder on his body."

"No."

Sly meowed and sat up, bumping Deena with his head as if to reassure her everything was alright, and she nearly lost it because that was what he'd done when she sat in the dark unable to move after her Mom finally passed. She wanted to grab him and run so it couldn't be true. Instead she took a deep breath.

"What do I need to do?" Be practical. Focused. It got her through everything else.

"At this stage, until we know what else is wrong, we need to stabilize his insulin levels. I'm going to show you how to give him shots and you should start off with four units twice a day and control his food intake. That's about all we can do."

Deena bent down to look Sly in the eyes. "What you doing getting sick on me, little buddy? You're supposed to live forever."

Sly who had been there through all the dark times as Deena's RCMP career ended, as she nursed her mother, as her marriage fell apart. It was like he'd been the sponge for all her pain. She supposed it was time she took some of that pain back.

She exhaled and faced Julie.

"Okay. I can do that."

"You're going to have to watch his water and food intake and his urination closely, because if things go off, there can be big-time problems. Understand? And he needs to lose weight."

The numbness only grew as Deena went through the motions, paid the bill and went through all the instructions and the trial giving Sly his insulin shot. By the time she left, her hands were shaking and she hated the sense of helplessness. She could fight criminals. She could run a center, but her hands shook when she had to give Sly a simple shot.

She carried Sly out to the car and got home without remembering how. It was all too much. Her mother's death three years ago after a heroic battle, her divorce last year, the affair, and now Sly.

She parked in the gravel driveway in front of the cobalt blue house with the ornate red scrollwork at the peak and over the broad front porch that her father had been so proud of. Carrying the cat cage, she headed across the toy-riddled overlong, green lawn—she really should mow her next days off—towards the red stairs, but the front door to the house burst open and a small carrot-topped tornado came tearing out the door.

"You're home. Mommy wants to talk to you."

Lana Miller was a sprite of a child, with a freckled face and huge blue eyes like her mother, and a wild spray of red curls that were only slightly shorter than her mother's mane of red.

If anything her eyes got a little bigger when she saw Sly in his carry box. "Is Sly better now? Did doctor fix him?"

The words left Deena not knowing what to say. How do you tell a little child about diabetes or unknown illness? Or death?

Lana poked small fingers through the holes in the carry box and giggled. "He's licking me."

"That's Sly saying hello, honey." Deena was going to ease past to the stairs, but Suz Miller came to the door and scanned Deena. Suz's lips tightened, probably at what she saw.

They'd been best friends in high school and university until Deena headed off to RCMP training at Depot. When she'd returned home she'd lived in the big old house with her ailing mother. After her mother's death she knew she didn't need all the space in the big old house, but was determined not to sell. That house might be a tad rundown and drafty in the winters, but it was her family's. She wasn't letting it go.

So when Suz needed a new place to live with her growing daughter, it had seemed like the perfect solution to a problem she hadn't known she had. They split the house into two apartments and she rented her friend the main two floors. It had also led to their joint business venture.

"Get your rear up here, Dee. Bring the cat. Lana can watch over him while you and I have a little talk."

The hard little gleam in Suz's eyes told Deena she wasn't getting away. She might be able to boss her staff around, but Suz Miller was another matter.

They'd been a formidable pair in high school: on the debate team, student council, the track team together, and all the time the two of them had been neck in neck for the number one spot. It should have caused a rivalry; instead it created best friends that had Deena right there when Suz got pregnant out of wedlock. Sometimes it sort of felt like they were sisters. Or like Lana had two Moms.

Deena followed Suz into the house, set the cage down in the sparsely furnished living room and followed Suz into the kitchen. The old cupboards and faded linoleum held memories of many afternoons of spiced tea with her mom, of homework at the kitchen table, but now Suz's life and Lana's artwork on the fridge were layered over top of the old memories.

Suz poured a cup of coffee, but Deena waved it off. Suz poured a packet of sugar replacement in the cup and stirred.

"It's bad, huh?" she asked quietly, glancing into the living room to see Lana hauling Sly up onto her lap, singing softly.

"Not the worst. I keep telling myself that. Diabetes as far as they can tell so far. Julie says we can control that. And that I have to recognize he's getting old." She left the rest unsaid. Things unknown were what populated nightmares. At least she could do for Sly what she hadn't been able to do for her mother.

"Oh god, Dee. That's the last thing you need. You've had him forever, haven't you?"

"Feels like. I feel like I've been hit in the gut." She rubbed her face. Somehow Julie's news about Sly had sapped all her energy. She just wanted to go sit in the dark—something she'd been very good at after her mom's passing and her divorce.

"Shit, I hate to have to be the bearer of more bad news, but we got a call from the fabric distributor. They've bumped our order. Sounds like one of the big manufacturers increased their order and so the distributor pushed ours aside."

A flash of anger ran through Deena and it took the last of her energy. She grabbed a chair and sat down. It wasn't fair. She and Suz were trying to break out of their respective ruts, trying to take their lives into their own hands by creating their own business designing and manufacturing uniforms that were specifically for female police, correctional officers, security guards etc. But if they couldn't get the material there was no way they could get their prototypes made up to advertise their creations.

"Deena, are you alright?"

She looked up and found Suz in her face. How long had she been zoned out?

"Of course I'm alright. I've just got a lot on my mind right now." She looked around. "Maybe I will have a cup of that."

Suz sized her up and went to the cupboard high above the oven.

"I'll do you one better." She hauled a bottle of Irish cream liqueur down and poured a healthy dollop into a cup before adding coffee. Then she put her own cup down and added some of the cream. "Might as well join you for a cup. Now tell Aunty Suz everything."

Where to start. Deena ran through her day tallying all the things that had gone wrong. Sly. Still dealing with the aftermath of the Stickley suicide. Ravi already sending her memos demanding she update him on the ISI when she hadn't had time to do a darn thing. She could almost swear he was using it as a way to spend more time with her.

And then there had been Rich Webster.

She stopped her dissertation realizing she'd finished her cup of coffee and was sipping at an empty cup.

"You want another one of those?"

"If I do, I might go maudlin."

"Maybe maudlin is what you need," Suz said with speculation in her eyes. She took Deena's cup and poured another round. In the living room Lana was reading Sly a story, and he was sitting beside her on the couch, purring his patient-cat purr. "This Rich Webster. Wasn't there a cop you used to work with?"

Deena could only nod.

"Dee, is this THE GUY?"

Deena jerked at the question. "What the hell are you talking about?"

Suz slid back into her chair and caught Deena's hands.

"We're old friends, right. I know you way better than most sisters, believe you me. And I remember those phone calls I got from you when you first started with the force. You talked about this guy you were working with and even though you never said it, it was pretty clear you were as attracted as hell. That was Rich Webster, wasn't it? I remember because I wondered at the name. Rick is what you expect, not Rich."

Deena almost squirmed in her chair, because Rich Webster had been everything she ever wanted—or thought she wanted—in a man. Tall, solid and smart, and sexy as hell, because he didn't even know it. She'd run for the hills when she'd realized he was engaged.

"It was just a crush. I was young. Nothing more."

Suz's scrutiny narrowed like one of the arrows the two of them used to shoot.

"You're not lying to me, are you, because I can always spot one of your lies?"

After the day she'd had, Deena didn't need Suz riding her as well.

"Whatever. I'm tired. I'm old and I've got a sick cat and a suspicious death on my hands and a Warden who's riding my ass."

"So long as that's all he's riding."

Deena glared at her friend for a moment. Suz knew about the torrid affair. She grinned.

"I think you need to get a life, Dee. How long can you continue just focusing on what everyone else needs?"

Suz went for the bottle again, but Deena covered her cup. Suz might know her very well, but she was wrong in this. Deena might not have much of a social life, and her sex life might be downright moribund since she broke up with Ravi, but she had a life. It was just work-focused, that was all.

"What I need is good run and a soak and a good night's sleep."

"So what's stopping you?" Suz sipped her cup, poured herself another.

"Sitting here with you?"

"Laying it all at my doorstep are you? Just like always. Gets herself in trouble and lets me pick up the pieces." Suz grinned, because they'd both picked up the pieces for each other so many times. "Listen, I'll take on the distributor. I was going to ask you to give them a call, because you are sooo much better at being sweet and bitchy at the same time, but I'll deal with it. You've got enough on your plate."

"Sweet and bitchy?" Deena didn't like the sound of that, even if it was probably true.

"Sort of like sweet and sour, only vocal—and in your face." Suz must have read the look in Deena's eyes. "In a good way, of course!"

"Damn straight. Don't you forget it." Then she realized she swore and almost swore again. With a grimace, Deena hauled herself off the chair and leaned in for a Suz hug, then went to relieve Sly of the pink bows and barrettes Lana had decked him in. Such an all-suffering old man. He'd do anything for attention.

"Sly's got to home, sweetie." Lana's lips pressed out in a showy pout. "He's still not well and the doctor said he needs to get lots of rest. But you can come upstairs and visit tomorrow, okay?"

Lana's eyes sparkled as she nodded.

"Maybe we can play doctor, Sly, and I'll fix you *all* up." She slid off the couch as Deena cradled the big cat in her arms and grabbed the travel cage. The cat's fur smelled of Lana's little-girl soap and water.

"Mommy, can you and me make bandages so I can make Sly better tomorrow?"

"Sure, honey. I think I've got an old shirt we can tear into strips." That was Suz. She might be on welfare right now, but only because she was the best mother in the world. She felt her responsibility was to be there for her daughter.

Carrying Sly upstairs she almost wished little-girl wishes could make everything better. If that were the case Deena would never have relinquished hers. But big girls don't get princes or three wishes. They get hard work and sadness and deaths that you never quite understand. All you could do was deal. And be responsible.

Upstairs she pushed into her sanctuary of peace, ancient greed shag carpet, pale couches, the green spray of plants around the windows that gave onto a view out over Mission, the river, and across Sumas Prairie southward to the mountains and the magnificence of Mount Baker. She settled Sly on her cream-colored couch, set out feed for him, and forced herself into running gear. Get out, do a few miles, make sure she came back, then the hot bath—maybe with bubbles and candles tonight. Something nice and relaxing with soft music, and then bed and—please God—a good night's sleep—because lately even though she kept her apartment like a cool green refuge, it hadn't been enough to relax.

The afternoon light through the large windmill palm and dieffenbachia placed striated shadows and a green-gold haze on the pale yellow walls. Through the southern sliding glass doors between the kitchen and her small porch/verandah, Mount Baker gleamed smoky blue in the distance.

Some of her favorite memories as a kid were zipping down those slopes and feeling like a goddess because if she could ski those slopes, she could do anything with her future. Nowadays she just got through each day one at a time. Today, the realization saddened her.

She finished tying her runners and was just stretching out when someone knocked at the door. Hopefully it was just Suz come to tell her she'd dealt with the distributors, because Deena didn't really need another problem dropped in her lap.

"Let me guess. The guy's going to do the right thing," she said as she yanked open the door.

Not Suz. Her gaze lowered to meet Anita Underhill's and Deena stiffened.

"Anita?"

The younger woman's long hair swung around her hips like a shawl. She wore cut-off white shorts and a short-sleeved, blue t-shirt that skimmed away from her body. Anita looked her up and down.

"I've caught you in the middle of something haven't I?"

"I was just going for a run. The only way I can seem to get rid of tension these days." Deena stood at the door, not knowing what to do. She wanted—needed—that run, but Anita had a look in her eyes that Deena recognized—that of someone needing to talk. Sighing, she stepped back from the door. "The run can wait. Come on in."

Anita stepped inside, took in the apartment. Even though Deena had painted it and brought in new furniture, she knew with the old plasterboard and fake fireplace the place still had the slightly beat-up look of old age.

"You know, it's just like I imagined it would be." She must have seen the puzzlement on Deena's face. "As a kid I always wondered what kind of place you'd gone to in Alberta. When you told me about your house, I thought of something like this. I guess it's your style or something."

Anita's face suddenly colored as if she realized she'd been prattling on and possibly insulting her boss. Trying to cover up for whatever her real purpose was in coming here, Deena supposed, setting aside the possibility that she'd just been told her style was old fashioned.

She motioned Anita to a chair and Deena sank down on the couch. Sly came in from the kitchen and made a bee-line for her lap.

"So what can I do for you?"

She didn't mean to sound so cool and professional in her home, but it was anything but usual to have one of her staff come here. She made a point of keeping work and her life separate. She knew Suz would groan at that one.

Anita was still scanning the photos of Deena's parents, the Moulin Rouge poster print, the antique tea cart that had been her mother's, but that now held catalogues and cloth swatches for the business.

"I wanted to talk to you about working at the Hat. It's all so strange I thought maybe I could ask you for some pointers? I thought maybe that would help me fit in."

"Fit in." Deena almost laughed, but Anita's face was so earnest Deena didn't dare. "You come to me to ask how to fit in. Anita, I'm an ADW—that means I don't fit in. I'm separated by rank."

"But you know how things work, don't you? You've worked the line. You know how the staff work?" Anita's small face was uncharacteristically tight with concern and she seemed to have forgotten her smile.

"What's happened?" Deena sighed, figuring she probably already knew, but talking about it would help Anita get through the hazing that always happened with a new staff member.

She settled Sly so his claws didn't cut through the black Lycra and into her thighs and made her peace with the fact this probably was going to take a while. Regardless of her own needs, right now she had a worried young woman in front of her.

"Well, you see, after my first shift Lucy and Rosetta and Janet took me out with the guys for a beer." She frowned a little and the slight look of confusion sent a small runnel of anger through Deena. The damn women could set Anita up just as badly as any of the guys. Here was a kid who just wanted to fit in to her job, just like anyone. She nodded her encouragement for Anita to continue.

"We went out to the Heritage Pub—you know, that new place that sits on the bluff by Heritage Park. There were a lot of other Correctional staff there, too. Lucy and the others, they introduced me around. So we sat there, had some beer. Some of the guys played a little pool." Her small hands fidgeted with the hem of her shorts. "It's just, well, we stayed for a long time and then the guys started a drinking game and I seemed to keep losing."

That was enough. Deena held up her hand, cutting off the rest of what Anita had to say. Deena knew the smoky environs of the Heritage Pub. It was a C.O. hangout and a place she avoided like the plague.

"Let me guess. They got you drunk. You did something stupid and now you're mortified at what you did and are afraid to go back to work. You're wondering how to manage the whole affair."

The blood seemed to drain out of Anita's face as she nodded and for a moment Deena regretted being as blunt as she'd been.

"Darn it, Anita, what were you thinking? That this is college? High school maybe? These are men, Anita, and they might play the same games, but they play a lot harder."

Deena stood up, sending Sly onto the floor. He sent her a look of disgust at being dislodged from the comfort of her lap, then he leapt up and took over the spot she'd warmed up. Deena was pacing now, as she glanced at Anita.

"You came here expecting sympathy and a shoulder to cry on, didn't you?" When Anita didn't answer, it only made Deena madder. She stopped and leaned down with her face close to Anita's. "Didn't you?"

"Y-yes." Anita gulped air after answering, but tears were trailing down her face. Her chest convulsed.

"Darn it, Anita. Stop. Stop right now. You wanted to be a Correctional Officer. You wanted to be strong. I saw that in you on the unit after we dealt with Stickley. You did good—as yourself. That's what you have to do on this job—not collapse and cry. What do you think the guys are going to do if you collapse and cry on the job?"

Anita was struggling to stop her little hiccoughed sobs. She just needed to understand what she was up against, what she'd hired on to work with.

"What did you think you were going to find when you came to work in a correctional center?"

Anita paused, swallowed.

"Don't think about it. Tell me what's the first thing that pops into your head."

"I thought I was going to work with convicts."

"What about them?" Deena hated what she was about to do, what it said about the place she'd chosen to work, that she had to do this, but she had to push. She couldn't love, support or appear to care for this special young woman. She had to push her to be strong and resilient and responsible on her own, because Deena wouldn't be there all the time and a correctional center would eat the weak alive.

Anita wiped her eyes with the back of her arm.

"They were probably going to lie and be hard to deal with. Because of the prison sub-culture and their pasts, I guess. It was going to take me a while to feel comfortable working with them, but I had to be confident and demand respect from them even though they might have trouble working with women."

Deena stared up at Mount Baker. The pink stains of late afternoon had found the lower flanks of the mountain. At this rate she wasn't going to get out for her run. She turned back to Anita huddled in her chair.

"Good description. It also describes most of the correctional staff at the Center—including the women."

Anita blinked and Deena could see her trying to make sense of the comment. She crossed the room to stand over Anita.

"They're just as institutionalized as the cons, 'nita. Don't you see it? They have their own subculture, too. To become part of that culture they try to erase the parts of you that are important to you—your values, for instance. And then they want you to learn theirs. They'll let you be one of them if you live by their rules. Understand?"

"I...I think so." The tremor in Anita's voice had lessened. "You're telling me I have a choice about whether to become like them or not. But whatever I choose, it will impact how I get along with the staff."

At last. Someone who sort of understood how the sociological principles came into practice in a jail. Most other young correctional staff didn't. They spent their first month or so looking like they'd just been run over by a truck, and then they were sucked into the 'way-things-are-in the-system' and quit even questioning the status quo.

Deena knelt in front of her and caught her hands. "Let me tell you a story. It's not from Corrections. It's from policing. If you tell anyone else I'll deny it, understand?"

Anita nodded and Deena wondered why she was baring herself again. Why tell anyone anything that might come back to bite her? But she knew the answer. Seeing Rich Webster had brought a lot of things back and she was trying to help someone else avoid her mistakes.

"When I first got into policing I wasn't much older than you. I started in the detachment and started hanging out with the guys. It was good. We'd work. We'd party. We'd cruise in the police car and feel tough when we did liquor checks or stopped a car. It goes to your head, that authority. It also becomes really important to be one of the guys. I swore like them. I talked down about the people we picked up, like them. I even talked down about women, like them. And then one day I was with another police woman—one who had been on the job for a long time and who was pretty much a ghost at social events, but a good cop nonetheless. She asked me if I'd always acted like a man. It stopped me dead, because I realized I had just about lost everything that made me different from the guys except the ability to fit part A into slot B. I didn't like what it meant. I was a woman and it was okay to be different. Better, even. Her words got me myself back."

"You're telling me I need to quit trying to belong and do what's best for me."

"Be responsible for yourself."

"But I did something stupid last night."

Deena rolled her eyes. "Girl, if we locked up all the people who had done something stupid when they were young, there'd be no one on the street."

"You?"

"Goodness, yes." She grinned. "Fortunately I'm old enough most of them are just dim memories." But not all of them. Sometimes, when you got old enough, you just started to repeat some of the stupid things you did when you were young. Like sleeping with Ravi Sandhar.

"But how can I face these guys?"

"That, I can't tell you. You have to decide. But I'll tell you what I hope—that you'll be proud of yourself, no matter what, because I think there's a lot to be proud of. You did a good job on that shift and dealing with your first dead body. Heywood even said so and he doesn't say much good about anybody. And at least you're asking yourself these questions, Anita. A lot of new C.O.s don't."

The color began to creep back into Anita's features until finally she looked—really looked at Deena—and stood up.

"I should get going. I'm sorry. I really didn't mean to take you away from your run. I just needed to talk to someone and I didn't know who else to talk to."

The way she half-hung her head and looked out of the tops of her eyes almost made Deena laugh it was so reminiscent of Lana and of how Anita had acted when she was much younger. A young animal asking for attention and approval. If it hadn't been for their professional positions, Deena would have taken her young friend in a hug.

"Fine. It's all fine. I'm glad you came by, instead of letting this all eat you up. Working in a correctional center, well, the cons are the easy part—and I've got a good crew. The others are way tougher." Deena meant it as she said it. She was glad to help Anita, just as she'd been glad someone helped her. Pay it forward, as the saying went.

At the apartment door, Anita paused. She started to say thanks again, but Deena wasn't having. Anita's face still didn't carry its customary rosy color. She was still shook up. Whatever she'd done, she was struggling.

To hell with professional boundaries. For a moment, Rich Webster crossed her mind.

"Come here." She caught Anita in a reassuring hug and then set her away. "You'll do fine. Just keep remembering who you are, what you think is right and you'll do fine."

"It's just...I don't know if I'm as strong as you."

"You're plenty strong. Remember how you used to beat me at arm-wrestling?"

A watery smile, then. "I was ten."

"See what I mean? Strong. Now get outta here."

Deena watched her thunk down the red stairs and then closed the door. She slumped back against the wall, wishing she could find the strength she'd coached into Anita. Well strength was what other people saw, even though you were falling apart inside. She'd gotten good at doing strength.

Chapter 8

MISSION RCMP DETACHMENT was a small, twenty-five officer operation operating out of a low-slung building on the bluff above the river. Inside, beyond the public counter, it was a single large room, with an office for the Watch commander, the Inspector, a coffee room, and a shared office separated from the main room by a glass block wall for the detective section where Rich and Chuck hung their hats.

The rumors about Rich and Ivy were the buzz this morning around the detachment and led to many truncated conversations whenever he went to the coffee room. He really didn't give a damn about all the sympathetic glances because his head was full of Deena Hunter. Like he needed the headache of dealing with all the feelings she'd evoked.

All those years ago and he'd never kissed her.

He'd wanted to. It had been one of the toughest things he'd ever done to stay a training officer and drive around all those night shifts and simply treat her as another cop. Damn thing was, he'd wanted to kiss her today, too, because when he first saw her it was like he heard his heartbeat for the first time in years.

Even now, twelve hours later, his nose still held faint traces of the scent of her hair that he'd first caught when he'd damn near run her over. Deena Hunter.

'F'ing amazing.

He sorted through the Correctional Officer reports again. Overall, they weren't bad. Even the report by the Underhill girl was not bad. At least as good as a new RCMP recruit, and Deena's—well—hers was just as complete and detailed as he'd come to expect when he'd trained her. She'd taken his powers of observation and raised them to the next level. She'd been a good cop. Damn good.

Morinville Detachment had been sorry to see her go, but she'd left as soon as her mandatory three years were up and gone to St. Albert's. At the time he'd told himself it was better that way, because then he wouldn't be tempted to tell her how he felt. His marriage had already been going bad.

A lot of water under the bridge since them.

"Hey." Chuck slouched into the office and slid into his chair, his briefcase thunking onto the desk top. "Whatcha got there?"

"Reports from Hatzic."

Chuck only raised his brows in that 'tell-me-more' way that old cops had. He busied himself snapping open the leather case and hauling out files he'd worked on at home.

"Had a good interview last night for that grow-op case. I think we've got a lead on a couple more houses tied into organized crime. Have to pass it along to the Integrated Drug Task Force."

"That so?" Rich tapped the stack of reports into a pile and felt Chuck's gaze on him.

"Yup. It'll look good on our stats. Now what's got you so quiet this morning?"

Rich shrugged and Chuck snorted his disbelief. "Don't try that on me, partner. What's going on with that Hatzic case. You look like your worrying something around."

Rich pressed his fingers up through his hair. He hadn't thought his preoccupation with Deena showed so much. Be professional, he thought, her words coming back to him. Focus on the case. He scanned the reports.

"Couple of things actually. The evidence of it being a suicide doesn't all quite fit. The Assistant Deputy Warden—she pointed out how the ligature laces couldn't have come from his own shoes—he wore Velcro. And then there's her description of the cell and how it doesn't fit with the subject."

He shook his head, not knowing where to go with the case and knowing that wasn't like him. Chuck would know it, too.

"You got corroboration of the cell and the laces?"

"Yup. Young C.O. describes the scene almost identical to the Assistant Deputy Warden. The others all describe at least part of it. Dead guy was apparently the ADW's snitch, too, which would give the inmates motive to do the guy in, but there's something that's just not working." He shook his head and raised a tired gaze to Chuck.

"Let me guess, you were at the hospital with Ivy, again." A little frustration came through in Chuck's voice. He was getting tired of Rich's ongoing guilt.

"Actually, I wasn't. I just couldn't sleep." Rich didn't want to go into who had kept him up. There he'd been, laying in the dark with his head full of memories of working alongside a certain tall blonde. It was downright ridiculous that she'd have more impact on him than the woman he'd slept with the night before.

Chuck's gaze narrowed. "So what's not working?"

"It's timeline stuff. The guy was evidently alive when he went into his cell. According to the staff there was no one other than the inmate in the cell all night, just the officers checking through the windows on prowl. But this morning the unit officer found the guy dead when he first went on the unit. So I'm wondering, how come he saw it, and the prowl officers didn't? How come the EMT guys and coroner don't report any rigor when there should have been if the guy was dead for a while."

"It sounds like a suicide. Maybe your Assistant Deputy Warden is barking up the wrong tree."

Rich glanced down at the papers and thought of Deena Hunter. If there was one thing he'd learned about her long ago, it was that you could trust her instincts.

"Nope. She's got something. I can tell."

This got Chuck raising his brows. He shoved his briefcase and files aside, suddenly more interested than Rich probably wanted his partner to be.

"What was the time of death?"

Rich flipped through the papers. "Still waiting on the full M.E. report, but preliminary T.O.D. is right around the time he was discovered." He raised his brows at Chuck and saw the wheels turning.

"Staff?"

Rich thought of Deena's immediate refusal to go there. She trusted her staff—probably because she'd hand-picked them so they were the best of the bunch, but she had always expected people to hold the same high standards as she did.

"It's not my first choice. Could be that the ligature made dying real slow. He ties off the shoelaces, but then it takes him all night to die. Pretty tough way to go."

Chuck's gaze seemed to look into Rich—so hard and deep a part of him squirmed. Then Chuck blinked and things seemed normal again.

"So this case seems to have you tied up in knots a little." It was casual, but then Chuck's long spider arm swooped in to snag the top report on Rich's pile. Deena's report. "So just who is the Assistant Deputy Warden that's got you following along on her suspicions?"

He scanned the report, nodded at appropriate places, then looked up when he got the end.

Rich knew the expression on his face was a dead giveaway—sort of a cat-that-ate-the-canary look, but in his case the canary was too big to swallow. He might choke, and he knew it. He certainly didn't need his partner knowing it, too. He stood up to grab the report back, but Chuck tucked it into his lap.

"D. Hunter?" Dry humor and a small bit of wicked delight came through in Chuck's question. Rich could only grunt the affirmative.

"D. Hunter writes a report like a cop," Chuck observed thoughtfully. "Seems to me I recall you mentioning a Deena Hunter. Worked in Morinville and St. Albert Detachments. That wouldn't happen to be the same D. Hunter, would it?"

"I don't need this, right now, dammit. I've got enough on my plate just trying to figure out what to do." Rich managed to grab the report back from Chuck and settled himself back in his chair. His bloody partner had this big stupid grin on his face. "What? What are you smiling at?"

"Didn't I just say to quit lookin' and something would happen?"

"Like I need this? I've got work to do, man. How the hell am I supposed to work when I've got her in my head?"

"Do something about it?"

"Shit," he groaned. It was almost worse this time out than it had been all those years ago, because then he'd at least been doing the right thing to his way of thinking. He'd never pushed their friendship because he'd been faithful to Ivy. And so he hadn't known how Deena would react to any overtures on his part.

But this time he did, because he'd made it pretty bloody clear by asking for her phone number.

"You think I didn't try?" He ran his hands through his hair again and tried to focus on the case. When he looked up Chuck was still studying him with a grin on his face. "Look, I asked for her number and she went all professional on me. There's nothing there as far as she's concerned. I just have to get over it."

And he would dammit, because Ivy needed him and frankly he'd gotten along just fine without anyone since the split.

"I guess we'll see about that, won't we," Chuck said quietly. "Cause from where I'm sitting, you still got it bad, boyo."

Chapter 9

ANY WAY ANITA LOOKED AT IT, Dee might be right about being true to yourself, but she sure as heck had a lot wrong, too. Which was kinda scary given Anita had always thought of Dee as more or less infallible.

But a half an hour before her first evening shift, in the quiet of the women's locker room, with the steam and perfume gone, and inhaling only the scent of her well-polished leather boots, it sure seemed that Dee had missed the boat by a mile.

Sure, her general guidance about being responsible and not letting the job erode your values, were good. But this wasn't about losing your femininity. This was about doing something that stepped way beyond your morals. What was she supposed to do now?

How did she live that down?

It was worse than how she'd reacted to the body being found.

"Heywood get her out of here. The last thing we need is her tossing her cookies."

Heywood hauled her out of the cell and she fought for breath while down on the main floor of Unit E1 came a buzz-click and the door burst open admitting a bunch of other officers, a blonde Valkyrie at their head. The buzzing in her head was so loud she couldn't hear her own thoughts. She was afraid to speak for fear of what would pop out. A scream? Collapse?

Then the Valkyrie was giving orders in Dee's quiet voice. Dee had given her the once over, then sent her down to take charge of the unit logs and clear the staff from the unit. As if Dee had given Anita the chance to prove herself.

Apparently she had to Dee—ADW Hunter—but after Anita's actions the night before, she felt pretty—well - trampy, walking in amongst all those guys she'd been French kissing last night. She didn't know what had gotten into her.

Going out with the guys after her first shift had seemed okay to start, but then the beer had gone to her head far quicker than it had anyone else. She supposed it was because she didn't often drink. She didn't know when or how, but she knew there were a few beer under her belt when there'd been a kissing contest with the gals all being judged by guys from all the shifts.

So there she'd been, French kissing all the guys and going back for seconds when one of them said they couldn't judge. At some point she seemed to remember she and Rosetta both French kissing Randy Johal while sitting on his knees, and all three tongues getting tangled up in the act. Just the memory set her blushing.

It had been Chad Preston who'd called the whole thing off, saying things were getting a little bit too out of hand and offering to give her a ride home when he headed out earlier than the others. Thank God she'd been lucid enough to know she was in trouble.

Thank God more, Chad had been a gentleman and had dropped her off with no more than a devastating smile.

She tucked in her blue shirt and zipped up her trousers, then checked herself in the mirror. She could swear that the lines around her eyes were put there by yesterday's hangover. At least she didn't look like someone who'd acted no better than a whore. Maybe, it wouldn't be that bad. Maybe all the guys would give her a break for being young.

Besides, Dee had been right when she said you had to take responsibility for what you did. She'd made the mistake, she'd have to fix it.

"That's it," she said to herself in the mirror. "No more expecting anyone to fix your mistakes. Learn to live with them."

"A good philosophy," Janet Lefevre, said as she pushed in the door. She was dressed in blue uniform and the loose strands of her hair and the fatigue around her eyes spoke of her hours as a control officer, watching computer screens and tracking inmate movements through the jail.

"God, I'm tired. One hell of a day. A whole slew of new admissions from a big drug bust. Had to do a total population reassignment to make sure we didn't have enemies together. If I hear one more radio call about a bust'em up, I'll scream." She reached overhead and stretched her arms back, her shoulders audibly cracking.

She sauntered over and peered at Anita's face. "Still feeling Monday night, huh?"

"A little." But Anita didn't shake her head in denial. Her brain still felt just a little too tender. Something like that must have registered with Lefevre.

"Don't worry about it. I heard Johnson—the afternoon ADW—talking. He's short staffed so he'd going to use you on prowl. You can take it a little easier 'cause you won't have Heywood dragging you around."

Lefevre patted Anita's shoulder and started to pull off her shirt, muttering about how tired she was and how she just wanted to get the hell out of this fucking place, while Anita considered the news.

She was going to have to find her own way around the Center. That meant she was going to have to remember everything on her own. A little trickle of fear tightened her gut.

She could do this thing. She would do this thing. She'd told herself that—now she just had to believe it and to heck with what she'd done Monday night. Heck, it wasn't like she'd slept with anybody. It had been simple kissing—in fun.

Hell, she'd probably even do it again. No one had minded. Lucy and Rosetta hadn't been upset. Probably no one would say anything at all. They accepted mistakes, just like Janet said they'd understand if she was slower at doing prowl. It eased the taut feeling in her stomach.

"Maybe I'll see you next shift if I get called in," she said as she pushed the locker room door open. Lefevre only grunted.

Down the hall and she stopped to knock on the door of the ADW office.

"Come," a male voice growled and Anita pushed open the door, trying to exude confidence she didn't feel. She found herself facing two people with those three stripes on their collars. Deena had vacated the chair behind the desk and a barrel-chested man sat there, but the way the desk hit him mid chest he looked like a kid in his father's seat. His round face and protruding eyes were dark and staring as if he considered her a different species than he was used to dealing with.

"Yes?" His tone said he wanted to know why she was here and who she was, but for some reason his two-word vocabulary just struck everything she'd wanted to say from her brain. She stood there like a bump.

"I..." It was a start, but not good enough. He must think she was an idiot. He blinked like he was a fish.

"Brent, this is the Correctional Officer I was telling you about. ADW Brent Seger. Officer Anita Underhill. She did a good job on Monday."

He looked her up and down as Anita shot a thankful look in Dee's direction. "I heard about you."

But the look he gave her made her wonder whether it was Dee's recommendation or a story of Monday night's escapade. Darn it, she wasn't going to let that get in the way. Not with Dee sitting here.

"Sir, I understand you want me on prowl."

"Hmm. Yes. Hmm. Prowl." Her statement seemed to have deflected him from whatever he knew about her performance. "You know the way around the Center after your shift?"

So he had the same concerns she did, but Dee had said she'd done well and she sure as heck wasn't going to show any other weaknesses.

"I'll manage, Sir."

With only a nod, he flipped a portable and a door card in her direction and Anita beat it out of the office only to meet Chad Preston coming down the hall.

"Anita. How's it hanging? You recover alright? The Heritage's beer packs a wallop." His grin was light, easy, friendly and frankly she really needed that right now.

She grinned back. "I swear I thought my head was going to explode yesterday. That interview with the cop. Oh. My. God. I could hardly hold it together."

Chad's hand tapped her shoulder. "I think we all feel like that when we get the cops in. But don't feel like you can relax now. Managers'll have an internal investigation, too. There are going to be more brass floating around this place than you ever wanted to see. Ask me, they should just thank us for relieving the world of one more con."

His smooth dark gaze was locked on hers as if waiting for a reaction as she pondered what he'd said. Just what had he said? Finally she gave a little nod. It must have been what he wanted because he reached up to give a loose strand of her hair a little tug.

"You might want to fix that. Con could catch it and give a pull. Would hurt like hell."

She smoothed the piece of hair behind her ear, liking the fact he'd touched her. It made her feel feminine—she thought briefly of Dee's story. Not a problem.

"Thanks. I guess I'll see you next time on dayshift."

"Nope." He shook his head. "I hope you brought a big enough dinner for two, because I'm doing a double and after my gentlemanly behavior the other night, you owe me."

Little alarms started to go off in her head, and he must have read it in her face because suddenly he started to laugh. It was a nice laugh, friendly as he shook his head.

"Don't worry Underhill. I'm not after your body. I was just thinking dinner some time would be nice, you know? Get to know each other?"

And it would be nice. Chad had been an all-around nice guy since she'd met him—aside from the teasing at the suicide. But she hadn't known him then. She could think of worse ways to spend an evening that talking to a guy with dimples like Chad.

"So how are you for carrot and broccoli sticks?"

His gaze fell and she grinned. "Won't cut it, huh? And that's all I brought for dinner tonight. So sad. How about we take a rain check and I'll make you a real dinner some other time? Manfood."

"Sounds good. Set a date and I'll be there." He started to turn away, then stopped. "Have a good shift, Underhill. You on prowl?"

She nodded as she headed down the hall.

"When you get lost, I'm available for rescue," he called after her and she could feel his gaze warm on the back of her neck.

Somehow being rescued by Chad Preston didn't seem like such a bad thing. Working in the jail might just be better than she'd thought.

Chapter 10

THE MAIN DOORS TO THE HAT opened with barely a sigh and released Deena into a cool gray day. The weather had changed, grey clouds settling around the cedar, hemlock and spruce covered mountains that formed the northern side of the Fraser Valley. The Hat sat in its own small valley beyond the first ridge north of Mission right where the clouds caught and held on the mountain tops. It meant the bowl of land that contained the prison sat in its own damp little microclimate that made her think of mold. At the moment it was threatening to drizzle.

Another shift and another fifty cents, Deena told herself as she dragged her rear across the parking lot that spread across the entire front of the institution and its side yards. From the barbed wire-topped fence came the soft whir of surveillance cameras on their poles. Walking straight-backed to her Camry through the drizzle took a lot of energy, but she'd be damned if she'd let anyone see just how beat she was after this shift.

Too many fights with the new inmates on the units, and one brawl had sent one inmate and two staff to the hospital for x-rays and stitches, and that required some of Seger's staff to come in early to backfill for the injured staff. A request from Deputy Warden Digneault for her to schedule another round of staff interviews for the internal review of Stickley's death had taken far too much time to arrange, and Ravi Sandhar's constant demands for updates on the Center's new ISI had finally led to her snapping that she would get to it tomorrow if he'd just let her do her job today. She darn well hoped she could.

Tossing her uniform into the passenger seat, she sat behind the wheel of her car, door open to just breathe the tree scent on the moist air.

Cedar and juniper seemed to ease away tension. The local Indian Elders who visited the Hat said both were medicinal, and sitting here with her eyes closed and the patter of rain on the roof, she just might believe. Finally she closed the door, put her car in gear, waved at some of the other staff and headed home.

Driving down the mountain the view showed Mount Baker was lost in cloud, but sunbeams caught on the cornfields of Matsqui Prairie and on the brown ribbon of the Fraser River. Even the sun couldn't dispel the darkening mood she found herself in.

There was just too much to do today and when she got home she suspected there would just be more of the same. She'd brought her files on the ISI with her so hopefully she could get a head start on the work she needed to do tomorrow, but whether she got to it would depend on what Suz had been able to do with the fabric distributor and how healthy Sly was.

The twenty minute drive took her across Hatzic prairie with its low rolling farmland and following the Canadain Pacific Rail tracks past the many-fingered hand of Hatzic Lake, then through the worn-down main drag of Mission and up the hill to her street and her house. Just get home and get a cup of tea and sit for five quiet minutes before the rest of the day intruded.

The tall figure draped across the bottom flight of red stairs to her apartment made a change in plans inevitable. It was the last thing she needed.

She climbed out of her Camry, resenting and yet unreasonably pleased she was dressed in clean jeans and a white blouse that she knew set off her tanned skin. Carrying her uniform she avoided the minefield of children's toys and reached the stairs. Rich Webster blocked her access.

"So," she looked up at him and cocked her hip. He looked good, a feast for very tired eyes, but she wasn't going to cut him any slack. She needed to figure out just what he meant to her after so many years. "You got a reason for disturbing my peace?"

That mocking grin spread across his lips and she really would have liked to find a way to wipe them clean, but her brain was just too tired.

"Just paying you tit-for-tat."

"Pardon me?" She tried to ease past him onto the stairs but he placed his hands on each rail, effectively stopping her.

"I'm just saying you sort of threw a wrench into my day when you sent that report into the police. Figured I'd return the favor and keep you posted on what I'm thinking."

She felt herself color a little and knew he saw it. She could only hope he didn't know she'd thought this was something other than a professional meeting.

So maybe it was just professional. Maybe all her anxiety about seeing Rich Webster was simply in her mind. But there was...

"So you took the time to track down my home address when you could have phoned me at the Hat."

It was his turn to look uncomfortable and that made Deena feel a trifle better. Uncomfortable didn't suit him any better than it did her. Both of them liked to be in control. It had taken some time to get the hang of working together even when she was in training.

"I thought you'd appreciate not being seen with me at the Correctional Center. If this investigation goes the way I think it might, it'll be better than way. But I don't want to talk about it here, either." He stepped sideways, opening the stairwell to her. "Can I come up?"

Deena frowned and eased her back. She'd really hoped this evening would be her own—even if she did have to work.

"Can't it wait until tomorrow?"

Like she needed more to do then. But it would keep Rich Webster out of her house—preferable given how vulnerable she felt around him.

"I think we should talk now."

So there it was. He was going to have his way and she wasn't. She didn't like it, not one bit, but she hid it and led him up the stairs and inside.

He seemed to fill the room with his presence, and the green-gold light seemed to coalesce in his eyes when he turned back to her from studying the space.

"I like what you've done here. It's got a sense of peace and permanence, even though a lot of your decoration is with plants. It feels like a place a person could grow."

It shouldn't surprise her that he could be so astute, but it did. Even Suz only thought Deena just liked to surround herself with life and growing things. Sly came wandering out of the bedroom all sleepy eyed and meowing his demanding, pay-attention-to-me-because-I've-been-alone-all-day, Siamese-style meow.

Before she could shush Sly, Rich had scooped the black cat up and settled him in his arms.

"Well aren't you a big fellow? Friendly, too." He said as Sly gave him a head-butt to the chin that could have left a bruise on a lesser person.

"Pardon him. Sly's a slave to attention."

"He's got some age on him, too. A lot of white on his muzzle."

Her throat tightened a little and she fought it back, ignoring the frisson of warmth from where their hands touched as she relieved him of Sly. She would not let him see vulnerability.

"He's fifteen. Still rules the household, though." She pressed her face to warm fur and felt the rumble of the purr through her chest. God she loved this cat. Hated that she couldn't make him well—could lose him.

She shook off the maudlin thought and focused on her unwanted company.

"You want a beer? Coffee? Water? Tea?" She was making offers as if she was nervous. Dammit, she *was* nervous because Rich Webster was standing too close to her. She moved off to the kitchen. "Well?"

"A beer would be good." He stood in the doorway, watched her take a glass from the cupboard that would never stay closed, a beer from the fridge. "I could fix that for you if you like."

She turned back to him, suddenly aware he was too close once again, standing just behind her so she could feel heat off his body as he examined the errant cupboard door. Those strong hands of his checked the latch, the hinges.

"I think it's just a matter of replacing the hardware. This stuff must be damn near original. Am I right?"

She looked at the cupboards, at the latch he was flexing with his fingers and hadn't a clue what the answer was. At home she never bothered with things like woodwork. Here, she relaxed, while at work she would have been all over fixing the darn thing.

She caught him looking at her, those blue eyes somehow warm, inviting, open, and quickly looked away. She'd had enough heartache to prove she was no good with men, even if his gaze caused a tingle through her skin.

"Thanks, but no. Things are fine as they are." She led him back to the living room and settled in the chair, watched as he sat on the couch and stretched those long legs of his out in a way that screamed he owned the room. Damn him. He'd left the glass behind, too, to drink from the bottle like she did. "Now what was it you wanted?"

She knew it was the wrong question to ask as soon as the speculation came into his eyes. Thankfully, he let it ride.

"I got the M.E. report and you're not going to like it. M.E. can't pinpoint time of death, but it's pretty clear your Mr. Stickley didn't die in the middle of the night. He died within an hour of being found. I thought you'd want to know."

He sipped his beer as Deena considered. She did want to know, but it was probably the worst kind of news.

"So what you're telling me is either it was a suicide or a staff helped him on his way."

"I don't see any other way it could have happened."

The trouble was, neither did she. She sat back, Sly purring on her lap, and sipped the cold, yeasty flavor of the beer. She should be feeling exhausted, but the challenge of Rich's information set her mind spinning. She met his gaze.

"No matter how I go over what I saw in that cell, I can't get it to add up to suicide. Last time I talked to Stickley he had all these grandiose plans for when he got out. Things he was going to do with his family. And he'd made that appointment to see me. Nope, he just doesn't add up to a suicide."

"And you don't want to go to the other option, do you? You always want to believe the best in everybody." His smile was gentle, and she didn't like the fact that he still knew her so well. "Strange trait for a cop or a screw."

She rolled her eyes, hating the nickname. "There you go and ruin it, just when I was starting to like you again. I'm not a screw, Rich. Just like you're not a pig. Got that?"

The smile had transformed into that mocking grin of his, but he held up his hands. "Point taken. I shoulda remembered how you always took offence at those names."

"Because they're bad names. They denigrate important work."

"Hey, you're preaching to the converted here. It was a little slip, is all." He cocked his head and his blue eyes caught on hers. Held. And the grin suddenly went serious. "You know, Deena, you are exactly like I thought you'd be."

It wasn't what he said, exactly. It was more the soft yearning undertone of his voice that left her momentarily stumped for something to say.

How do you tell a guy that you've thought of him forever? Have dreamed of him? Her body went cold. The answer was, you didn't if you didn't want to get hurt in the ruins of another relationship.

"Some people just age well," was the best she could do.

Chapter 11

"SO WHAT YOU'RE TELLING ME is you're well-preserved?"

Deena's eyes had gone momentarily vulnerable, then guarded and Rich could have sworn he'd seen a moment of desire, but now he just wanted to swear at himself for being so stupid. He'd shown he'd thought about her, and the last thing he wanted was to put himself out there and get shot out of the water.

He'd rather just have the illusion of what might have been than the truth of there never being anything at all. He smiled, trying to keep his feelings out of it. Keep it light, because by the look of her, and the fact she was living in this small apartment that seemed all about fostering growth and change, there was a history he didn't know.

"Like a jar of my mother's strawberry jam." Her voice was dry, soft, but the tension went out of her shoulders as she settled back into her chair. Take it slow, he thought. Easy. He was used to easy from dealing with Ivy.

"You know, I was pretty shocked yesterday, when I saw you. It has got to be what? Fifteen-sixteen years since we last saw each other?"

"Twelve. It was twelve. I figured it out last night."

The fact she knew it so precisely made his stomach tighten a little. So she was just as aware as he was of the passing of the time. Maybe—just maybe she'd been kept awake by their meeting, too.

"Hard to believe. I heard you'd pulled the pin—that must be, what, about ten years ago?"

"Eight. I came home because my Mom was sick. I couldn't wait for a compassionate transfer."

"So you came here and got a job in the jail."

She nodded, her blonde hair falling around her face in a way that made him want to go over to her and tuck it behind her ears. "It must have been damn hard choosing. I remember how much you loved policing—and your mom."

She got that Madonna look again and it heated his blood. She nodded.

"Toughest thing I ever had to do, but it was the right thing. The responsible thing. It helped Mom to know I was there for her. After Dad died, she'd been so lonely." There was a misty look to her eyes that spoke of pain that was still not healed and he wanted to ease it away.

"I'm sorry."

Her gaze flipped up to him. "For what? You didn't give her kidney disease and no transplant in sight. You didn't make the choice."

There was that guardedness again and it saddened him that there were so many years separating them.

"I guess I'm sorry I wasn't there to help you through it. We were pretty good friends when we worked together. I always remembered that." He let it hang in the air, waiting to see what she would do.

Finally she smiled around another sip of beer, and his mouth went dry.

"We were, weren't we? It was one of the best times of my life." She swallowed and he watched the fine shift of her throat. Whatever was coming was hard for her. "So how's Ivy?"

He could have almost laughed at the hard look in her eyes. That was Deena Hunter all right. She never failed to name the elephant in the room—not with suspects, not with him.

"Ivy. God, there's a story to tell. We split up five years ago. We'd moved out here to be closer to her family—sort of hoping that might work some of the problems out. It didn't." The sigh escaped before he could stop it.

"Now it's my turn to be sorry. It's tough when things don't work out like you planned. You had such hopes. I remember you used to talk about Ivy all the time."

"Did I?" He didn't remember it, but he supposed he might have had to remind himself of his commitment when he'd been sitting next to a woman he was truly attracted to. "We were engaged."

"Yes. You were." That soft smile that seemed to come right from her heart. It stole his breath away, made him want to get up, go to her and apologize for being such an idiot all those years before.

"I heard you were married, too."

"I was. It didn't take. 'Nuff, said." She sipped her beer and this time there was speculation in her eyes. "So here we sit, two old friends with failed marriages. Here's to old friendships." She hefted her beer bottle and he clinked his against hers, then couldn't stop himself.

He caught her other hand and felt her tighten, her gaze still, her pupils as huge as the chance he was taking.

"I missed you Deena. I thought about you way more than is healthy."

"So you're telling me I make you sick?"

She was trying to cut through the energy he felt flowing across their fingers, but he wasn't going to let her get away with it. He needed her to understand, damn it. It was the only way he'd know if this was all a figment of his own active imagination.

"I'm telling you I made a mistake all those years ago. I should have held onto you."

"Don't, Rich. Just don't." She squeezed her eyes shut, pulled her hand back. "You don't know what you're doing."

"Don't I? I'm taking a big chance here. I'm trying to make things right. Are you telling me you don't feel anything?"

Her eyes jerked open and he could see the raw need there, even as she was shaking her head, cutting him off.

"What I'm saying is that I've got no place in my life for a... relationship. I'm no good in them. They only cause me pain and frankly I don't think I could stand anymore right now."

He opened his mouth to say more, but she stopped him with a pleading look.

"Please, Rich. Don't. Don't make this any harder than it is." She stood up, paced around the room, the black cat trailing behind her, meowing pathetically. Right now he felt a particular affinity for the animal.

"He looks like he's your familiar or something."

She glanced at the cat and smiled. "That's just Sly. He's my buddy."

Rich stood, faced her. "I'd like to be your buddy, too. At least that. I think it's important we have at least that." Because with friendship came closeness, and with closeness she might remember how she felt. He could hope that. At the least he'd still have Deena Hunter back in his life.

Another part of him crowed derision. Like he needed another woman to walk on egg-shells around. He already had that in Ivy and what he wanted was Deena—all of her—because she—she was his, damn it.

She stood framed in the window like something about to take flight. With the mountain's bulk behind her and those little arrow earrings glinting, it made her look like a goddess come to hunt the earth. He knew she'd already caught his heart.

"Guess we can do that. After all, we have a case we're working together." It came out soft and thoughtful, as if she was considering what friendship might bring. Maybe it would ease her fears a little, because obviously something had happened in her marriage, even though she wouldn't talk about it.

"So let's strategize about the case, shall we?"

Always the cop. He left her to pace and settled back into the couch, hoping it would be like catching Ivy's Majority Report—act like you were doing something else and the damn horse was sure to come nosing around where you could catch him.

To his satisfaction, she came back and settled in her chair, kicking off her shoes. A good sign. As if settling the nature of their relationship had been what she needed to relax.

"Another beer?"

"Mine's dead, so yeah."

She accepted his empty and padded into the kitchen, brought him another and settled into her chair, curling her legs underneath her. Sly, of course, was immediately up and settling into her lap. He could envy that cat and his closeness.

"So what do you think?" she asked. "Cause I'm sort of feeling like I should interview the inmates on the unit. They'll have information about Stickley's frame of mind. They might also be able to say whether they heard or saw anything—if we can get them to talk. And then there's the computer logs and videotape from the institutional cameras to see when the door was cracked and who had egress. I've already got them locked in my office for the internal investigation."

He shook his head, letting his admiration show. "You are a piece of work, woman. Does that mind of yours ever shut off?"

"Nope. It's a curse. Keeps me up at night." A quick grin, as erotic to him in its playfulness as another woman's strip tease.

"I guess that leaves interviewing the widow Stickley to me."

"Guess it does." She grinned over her beer. "You know, this is kinda nice, Webster. I think I might have missed you."

His heart did a thu-thunk and he knew he was damn-well lost and he wasn't sure how to handle it in front of her. He checked his watch, sorry he had to cut this short, but knowing it was better that he did, before he blew it.

"I better get going. You'll take care of those interviews?"

He stood up and she led him to the door, stood close enough he could see the tops of her breasts through the shirt's open v-neck. She nodded.

"Better you're not involved, because police'll just spook everyone." She grinned. "The staff probably more than the cons. But I'll let you know what I find out. You'll do the same?"

"Sure." The apricot scent of her hair kept catching at his thoughts. "So…I'll pop by tomorrow and we'll share notes. I'll bring my tools and fix that cupboard for you."

"Not necessary, I told you." This time it was him that stopped her.

"It's what friends do, Deena. Help each other out. Fix things."

It seemed to force her to acquiesce as he handed her his mostly empty beer bottle and went out the door.

"So tomorrow, then. I'll meet you here."

He went down the stairs and realized he was whistling.

Chapter 12

DEENA BARELY HAD THE DOOR shut behind him, barely had a chance to breathe because Rich Webster had that effect on her, when there came another knock on the door.

Maybe he'd come back.

If he had, she didn't know if she could let him out that door again, because he'd just worked her and worked her hard, like only an experienced cop could work a con. For some reason she didn't mind that she'd seen what he was doing. In fact, it kind of turned her on that he'd actually been willing to work so hard.

The damn apartment was too hot, she thought, as she crossed to the door. She ran her hands over her hair, fanned herself with her shirt and opened the door casual-like.

Unfortunately—or fortunately because she just might have embarrassed herself and kissed him—it was Suz standing on the small landing.

"Okay, girl, tell all." She was shaking her head, pushed Deena one-handed back into the apartment and closed the door. "Lana's playing at the neighbors. That was him, wasn't it? The guy? That Rich Webster?"

"Yeah, that was him."

"So what'd he want?"

"Me, apparently. Until I set him straight."

"What!" Suz grabbed her hand and dragged her in to the couch, pushed her onto one end and then settled herself at the other. "Start talking, because I'm going to slap you if you've gone and done something to chase that guy away. That is a sweet piece of man-flesh."

"I'm sure he'll be pleased to hear that," Deena said dryly. "One always wishes to be compared to a piece of meat. I know it makes my knees go rubbery."

"Stop avoiding the question. What was he doing here?"

Deena couldn't avoid Suz's questions, because Suz, when she got a bee in her bonnet, was a lot like a barnacle on a tugboat hull. It just wasn't going to let go unless you pried it off, and the prying would likely do serious harm to the barnacle. Deena wasn't prepared to harm Suz.

"Alright-already. He wanted to talk about the case and then he was suddenly talking about us and how we'd worked so well together as partners, and how his marriage didn't work out and how mine didn't either."

"Oh goody. So you both cleared the decks. Good going, Dee."

"No we didn't clear the decks. Darn it, Suz. You know as well as I do that I'm prone to relationships like train wrecks. I don't want to do that again. I couldn't stand the pain and frankly I don't want to lose him that way either."

"What are you talking about? Did you ever think the reason for all the train wrecks is because you haven't found the right relationship?" One of Suz's brows had arched up until it almost looked like it could touch her heart-shaped hairline. She did not look pleased. As a matter of fact she looked like she could pick Deena up by the scruff of her neck and just, well, shake her.

"He's my friend, Suz. At least that what I'd like him to be. He was my friend before, too. Maybe I'm better at friendships with men than with anything more. I've kept male friends."

"Name one."

"Well there's Brent Seger and Mitch Digneault from work."

"Puh." They don't count. Those are coworkers, not friends." Suz shook her head so adamantly, it almost pissed Deena off.

"Since when can't co-workers be friends?"

"Since you work in a jail. When was the last time you had any of those so-called friends up to your place?"

"Well...never." Damn. Suz had her there.

"The defense rests."

"And the red-head is a lawyer now?"

"I could have been."

"Yes. And now you're pissing me off like a lawyer does. Suz it just isn't meant to be. We're going to keep this professional, friendly. That's all."

"So when are you seeing your professional friend again?" Suz's avid expression latched onto Deena and she couldn't deny she felt a little bit excited that she *would* see him again.

"Tomorrow." She held up her hand to stop Suz's crowing. "He's coming over to talk about the case, is all. And he's bringing some tools to fix that darn cupboard latch. That's all."

Suz's face split in a loud guffaw and Deena was about ready to pick her chortling friend up by the scruff and dump her out the door.

"Tools. The man's bringing tools and she can't see it. For god's sake Deena, men don't bring tools to fix things in just any woman's house. They bring them to a girl-friend's, a mother's, someone they care about."

"Like a friend."

"No—they bring tools to someone they're interested in. Sort of like a bird of paradise will show potential mates the sticks and stuff they've gathered for a nest." Suz puffed up her chest and made her voice deep. "Here, woman. Me strong man with tools. I fix things. Good provider."

"And you know this how?"

"Hey, I watch wild kingdom. Lana likes the animals."

"I really should just dump your ass out the door."

"You just don't like the truth 'cause it might mean you're desirable instead of just a kick-ass ADW."

Desirable. Now that was an unfamiliar thought—at least not one she'd thought of in terms of anything as positive as the flutter Rich raised inside her.

Her short affair with Ravi had left any feeling she had of being attractive sullied with the knowledge that she'd been the other woman. Truth be told, when she'd found out he was still married she'd felt cheap and tawdry. She didn't like feeling that way. When she'd broken it off, she'd done everything in her power to make herself less desirable.

"It's okay to be desirable, Dee." As usual, Suz had read Deena's insecurities. Her red-haired friend was far too tuned in. "Sometimes I think you just hide behind being tough, you know. Like a guy."

That rocked Deena, but again Suz seemed to know what she was thinking.

"It's not like you're masculine or anything on the outside." Suz's pert mouth was firmed into a line as she assessed Deena. "Nope, if I was a guy, I think I'd find you eminently desirable. It's that blonde thing I guess." She sighed and fingered her mess of red curls. "I think it's something you've done to yourself inside. All this being strong has cut you off from the other side. The soft side I remember from school. Instead you seem to keep everything locked up tight."

"Yeah, like I can be all soft and weepy as a cop. Or a Correctional Officer. Or an ADW for that matter. Tell you what, I'll try to cry at least once a day, okay? In private."

"That might be a good thing, Dee. I haven't seen you cry since your Mom passed, and I know things get to you. Heck you just sucked it up when you and Blake fell apart. You even seemed to take pride in the fact." Suz reached in and caught Dee's hand, an expression of worry on her face that Deena didn't want to see. The wreck of her marriage to Blake had been something that almost took her down until she decided to be strong.

"I'm worried about you, Dee. You're locking the world out, except for me and Lana and sometimes I think you'd even rather we weren't here."

"Hold on there, partner. That is never going to happen." Deena caught Suz's shoulders and gave her a little shake when she saw the way Suz's eyes were filling. "We're partners, right? Through thick and thin, right? Besides, Lana's my Goddaughter. You think I'm going to let you make her all girly without some sort of counter-balancing influence?"

"So you're the man in my daughter's life?"

"Could be." The two of them looked each other hard in the eye and neither could hold it very long. Deena fell back against the couch laughing. Suz caught her in a hug that felt so darn good.

Then Suz went serious. "Listen, I didn't really just come up to bug you about your delectable guy-friend with tools." She grinned when Deena fisted her hand. "Hold on. I came up to tell you I got in touch with the fabric distributor. It didn't go well, Dee. He left it that he might be able to get us the fabric, and he might be able to get it to us in time for us to get the prototypes made. I don't know what more to do. My sweetness just didn't seem to cut it."

Deena sighed. Not what she needed, but she knew Suz would have given it her best shot.

"See, this is why you want me to be like I am. A bitch. I'll give him a call in the morning. Now I need some time to take care of some work stuff, okay?"

At the door Suz gave Deena another hug. "Thanks, okay. Sorry I'm not quite as tough as you. I promise I'll make it up to you."

"Yeah, right."

"Really. Between Lana and I, we will."

"Tell that to someone who hasn't known you as long as I have."

Suz snorted her disagreement, then started down the steps. Half-way down she started chortling and glanced back up the red stairs. "Silly woman doesn't even know what a man with tools means. Go figure."

Chapter 13

HALF WAY THROUGH SHIFT AND Anita already felt like she was so far behind she might never catch up. She jogged down the Center's long, antiseptic-smelling halls, the prowl time punch heavy in her hands, and hoped she was headed toward Living Units E1 and E2. She knew she was already five minutes late on the clock and that wouldn't look good on either the computer monitors or her work record.

If only she hadn't gotten lost in the program area, things would have been alright, but one door looked much like another in the jail and she'd missed the entrance to the fiberglass shop when a work crew came by. She'd gone all the way to the outside door and then realized her mistake because the darn punch clock wouldn't accept the check-ins in a different order than programmed.

Her footfall echoed back at her, but otherwise the halls were mostly quiet. The inmates were all in their living units, and the day was winding down as the dinner hour approached with the expectation she would relieve the officers in the living units for their half hour dinner breaks.

They wouldn't appreciate her lateness either, because if she was late for the first officer, she was going to be late for all the rest.

She came to a hallway junction, turned left and spotted the familiar doors with the large E1 painted on them. Half running, she reached the door, passed her card over the monitor and yanked the door open to stride inside the unit where the death had occurred.

At least it only reeked with what she had come to think of as the heavy scent of 'cons'—sweat and clothing that could use a laundering. The

T.V., purchased by the inmates through money earned through their work, blared a game show. Four men played pool in the next room.

One of the men watching T.V. looked up, then raised his chin at her. She felt his companion's gazes and was uncomfortably aware she was alone with a roomful of men who didn't mind breaking rules. It scared her a little—until she remembered that she was strong. Hadn't Dee said it? Hadn't Chad accepted her?

And speaking of Chad—he waved her over from where he was talking to an inmate at the miniscule Correctional Officer's office.

"Okay, so I'd advise you to make this last," he said to the inmate as she arrived. The other man stuffed something in his pocket. "You don't know when I'll be on this unit again, understand?"

The inmate, a big, barrel-chested man with shoulder-length bushy hair and prison tats spelling out 'love' and 'hate' across his knuckles, went to say something, but Chad cut him off.

"No discussion, Corvin. I'm going on dinner break. This is C.O. Underhill. I figure you better listen to her like you do me, or there'll be hell to pay, understand?"

The inmate, Corvin, turned watered-blue eyes on Anita and she fought back the urge to shiver. They were cold, without much humanity left in them. Then he smiled and it was like he pulled warmth up from hidden depths.

"Pleased to meet you, Ma'am."

"Corvin," she returned the nod.

Corvin glanced at Chad and then eased away from the door walking so quiet, it made Anita a little nervous.

"Corvin."

The big man turned back to Chad.

"See the others know what I said."

He nodded and went into the pool room, as Chad turned back to Anita. "So how's it going?"

She lifted her chin at the clock on the wall and pushed a loose piece of hair behind her ear. "How does it look like it's going? I got lost—almost had to send out for search and rescue."

She grinned, cocked her head up at him and realized she was darn well flirting, but he didn't mind. So much for Dee's worries about femininity, but then being not much more than five feet tall, it was a lot easier for guys to see you that way.

"So you should take off. I don't want to keep the other Unit Officers even later. What do I need to know about the unit? That Corvin—you gave him something—anything I should know about?"

"Come on, Underhill. Don't go all Hunter on me. No one does the rounds on time—except maybe Heywood." He closed the door behind them and motioned her to the chair so she found herself sitting crotch height to him. She felt herself warm and knew her face had colored. Nope, she was no Dee, because Dee wouldn't have allowed herself to be in this position, and she sure as heck wouldn't be so aware of the male anatomy.

Chad simply looked down at her from his height.

"So the guys have been pretty quiet tonight. I guess all the fights today took it out of them. Keep an eye on the pool game, though. Rogers and Henry can be dynamite together, but so far they're playing nice. If you need to get information out to them, talk to Corvin. They respect him. Got it?"

She nodded, went to stand, but for some reason Chad seemed to fill all the space in the office. If she stood, she'd be pressed against him.

She stayed where she was. "You should get going, 'cause I really need to keep breaks going around the Center."

"Underhill, would you relax? Yeah, you need to keep the check-ins going and to relieve the officers, but it's not life and death. We're here for each other, right? If you miss meeting the times or relieving us for dinner, we understand. Okay? And you'll get better. We don't mind carrying you - for a while. Besides, we all need someone to watch our backs."

He opened the door, smiled back at her. "When I get back, I want to hear about the menu you've got planned for our dinner. Make sure it meets my approval and all that."

He left her with the nice smile and the tight feeling inside that came from knowing the rest of this shift were carrying her. She darn well was going to get better. Dee had been so wrong. What Anita had done at the bar didn't seem to matter at all.

What mattered was being there for the guys, showing them she was dependable and could carry her weight. She was going to make these guys want her on their shift. She had to.

Chapter 14

SEATED IN THE FAMILIAR CONFINES of the SCO office, Deena shifted in her chair and ignored the tired squeal. She shifted the papers in front of her, feigning total interest, when all her focus was on the man seated in the chair across from her. She'd even advised Control not to disturb her unless it was an emergency.

Jim Henry was the last of the inmates Deena planned to interview. He was an old con, big man, big in the biker gangs, and solid enough he wasn't going to give anything away without a battle. He wore his prison greens with sleeves rolled up to display his massive forearms with the snake and skull tattoo that matched the leathers he no doubt wore on the outside. He had dark eyes like pits that right now were trained on Deena.

The trouble was all the other things in Deena's life kept creeping into her brain and the effort of focusing on Henry just left her tired and wanting to be home.

Sly had had an accident again in the morning. That and having him cry for more food just about broke her heart before the day even started. She needed to get his insulin evened out, but work took her away. She was beginning to think the job just demanded too much. Suz had said it often enough. She'd always disagreed before.

"So you know they call you the bitch-goddess of day shift."

She glanced up at him from the papers and smiled at his opening gambit. Inmates were born conmen, always looking for your weakness.

"That's nice. Goddess shows respect, don't you think?"

The guy looked around her office—it wasn't usual that a con would be brought here, but she wanted to interview in private, before the

Internal Investigation started. Those big-wigs rarely interviewed prisoners. They were more intent on preventing suicide deaths—not on identifying a murderer. But if she could get evidence by interviewing the inmates, it would help the police investigation. It was also something she could say she was doing as part of the ISI Ravi still pestered her about.

"So why'd you have me brought here. I haven't done nothing wrong." He crossed his arms over his chest and leaned back in the plain wooden chair so its joints creaked and she had to swallow her smile at the man's bravado. He was nervous.

Deena studied the papers again. Let him think she knew something, even if she didn't. He obviously didn't like the fact he had been pulled from his work and made to sit in a holding cell awaiting her pleasure. The wait had made him cranky and cranky men sometimes let things slip. She counted on it.

"So. We know Stickley didn't commit suicide." She saw the slight widening of his eyes, then awareness of her observation slammed down like blinds over his eyes. Just like a good ol' con. "Why don't you tell me about it?"

"I'm not telling you jack shit."

"Mr. Henry, you occupied the cell next to Stickley on the night he died. You're an observant man. You know how things work." She nodded at his tats. "When things happened, you would have seen it. I want you to tell me what and who you saw."

"I didn't see nothing."

But the flicker in his eyes told her otherwise. She matched his body language and leaned back.

"You certainly saw Mr. Knight take your candy bar. Beat him pretty bad from what the medical report says. Going to go badly when you come to Warden's court. I'd say you could expect to be in isolation for a good stretch."

"I can do hard time." But his down-turned lips said he didn't like it and that was something she could work with.

"I'm sure you can. You've got a lot of years inside and this is just a short stint. But things could go a lot better if I can put in a word about how you cooperated."

"You trying to bribe me?"

Deena just smiled sweetly.

"Warden's court doesn't have the same rules of evidence."

She watched him mull that over, but his gaze when it met hers was still solid con. Too solid. He wasn't buying and that meant all her plans were really going down the toilet today. She hoped Rich was having better luck than she was.

"I'm not a rat. I don't plan on being one. Now if you'll just get one of those screws of yours to take my sorry ass back to work, I'll let you get on with your day."

He half-rose out of his chair and that was not something to be tolerated.

"Sit down," she said quietly.

He didn't.

"I said sit down!" She was half out of her chair, standing eye-to-eye with him and maybe he wasn't used to a woman ordering him around, or maybe it was the fact he saw her flash of anger and knew what it could mean to his stay at the Hat.

He sat.

Deena eased herself back into her chair and let the anger dissolve off her face so she smiled pleasantly.

"You know, Mr. Henry, I have a lot of paperwork to do here, and I can see you need to do some heavy thinking about how you plan to spend your time at the Hat. Now I'm going to sit here and work and you can sit here for the rest of the bloody day until you decide to talk. Of course if you're in here that length of time people are going to think we had a nice long chat. They're going to wonder what we had to talk about. Understand?"

He snarled an epithet at her, his fingers clenching the arms of the chair so she could actually hear the wood groan. For a moment she thought he might throw it at her and she readied herself to move.

He glared. "You'd really do that?"

"Did they tell you I used to be a cop?"

"Shit." He closed his eyes. "Look. I ain't no rat. If I do, I'll end up dead on the outside and I got a wife and kids."

"So I'm supposed to feel sorry for you?"

"No, you aren't fucking supposed to feel sorry for me." He was clenching the chair arms again, shaking his head. "Fuck this. Fuck you. Fuck the whole fucking institution."

"Not too helpful, Mr. Henry. And you really do need to work on your vocabulary. The staff here are Correctional Officers. See you refer to them that way."

She knew she was treading on the edge when he stopped. His chest heaved with his anger, the same anger he'd used on his whores when he caught them trying to stash some of the cash they earned on their backs. But she was no whore and if he came at her, she had the skills to fight back and an institution full of back-up. Of course, they both knew him trying anything would be a very stupid move.

Henry met her gaze.

"Lady, you need to listen. You want to know how Stickley died, stop talking to the cons and maybe try talking to your staff. That's all I got to say. You can keep me here for the rest of your damn life, for all I care."

He crossed his arms again and leaned back in the chair with his eyes closed as if he was settling in for the proverbial long winter's nap.

The conversation was over, she knew. Henry had shut down and he was the kind of con who could keep his counsel no matter what kind of pressure she brought to bear. She picked up the phone and called control for staff to remove him.

When she finished she found him looking at her.

"I don't like you Mr. Henry. And I don't like what you're trying to suggest about my staff."

"You think I give a flying fuck?"

"If you're trying to create suspicion between me and my staff, it's not going to happen."

A smile lifted the corners of his lips as if they were on a string. Uneven yellow teeth showed.

"You really don't have a fucking clue, do you? Expect everyone to be like you."

A knock came at the door and he stood as Randy Johal stepped in. Randy glanced at Deena and looked Henry up and down. He was a good officer—a little too impressed with himself perhaps—given he was Supervising Officer on Deena's shift—but then he'd impressed Deena, too. That was why she'd give him the job and was grooming him for promotion.

"You done grilling this guy?"

Deena gave a tired nod.

"Don't put him back in population. Put him in observation 'til the end of the shift."

"You got some concerns the shift should know about?"

She felt Henry's gaze on her. She didn't even want to think about the potential for his story to be right, but she also couldn't ignore it.

"Let's just say Mr. Henry and I had a disagreement and I want him to have time to reflect on the error of his ways."

Henry snorted, but Johal already had him by the arm and was hauling him out the door. When it closed behind them, Deena leaned back and copied Henry; she closed her eyes. God, she was tired and the last thing she needed was to have suspicion separate her from her staff. Which was probably what Henry intended by saying it. For a moment she wished the shift was over and she only had Rich Webster' visit to 'get through' before she could focus on Sly.

Look forward to, was more like it, but she wasn't going to allow herself to go there.

Nope, she had to focus on what Henry insinuated. For all her desire to deny it, a part of her had the little alarms going off that had always served her well as a Police Officer. It had even saved her life once, when they'd responded to a complaint of a family dispute. When she'd attended with her Auxiliary Constable partner, something hadn't seemed right. The place had been silent and she'd forced her partner to stay in the car calling for backup while she decided how to go in the front door.

Usually she'd simply knock and stand by the door. This time the tingly sensation reminded her of all the stories of shots fired through a door. Good thing, because the three shotgun blasts through the door and door frame would have cut her almost in half.

So something she trusted was giving her a warning and when she had these feelings she needed to understand why. That need to know had led to her rapid promotion and right now it was leading her to do something she really didn't want to do.

She picked up the phone and just sat. Damn, this was the last thing she needed to be doing, but she supposed it was only putting off the inevitable. At least she could probably kill a couple of birds with one stone, as the saying went.

She dialed, and the phone picked up after only two rings at the other end.

"Fraser Regional Correctional Center."

"ADW Roberts, please."

"One moment."

A click and a ring and then the phone picked up and a voice said 'hello'.

Deena thought she was going to be sick then and there.

Chapter 15

T HE SCO OFFICE AIR SUDDENLY became too hot and cloying and she struggled to loosen her collar and stood up to shift around the office. Didn't help—not when she felt like she should be running and should keep on running for a hundred miles.

"Roberts."

His voice was crisp, professional, emotionless, but Deena remembered too well all the emotions that low voice could carry. Like the heat of passion, the low, sultry tone of seduction, and the cold flatness of disdain. It had been worse than hate, and it made her almost hang up except she knew he'd be reading the caller ID on his phone.

Still, she hesitated.

"Deena, that you?"

She grimaced and returned to her chair.

"Blake. Hi." She was pleased at how professional she sounded. "Long time no talk to."

"So you needed to break the tradition?" Her ex put her in her place, just like he'd always done, and she took a deep breath to stop all the old frustrations from coming back. From the heat of mutual passion, their relationship had quickly fallen to the depth of hate. He'd cheated with just about anything that walked and she'd thrown herself into her work to ignore Blake's innuendo that she was a manipulative bitch and a cold fish in bed.

Two years later she could no longer be responsible for how he acted, only for herself, and she was damn well going to be bigger than him.

"Ravi Sandhar has decided he wants to establish an ISI at the Hat. I understand you're the ISI guru, so I thought we needed to touch bases."

Let the compliment salve him; make him feel as big as his ego had always demanded. For a tall man, Blake Roberts had always had unbelievably low self-esteem—to the point where he constantly accused her of fooling around when he was the one screwing around on her.

She'd put everything into their marriage—her whole heart and soul—so when she'd found out the truth she'd been humiliated and broken, and it had taken throwing herself into her job, and the project with Suz to get her life back in order.

Until Ravi Sandhar came along. That had been the final lesson not to trust men. Focus on her responsibilities—that was a whole lot safer.

"What do you want to know? You read my paper on it then you know everything."

"I didn't know there was a paper. Sandhar didn't provide it."

"I'll fax it over. Is that everything?"

"I'd like to talk about this a bit, if it's not too much trouble." She damned herself for the way her bitterness came through in her tone. He must have caught it.

"Shit. Like I need this."

"If this isn't a good time, we could set another, but I need to talk this through. Tell me what your objective was in creating ISI and how you got started. I'll be able to build from there."

"My paper will cover that..." Deena sat back in her chair, hating the fact she was having to wheedle him for information. He probably thought she was pathetic, looking to rekindle contact with him or something.

"So how's Renneth? I heard she had her baby." She put it all on the table and the phone went silent.

"So you heard." He asked it almost gently, as if he was afraid she might break apart because her ex-husband's new wife—one of the women he had screwed around with while they were married—had had the baby Deena had never produced when they were a couple.

"Yeah, I heard. Congratulations. I heard it's a girl." The fact she kept herself cool, even, seemed to defrost a little of his attitude.

"Amber Pearl Roberts. Both our mother's first names. She's a doll."

"You always did want to be a dad. Bet you're a good one." It almost choked her to say it.

"I try, but the cost of all the damn baby equipment is darn near breaking the bank."

"Why do think I never got pregnant? We wanted holidays."

"We did, didn't we?" It was soft, and Deena blew out a breath. He might just help her. At least the worst of it had settled and she only felt like a knife was embedded in her gut when she heard his voice.

"So—I proposed the ISI to my director because he kept hearing rumors about drugs coming into the Center. I thought myself and maybe a couple of good officers could collect intelligence in the Center that might help to determine what was going on."

"So it was intended to deal with drug problems."

"That was how it started. Now we deal with a lot of things—other contraband mostly. Stills and so on."

"And how is this better than just using snitches?"

"It's coordinated. People get different information depending on who they talk to, or what shift they're on. ISI is a clearing house. What we can't do anything with, we pass along."

Deena stayed silent, letting Blake talk, because he did like to expound on things.

"Like we got intel that some drugs were moving into Surrey, so we passed it along to their intake guys and they stopped a few vials of cocaine from getting in. I know it doesn't sound like much, but our snitches are starting to get confidence in us and we're getting better information all the time. If those rumors about drugs in the correctional centers are true, we're going to shut it down. It's been a good program—one you probably should have at the Hat."

That brought her upright, because he was clearly suggesting something about the Hat and Blake Roberts wasn't the kind to trade that kind of information for free. He was more the kind to gloat when something went wrong.

"So you're hearing about the Hat, are you?" This was her opening— what she'd hoped would happen.

"You always hear rumors, but nothing definitive. You run a good Center there, and I know it."

"So what kind of rumors do you hear?" Keep him talking and he might not notice what he was telling her.

"Shoot, Deena, you know. The usual crap. Drugs coming into the Center. Organized crime. And so on."

She allowed herself to laugh. "Oh you mean the *crazy* stories. Like stories of staff doing stuff?"

There was a moment of silence on the phone that spoke as loud as rock concert.

"Of course not." He laughed with her, but the sound was forced. He knew something, but some things were just too uncomfortable to be spoken. Besides, Blake Roberts was a serious Union man and would do nothing to sully his coworkers. Sis-boom-ba, she thought. Correctional Officers forever. Guys like Blake treated their coworkers like a friggin' fraternity—complete with initiation and a solidarity that could be as tough for management to crack as it was to crack the inmate code of silence. Heck, the C.O.s had their own code of silence.

"So it sounds like you're really liking this added responsibility."

"It keeps me in the loop, you know?"

She did know. Blake had always wanted to control her and when he couldn't he went looking for women he could, so now he got to control information in his Center and look like a big man to boot. That'd be his style.

"And you figure it's doing some good."

"It's doing a lot of good, now that I've got the right people working with me. The gangs outside the institution are always trying to get drugs into their crew inside. Lucrative business with a captive market. We stop 'em. You could do worse than to start an ISI at the Hat. As a matter of fact, a couple of your guys have even asked me about it—and if they could help out from your end."

Deena stiffened. This was Blake's way of trying to get her to thank him for doing her a favor by keeping tabs on the Hat as well, when in truth what he'd been doing was keeping a little bit of power over her.

"And who would these helpful souls be," she asked so sweetly it made her want to gag.

"A couple of your guys, actually. Preston. Johal. Sihota. Heard something once from Heywood, but he's dropped out of sight."

"Well, thanks for the heads up. Do you mind if I call to pick your brains again?" And she really did mean pick his brains because this whole conversation had just turned the little alarm into a claxon. Trouble was, she wasn't sure if her reaction was to his information or to him honing on the Hat.

"Nah. Any time. And Deena—I'm glad I can be of help. I was saying to Renneth the other day how I wished you could be as happy as we are. Anything to give you a hand getting your life in order."

He hung up and left her sitting there, staring at the phone and seriously wanting to march right over to Fraser Regional Correctional Center and throttle the life out of the guy. Or strangle him with the phone cord.

Like she needed to get her life in order.

"Asshole. Bastard. Frigging asshole bastard." Shit—she was swearing and the epithets just weren't frigging bad enough to convey the twisted feeling she had for Blake Roberts. And after she'd tried to be nice.

Well, with her team she'd have the best friggin' ISI in the B.C. Corrections pretty damn quick. At least she had the information she needed to get Ravi his implementation plan.

"And then you can eat my shorts, Blake Roberts. Just you wait and see."

Chapter 16

THE WIFE OF THE DEAD INMATE lived in a mildew and moss covered rental house at the end of a narrow driveway into the woods near the remote neighborhood of Stave Lake Falls. The area sat in the narrow folds of the mountains amid moss-draped trees and huge spear ferns that grew along the rushing Stave River. When Rich pulled up in front of the faded green rancher, he stepped out into mud that almost covered his shoes. Grace Stickley met him at the front door and led him silently into an olive-drab painted kitchen. Fitting.

Grace Stickley suited her name. The narrow woman fidgeted across the scarred kitchen table from Rich. The air carried an undertone of mold and an in-your-face odor of fried onions, grease and cigarette smoke.

The combination wasn't as bad as some places he'd been in his career—there *was* that murder at the abattoir—but it was enough to make him want to cover his nose. The olive walls and the dirty-white cupboards seemed to carry a yellow patina of all that grease and smoke so he knew it would be in his clothes when he left.

The way Rich figured it, there were two kinds of women who were married to cons. The first, and thankfully the most frequent type, were the blousy, bar-mama kind with too-big breasts and too-small clothes. The second kind were the women just too beat up by the world to think they had options beyond standing by their man.

Grace Stickley was of the latter variety with her mouse-blonde hair fading to grey, her thin body that looked like it could be broken with one good blow, and a weariness that suggested it took every bit of strength just to wear her faded sack-cloth dress. All this and the bowed shoulders and the woman was barely in her thirties. This kind of sad woman always made Rich feel like the world really was unfair to some people—and that his problems were pretty small by comparison.

"I don't know what else I can tell you, Officer. I haven't seen Jim since last week." She spoke with the practiced, guarded voice of a woman used to covering for her husband.

Rich shifted the barely touched cup of coffee on the table in front of him. Just the look of the stack of dishes by the sink didn't give him any comfort the cup was clean. And then there was the dog, half-defurred by fleas or mange - he didn't care to look close enough to check which—that kept coming up to him for attention.

"Mrs. Stickley, this is very important. I need you to think about whatever he told you about being inside. How was he feeling last time you saw him?"

She shrugged, the bones of her shoulders jutting like mountain ranges up through the thin, flowered fabric of her dress.

"He said stuff like he always did. When he got out he was going to take me out some place special. He told me to go buy a new dress to celebrate in. He was planning that his Parole hearing was going to go good." She shrugged again.

"What did he tell you about how he was getting along in jail? Did he ever say anything that made you think he was depressed?"

Grace regarded him with faded out brown eyes. "My Jim never held with those psychiatrist diagnosis, eh. He was a happy man. Said you made your bed, so you better lay in it. Take your medicine, he always was saying to little Jim. He tried to raise the boy right." She nodded at the doorway into the living room, where a ten year old boy was glued to the big screen television to while away the last days of summer. Judging by the kid's obesity, greasy hair and pale face, the kid probably wasn't exactly Mission's leading light.

"So tell me how he seemed the last time you saw him."

She gave him a helpless look as if he was asking her things she didn't understand. Either the language was too hard for her tired brain, or she didn't even think in those concepts. He thought it was probably the latter.

"Did he seem happy? Did he have a job lined up for when he got out?"

"I told you." Her shoulders sagged a little more. "He was fine and he was going to take me for dinner. He probably would have gone right back to work at Justin's Mill, because Hank Justin always took him back when he'd been away for a bit."

She looked like Rich was abusing her by even asking her brain to fire enough to come up with answers. He could barely imagine what had aged her so quickly. She was what—nine years younger than Deena and yet Deena was still a woman filled with life, while Grace Stickley was sputtering along on empty.

"Did he ever say anything that might make you think he wasn't safe in jail?"

Just wanting to get the interview over with, he waited for her yes or no answer, because that would take the smallest amount of her energy. She surprised him when she met his gaze and placed her hands flat on the kitchen table.

"My husband never felt safe in that place, Officer. That's why he wanted that Parole so bad. He said it wasn't a safe place at all."

That set Rich back a bit. "What did he tell you?"

She shook her head with more energy than he'd seen in her. "Didn't tell me much, Jim didn't. He didn't want to worry me."

"So how do you know he didn't feel safe?"

She shrugged again. "You marry a man, you know how he feels."

"So you just *know* he didn't feel safe."

"That's right. You see it in your man's eyes and you know something's got hold of him. I asked him once if it was the inmates and he said some."

"What were the names of the men who scared him?"

She shrugged again, the movement like an earthquake through her body.

"I don't like spreading around names—it's like spreading around trouble and those as sew a little trouble, sure as heck are going to reap it."

"It sounds like you knew more about Jim's business, Mrs. Stickley, but you're afraid to tell." He had to do this. Had to deal with her hesitation and make her feel at least a little secure. "It also sounds like you're afraid to tell me anything. Let me tell you, there are staff at the jail who are really worried about what happened to Jim."

Her eyes said she didn't believe him, but he was determined to show her that someone thought she deserved the truth and was prepared to dig for it regardless of safety.

"Those staff think Jim didn't kill himself."

She stiffened now, looking like she might just plain melt away. "They think someone murdered him."

"You're sayin' a staff's worried about what happened to my Jim?" she almost laughed, but the energy disappeared as quick as it had come.

Rich nodded. "That's what I'm trying to tell you. We want to find out the truth and we can't do it without your help—what you know."

But her eyes had gone large and luminous with fear. "Staff are asking about me? They want to know about what I think?"

Rich watched the fear take control and the way shutters fell over her eyes, then: "I told you. I don't know anything. Nothin' at all."

But there was a tremor in her voice that said she was afraid and weakening. If he pushed, he just might get something more, like that name.

He opened his mouth to press, but his cell phone burred at his side. He was going to flip it off, when he saw the number. MSA hospital. Ivy.

"Just a moment, Mrs. Stickley. I have to take this."

He flipped the phone open and walked into the living room for the privacy the television noise would provide.

"Webster."

"Rich, I need you to come and get me. The hospital says I can go home."

Ivy's voice was thin and wavery, but as together and focused as he'd heard it for weeks, months, hell—years.

"I'm in the middle of things now, Ivy. Is there any way you could get your parents to pick you up? Maybe a friend?"

He heard the quavering intake of breath as if she was fighting for the strength to answer and all the guilt rushed over him. Once Ivy wasn't like this. She'd been strong enough to attract him. But now she wasn't much better than Grace Stickley and he knew damn well that he'd helped Ivy become what she was.

"Alright. Let me finish off here and I'll be there."

"You won't be long, will you?"

God he was tired. Her voice seemed to suck away his energy like a galactic black hole. "No. I won't be long."

"Can we run a few errands on the way home?"

"We'll get you all set up. I'll see you later."

He clicked off, knowing she'd answered with a 'don't be long'. Grace Stickley still sat at the kitchen table.

Unfortunately the moment of opportunity had passed. She had her arms clasped over her sagging chest and was holding onto her thin arms so tightly he doubted he could pry her fingers loose any more than he could get whatever information she had. Her face said her fear had gone far beyond her usual distrust of authority.

He wasn't going to get anything more, but he supposed he'd got enough to send him back to look at things in the Center a little more closely. How Deena would respond to that suspicion was another matter. Hopefully she had found something a little more concrete that would deny the suspicions that Grace Stickley was creating.

"Mrs. Stickley, I'd like to thank you for your time. If you decide there's anything else you'd like to tell me, please give me a call."

"I don't have anything else to say." Her face was shuttered to him now; there was only fear at his presence.

"You might think of something." He placed his card on the kitchen table when she hesitated to take it from him and he figured it would probably end up in the garbage soon enough.

He left her at the kitchen table, probably trying to find the energy to move, and went out to the blue suburban he'd snagged from the detachment. It wasn't a bad day. Sun was shining, but there were a few leaves on the ground and there was a haze in the air he knew only came from autumn. It always perked him up a bit, remembering boyhood camping trips up into the Rockies. Today it wasn't the sour smell of leaves or the feel of the air that cheered him—it was a certain blonde woman he was going to see in a few hours.

He checked his watch and it was almost two o'clock. He could picture her—all starched and stern in her blue Corrections uniform, the fine hairs of her neck catching the light. The length of her neck. The curve of her breast. Even in that stodgy uniform, she was a woman through and through. He'd seen it years ago even as she'd developed the outer police persona. He'd wanted to explore it, get to know that other side of her. And maybe he would now.

"Fix her cupboards and maybe fix a few other things as well."

But first there was Ivy.

Chapter 17

IVY MCLOUD-WEBSTER LAY FULLY clothed on the hospital bed, her forearm over her head as if she was as overburdened by life as Grace Stickley. When she sensed Rich's presence and uncovered her eyes, Rich knew his guilt probably helped overwhelm her.

"So. How you doing?"

She looked so pale and thin in the clothes he'd brought her on his other visit. It had been her favorite—a sweater of crème brûlée-colored cashmere—a gift he had given her on their last Christmas together. Now it just displayed the bones under her flesh.

"I've had better weeks." She smiled, but it was a faint reminder of the radiant nurse who had asked him much the same question way back when in the Edmonton General Hospital. She raised her arms to him. "Help me up."

He did, ending up with an armful of Ivy, which was about the last thing he wanted right now. Her hair felt brittle against his cheek and the weight of her was like one of the old women police rescued when they became too decrepit to live on their own.

He disentangled himself and Ivy swayed on the edge of the bed. He felt sorry for her, sorrow for her, but he didn't want Ivy. Never had and the guilt that surged through him made him catch her hand.

"We'll get you home and all set up. Have you got someone to come by and help you get a meal together?"

Her dark, haunted gaze caught his. "I thought you'd give me a hand."

All the things left unsaid came through in her eyes. *You got me into this mess. You did this. You never loved me.*

Rich broke the look and glanced at his watch. He just might get this done and still get to Deena's on time. Or maybe he should phone and cancel.

He helped Ivy off the bed and grabbed the small suitcase he'd brought her, then headed out the door with Ivy on his arm.

No, he wouldn't cancel because Chuck was right. It was time to move on and there was a good chance Deena Hunter was the person he wanted to move on with.

The drive from MSA Hospital took them to a pharmacy for Ivy's prescription, then to the Supersave Market for groceries, and then south to the property they'd bought hoping that the change of scenery would also change their marriage. Instead the property had just become symbollic of their marriage's demise. Every time Rich came here, he felt like he was returning to the scene of a crime.

At least this time he could take it because there was a bit of hope in his life.

At the house Ivy fumbled the house keys and Rich almost took them from her, then forced himself to wait. She had to do for herself. He couldn't always be here for her. He wouldn't be. She tried again, then offered him the keys, but he shook his head.

"Your keys, your house. You do it."

Something dark crossed her eyes like a shadow on a shade. She rammed the key home and twisted, so the door opened and she stalked into the house. Then she stopped and got this lost look on her face that made Rich wince worse than the stale air across his face. No, he was going to do this—get her settled and start her on the road to taking care of herself.

"Why don't you take your bag upstairs and I'll bring in the groceries?"

He didn't wait for an answer, simply put the bag by her feet and returned to the suburban, inhaling the clean air and wishing this was over. He checked his watch. Three-fifteen. Forty-five minutes and his shift was technically over and he could be headed to Deena's. Just get Ivy settled and he could roar back to the office and pick up the latches he'd bought on his lunch break. If he was a bit late it wouldn't matter, and he'd be able to avoid Chuck's knowing look as well. Rich knew he couldn't disguise that this wasn't just a mutual investigation. One didn't generally fix the latches of a fellow investigator.

Lugging the plastic bags of groceries, he went back to the house. Ivy had only made it up three stairs. She now sat there, weeping.

"I can't do it. I just can't." The tears streaked down her cheeks and Rich's stomach clenched. He hated to see anyone so helpless, but darn it, she had to try. If she was trying, she'd be pushing that suitcase up the stairs or dragging it behind her, not waiting for someone's rescue.

Feeling both frustrated and heartless, he headed for the kitchen. "Just get the bag up there, Ivy."

He unloaded the bags onto the kitchen table, then went to put milk and cheese in the fridge. It was filled with old take-out cartons and mold, and the stench sent him back a pace. This was going to take more than a couple of minutes.

He ran his hands through his hair. Sure, he could toss stuff, but it should be Ivy's job. Ivy learning how to live again, just like he was.

He went back to the front hall and she'd reached the top of the stairs, suitcase in hand: so she wasn't as weak as she'd said.

"Good job, Ivy. Just put the case on your bed and then come on down here, because I'm going to make you some dinner while you load the fridge."

She looked down at him, uncertainly. "Can't you do it?"

"Nope. You need to." Tough love and all that.

He went back to the kitchen, hunted for the fry pan and a bowl and found them in the stack of dishes in the sink. Okay, that he would take care of because he'd be here all night if he waited for her to wash them.

He ran hot water, searched for dish soap and swore when there wasn't some. He'd tried to remember everything at the grocery store, but he'd focused on food, not cleaning items. Doing further shopping was a task Ivy would have to take on.

He poured a little dishwasher soap in the water and by the time he had a clean fry pan, Ivy had wandered into the kitchen. She opened the fridge and began putting the new food in amongst the moldy-oldies.

"Maybe you should clean the old stuff out first?" he tried to keep it casual but he still saw her shoulders curl under the load of his words and he wanted to grab her, shake her, tell her to wake up and live.

Silently she removed the things she had put in the fridge and started pulling things out of the fridge to the floor. Rich held his tongue, forced his anger into curled fists. She should get a garbage bag for the old stuff, but she just doggedly piled the old cartons on the floor. The stench of rotten food flooded the room and he pulled open the kitchen door, looked out to the field where Majority Report stood in the field looking dusty and uncared for. The horse looked nothing like the $30,000 animal he was still paying off. That horse had been fit and ready for competition.

She'd allowed the animal and this place to go fallow as an Alberta wheat field in the fall, just as he'd allowed her to go fallow and uncared for.

How long was he supposed to go on taking care of her? He realized this was the first time he'd really asked himself that question. Other people had asked, but it had never sunk in. This time something had changed.

He returned to the kitchen in time to see Ivy start to refill the fridge again.

"You might want to wash it out. It smells pretty bad and there's old rotten vegetable juice dried in the vegetable crisper."

She looked at him. "Can't you do it?"

"No. It's your place. You have to keep it clean. You have to want to."

She looked around helplessly at the mess she'd made on the kitchen floor at the clean dishes on the counter and he could see her confusion.

"But I don't. I really don't give a damn, Rich. I don't give a damn about much of anything anymore and I don't know why." She turned back to him, her eyes filled with frightened tears. "Help me, Rich. I don't understand why I'm like this."

When she begged like that it just all-out broke his heart. He crossed the room, grabbed her shoulders.

"You have to want to do for yourself, Ivy. I can't do it for you."

"But, you—you have."

"I'm not your husband anymore. I'm a friend. Only a friend and friends help, but you have to help yourself."

She shook under his hands, sobbing as she clung to him. He should just leave, but that wasn't what he was trained to do.

There were too many people who just ignored people in distress— like the people who had ignored his father collapsed with a heart attack behind the wheel of his car. Everyone said they just thought he was a drunk. They'd left him and so Mike Webster had died when his son was just twelve.

He groaned and set Ivy away from him, slammed open the pantry cupboard and grabbed the bucket there, threw it in the sink and poured in some more of the dishwashing soap.

"Fill it with hot water. I've got a telephone call to make."

He left her hollow-eyed and staring at the sink while he went outside and dialed Deena. He didn't want to do this. In fact all he wanted to do was climb in the suburban and drive like mad to the cool green silences of her apartment.

But he couldn't because Ivy was waiting. He listened to the buzz of the ring-tone and then the click of pick up, hating himself as he prepared his excuses.

Chapter 18

"HEY, RICH. WHERE ARE YOU?" she said and instantly regretted the warmth she knew came through in her voice—like she was looking forward to seeing him or something.

This was business, even if she'd just finished her fifth ridiculous round of tidying the apartment. Hell, she'd even dusted the philodendron and cleaned the fly carcasses off the window sills. Sly had been ecstatic when she brushed him to get rid of any excess fur that might sully her cream colored couch.

A moment's hesitation and then: "Abbotsford. Thing is, Deena, something's come up."

The stiffness of his voice told her everything she needed to know and instantly she was on her guard. She'd been an idiot letting herself even slightly consider Rich Webster.

"So let me guess. A rain check, right? We'll both keep on with our respective investigations and we can catch up with each other next week or something. Works for me."

There. She'd taken control and dealt with it so he didn't have to hem and haw his way through a difficult apology. It didn't matter to her. Really, it didn't.

"That wasn't what I was going to say."

"Don't worry about it, Rich. I understand. I was a cop once, too. Duty calls and all that. You got called out." He must know she was giving him the easy out. Just say yes, you fool, and she could be sure it wasn't her and just let it go.

"Deena, would you just be quiet for a minute. It's not work. Work I could deal with. This is personal and I'm not sure how long it'll take. I know I was supposed to be over after shift, but would it be okay if I came later?"

He just couldn't just say 'yes', damn him. He had to sound like he *wanted* to come and get her heart beating erratically again, just when she'd thought she had it under control.

"How much later?" was all she could manage to say.

"That's the trouble. I don't really know." She heard the reservations in his voice and didn't have the heart to push it for fear of what he might have to say. Another woman, perhaps. She'd heard hesitation like that in Blake's voice before she figured out he was screwing around on her. She wasn't going to trust like that again.

"Listen, Rich. Personal stuff takes it out of you, so you want to call it off, just say so and I can deal." She'd managed to put cool in her voice and that was good. Keep this *mano-a-mano* regardless of Suz and her story about tools. That's all this was to Rich Webster—a chance to discuss a troublesome case he'd been handed.

"And this is me saying I don't want to call it off. Damn it, Deena, don't you listen?"

That got her dander up.

"I listen just fine, thank you very much, Corporal Webster. That's why the cons talk to me and that's why my boss has me starting an Internal Security Initiative. All cause I listen so fine to whoever wants to talk. I'm just saying if you don't want to come over, don't suggest you might. A night in alone is fine by me."

"Dammit, Deena, I don't need this right now. I've got enough on my plate without you doing this."

Now she was pissed. So she was doing this to him, was she? Just like she'd been the cause of Blake's stepping out? And the cause of their failed sex life. And "too much of a ball buster for any man".

Just like she'd *made* the fabric distributor tell her to just take her business elsewhere and leave Suz and the business high and dry?

"You know what, Rich? Just don't bother. I've got enough on my plate and I really don't think it's a good idea for you to come over. Now good night."

She didn't quite slam the receiver down, but Rich Webster would sure enough get the message. She wasn't some bimbo waiting for her Richie to come calling. She had a life. She had things to do.

She slumped down on the oh-so-creamy couch and forced her lower lip into a major pout as Sly leapt up and insinuated himself onto her lap. She palmed his little round head.

"That did not go well, buddy."

He looked up and meowed the throaty Siamese-style voice that you either obeyed or took your life in your hands.

"What? You think it was my fault?" She shook her head. "What do you know? When was the last time you were really interested in a member of the opposite sex?" His golden gaze met hers and she thought of Morinville and long nights on patrol. "Probably about the same time I was, right? Feels about that long."

She hugged the cat, inhaling his warm fur and realizing that she really had probably been a bit of a bitch when Rich was trying to deal with something personal and all she could think of how Blake had messed around.

"Messed you around, more like." She sighed, thinking Rich really wasn't a bit like Blake. Blake had been all about blame and she'd accepted it. Rich didn't seem the type.

"Come on Sly. Let's see what's good for you to eat."

She carried him into the kitchen and set him on the floor while she pulled his specialty food from the fridge. Sitting on the stove top was evidence of her temporary insanity where Rich Webster was concerned.

Freshly baked cornbread still steamed, filling the air with its nutty-sweet scent. She'd remembered long ago when Rich had said it was one of his favorite comfort foods. For some reason it was one of the few things she'd ever bothered to learn how to bake from scratch.

Stupid, stupid, stupid. She should toss the whole thing out and forget it. Get Rich Webster out of her head, because she really did have other things to worry about. Maybe she would toss the cornbread out, or maybe she'd just eat it all herself and be done with it. In the meantime she'd think about something else while she fed Sly.

The diabetes had made it bad practice to leave Sly with free-choice feed. The old cat had a tendency to over eat—boredom she supposed. So that meant she had to give him small amounts of food at regular times of the day. Impossible to do, if Suz hadn't been available to help. The tough thing was Sly's little pot belly was shrinking and it almost broke her heart. And she still didn't have the results of his blood work.

She measured a scoop of tinned food into Sly's kitty bowl and set it on the floor. Sly scooted over like he was on a starvation diet and started to purr. The rumble filled the room, and he glanced at her. Possibly recriminations that she'd made him wait when all he had ever done was try to accommodate and comfort her.

"I'm sorry, fella. I guess I'm not too good at that."

Nope. She just tried to control things like Sly's diabetes. The trouble was, she just didn't have enough hands or time to control everything in her life and that fact left her helpless and angry And all she could do was breathe deep and watch an old friend try not to live as long as possible.

Not the Julie had said he was terminal or anything—but her emphasis on Sly's age...

Deena's chest tightened and she wanted to hit something. Instead she stroked Sly's fur as he finished the small amount of food. He gave her a meow that let her know what he thought and went over to the sliding glass door to curl into a pool of sunshine. She heard his stomach growl and felt mean as heck, but stayed where she was to watch the sunset color Mount Baker.

The mountain was why she'd chosen to live in the third floor apartment with its cracked linoleum and ancient turquoise appliances, rather than in the main part of the house. Aside from Suz and Lana needing a place to live, this room had the best view of the mountain that had fascinated her forever. As a kid she'd dreamed of living at the peak. There was a magic place there. A place where all the people were gods and goddesses and sought justice and rightness for all. It was a pure place. A good place. A true place.

Unfortunately it didn't exist.

As a kid there was such a thing as justice and rightness and belonging, but at this point in her life she'd come to realize most things came in shades of grey and that she was one of the few people in this world that had such strict ideas about what was right and wrong. It meant she rarely belonged anywhere.

Now the mountain was just a wonderful creature that changed moods with the light as she sipped her morning cup of coffee at the battered wooden table she'd liberated from her mother's kitchen. She kept meaning to refinish it, but somehow just never found the time.

Well she had some extra time right now—a gift really. She could take the table apart, carry it outside for sanding and then pick up some varnish at Home Depot. While she was at it, she'd pick up some new door latches for the kitchen cupboards and wouldn't that just show Mr. Rich I've-got-tools Webster.

"Sorry, Sly." She stood up, turned the table over to expose the screws and that made Sly head for the couch. No problem with black fur, now. Then she went to find her lone, multi-head screwdriver.

§

By the time the knock came at the door all the light had leached out of the mountain and all Deena's certainty about her ability to refinish the table was just about gone, too. She was sitting under the lone kitchen light bulb with the table still on its side, Sly crouched in the doorway flicking an ear at the epithets—she was doing it again, darn it—that were coming far too frequently from her lips.

The darn Phillips screwdriver head just kept slipping in the table screws. Over the years they had been damaged by some other person's ill-trained efforts—probably her mother's. Knowing she was doing something her mother had done almost left her immobile on the floor.

That had been her first thought. Now she was thinking that the whole idea had been really stupid—like she needed *another* project— and why didn't she just turn the table upright and forget the whole thing.

"That's what you've thought all along, isn't it Sly? This was a stupid idea." He just gazed at her with those golden eyes.

At the light knock she hauled herself up off the floor, brushed the hair out of her eyes and wondered how she was going to explain to Suz just how disastrous her conversation with the fabric company had been. She'd avoided her friend all day.

When she opened the door the broad chest and the red toolbox of Rich Webster stopped her dead.

She looked up to his eyes, then down to the tool box—the red one—then back up to his face again. Concern there. And apology. And a certain humor as he lifted his finger to push a strand of her hair back from her eyes.

"I thought I told you not to come." She managed to pull herself back together, but darn it, she was running her hand over her hair like a bloody school girl and really she should be apologizing.

"You did. But I don't listen any better than you do." He looked past her into the apartment as Sly meandered over, his tail upright as a flagpole.

"Howdy there, Mr. Sly." He crouched down and held out his hand and Sly—the traitor—immediately rubbed his face across Rich's fingers and waited for the obligatory ear scratch.

He glanced up at her. "You know, I was remembering. This is the kitten you got when you first moved into Morinville, isn't it? You named him Sylvester Talone—stupid name, if you ask me, but you always laughed at it and said he with his sharp claws he was forever starring in a movie called 'First Blood'. But this is him, all these years later, right?"

She nodded as he ruffled Sly's ears and stood—too close to her. Sly gargled a demand for more attention, but Deena was too aware of Rich facing her and of how her skin felt hot and tingly.

"Aren't you going to ask me in? I know it's late, but I did bring tools." He hefted the box and manly things rattled inside.

Damn his winning smile. "All you need is a tool belt and you're a regular Tim the Toolman."

He eased past her without waiting for an invitation and carried the red box toward the kitchen, then stopped.

"Be still my heart. Is that cornbread?" The toolbox went on the floor at the kitchen door and he had his nose over the now-cooled loaf. He groaned. "Heaven. Simply heaven."

He turned around to look at her where she leaned against the doorframe with her arms crossed because she was still pissed at him, wasn't she. She wasn't going to let him off the hook for just letting her hang, but he was soooo like a kid with his dark tousled hair falling across his forehead and the way he stood there positively panting for cornbread.

She couldn't swallow her smile.

"You're lucky. I was going to throw it out. Or eat it all myself."

His hands went to his heart. "Sacrilege. You wouldn't do that."

"Right," she said dryly. "Try me."

She hip checked him out of the way and pulled a plate from the cupboard and a knife from the drawer and cut him a piece.

"This is payment for the kitchen latches, nothing more. You want butter with that?"

He nodded, his face too close to hers as he did a vulture act over her shoulder.

"And maple syrup if you've got it."

She rolled her eyes and went to the fridge, set it on the counter for him.

"You always did have simple tastes," she said, watching him slather the syrup over the cornmeal, then take a huge bite. Ecstasy flooded his face.

"I feel like I shouldn't be watching."

Rich grinned and put the piece of cornbread down, crumbs peppering his lips.

"Sorry. It's been a while since anyone made cornbread for me."

He cocked his head at her, and the way he studied her made her regret that she'd done it. At also sent a little flash of knowledge through her. He wanted her. Hopefully just as badly as she wanted him, but she wasn't going to be the one to show it or initiate anything because there was no way this could end in anything but another disaster. At her age she was better off sticking to the memories of what might have been, rather than trying to force them into being now.

She broke their eye contact and nodded to the living room.

"I think it's too late for you to be banging around in here. Lana'll probably be in bed."

"Lana?"

"Little girl downstairs. My goddaughter, and a tough sell when it comes to bedtimes. I don't want to wake her up."

"Aah. And here I brought tools..." He glanced over at the upturned table. "Whatcha doing?"

A little squirm of discomfort ran up her back because she really didn't want to appear incompetent to this man.

"Given I had extra time tonight, I was going to take it apart so I could refinish it."

She knew his toolman glance took in the worn screws and forlorn screwdriver she'd left on the floor, and she clenched her teeth waiting for the comment that she knew would be coming.

"Had a bit of a problem with the screws I see." He went over to the table, inspected it. "Nice piece of wood. Should turn out real nice. You want a hand with the screws?"

She knew she should just say yes and get it over with, but that just wasn't the way she did things.

"I'm not someone who needs to be rescued, Rich. I don't need you to fix things. I just haven't got it done yet."

"Well why don't we just get it done—quietly—and then we can talk about the case. I saw the Stickley woman today."

He already had his tool box open and had pulled out a screwdriver that looked way more proficient than her little multi-head, and was setting up to take on one of the old screws.

"Hold on there, partner. I didn't ask you to do that. Me and my friend here will take care of this just fine."

She hefted her screwdriver, trying to ease herself between Rich and the table, but unfortunately that just brought her into far too close a contact with Rich. She held up her screwdriver trying to cover for the flush she felt roaring up her neck.

"Mine's bigger than yours," he said softly. "The screwdriver, I mean."

He held up his screwdriver. The damn man was enjoying her discomfort. Then he took advantage of it and leaned in to place a light kiss on her lips.

Chapter 19

SHE FROZE UNDER RICH'S TOUCH and yet her lips were as sweet as he'd imagined. Soft and full and tasting of—it reminded him of the subtle-sweet taste of rosehip tea—just as the scent of her hair reminded him of apricots and the wild roses that bloomed so delicately in the foothills of the Rocky Mountains.

But for all Deena's softness, her lips weren't just going to give in to him. This woman had strength, spine. When she gave back to him it would be incredible, mutual, he knew.

He grazed his lips across hers, touching, tasting and still she didn't move, didn't breathe, a veiled look coming into her dark eyes, and he felt her soften, yielding to his touch. Then suddenly she jerked away.

"What the hell was that?"

She held the useless piece of metal and plastic she called a screwdriver between them like a weapon and it almost made him smile except for the anger he saw brewing in her eyes. After the day he'd had, evoking Deena's anger was about the last thing he had on his mind. The kissing, however...

He stepped back, knowing she needed the space.

"What do you think it was?"

The confusion in her eyes, the flush of her cheeks were enough to let him know he'd had the desired effect. That was good. Very good, in fact.

"I thought you came over here to talk about the case and maybe do something with those tools of yours."

She eyed the toolbox warily. Almost as warily as she looked at him. God the way her hair fell so golden across her forehead and shielded her neck. He wanted to taste the shadows under that hair, already suspected they would taste of roses, too.

"I was just using another tool. Wasn't it you who once said the mouth was the most important tool in policing?"

"Don't throw all my idiocy back at me. I was talking about talking and you know it."

"Well I was just being creative. Thinking outside the box and all that."

"Well I'll have you thinking outside this apartment if you try something like that again."

She was furious, but it was a cover for something. A kiss as gentle as his shouldn't have her this riled. He looked more closely and saw it— fear underneath it all. And suddenly he understood. Someone had burned Deena. Maybe more than one someone, but something had left her very afraid. Being Deena, she tried to get through on strength of will. So different than Ivy.

That Deena had been hurt enough to fear made him angry. No one should have hurt her like that. She was—precious—perfect—his, dammit. She was his and he didn't like people hurting what was important to him.

No, you do that all by yourself.

He exhaled.

"Listen, I'm sorry. I overstepped boundaries. I shouldn't have. Don't send me packing. We've got the case to discuss."

He set his screwdriver down like food left for a wary animal. She could use it if she so chose, but he wouldn't push it.

"Besides, I haven't finished my cornbread. You can't deprive me of that."

Her look said 'try me', so he grabbed the plate and went into the dimly-lit living room to settle in the chair. That would give her space. He took another big bite of the truly heavenly snack.

"You want some coffee with that? I've got decaf." She still stood in the kitchen, her arms crossed over her breasts protectively.

"Sure. If you'll have some."

She turned back to the kitchen and he heard her movements. It allowed him to study the apartment. Tidy as hell. Seemed to hold a glow even in just the light from the kitchen, just like she did. It must have been the green plants that gave the place such a sense of life. On the bookshelves against the bedroom wall was an eclectic collection with everything from

Steinbeck, to Robertson Davis, to Asimov and some ancient Heinlein juveniles. He remembered she'd been a science fiction fan as a kid. And on the walls were old photographs—one he recognized of the two of them during her time in training. Its presence gave him hope.

From the kitchen came the gurgle and pop of the coffee maker and the oily scent of good coffee. There was also the sound of screws turning.

He smiled. Chuck had once told him women don't always want men to fix things for them, they just want to talk about the thing that needs fixing. A wise man, Chuck. Rich really should listen to him more often.

Then Deena came in carrying an old wooden tray painted with flowers and laden with two coffee cups and cream and sugar. She set them on the tea wagon by the wall and wheeled it over. "My mother's. Might as well use it."

She settled herself on the couch with her coffee, and as usual Sly was there. Rich had to smile. The old cat was the constant that had been there through all the years they'd been apart.

"I had an interesting day as well," she interrupted his thoughts. "I decided to get into it and interview the inmates. My boss is going to have my ass because I didn't get a report done, but the interviews were more important."

Rich sipped his coffee and nodded his appreciation. "Good coffee. Seems you're not just a pretty face."

She stiffened and Rich knew he had to watch himself. She knew he was interested, so cool it, Webster. Give her space. It was darn hard to do when he'd just felt the promise of her lips.

"So what did the interviews tell you," he asked, this time keeping it professional—he hoped.

"Not much. None of them would talk. As a matter of fact, now that I think about it, their absolute inability to provide any information is suspicious in itself. Usually in this sort of case if they're interviewed they'll tell you about the guy being depressed or being a bug or a snitch or whatever. Or they'll use the chance to air old grievances against other cons. They can usually give a pretty good sense of where people were in the unit as well. But this time it's a total wall. I mean nothing. Zip. Nada."

"Like they're afraid."

She nodded, the light from the kitchen catching on her earrings.

"My thoughts exactly. There *was* one interview that was different. A con named Henry. A made-man with the Vancouver Chapter of the Angels. He's solid—or I thought he was. Enough to threaten to make his life hell if he didn't talk."

"Geeze, Deena. I didn't think you had that in you."

She just grinned in response and the hard part of Deena Hunter, the part that made her such a solid cop, came through. She could care for and take care of people, but stand in the way of the truth, and she was relentless.

"Anyway. He wasn't going to tell me anything, but these guys— they'll feed you something sometimes."

"If it'll get you off their back."

They nodded in unison, just like old times and the tension that had been in the apartment melted away. In the dim light they could almost be in a patrol car together, cruising through night shift on the flat prairie that surrounded oil-rich Edmonton.

"So he said I should be talking to my staff if I wanted to know what happened to Jim Stickley." She let it settle between them, like a piece of evidence to be examined.

"He could be trying to sew suspicion." He watched her eyes as he said it. They were cop eyes again.

"He could be." But she didn't believe that, even if she wanted to. Even if considering the alternative caused her pain. God, she was an admirable person. He didn't know if he could consider a co-worker as a potential suspect. He'd never been put in that position.

"So you think it's possible."

Finally she nodded, as if it took way more than she liked to admit to do it.

"It's not only possible. The one thing the inmates did talk about was the time before lock down night before and all their stories were consistent no matter how I questioned them. Stickley was down watching T.V. with the others until the last minute. The guys on his tier and the staff from the night all corroborate that he went into his cell just at lockdown. There were no altercations and no distractions on the unit to take staff's attention away that they could recall."

She went silent a moment as if letting that sink in, and Rich could see that it bothered her. The whole thing was a blow to her sense of the order of the world.

"I also looked at the computer printouts. According to them the only time that cell opened after lockdown last night was when the C.O.s on my shift entered the unit and then after the code blue. I don't want to believe it, but it is possible that they could have gone into the cell and killed Stickley and then administered first aid when the responders got there. I haven't had time to see the corridor videos yet."

Her pupils had gone huge in the dim light and the pain of what she was suggesting was painted across her face. He wanted to do more than nod his sympathy, but that was clearly all her boundaries allowed.

"It's not proof, but it is a theory. I have to say it's born up by Stickley's T.O.D. and maybe by his wife's reaction. Grace Stickley knows something, but she's scared and she isn't talking."

"Shit." She sighed and leaned her head back, to ease the long column of her neck. Funny how the epithet coming in Deena Hunter's musical voice, was almost sexy. Almost? Hell, it was sexy. "Just what I need."

He knew what he needed, but it wasn't going to happen right now.

"So what are you going to do?"

"What else can I do? Keep looking into it. I've got to alert my boss, which is not going to earn me any favors."

She rubbed her eyes and he could see the fatigue sapping her, and yet she still sat there working it all out.

"It's going to be a tough situation because I'm staff. I shouldn't be investigating staff."

"I could come in."

She looked at him over the rim of her coffee cup.

"Like that'll work. You've already interviewed the staff. You saw how they close ranks. No, I need another way and my boss might just have given it to me with this Internal Security Initiative he wants set up."

She stood and started to pace, leaving Rich to enjoy her lithe movements, and the intense way she considered her options. Then he checked his watch. It was almost eleven p.m.—fine for him, but not so fine for anyone who had to work shift work like Deena did. He stood up.

"You're still on days, aren't you?"

She nodded, looked at him as if it was a surprise he was still here. "For the rest of the month. Why?"

"Because I should get my rear out of here so you can get some rest. Five a.m. comes early."

She looked at the solid man's watch on her wrist. Frowned. "Try four-thirty. You want to take the rest of that cornbread with you? I can wrap it up," she offered as she followed him to the door.

He turned back to her and saw she had allowed the distance between them to diminish. She stood close enough he could lean in again, but he held back on that instinct.

"Nah. I'll eat it here." There was that flicker of guardedness again. He smiled. "I have to come back to do those latches. And get my tools."

He couldn't help himself, it felt so natural to run his hands up her arms, feel the little thrill of friction before letting his palms rest lightly on her shoulders.

"Deena, I just want you to know—I've thought about you for a long time and I'm prepared to wait however long it takes until you feel comfortable with me. Until then I can be a friend and a partner, but that's not all I want. Okay? I just thought you'd want to know because partners are honest with each other."

He didn't wait for an answer. He'd put himself out there and he didn't want to wait to see if he'd be shot down. Just let her stay silent and think about it. He took his hands off her shoulders, ran his thumb across her cheek and felt her shiver. It wasn't like Ivy might tremble. This was the shiver of a ready steel blade.

Then he was out the door and down the stairs, still holding his breath, still waiting for her protest.

It didn't come.

Chapter 20

THE LONG ROAD UP THE SLOPE of the mountain to the Hat with the sun and shadows alternating blinding and her and letting her catch glimpses of the road through the windshield was a lot like how she felt about Rich. He'd blindsided her with that kiss and the stupid thing was that it kept cropping up too vividly in her thoughts—like a bad smell that just wouldn't go away. That was it: Rich Webster, bad smell.

Putting her on notice, indeed.

Deena would see about that.

She swung the car into her spot in the Hat parking lot, then clambered out, swinging her uniform on its hanger and letting the cool, dim air of the early morning wash most of the exhaustion out of her. Smelled like fall—the scent of old leaves and cut hay.

Rich's suggestion had kept her awake a good chunk of the night—so much for him leaving so she could get some rest. At first she'd fumed about it and the fact she had missed her chance to retort. In the darkness she'd come up with all sorts of good responses. Far too late.

Then she'd considered what would have happened if she had just taken the initiative and leaned in to kiss him there by the door. That and the thoughts of his hard body and broad shoulders and that kiss that had just about collapsed her legs under her, had made sleep impossible.

Inside the Hat, she changed, then headed down to the ADW office hoping to catch a few minutes to sort her thoughts before shift change and the morning briefing.

Matt Jaeger looked up from a file when she pushed into the office. The guy looked like death warmed over, suitcase-eyed, but then night shift did that to people.

"Hey," she said. "How was the shift?"

"As good as night shift usually is."

"Let me see," she tapped her finger on the side of her face. "Good shift, no problems?" The tried and true phrase of every lazy C.O.

"I don't need your wise ass comments. I've got a whole watch full of wiseguys."

And that was true, because Jaeger's crew was where a lot of the troublemaker C.O.s ended up, and it was also where the most rabid Unionists came from for exactly that reason. Most were people she wouldn't have on her shift. Given she'd always thought that the quality of the staff reflected the quality of the supervisor, that didn't say much about Matt.

She settled into the guest chair across the desk from him. "So really. How was it?"

"No issue except for one incident. Don't know how it happened, but an inmate took a bad fall in the showers. Apparently he called in he was sick and two C.O.s allowed him into the shower room to clean himself up. When they went in to get him, he'd fallen and broken his nose. Blood all over the place and he's got a couple of shiners you wouldn't believe."

"Who's the oaf?"

Jaeger was busy reading again, flipped a unit log page, another, before looking back at her.

"What was that? Oh. Yeah. Big guy. Henry's the name."

A little jolt ran through Deena and she frowned.

"That the incident report there?" She reached across for it, scanned the write-up by the officers reporting how the unit officer had found the guy unconscious in the shower room.

Both C.O. reports were almost mirrors of each other. The nurse's report spoke of an apparent blow to the bridge of the nose that would be consistent with a fall or a significant blow to the face with a large object. Deena eyed the thick unit logs Jaeger was reviewing. Those books, wielded with power, could be just such a large object.

She was appalled that her mind went there. It wasn't fair to the staff.

But Henry had been in her office longer than any other inmate yesterday. Someone could have taken notice of that fact.

"He doing okay now?"

"Yeah, he's back on the unit. Going to be pretty quiet, I'd bet. So much for all that biker bravado. Sometimes it just takes something to bring a man down, you know?"

She avoided joining him in a sage nod and instead flipped through the rest of the night's reports. Overall, a quiet shift. Prowl had found a packet of drugs tossed over the perimeter wall and was recommending a more intense check when the visibility was better.

Something else to arrange for the day. And that meant that until the search was done no inmates were allowed into the yard. That was going to go over like the proverbial lead balloon. It wasn't going to be an easy shift. Then she checked her e-mail messages and found a long missive from Brent Seger, the afternoon ADW.

It set out a litany of complaints about her staff—that was always his favorite pastime—but then he lit into Deena for recommending Anita Underhill for prowl. She'd been late for every one of her time checks and that didn't look good because those checks were what confirmed the required fifteen-minute bed checks of inmates.

A knock came at the door and she checked the clock on the wall and her watch, making sure they were in accord. Her staff crowded in waiting for assignments. A blonde head half-hidden amongst all the male chests made Deena look around. Underhill. Must be pulling a double.

Deena cocked a brow at Jaeger. "Lucy called in sick so I was looking for an auxiliary who met your high standards." His sarcasm wasn't lost on her.

"Good choice." She turned to her crew and ran through the briefing as Jaeger left for home and bed. Henry's accident. Unit and program assignments and sent staff on their way, until only Heywood and Underhill were still in the room.

"Heywood, I want you out checking perimeter today. Someone tried to throw something over the fence last night. All outside activities are on hold. When you're done I want your report. Got it?"

The big man nodded his shaggy head and left. Then Deena turned to Underhill.

The petite blonde fidgeted where she stood. Good. That showed she had enough sense to know something was the matter. She probably even had a sense of what the problem was. Deena shuffled papers to let the young woman stew. Finally, she looked up and could see the pallor in Anita's cheeks.

"So—any idea why I kept you behind?" Deena settled back in her chair, riding out the low squeal that had developed from years of wear and abuse. Anita winced at the noise, but Deena was long used to it.

"I'm not sure, Dee. Something about my performance?"

Deena narrowed her eyes the way she knew had earned her the nickname 'bitch-goddess' and if anything Anita blanched further. Good. A little fear of rank would do the youngster good.

"That'd be Sir, or Ma'am, to you, Underhill. Got that?"

A voiceless nod and wide, wide eyes, and Deena couldn't help but marvel how at forty she was able to do to Anita what had been done to her by RCMP Sergeants in the past. It felt like only yesterday, actually.

"Yes, Ma'am."

"See you remember."

"Yes, Ma'am. Is that everything, Ma'am?"

Dammit, the kid wasn't getting it at all and that sent Deena right up out of her chair so she could make a point of towering over Anita.

"No, it sure as hell isn't everything, because I made a point of putting in a good word for you with ADW Seger and I've got an e-mail from him saying you fucked up royally on his shift. Care to comment?"

She loomed over Underhill, glowering at her so that the woman couldn't help but get the message. She was nothing, worthless, just as their past relationship was worthless compared to the well-functioning of this institution. If she let Underhill's performance go uncorrected, it would only breed the same mediocre performance found on other shifts.

"I tried. I really tried. But I got lost, okay? And when I found my way to the units for break relief, staff said the checks weren't all that important, so I guess I took my time the rest of the night. That's all. No one got hurt. No one died."

Deena held her gaze until the younger woman looked away. The motion told Deena Anita knew she'd done wrong.

"So what you're telling me is you're not only incompetent—you're a slacker. You see the problem I have?"

If anything Anita paled further as she swallowed. "Someone could have died because I wasn't doing my checks on time?"

"Bingo. Inmate Henry was badly injured last night. If someone tried to commit suicide, would you have found them on time? Or didn't you know that suicides seem to come in batches? One inmate does it, so a bunch of others get the idea. We have to be more vigilant." Deena returned to her chair and leaned back, ignoring the squeal. Underhill stayed at rigid attention in front of her. "So what are we going to do about it?"

"I'll—I'll do better."

"You will." Deena made it an order.

"And I'll—I'll—"

Deena decided to take pity on the youngster and sat up to fold her hands on her desk. "Sit down Underhill. I have a proposition for you."

Anita scrambled into the chair, leaning forward like a puppy straining to its master. Not exactly what Deena wanted. She needed workers who thought for themselves, who had work ethic and drive.

"I need your help Anita and it's not something you can take lightly. If you say yes to this job, you could be a target for others in the Hat."

The little frown on Anita's face said she wasn't following, so Deena had to make it clearer and she wasn't exactly sure herself what she was asking Anita to do.

"I've been given responsibility to create a unit in the Hat called the Internal Security Initiative. It's going to be small. Me and maybe two staff, but I need staff I can trust."

Anita was chewing that information over. "What's an Internal Security Initiative?"

"Good question. It's a unit of staff who coordinate the security information in the Center. They work to keep drugs out of the Center, gather intelligence on things. That sort of thing."

A slow nod and a little color came back into Anita's face. "Are you asking me to help you?"

Deena nodded. "I need staff that I can trust and that aren't so totally caught up in the institutional mind set. You're new. As an auxiliary you cover all shifts. People won't think of you as a threat and that means people might tell you things that they wouldn't say to me or other senior staff."

Silence and Anita's thoughtfulness again reminded Deena of herself as a new Police Officer. The girl could go far in the service if she was so inclined.

"You're asking me to spy on staff, aren't you?"

And there was the kicker, because she was, sort of.

"I'm not asking you to report on staff. The unit will be set up to focus on crime within the Hat. Drugs will probably be our primary focus, but if something else happens, an assault, a murder, that sort of thing— well any information we can get will be collected, too."

Deena tightened her folded hands and waited for Anita to chew that over. When the younger woman's eyes met hers, she knew she had her answer.

"You're putting a lot of faith in me after I messed up."

"Yes. And if you screw up again, it'll be another story because I won't have a screw up in the Center. You're still on probation. You mess up, you won't make it to permanent. Understand?"

"Yes—Sir."

"Good." Deena checked the wall clock. "With Heywood checking perimeter I'm putting you on prowl. This little talk has put you behind. See you have the time made up by lunch break."

She nodded Underhill out the door, then sighed. She hated doing that sort of thing, but darn it, the kid needed it now, before she became another drone in the Corrections hive.

§

She used the excuse of awaiting Heywood's report, and the results of recruiting him for ISI, to put off reporting to Ravi, but by eleven a.m. she knew she had to get it done. She had a concise plan for the ISI that she could use as an opening for discussion, and then she'd lead him into discussion of the Stickley case and the need for further investigation. She just prayed she could make this fly.

She nodded at the reception staff and ducked her head into Mitch Digneault's office.

"Just wanted to keep you in the loop that I'm taking the ISI plan to Ravi."

Digneault just waved her away. "That's Ravi's baby and he doesn't want me or anyone else messing with it."

"Well, you're still my direct supervisor, so I report to you."

"I still don't want to know—unless you turn up something that can be confirmed. Or you're going to impact staffing." He looked back at the papers on his desk in a clear signal the subject was closed.

"Mitch?"

"Yeah?" He looked up at her with dark intelligent eyes. He too-often hid that intelligence behind his cherubic expression and so he'd been passed over in promotion, but he was a career officer and one she respected.

"You ever hear anything about staff being involved in stuff in the jails?"

She knew she was taking a chance even asking such a question, but he was management and he was on her side. He'd been one of the people who had pushed for her promotion even though she didn't have a lot of seniority. He'd had her back before, and she sure as heck had his. He set his pen down and all his attention was finally on her.

"That's one hell of a loaded question, Deena. One I don't like to hear. What's got you asking?"

Tell him?

"It's just this Stickley death. Things aren't adding up. Things seem to be leading right back to staff."

Digneault looked down at his desk and then back at her and his face had gone dark. He wouldn't like the idea anymore than she did.

"An ugly suspicion, Hunter. You want some advice? I'd say that sort of investigation is way outside your authority and scope and you should leave it alone."

She nodded. Sighed.

"And if I can't?" She smiled, knowing he knew her well enough to understand how she was driven by the truth.

"Then I'd say to think hard about your decision and seriously watch your back. It's not something I'd advise you to get involved in. In a center like this, you need friends, Deena. Remember that."

"But it's wrong, Mitch." And she saw by the shake of his head that he understood. It was how she was built.

She left him for Ravi, but he must have seen her coming. His desk was cleared. He already leaned forward, eyes too firmly on her, hands out for the report.

Breathing through the mouth to avoid his too-florid aftershave, she handed him a copy and slipped into the too-low chair to wait.

When he'd finished scanning her report he smoothed the papers and considered her for far too long.

"As complete as I expected. So who have you selected as your assisting officers?"

Hating to lock herself in a room with this man, Deena snagged the door closed. He might trust the reception staff, but biker wives had been known to work in Corrections before and a unit like ISI was only as good as its ability to stay relatively anonymous. The word would get out soon enough.

"I've approached C.O. Heywood and a newbie—Underhill. You likely haven't met her, but I've known her a long time. She's reliable, I believe. Between the two of them we've got experience and the capacity to work all the shifts. It covers more of the Center than just having staff on my shift."

His look was appraising, and yet the way his gaze too-frequently flicked down to her breasts made her want to cross her arms. She didn't give him the satisfaction. Finally he shook his head.

"I'm not sure I feel comfortable with you using someone so new. Draw on staff from the other shifts. This is an institutional priority."

She just looked at him. Ravi Sandhar might have an overwhelming need to control, but she wasn't having any. Just like she wasn't having anything else to do with the man.

"You want me leading this, I choose the people I work with. That's it, plain and simple."

She didn't add the warning to quit pushing her, because Ravi didn't listen to those sorts of warnings. They'd locked horns before, and the only reason he hadn't had her job was because he was convinced he championed the role of women in corrections. That, and he wasn't threatened by women. In Ravi's world what was a woman other than a subordinate?

"You've got more balls than most men, you know?" He sank back in his chair, shaking his head in almost admiration. She supposed his inability to control her had been part of what had attracted him to her. Like a man drawn to chase a wild horse or hunters drawn to big game.

"I wanted to talk to you about Stickley," she said, changing the subject and his gaze shifted from mildly annoyed to guarded. He looked down at his gleaming desk top as if wishing for something else he could focus on, perhaps use an excuse to end the conversation altogether.

"We've got the Internal Review Team coming next week. Was there a problem with the scheduling?"

Deena shook her head and dove into the discussion she'd been dreading.

"No scheduling problem, just a cause-of-death problem. I've interviewed the inmates and have been in touch with the police." Rich's face, his kiss rolled through her mind and she knew she'd been a trifle more than in touch.

And then there were those tools still in her kitchen…

"And I recall telling you not to make a mountain out of a mole hill on this." Ravi's dark eyes had turned almost black. He was clearly not pleased. He had plans for his career. A smoothly running correctional facility was the only way to do that and she was risking it by asking questions. "So what are you saying?"

She figured the storm might break faster if she just got it all out in a rush. She could deal with Ravi's swift rages. It was his slow sulks that had made the end of their affair bad. He'd had her working night shifts for three months straight before the Union took action on her behalf.

"So the evidence is pointing to potential staff involvement. I know it should be a police investigation, but there's no way an undercover officer can get in here to investigate and a head on approach yielded nothing. I want your permission to pursue this on behalf of management."

She held up her hand to stop his interruption and knew she was treading very dangerous ground.

"We can't let this go, Sir. It's critical to institution security and you've just told me that institutional security is your number one priority. If we've got staff who feel they can just take a life—well we're truly letting the animals run the zoo, then aren't we?"

"You can't investigate staff. You are one. Investigating staff is a management function."

She just looked at him from under raised brows.

"You think you're going to learn anything from this office? Or maybe you'd like to get down on the line for a while. Get your hands dirty." She pointedly looked at those long manicured fingers of his and shivered. "Besides, won't it look good on your resume if you were responsible for rooting out rot in the Corrections Branch? Even if nothing is found, the fact you were vigilant looks good."

The way he settled back into his throne of a chair told her she'd won. At least for now. And with his permission to conduct the investigation, her back was covered as well. She stood up.

"Thank you, Sir. I'll make sure we do this right." When she saw the question in his eyes she nodded. "Both things, Sir."

"See you do."

Regardless of the chill in his voice, she had her mandate and that was the first hurdle won. Now she just had to tell Mitch things were going to get hot.

Chapter 21

THE DOORS ALMOST FLEW PAST AS Anita raced down the corridor to the next unit. The hallway echoed with her footfall. The air stank of men and cleaning fluid and air-conditioning.

Even though she hadn't gotten lost this time, she was still running late and it was getting hopelessly close to noon, and just how the heck was anyone supposed to get these checks done in the time allotted, anyway?

Deena just wasn't being fair. The whole darn jail wasn't fair to expect anyone to do this job so quickly. Anita didn't know how Heywood managed—how she had done it with him. They hadn't seemed to be moving that fast, but Deena never had a hissy-fit over their work so they must have been on time.

Or maybe Deena just gave more leeway to guards like Heywood. He'd been on the job longer. She probably cut him some slack.

This was Deena she was talking about.

So no slack. He must just have a system to get it done. Anita would have to talk to him about it, but in the meantime she'd been seriously reamed out. Her first inclination had been to cry, because causing Deena problems was not what she intended. Then, after she'd started actually running the hallways to make her checks and found she still wasn't making up time, she'd gotten angry.

Deena was riding her because of their old friendship and it just wasn't fair.

She flashed her card at the black plastic reader and heard the door of Unit E2 click. Pushing inside, she saw Chad Preston look up from what looked like an intense discussion with the big inmate, Henry. He was looking pretty banged up, white tape across his nose. Swollen bruises around his eyes that bled black and blue down his cheeks.

Anita waved in Chad's direction and pushed the time clock at the wall-reader. It clicked the reading and she turned to go.

"Hold on, Underhill." Chad motioned her towards his office.

"I can't. I'm running behind."

He must have read her face because his lips formed a grim line as he crossed to her. "Let me guess. The bitch-goddess read you the riot act."

Anita glanced at the inmates. They were always listening in. She wasn't going to telegraph everything around the Center.

"She said she'd have my job if I can't prove I can do it. Now I gotta go." She headed for the door.

Chad stopped her with a hand on her shoulder, smiled down at her when she gave him a cross look. She needed to get out of here, because all her future plans depended on having a job. How else was she going to earn the bucks she needed for school?

"I gotta go."

"I know. But after shift, don't run away. We need to talk."

She gave a nod and scooted out the door. Chad had become a friend—both at work and off. She'd cooked him that meal—a nice roast of beef with roasted potatoes and mushroom gravy that he'd said was to die for. They'd drank wine and talked for hours, and then he'd gone home after placing the lightest of kisses on her mouth. The perfect gentleman.

Just like the rest of the staff were perfectly reasonable even though Deena rode them hard. She was like a frigging general—not a Valkyrie. And certainly not the admirable Big Sister she'd known so long ago. The years had changed Deena. She was an autocratic control freak who was trying to get more control over staff through her sleazy little special unit.

Anita buzzed herself into the Observation unit, pushed the time clock at the timer and heard the click. She was already carding herself out the door and heading down to Programs as she checked her watch. She'd cut a minute off the time. If she ran like this she might just do it, and then she could shove the whole damn thing in Deena-'f'ing-Hunter's face.

Chapter 22

THE SCENT OF BURNED OFFICE coffee preceded Chuck's arrival like a bow wave. Rich looked up from his office computer—he'd been trying to do paperwork on a couple of other cases, but Deena Hunter seemed to make putting words on the page just a tad difficult. He'd heard buddies describe a woman as a drug. Deena was making a believer out of him. His drug of choice. God knew how bad he'd be if things finally did get going.

Rich glanced at the office Mouse clock on the wall and raised his brows at his partner.

"I thought you were supposed to be first witness this morning."

Chuck nodded as he set down an extra tall disposable coffee cup. The grey suit and subtle checked tie he wore for court couldn't disguise how lean the man was, nor could a tall suit seem to fit the length of his arms. Boney wrists stuck out of his suit cuffs, making his hands look even larger.

"It was a slam dunk, but I got a chance to go for coffee with a couple of Surrey drug squad guys. Since Surry finally got recognized as almost the size of Vancouver, they get more intel than we do."

"And you didn't bring me a cup? I thought you were my partner."

"And I thought you had coffee to drink here." Chuck slid into his chair across from Rich, taking in the stacked files and the computer screen. "So you get much done this morning?"

"Hell, no." Rich scrubbed his face, knowing Chuck had already 'sussed that out from the almost-blank computer screen.

"You got a stunned look on your face, son." Chuck leaned back with a satisfied smirk. "You saw her yesterday afternoon, right?"

"Evening. I got delayed." He let his eyes slide away from Chuck's, knowing that letting Ivy get in the way of time with Deena was just about the stupidest thing he could do, but also knowing he couldn't do anything else.

Chuck stayed silent, waiting for Rich to come clean.

"Alright, damn it. Ivy needed a ride from the hospital, and then she needed help with a few things. I still got to Deena's." Godallmighty, why did he have to defend doing what was right?

"So how is she?" Chuck's casual question came as he bent down to turn his computer on, and waited for his system to boot up. It was left to Rich to decide who Chuck was asking about—a test, Rich supposed.

"Fantastic. Great. Stubborn and bitchy and wow."

"Sounds like a different kinda woman. Your kind. I haven't heard mention of a wow factor before." Chuck's nod said he approved, but...

"You haven't even met her."

Chuck met his gaze. "She's not Ivy, is she? She's a woman who's managed to make her own way in the world—taken its punches and still come up swinging. I like that in a person. I'll probably like her. Hell, I like my ass-hole partner."

"Hey. I resemble that remark."

"Sure as hell do. So it was good last night?"

"A little rocky at first. She's so friggin' independent it could make you scream."

"What'd I tell you: women don't want men to fix things for them." A knowing nod. In the school of male/female relationships, Greta had taught him well.

"Yeah, yeah. But I did get my tool box in the door."

That got Chuck's attention.

"Latches. She's got these ancient cupboard latches that are all giving out and I figured to weasel my way into her heart fixing them. Make myself indispensable and all that." He nodded his satisfaction at the result. Frankly he was feeling kind of proud of himself for that one, but Chuck was shaking his head.

"Careful, there, fella. You don't want another one dependent on you."

"Not going to happen. Not with Deena. Sonofabitch is she strong. My biggest challenge is going to be feeling like she wants me around at all."

A snort from Chuck, that passed for a chuckle as he swung back in his chair.

"So after all these years of mooning over her, she's not making it easy. Not quite what you thought would happen if you found her again, is it?" He shook his head. "God I love women. Just like that proverbial box o' chocolates."

Chuck's humor wasn't quite what Rich needed right now, 'cause frankly he could use a few helpful hints about how to woo a woman who obviously carried some dark spots inside, but he found himself suddenly loath to share his suspicions with anyone. Whatever had happened to Deena was obviously private. If he figured out what it was, he'd keep her confidence.

"So, what did you get out of your coffee with the Surrey guys?"

Chuck's brows rose at the abrupt change of topic, but he followed along, sat up.

"Interesting info, actually. Seems there's a little war brewing. Hell's Angels are getting a run for their money. There's some new players in town. There's always been the Tongs, given Vancouver is so closely linked to the orient, but there are other groups moving in pretty solid, too. You got your Russian mob, a few Vietnamese gangs, but they're nowhere near the power of the Chinese, and then you've got the new guys on the block—the Independent Army."

He hauled out a note pad. "Vancouver's had a problem with the South Asians for a while now. All seems to stem from some of the stuff coming out of that Independent Khalistan movement for a Sikh homeland. It's metamorphosed, though. Up until the last year or so it was mostly young guys dealing a little ecstasy and taking out their frustrations on each other—thus the escalating number of shootings in the city. But the Surrey guys are saying something's changed. Someone's taken control and the undercover guys—Special O, Coordinated Law Enforcement, etc.—are still tracking back who."

"Interesting, but not exactly pertinent to sticksville-Mission. Aside from grow-ops and being the drop-off capital for most of greater Vancouver's stolen cars, what the hell is there to bring a major mover to Mission?" Rich shook his head and tried once more to get Deena out of his head and focus on his files.

"That's where you're wrong. According to the drug guys there is activity. They're not sure, but they think it's something like what's happened south of the border when some of the Latino gangs moved in on the black gangs. They took over and they moved in. Into the jails, too."

The mention of jails brought Rich right back to Deena and their mutual case. Chuck was already nodding.

"So what you're saying is the South Asian gangs might be moving into the jails. To what—sell drugs?"

"It's a closed market with high demand."

It was true. Most of the cons had drug problems and while the jails might offer some treatment programs, most of the cons only attended to have a gold star on their parole application. Chuck was still talking.

"Jails're also a good place to get your hooks in guys who aren't using, and a place to recruit into gang ranks. You put a bunch of losers together, they still have to figure out a pecking order. Those as control the drugs, control the jail."

"With staff like Deena on watch, there's no way drugs are going to be coming into the institution that frequently."

"Spoken like a man infatuated. Deena Hunter sounds pretty unusual compared to most of the institutional types I've met."

"She is."

Chuck didn't look like he really believed. "Too many of them work from the 'that's good enough, fuck it' perspective. It's why I don't share information with most of the jails. You never know who's going to see it."

Damn it, Chuck was painting everyone with the same brush—a tendency like racial profiling—that Rich despised.

"Deena wouldn't work under conditions like that. The law is front and center for her."

Chuck just looked at Rich hard enough so he had to look away.

"Alright. So I'm letting personal feelings enter into this a little. But I know what I'm talking about."

"There's been a lot of years go by, Rich."

"Sure." There was no hesitation as he said it. Deena Hunter was committed to the law. "Hell, it was her that pushed her management to investigate the Stickley case."

"I'll give you that," Chuck capitulated, but the fact he'd given on that point meant Rich had darn-well better consider the potential of what his partner was saying.

"So how are they getting the drugs in?" He knew it was the million dollar question, but Chuck's smile gave it all away. "Don't tell me. You're friends were thinking staff."

"Bingo. And welcome back from the la-la land of lust."

"Sonofabitch." The news sat like a stone in his belly because it tied so neatly into Deena's whole case. "If Stickley was going to pass news about staff involvement to Deena, then the staff would have to get rid of him, wouldn't they. If Stickley told his wife what he thought, it would explain why she shut down when I mentioned them."

All the puzzle pieces fit too neatly into the picture.

"It's all coming together, isn't it partner. And if the Corrections system gets badly corrupted, then there's a good likelihood it'll bleed into the rest of the justice system. Hell, the jail system feeds information to parole hearings, court decisions, pardons, the whole shittery. A lot of cops are recruited out of the institutions and let's face it, half the auxiliary cops and police reserves in the lower mainland work for them. That gives them access to police computers and information about police operations."

It was big. Too big and yet it had to be dealt with and the only way to do that was to take it apart into bite-size pieces so he could hold onto the thing.

"So the South Asian gangs are doing what the Italian mob did in the east years ago. Recruiting from within and letting the glossy uniforms hide the rot underneath, or recruiting young guys who then get employed as correctional officers."

He dug the Stickley file out from under the others and started shuffling through the staff reports.

"A third of these names could be Indo-Canadian." He met Chuck's gaze. The thought that Deena somehow might know—he didn't want to go there. "There's no way we can get an undercover guy in the jail. Hell, those staff are so unionized they'd complain if someone volunteered to babysit."

Chuck shook his head. "You got a bigger problem than that, my friend. If I recall correctly, isn't the Hatzic warden Indo-Canadian? This thing could go right to the top."

Chapter 23

WHEN DEENA GOT HOME FROM work, she was still reeling from her last confrontation with Anita Underhill and even the calming cream and green of her apartment and the glorious view of the huge white mountain couldn't settle her. It was like the pristine white peak of the volcano was a lie for all the destructive power down below and right now she felt all that stymied power locked up inside. Just how was she going to deal with Anita?

The darn newbie hadn't made her rounds on time and showed an uncharacteristic resentment when Deena pointed out that Anita had let the shift down. It made Deena wonder if Ravi had been right regarding her choice for the ISI.

Concern over Anita, the Stickley case, and the disaster of her call to the fabric salesman made her avoid Suz, climb into her running shorts and sleeveless 't' and go. She needed to work out her frustrations before Rich arrived or she might just do something stupid.

Too quick a stretch and then she was pounding down the hill to 1st Avenue allowing gravity to pull her along. Wind off the nearby mountains streamed in her face and, across the river, Mount Baker gleamed. Just run. Just get the heck away from all the confusion. Muscles pull. Impact of earth. Sear of breath.

It had been a while. She felt it in her breathing, in the tightness across her butt and the weight of a few extra pounds. Gotta take care of that. East through the area of town that held most of the characterless government and service agency office buildings and then up the steep hill past more gingerbread houses. Puffing. Pull on the calves and shins.

Sunshine on her face, her shoulders. Salt sweat in her eyes and a stitch in her side as she reached 7th Avenue. Mother of God, she'd made it.

Turn west. On the flat she let her stride out like a long distance runner. Ignored the traffic, the honks of people who knew her, noticed a gleaming blue truck coming out of a little strip mall near Mission Senior Secondary School. Nice wheels. She'd almost owned a truck like that once. Blake had wanted one and had pushed her to get rid of her car.

Thank goodness she hadn't made that stupid mistake. Trusting him. Trusting Anita might be a mistake, too. Her mind mulled the options for the woman as she paused, turned downhill toward the house and checked her watch. Time enough left for a shower before Rich arrived. She'd pushed the run and knew she'd pay for it later, but no pain, no gain.

The house with the red stairs and the white picket fence was just ahead. She slowed, let gravity pull her home and saw Lana in the yard. The kid was great.

One of Deena's favorite people and the feeling was mutual. Lana saw her and came dashing out the gate.

"Aunty Dee! Look what I did!" She held up something—stuffed animal?—all wrapped in gauze—and then ran out to meet Deena.

Right into the street.

Traffic sound suddenly pierced Deena's runner's focus. Engine just behind her, revving. Glimpse of blue, moving fast and Lana in the street.

The truck was moving fast. Too fast. And the driver obviously hadn't seen Lana.

Deena leapt. Grabbed Lana, bounded for the curb as truck tires squealed.

It was still coming at her!

Like it aimed for the curb. For Lana. For her.

She threw herself at the front gate and heard the engine roar.

"Bitch," someone yelled and then the truck was gone down the hill before Deena could get to her feet.

Chapter 24

SHE SAT ON THE LAWN, IN FRONT OF the three story house, the overlong green grass damp under her bum, the precious, squirmy, little girl in her arms. The scent of baby shampoo from the mass of red hair in her face.

"Aunty Dee, what are you doing?" Lana finally forced Deena's arms loose and sat back to look at her godmother crossly. "I wanted to show you I been practicing my bandages. Now you made me drop Buster Bear and he's going to be all dirty and broken."

Deena almost cried in relief, felt the tears press her eyes because she knew she'd almost lost something precious and it was her fault. Bitch, someone in the truck had called. She knew a warning when she heard it.

But Lana didn't and Suz didn't and she had to keep them safe, secure.

"Lana, honey, you gave me a scare. That truck could have hit you. You remember what we talked about—always looking both ways before you step off the curb."

Solemn little-girl eyes. A nod.

"Did you do that?"

A shamed shake of head. "I always will, now."

About the best Deena could hope for. She squeezed Lana tight and stood, swatted Lana playfully on the butt. "That's for taking about fifty years off my life."

"But Aunty Dee, that makes you very old."

"You're right." She went out of the yard, retrieved Buster Bear and wiped him off, then handed him back to Lana. Very old about hit the nail on the head. All her muscles still jumped with adrenaline and her hands shook.

"A very nice job. Now I need to have a shower, sweetie. Go show your mom."

She swiped at the dirt smeared up her side. Dust and sweat, but only a minor scrape on her thigh below her shorts. They'd got off easy.

A warning. The question was whether or not she'd take it.

The new problem increased the shaking in her hands, but then Suz came out the front door, a big, triumphant grin on her face. She clattered down the stairs to grab a very sweaty Deena in a hug.

"I don't know how you did it my friend, but let me just bow to your greatness." She stepped back and did a mock curtsey and almost fell over—grace never having been one of Suz's better traits. Deena just tried to hold the shaking in check. Maybe Suz wouldn't notice how all the blood had probably left Deena's face. She checked her watch—Rich would be here soon and she needed that shower. Needed to get her head on straight.

"Care to share what you're talking about?"

Suz's smile only got broader. "The fabric, you ninny. I don't know what you said, but he called this morning. Apologized for acting like he had on the phone to you. He said he can't come up with the amount of fabric we'd ordered, but he wondered if there was a smaller amount we could make do with short term."

Deena had to close her eyes, because she was feeling unsteady enough and the way the fabric guy and she had left it, it was pretty clear hell would freeze over before he would deal with her again. She'd threatened to go to the guy's boss and he'd told her he was going to black list her with the other distributors. She hadn't had a chance to go to the boss yet.

"I'm not tracking, Suz. The call was a disaster. I just hadn't had the guts to tell you yet."

Suz was positively vibrating with her news, oblivious to the shock Deena had coursing through her veins and the road rash on her leg. Stung like heck. But nothing Deena could say was going to take the wind out of Suz's sails.

"I don't care how it happened, but it did. I told him exactly how much I needed to make up the minimum of your design prototypes and he said he could do it. He's overnighting the shipment. I can start sewing tomorrow! We're going to have the prototypes in time for Police Expo! We're going to do it!"

Again a hug, but this time she did a little dance that Deena couldn't stop herself from being dragged into when all she wanted was a shower, a chair and a chance to figure out what to do.

"Mom, can I dance, too?" Lana was standing at the corner of the house observing.

"Certainly, sweetie. You show Aunt Deena how you can dance."

The little girl scuttled across the grass and was standing on Deena's runners, her body pressed against the scrapes on Deena's leg before she could say anything. She winced, but what the heck—you only live once. The three of them rocked across the driveway and into the front yard, Lana giggling, until the three of them toppled onto the grass.

"Now that's a dance," Deena said, composing herself by mussing Lana's red curls. "And I'd have another, but I have this thing I need to get ready for." She checked her watch again.

"Would it involve a certain cop?" Suz caged as she hefted Lana into her arms. Deena tried to play it casual for too many reasons.

"We've got work to do on the case."

"Uh huh. I heard tools last night, didn't I? A whole case of them rattling up the stairs."

"Uh," Deena tried to avoid her friend's gaze, then gave up. "Yup. There were a whole box of 'em all right. Seems he even knows how to use them."

She thought of the kiss and a warm, fizzy feeling helped to dissipate the distant feeling she had.

"Well, isn't that just the darndest thing." Said in a southern-belle drawl it got Deena smiling.

"I'll try to make sure they aren't too noisy tonight."

Suz just caught her hand, missed the wince as she squeezed a scrape on the heel of Deena's hand.

"It's been a long time since I've seen that look on your face, Dee. You make all the noise you need."

§

At precisely four-thirty Deena, showered and changed into jeans and a green t-shirt that set off her eyes. Out her window Mount Baker looked good enough to eat with the sun turning the glacier apricot and hazing the farmland across the river with early evening mist. Closer in, trucks stirred impatiently up and down the street—until Rich drove up. He parked out front and climbed out of a swank-looking black SUV, wearing dark-tinted aviator classes, faded jeans and a plain white t-shirt. She watched him from the window as he strode, loose-limbed and looking mighty fine, stepping over the toys spread on the decidedly disheveled front lawn—she really must get to mowing—stopping to talk to someone—either Lana or Suz—probably Suz by the way he threw his head back and laughed.

Then he rounded the corner to the stairs and the regret she had over Anita was completely erased by the sound of those long legs of his taking the stairs two at a time. Only problem was, she still hadn't gotten rid of the slight shake in her hands. Or the fear.

She needed to be on guard, keep it professional because maybe she was blowing this whole close call out of proportion. It could have just been an accident. There were a lot of bad drivers in Mission.

But this bad driver had *aimed* for her.

She was being stupid. She'd been terrified for Lana. She could have imagined the aiming, but it was a bad sign that Rich Webster brought this soft, warm vulnerable feeling deep in her gut. She kept thinking of his hands on her arms. She could use them around her at this moment, which was about the last thing she should be doing.

Still, she couldn't help the big grin when she threw open her door before he could knock and saw the surprised look of pleasure on his face.

"You're a sight for sore eyes," he said stepping in close and ran his hands down her arms as if he knew just what she needed. She wanted to grab him and haul him down for a kiss right now, feel those arms wrap around her. Be safe.

When he removed his hands without trying anything it was almost a disappointment.

"You look pretty fine yourself, Mr. Webster. *Mi casa es su casa.*" She bowed him into the house, but eyed the fine way he filled out the rear of his jeans, and the way his t-shirt stretched just the slightest across the breadth of his back. Yup. He still had all the muscles she'd imagined, though she didn't remember him being a fitness freak or anything. And at least his presence set the fear away. "So you ready to use those tools?"

He glanced at her oddly. "The woman downstairs asked me pretty much the same thing. You telling tales, Hunter?"

"Me? Heck, what's there to tell?"

He lowered his chin to eye her over the top of his sunglasses in a manner that promised lots of fodder for rumors if she just wanted to play. But she didn't. She had too much on her mind. She swallowed and managed to look at the kitchen.

"Tools. Well." She cleared her throat, but two could play at this game. "I told her you were going to fix my cupboard latches. You still game for that, or you got something else in mind."

When he stepped up to her again she thought she just might have gone too far, pushed until she wasn't going to have a chance to step back again in this strange dance they had going on. When he just brushed a stray strand of hair out of her eyes and then turned to the kitchen, it left her breathless, aching. Darn him. She wanted him to try to kiss her again, because this time she just might kiss back.

Maybe she did. Would. Should.

She was being a darn fool.

Shaking her head at the muddle of her emotions she followed him into the kitchen and caught him looking at her kitchen table. It stood against the kitchen wall in pieces. After Rich had left last night she'd dismantled it using his screwdriver and way more effort than she imagined it would take him, but at least she'd done it herself.

"So what's the plan for the table?" he asked as he sorted through his tools and began unscrewing the cupboard door from the shelves.

"I'm going to move it out onto the verandah so I can sand it down and varnish it without messing up the house. What the heck are you doing?"

Without even asking if he could, he'd started removing the screws holding the hinges of another cupboard door. And another. And another and it pissed her off.

He threw a glance in her direction. "What's it look like? I noticed it wasn't just the latch that was going. The hinges are ancient too. And if the hinges and latches are going on one door, then they're probably all on their last legs. No reason to do a job half-assed I always say. We'll replace them all."

"But..." He didn't need to do all that. He might see how messy her kitchen cupboards really were. Heck she didn't even know if there might be bugs in some of them. After all, it wasn't like she cooked a lot. Salads and take-out were her standard fare.

His look told her there were no buts. Just like she didn't take a half-assed job at the Center, he had his standards with hinges and latches. Okay, well a man of his age was allowed to be set in his ways about some things.

She leaned against the doorframe and watched him work considering whether to tell him about her little escapade with the truck.

Quick, methodical. All the upper cupboard doors off, all the hinges replaced with quick, neat twists of the screw driver, held in those strong, neat hands of his. She wondered if things would be so neat if those hands were on her and somehow she sensed not. She caught his glance at her and felt that little frisson of energy again.

Nope. Definitely not neat, and things were already too messy in her life.

"This'd be mighty thirsty work, Ma'am. You got anything in this house to drink?" he said pausing after he'd replaced all the hinges.

"Oh for god's sake, cut the southern boy charm and ask like a man."

"I've been told by experts that southern charm works great on the ladies."

She looked him hard in the eye. "That would require one of us to be a lady."

His gaze raked up her form, found her face and stuck. "I'd say you got the tools for it."

She knew color followed the heat that flooded her face. Damn him. She yanked open the fridge and stuck her head inside to cover her reaction, but knew it was too little and way too late. He was standing behind her now, his hips brushing hers in a way that left her entirely too vulnerable. She didn't like the feeling—not after today—and yet...

"If that's a beer, it'll do just fine."

"Here." She thrust the beer at him and backed out of the kitchen to give herself a chance to recover. Unfortunately Rich followed her, plunked himself down on her couch to pat Sly who chirruped a sleepy hello. He'd been sick again when Deena got home.

"I make you nervous," he said, stating the obvious, but it still bugged her because she was trying for cool. "You know why that is, I suppose."

She made a point of not looking at him, of going to the verandah's sliding glass door to stare at the mountain standing glorious and strong against the deep blue sky.

"You stand too close to me. You don't respect my personal space."

She felt him come up behind her now, but he didn't impose himself on her, didn't touch her.

"I do it because I want to touch you. I've wanted to for years. Even back then."

"Rich this isn't any better an idea now than it was then. We're older. Have learned things."

He did touch her then, caught her hand and came around beside her the way a cop would who was trying hard not to scare someone.

"Someone hurt you pretty bad, huh?"

Deena clamped her eyes shut, ignoring the sting in her hand and leg and shook her head. She didn't want to see his face, because if she saw his face she'd forget the hard lessons learned and her resolve.

"Let's just say I've had great lessons in why you should never let yourself be vulnerable, and leave it at that."

Silence a moment and she opened her eyes. He was still beside her, still holding her hand and stroking its back with those strong fingers of his as if he was considering what to make of a fine piece of wood. He caught her looking at him, nodded, and released her hand to turn back to the kitchen cupboards.

"Better get these done." He took a long pull of his beer, set the bottle down and started hanging the doors, checking the level, and that they all latched, with such careful competence that all she wanted to do was stand back and watch. Suz had been at least half-way right. A man and his tools were sexy as hell.

When he was done she hauled out the cornbread.

"Reward time."

"Be still my heart." He stood close again, as she started to cut him a piece, caught her hand to shift the knife. "A man needs fuel to use all these tools, Ma'am."

She swung to face him, knife in hand and plenty of attitude. "You want I should just put it all on a plate, 'cause I can do that. Or maybe I should just hand you the pan and you can eat it from there."

"Can I still have maple syrup on it?"

"Oh lord." She looked heavenward, then went to the fridge to retrieve the syrup. Handed it to him. "Fill your boots. Have it any way you like."

His glee was almost embarrassing to behold as he poured the syrup over the pan, grabbed a fork from her, then licked a bit of syrup from his fingertip.

"You know, there's this experiment I've been wanting to do." He stepped past the waiting feast of cornbread, stepped in close enough their chests almost touched and he caught her chin, gently lifted her face so she had to meet his eyes, and she realized she was lost, because she wanted that touch, and what came next.

Rich leaned in and his lips found hers, soft, trailing across her lower lip to the corner, holding, a tongue tip passed across her upper lip until her mouth parted, answered. The taste of maple syrup and man. Copper and sweat and the woodsy scent of his soap. All the scents of him filled her nose and his lips asked, asked and damn it she wanted him. Wanted him. And all the problems she had went away.

Her hands came up to his face, discovered the angles of his cheekbones and jaw, the thickness of his hair and his fingers that had been so gentle on her chin, slipped down her sides, sending a shiver through her, rounded her back and pulled her in tight against him as he ran his mouth across her face to her ear.

"You know, I think I found my answer."

"Answer?"

"To my experiment."

"Aah, that." She nibbled on his neck, loving the way the shadow of his beard was rough against her lips and wondering at how quickly the human psyche could adjust to new stimulation. "What was it?" she managed around kisses.

"It?" He caught her earlobe in his teeth and she hissed, felt warmth between her legs, and the way her knees wanted to buckle right there.

"The answer."

"You are."

She somehow extricated herself then. Pulled back and looked at him. "I'm what?"

"You are sweeter and more satisfying even than cornbread, and that's going some, because that's mighty fine cornbread."

He leaned in for another kiss, but she batted him away knowing that what had just happened was all wrong and yet felt all right. But she wasn't ready for a relationship—not even a lusty one-night stand with an eminently eligible man like this.

"I need to think about this," she said warding him off. "Go make do with number two."

She followed him into the living room and plunked herself down in the chair because she knew if she sat on the couch he'd sit beside her.

She needed to figure out how to control the feeling she had so things didn't get out of hand. So she could focus on the other things in her life.

Like a warning.

Chapter 25

THE COOL GREEN AND WHITE OF Deena's living room was a clear reflection of the woman—cool. Leastwise she'd managed to cool everything off, or looked that way, when the heat of her kisses made it hard to think clearly. He'd been an idiot to take a chance like that; she could have just thrown him out.

But she hadn't.

No, she sure enough hadn't and she was sitting across from him now, looking cool and yet she couldn't hide the flush of her cheeks and the slightly stunned fluster of her gaze. So maybe she wasn't quite the cool one he'd thought. Chalk that one up, buddy. But Deena just sat there in her simple jeans and v-neck t-shirt that from the side showed the delicious curve of her breast.

What she was doing was trying to put all her armor back on so she could be the formidable Deena Hunter again. Frankly, he might admire and even lust after the formidable Ms. Hunter, but he thought the flushed and flustered one might just have stolen his heart.

Well he'd let her have her space right now, even though it cost him, because another moment of those kisses and he'd have had her on the counter and been using an entirely different set of tools.

He looked down at the platter of cornbread in his lap. Good, yes. But definitely numero two.

"So today I took a step to begin internal investigations at the Hat." She was trying to be cool, professional, but a slight tremor came through her voice and gave him just a little satisfaction. "It's pretty unusual for someone in my position to be investigating staff. I mean I supervise staff, but to actually go further than that—well it's frowned upon by the union. They see it as a management job."

Rich nodded slowly. He hadn't known the position she was in and it filled him with a little discomfort when he thought about Chuck's information. He'd prefer to just be enjoying the company of a woman he was intent on seducing, not thinking about gangs and investigations.

"I thought you could deal with problem staff."

Across the room, Sly rousted himself from a pool of sunlight and sleepily sat at Deena's feet until she settled him in her lap, and stroked his black fur. A woman and her familiar. She smiled affectionately at Sly, then looked back to Rich.

"And I can, as far as it goes. But if it's serious, it goes to Management for decisions about whether to suspend or fire or send letters of reprimand. And they do investigations."

"Well then maybe it should be management who take on this one."

She glowered at him—actually glowered, but there was something else there, too. He couldn't quite make out what it was.

"Are you saying you'd rather not deal with me?" Her eyes, dark and luminous in the shadows of the room's glow, said she didn't believe it, that she knew something was happening between them.

"I'm saying maybe it should be your management leading this charge." He looked away because he didn't want to think that there could possibly be danger to her, but at the same time the knowledge was there.

"Rich?" His name sounded just right on her tongue. He looked up at her and found her smiling at him. "I'm a good officer. I know how to investigate a hell of a lot better than anyone on the management team. And I'm not afraid."

Had she known what he was thinking?

"Besides, have you met Ravi Sandhar?"

She looked grim, and there was a hint of distaste in the way she said the name. Maybe—maybe she already sensed what Chuck and he suspected.

"Tell me."

"In a word, 'slime'. He's smooth, oily, even—one of those guys with perfect teeth and hair, who truly believes his own press. He's self-satisfied that he'd gotten as far as he has, as quickly as he has—he was a Probation Officer once, but then transferred over to the jail system into a Deputy Warden of Programs—that's the position responsible for all the work and treatment programs at the Center. He made a splash when he arrived. Pissed C.O.s off that he'd jumped the queue of promotion from within the institutions, and impressed the hell out of headquarters for his progressive programs and policies. When the last Warden retired he was a shoe-in. Problem is, like I said, he's slimy."

It was good information, but not enough. He chewed on a piece of the satisfying cornbread, thinking.

"So what is it that makes him slimy?"

"How he works." The lack of hesitation and the way she shook her head told him she was getting to the heart of the matter. "He uses people. Mitch Digneault, the Deputy Director of Operations who basically runs all the jail was the acting Warden until Ravi won the competition for the job. He was a gracious loser, but Ravi's one of those insecure guys. He started doing things behind Mitch's back— taking over operational things that were Mitch's responsibility and when things didn't quite work out, then the shit ran downhill right into Mitch's lap. It's left Mitch's rep tarnished and him just trying to keep his head down."

She went quiet and Rich saw something else was coming; she was just trying to figure out the best way to say it.

"And there's his attitude towards women. He crows about how he promotes women. Then he goes and hires babes to work in his office and, I suspect, harasses them. He's got this damn plant in his office that when you brush against it, it's like his eyes light up and he says some damn-fool thing like he wishes he were the plant."

By the twist of her mouth he knew she'd experienced what she described and that this was the reason for her distaste for Ravi Sandhar. Deena was a supremely sexy woman, but she had always put her sexuality aside for professionalism. Sandhar's attitude would drive her nuts. He'd like to bop Sandhar a good one for making her work in that kind of environment.

"My partner says there's intelligence information that South Asian gangs are infiltrating the correctional systems—both Federal and Provincial."

He saw her eyes widen as she computed his information. "Sandhar?"

"You tell me."

It was a considering gaze she gave him as her thoughts turned inward, assessing in that careful way she had. Finally she shook her head.

"I'm not buying it. Ravi's slime in oh-so-many ways, but he's law-abiding slime." The little snort she gave as she said it eased the tension of the discussion.

"I have a vision of algae with six-shooters."

"Nah. Ravi'd have a glock but he wouldn't know how to load it."

She grinned and the connection he knew they'd had long before bloomed bright and renewed between them.

"You done with that?"

He looked down at the pan. Somehow he'd managed to devour almost a full pan of cornbread while they'd talked. The tightness of his jeans confirmed it.

"God, yes. My waistline will never be the same, but it was worth it."

She set Sly down, stood with that innate grace that always took his breath away and retrieved the pan, but then she totally surprised him by leaning down to place the lightest of kisses on the corner of his mouth.

"You taste like maple syrup," she said as she straightened and took the pan to the kitchen.

"Sorry about that."

"There are worse things." Returning to the room she settled herself at the other end of the couch. Close enough he could touch her, could feel the heat of her presence and catch the faint scent of wild roses. The intimacy of her choice made him swallow.

He was *so* not going to blow this.

Then her gaze went business again, as if regretting what she'd done and forcing him to put aside all thoughts of what might happen between them.

"So if that's the case, then any of my South Asian staff might be gang connected." She was shaking her head, not wanting to believe. "Do you know how many Indo-Canadian staff I've got? How many there are in the jail? Amarjit Sandhu was first on scene with Stickley. He was working chest compressions on him."

"A fact that seemed a little too in keeping with our suspicions."

"But Chad Preston was there, too. He comes out of a cop family in Toronto."

"So something to look into."

"Damn. The last thing I need." She stood and started to pace, avoiding Sly's head-bumps, her long, runner's legs taking her across the hardwood in just a few paces. She turned back to him and must have caught his admiring gaze, because a slight flush appeared in her cheeks.

"I've got an absolute rookie and a seasoned old bear trying to gather information in the jail. I could have placed them both in real danger—especially Anita."

She must have seen his look of confusion, because she crossed back to him, settled beside him, her legs crossed.

"It's what I did today. I recruited two officers to help me— Heywood because he's been around forever and people trust him. The other one is Anita Underhill—a newbie, but I've known her for years. She's got a good head on her shoulders and has the advantage of being new. It means she'll be working all the shifts and people won't see her as a threat. They'll be more prone to try to indoctrinate or recruit her."

"Sounds like they were reasonable choices," he hedged, because he saw the concern in her eyes. "Who else could you have chosen?"

"I could have chosen no one and done it myself."

"And all the staff are going to talk to you—an Assistant Deputy Warden? Aren't you the one who just said you can send staff up for discipline?"

"Yeah, but..."

"Deena, they wouldn't talk to you, just like they wouldn't talk to a manager. Give yourself a break. They're probably safe enough. Just tell them to be careful."

She got up again and strode across the apartment. He could see there was something more on her mind. Finally she turned back to him.

"I should warn them, and we're off now for four days. I don't even have their home phone numbers. I can't call the Center for them, because that'll get people talking."

The way her gaze went unfocussed told him her mind was racing, considering her options, assessing what she knew.

"Henry."

"Sorry, but the name's Rich," he said softly. "I could pretend to be a Henry if you like."

That brought her back to him, but she shook her head, brushed her blonde hair back as her eyes lit with an angry fire.

"Henry. The inmate that mentioned staff. He had a shower accident the other day. I read the report, but I let it go. Damn it, how could I be so irresponsible?"

She was pacing again, leaving Sly protesting as he followed her back and forth. Finally he gave up and came over to Rich. Rich met the challenge of head-butts and meows, and hauled the cat onto his lap.

"Sorry I got her riled, little fella. Do you think she might come sit with us again?"

The cat chirruped and Deena stopped her pacing.

"You think you're being cute, don't you?"

He grinned his best grin. "Is it working?"

"Dammit, Rich, I've got a case to work here and people are in danger of getting hurt."

"And we've both just come off shift and this sort of thing takes time. Your staff are safe at home right now, aren't they? Henry is still in jail. How badly was he hurt?"

"Broken nose."

"Then he'll live, too."

He saw her jaw flex in anger, or he thought it was anger.

"You need to get a life, if all you've got to do is worry about your job. Balance, remember? We used to talk about it while we drove."

"Damn, you've got a memory like a horse."

"Elephant."

"What?" She looked at him a little crossly, and he uprooted Sly from his lap with an apology and went to her.

"Elephants are the ones with the memory. Horses eat, as in before I ate that cornbread I was hungry as a horse."

She stood quietly under his hands as he ran them up to her shoulders and the shadows under her hair. Her skin was warm, smooth, and the sleek feel of it brought all of his senses to attention.

"There are other things we could do with your time. Like this." He leaned in and placed a soft kiss on her lips. She stiffened.

"And this." Another kiss, this time on her jaw and the scent and taste of her flooded his senses, aroused him so he was almost afraid at the power of it.

"And this." His lips found the soft spot between her ear and her jaw, ran lower into her shadows and she softened under him, the rigidity melting, her neck easing over to allow him access and her breath hummed a little surprised 'oh' in his ears.

"You see. Other things." His lips trailed lower, down to the collarbone that so delicately ringed her neck. He pulled the v-neck of her t-shirt aside to show more skin.

"Other things," she whispered and her hands came up to his head, lifted his face to hers so she could meet his gaze.

"You hurt me and I'll die." There was such fear there, and longing, it could almost break his heart.

"I've waited too long for you, Deena."

And then she was warm in his arms, her body trembling, pressed into his, his arousal clear between them and all he could hope was that this wasn't too fast, too soon, because he bloody well knew that it was happening now.

Chapter 26

SOMEHOW THE AFTERNOON HAD disappeared and evening had sprung up outside her apartment. It left her standing in the half-glow of sunset, the green and cream of her living room making Rich look like he was a mythical god in the glade of a forest.

Deena's heart yammered in her chest and her hands were shaking. Dammit her whole body was shaking because she wanted him so badly, was afraid of the feeling just like she was terrified of the threat on Lana today. But Rich was here. After all those years of setting him aside, of trying to make him just a memory, and she was young again and very much obsessed with this man.

The difference was this time she could do something about it. Give in to it. And mask the fear.

His lips found her neck again, his hand pulling the neck of her t-shirt aside, exposing the slope of her shoulder, the indentation of her collarbone. Trailing kisses up the tender skin of her neck he reached her jaw, her lips, kissed and rested.

A light kiss. Rested again.

Those blue eyes of his smiled down at her and it was hard to focus, because all her attention was on the electric feel of him under her hands, the tremors that quaked through her core.

"Not so bad?"

She had to swallow to find the strength to reply; she was not going to rush this. She had waited too long, and wasn't control almost her middle name.

"Let me show you."

She planted a light kiss on his lips, used her fingers to hold his face, as his hands came around her waist, held her to him as she ran her cheek over his, kissed his jaw, his earlobe, caught it in her mouth and bit oh-so-lightly, half-laughing as she felt his body tighten against hers and the rising heat of his erection. She ran her lips down his neck to his broad shoulder and down further, pushing his shirt up, letting her breath heat his skin, her kisses leaving a small moist path down into the chest hair that just showed. Her hands followed as she paused there, ran fingertips down over his chest, lightly up his side and his hands clenched, slid down to her buttocks and tightened there, pulling her into him.

She pulled back, cocked her head at him. "Did I do something?"

All innocence, but there was a wild fire burning barely checked in Rich's gaze, that sent heat and moisture flowing in her body.

"Oh, God." It was all she got out, before his mouth covered hers and she answered, opened, pressed into him, half-lifting on her toes to better fit herself to his hardness and need. His hands ran up her back, found the bottom of her shirt, found skin underneath. Hard callused hands, knowledgeable hands.

For some strange reason her mind went to tools, and she wanted to be used by him, knew he'd use her as expertly. Her fingers pulled the back of his shirt free, found the hard sheath of muscle over his ribs, as his hands slid to her sides, his thumbs grazing the sides of her breasts, then sliding forward to palm her taught nipples.

"Here." She fought free of him, pulled her shirt off and faced him, knew her chest was heaving like a fighter's, and this was a fight—to hold herself back, to make this last because God knew it was a stupid thing to do and she would probably live to regret it, but right now she was getting her wish—the wish she'd carried locked away for too many years.

And hiding the fear.

"Come here." He reached for her, closed his eyes as his hands trailed over her skin, lightly touching as if he wanted to memorize her flesh with his hands. Then he kissed her, slid down her neck, his quick fingers flicking her bra loose with ease, freeing her breasts to find them with his tongue, his fingers.

When he took her nipple in his mouth, she groaned, arched her herself into him, wanting more. She raked her nails over his skin and he pulled back long enough to pull his shirt off, then yanked her to him so their flesh finally met.

His arms tightened around her and he was shaking just as much as she was, as his kisses trailed over her hair, her face.

"We're passing the point of no return here." It was a whisper, heated with passion. The fact he was trying to let her make the decision only made her want him more.

She just caught his hand, led him to her bedroom door.

It was a simple room, quilted white bedspread, antique dresser, pale yellow walls, the walls covered in art photographs of doorways of Europe lit up by the late afternoon sun.

She faced him in the slatted light through the binds and unbuttoned her jeans.

"I'll warn you, I'm not a girl anymore. I'm afraid I've got a bit of topographical map for a butt." She knew she was using humor to try to lighten this moment, this intensely, supremely, important moment. She slid her jeans down, stepped out of them, feeling vulnerable and foolish and sexy all at the same time and please God, just don't let him laugh as she looked for his reaction.

"Jeezus, Deena. You're beautiful." He had her in his arms, his hands on her, like he was taking possession as his kisses explored more of her body.

He went to his knees in front of her.

"More than I ever expected," he whispered into her belly, as his kisses found her navel, his hands hard on her butt, catching the silky fabric of her underwear and sliding it down so his lips found the tight blonde curls of her. "All I ever wanted."

His mouth took her and she thought she would explode right there. Her hands caught in his hair as his tongue worked magic, as his hands parted her and his fingers found the slick moisture of her. Her breath came in small jagged sobs as the heat in her mounted, as her body constricted, fell inward to only the sensation of his hands, his mouth and the explosion that was going to...

Almost...

Not quite...

There.

The climax rocked her. Sent shudders through her so her knees gave, but Rich was on his feet, caught her as her body spasmed.

Need. She pulled away from him, running her hands down the broad "Y" of his chest, following the thin trail of fur that led down past the faintest hint of a belly to his narrow hips. Shaking fingers quick on his fly, hauled the jeans open, running her palm up the fullness of him. She ran her kisses down his chest as she forced the denim down, as she slid his underwear off and kissed him.

He shivered and she felt the power of him like a huge engine under her hands, her lips. She would have taken him in her mouth, but he pulled her up, took her mouth, pulled her into him so their bodies meshed together, lifted her up so she could spread herself around him, feel the thrusting heat of him.

He pressed into her and she stopped breathing as he filled her, at the strangeness of it and the comfort as he slowly began to move, edging deeper until he was home.

It was like they couldn't believe it. Simply stood there not moving, shocked by what they had done. His blue eyes on hers, caught in the pulsing sensation that was whatever they had become.

Then he moved and she answered. Answered as she met his kisses, as his hands held her to him, as his hips thrust, softly at first, then harder. Then deeper as he turned, carrying her with him, pressing her into the wall, bracing them both as he stroked into her, each movement sending shockwaves through her body that left everything singed with fire.

She couldn't think. Only feel. This was him. This was home. This was the tightening of the body into a coil, a spring that was explosion. This was reaching down for his ass, sliding her fingers there, even as he bit her neck, her shoulder, the top of her breast. As the spring inside tightened to the point it would break, to the tension no steel could take and his gaze was on hers, blue flame burning, and she was burning, on fire, and oh God.

The room exploded as her body shuddered, as he slammed into her and she heard him groan, heard her own shout as if from a great distance. Her legs clutched his hips, not wanting it to end, not wanting him to leave, to ever leave her again.

He must have felt it because he rested there, kissing her neck, her lips, her lowered eyelids.

"Deena," he whispered and swung them both around to the bed to collapse there, still joined, his long body over hers.

"You know we could have used the bed," she said, smoothing the sweat and his hair back off his brow and loving the covetous look in his eyes. Her body steamed with the heat of their joining, and the trouble was, even in the afterglow of the explosion she only wanted him more. There were too many lost years to make up for.

He smiled down at her, pulled a stray hair from the corner of her mouth.

"Don't worry. We will. By my reckoning we've got a whole night to mess up your bed."

"That's mighty assumptive of you, officer."

"I'm real good at reading body language. Got tops in my class in forensic interviewing."

"That right?" She clenched a set of muscles she hadn't used in a while and saw the blue fire suddenly darken. His hands ran up her sides.

"You do that, you're liable to get yourself in trouble, little lady. I might have to do something about it, even if I'm an old man."

"Now there's a thought." She took the dare, loving the way he filled her, the way she could feel him wanting her, the way he touched her—almost with reverence—and the way their bodies just seemed to fit. "By the way, you're not feeling particularly old right now."

"I think I'm in training." He lifted himself onto his elbows and did something inside her that left her totally breathless. "Let me show you."

Deena could only smile her delight.

Chapter 27

CAFÉ CRÈME BRÛLÉE, SAT unobtrusively between a gas station and a pizza shop in a little strip of stores near Mission Senior Secondary School.

It was a little hole-in-the-wall kind of place, accessorized with slightly bad modern art and slightly wilder music and free internet access, all designed to bring in the high school crowd for their iced lattes and cappuccinos. A few other hardy souls who could get beyond the music and the warring scents of incense and coffee also patronized the place. Seemed they knew what Anita was discovering: the swarthy little man behind the espresso machine made a darn fine cup of coffee.

Anita nursed her extra-tall, no-foam, no-fat latte and tried to stop her chair from wobbling as she faced Chad Preston across the postage stamp-sized table.

She had followed his red four-by-four with the over-sized wheels in her little red hatchback from the Hat to the shop she hadn't even known existed. She thought she knew Mission like the back of her hand, and yet things were happening around her that she wasn't even aware of.

Like Deena Hunter. Contrary to what Anita had thought, the woman was no friend of Anita's. She shook her head.

"You're still letting her get to you."

Anita lifted her gaze to meet Chad's concerned grin. The guy had been really decent to her. She hadn't expected him to follow through on his offer of getting together after work. Frankly, after the run in with Miss ADW Hunter, Anita hadn't really been in the mood for socializing. Chad

had taken one look at her face, grabbed her elbow and led her to her car. They'd been here an hour now.

"So how'd you find this place?" She asked as a girl of about fifteen smiled at Chad. She was followed by a youth with the typical ripped jeans, oversized hockey jersey and slightly pimply face found on half the teenage boys in Mission. Behind them came Julie Brar, the Veterinarian Anita had volunteered for way back when Anita was sure that working with animals was what she wanted for a career. Now Anita's father said she was just working with a different kind of animal.

"Julie! Hi! Gosh it's been a long time."

Julie looked a little surprised but came over, her characteristic grin growing bigger when she looked from Anita to Chad.

"Little Anita Underhill. Well I'll be. I heard you had aspirations of becoming a lawyer or something."

Anita ducked her head, momentarily embarrassed for Chad to hear.

"I still do. I'm working at the Hat for experience and to pay tuition."

Julie eyed Chad, her hands on her hips. "Let me guess. That's where you met this reprobate."

That brought a grin from Anita. "I see you know Chad."

"Hey! I'm sitting right here!"

"And so you are," Julie said, then turned back to Anita. "He brings all his women here, so watch him."

"Don't listen to her; it's all lies. Everyone comes here. This place is the worst kept secret in town." Chad grinned those dimples at Anita in a way that made her feel a little mushy inside. She had to remind herself this was a co-worker and she needed to keep this professional.

Julie nodded. "I'm afraid that's true. Randy Johal is my husband's cousin and has got to be the biggest blabber mouth of them all. He told the world."

"And now the whole shift comes here. Nice being with the kids. We're role models I guess you could say." He glanced over at the coffee counter. "Would you excuse me a moment?"

He was up and over to the counter talking intently to the hockey jersey-clad boy, then clapped his shoulder, nodded something at the coffee-shop owner and came back to settle in his chair.

"So where were we?"

Julie checked her watch. "Listen, Anita, I got to go—appointments and all that, but come on down to the clinic some time. I'd love to chat over a coffee or something."

She left them and Anita looked back at Chad.

Where were they, indeed? The tension from her run-in with Deena still made her want to hit something, even though seeing Julie reminded her of a simpler time in her life.

"I just can't get over it. Dee—ADW Hunter was my friend, my sister. Heck, she helped me get hooked up to volunteer at Julie's. Then she goes and treats me like that."

"I told you, she didn't get her nickname for nothing. But even Bitch-Goddesses get older. Pretty soon she'll just be the Bitch."

Anita shook her head, appreciating the support even if she didn't totally agree. Dee might be forty, but it wasn't really showing. She was still an attractive woman.

"I tried so hard, you know? I listened, even if I didn't like it when she reamed me out at start of shift. I really tried to get the checks done on time. Heck, how am I supposed to help the fact an inmate wanted to talk to me on West1, or that C.O. Johal had a message he needed me to pass to Rosetta?"

Just thinking about the unfairness of it all got her shoulders so tense she knew she was going to give herself a migraine if she didn't watch it.

"Things just aren't turning out like I'd planned, you know? I want to do a good job."

"Hey! You are doing a good job. Heck, you've only been on the job a week. You've learned the Center and you're fitting in."

"But no one's going to trust me if I can't do prowl right. Everyone depends on you." She knew she was feeling sorry for herself and she knew she was kind of liking the way Chad was trying to help her. She looked up at him and found those dimples turned on again.

"I trust you. I'd say the other guys do too. Mostly. Prowl's a tough job what with the distance, and the time. If you can do prowl, you can do anything pretty much. Hunter's testing you."

"And finding me lacking, I'm afraid."

"And she's just a bitch who likes to prove she's better than everyone. She thinks she knows everything, runs everything and we let her think that. I mean, she sits in her office and tells us what to do, but we decide how we're going to do it. We stick together. That's how we put up with her. We work hard to keep her off our backs and let her be the Warden's showpiece."

Chad's face had gotten hard as he spoke and it was clear he didn't like Dee Hunter. That fact surprised Anita and made her cringe a little, because Chad hid it well. He was pretty darn civil to everyone else.

"You're trying to tell me something, aren't you?"

"Hunter's risen like a rocket in the Hat. Over solid guys with years of service. I figure she's been sleeping around with the high mucky-mucks, but no one's been able to catch her at it. It would bring her down a peg if we could. Might get her off us a little."

The poison in his words surprised her. It was hard to believe, because Deena seemed pretty tight with her shift.

"Heywood described her as one of the best ADWs in Corrections. Solid, he said."

"That's Heywood. God, look at the man, ancient. He started in the Branch when we were just kids. You might not have been born yet. He thinks this job is a career."

"And you don't?" It was strange to think of Dee's seemingly tight group of CO's as something different. She'd been totally wrong about them—naïve, actually.

"Hell, no. This is a stepping stone. A friggin' dead end if you stay. That's why I was so pissed when Hunter rained all over me, too, because I've got my application into the Vancouver police and I don't need bad evals."

He shook his head, tipped back in his chair with his arms crossed over his chest, his dark eyes studying her.

"I think we should get off the topic, don't you? It's just keeping you tense and the reason I brought you here is to see you laugh."

The look in his eyes stopped her and she felt a little heat flush through her face. He was flirting with her again.

"And why would you have an interest in me laughing?" said over the top of her cup.

He let his chair thunk down and covered her hands with his. They were big, warm, and his thumbs lightly ran over hers.

"What would you say if I told you I think you're cute as a bug and I have this urge to run my fingers through that mane of yours?"

The overt pass was a bit forward for her taste and for a moment Anita didn't know what to do. A guy as good-looking as Chad Preston would have no trouble with the ladies. She was probably just another conquest.

She met his gaze, trying to think how to slow things down a little, when the opening of the coffee shop's door saved her the trouble. Randy Johal sauntered in.

The good-looking, dark-featured, guard was in civvies—dark jeans and a red shirt that set off his golden skin. His face broke into a grin when he saw them.

"What the hell are you two doing here?" But the grin on his face seemed more trained on Chad and there was a forced look to Randy's eyes that said he wasn't quite as pleased as he said.

"What the hell's it look like? Anita, here, was in serious need of some moral support. Hunter rode her ass good today."

Johal swung an interested glance in her direction. "I thought you were buds?"

Anita sighed and shook her head. Apparently other people had been taken in, as well.

"I thought so, too—once. But after today I'd say the Bitch-Goddess and I are more in the realm of people ending a relationship—we got a past and no future."

"That's harsh." Johal shook his head. "What happened? Mind if I join you?"

Chad looked at her and nodded. It was pretty clear that the guys were rallying around her and that made things better. She could feel the tight pain ease between her shoulders; she understood what it meant to have people backing you up.

"I knew she was going to give me a hard time as soon as I came on shift. The way she looks at you sometimes."

"The don't-fuck-with-me look. We know."

"She fuckin' read me the riot act after she sent everyone else to the units, and then she fucking has the gall to ask a favor. Like I'm going to do anything to help her." It just felt so damn good to vent, to have sympathetic ears, and not bad looking one's to boot.

"So I go out and do my darndest, and when I miss getting the time checks on time by one minute—one fucking minute—she rides my ass again."

Just thinking about the unfairness of it all had her clenching her cup so hard she thought it might break. Venting like this, using words she didn't usually keep in her vocabulary, felt right, older, more in keeping with the men around her.

"That's rough." Randy glanced at Chad and the coffee counter. "I'm going to get me a coffee. Want anything?"

Chad assessed Anita, then shook his head. "We're fine. We'll be leaving soon."

He said it in such a sure, proprietary way it left Anita a little uncomfortable, but she had her car. She could decide to stay if she wanted. She sipped the dregs of her coffee and watched Randy order an espresso. A kid came in—high-schooler by the look of him in his low-rider jeans and brow-ring—and went up to Randy.

"You guys come here a lot."

Chad shrugged. "Yeah. So? Listen, I know we could sit here all night talking, but I thought it might be better to get outta here. If you're interested I could buy you dinner. Make up for the bad day you've had?"

He must have seen her suspicions in her eyes, because he held up his hands.

"Hey. No strings, here. Just dinner for a co-worker who's had a hard day." He gave her a grin she figured could just about melt most women's panties, but she knew she could handle it. She was handling working at the jail, wasn't she? Except for Hunter.

"Course I might expect that smile of yours in payment."

That made it almost a point of honor that she not smile, but the corners of her mouth trembled and she saw the appreciation in his eyes. It gave her another warm flush.

"You know, that might just be a plan." She drained the last bit of foam from her cup just as Randy came back, the kid in tow like an acolyte.

"'Nita and I are going to head. I'm still trying to get Hunter out of her head, so I'm going to buy her dinner."

Randy looked at her, but when his eyes met hers they were friendly.

"Watch out for the hands. That's what I heard Lucy say." He turned to Chad. "And you mind your manners. She's a good one."

Chad told Randy what he could do with his advice and caught Anita's arm.

"What d'you say we just leave your car here and take my truck down to the restaurant? I'll bring you back here when we're done."

The thought of leaving her car made her a little insecure, but she knew Mission wasn't that big—she could walk home or catch a cab without too much bother. Nodding, she followed him to his truck, waited while he unlocked and then gave her a hand up into the over-height cab. It felt like she was sitting above the earth and the truck cab carried the not-unpleasant scent of Chad's mild spice aftershave and a warmth that grew when he eased himself into the comfortable bucket seat beside hers.

He smiled down at her, caught her hand in a very non-coworker way. "So we're going to relax, right?"

Anita nodded.

"Good. Then take a deep breath and enjoy the ride."

The engine grumbled to life and he drove them out of the tiny parking lot to parts unknown. It was a little exciting because Anita knew she actually like this guy.

"So what was the favor Hunter asked you?" He glanced sideways as he drove.

Anita considered. Dee had never said the request was confidential. Besides, what did Anita Underhill owe Deena Hunter?

"It was like this...," she said, and began to talk.

Chapter 28

THE GREY MORNING LIGHT WOKE Rich. That and the slow, glowing feeling that something was very right with his world. He hadn't had the feeling for a long time.

Of course it helped having Deena's smooth bottom spooned into his belly. So did the scent of wild roses and the curve of the hip under his palm. He slid his fingers down the slope of hip to the slim waist and up her sleek rib cage to find...

...fur.

He yanked his hand back as Sly gave a sleepy meow from his place curled into Deena's chest.

"You know we shouldn't have done this, don't you?" The decisiveness in her voice said Deena had obviously been awake for some time. So did the undertone of regret.

"Seemed like the right idea to me." He pulled her a little tighter into his belly and felt himself harden at the pleasure of her skin's friction. They'd made love so many times last night and still he wanted her. He shifted his hips so she would know just how much.

"It'll cause trouble." This time her voice was a little softer, a little distracted as his hand sought past the darn cat that seemed jealous of Rich's time with Deena, and found the tender point of her breasts.

"Now why would a little thing like this cause trouble?"

Silence a moment, and he used it to move a little more, slid his hand from her breast down to the warm "Y" between her legs. Her sharp intake of breath only made him want her more.

"I...I seem to have a habit of relationship disasters..."

"That so?" His fingers stroked her and she shuddered. "Then why are you shaking?"

"Bastard. You know darn well why. All I want to do is stay right here, right now, with you, and forget everything else." Her breath came in quick little gasps that were so damn sexy he wanted to flip her on her back and take her right now, but he knew slow was better with Deena.

Slow and easy to gentle her into what she really wanted to do. Then would come the same fire she brought to everything else in her life.

"So we will."

"In an hour you have to be at work."

He bit her shoulder, lifted his face to kiss her cheek, her lips as she turned her head to him. "That's a whole hour away. Live in the now, babe."

She arched her back to accept him as his hands stroked her breasts. He wondered at the ease of being with Deena. Sure there'd been plenty of other women both before and after Ivy, but then it had been an athletic pursuit—two bodies and simple sexual hunger. This, however—this worked in a way he hadn't found before—their bodies fit so well, so clean and close. The tangle of his emotions heightened sensation to a point he didn't want to end.

In one swift motion he rolled her towards him. She fended him away from her face. "Caution, Will Robinson, I've got morning breath."

He caught her hands and pressed them back, found her mouth and a heavy sweet kiss sent his hot blood pounding. "I want to see your face," he said between kisses. "Your eyes."

They were heavy-lidded with desire as she reached for him, lifted one tanned thigh over his hip and he rolled her onto her back, her legs twining around him, reeling him in.

The warm sheath of her could almost stun him, almost send him raging he wanted her so much as she shuddered at his entry. Her pleasured look set him moving. Slowly.

An hour, he thought as the sunlight brightened through the window and caught the amber in her dark eyes. They were filled with the same desperate need he felt.

An hour would never be enough.

§

Deena raked her fingers through her still-damp hair and chided herself—again—for feeling so damn satisfied when she should be worried as hell.

Rich sat at the card table she'd set up while refinishing her kitchen table, Sly on his lap, his keys and cell phone beside him as he chewed on a piece of toast and peanut butter that were all she could manage for breakfast. He looked just slightly too pleased with himself, the way he kept glancing up at her.

As if he still saw her naked under the thick fleece robe she'd belted around her, and was certain he could reclaim that view any time he wanted. Trouble was, he was probably right. Was it possible to overdose on too much good sex? Because she was seriously considering trying.

She went to refill his coffee cup, but he covered the top, checked his watch.

"I should just be able to make it home and get changed and still make it to work on time."

She set the coffee pot back in the machine and leaned back against the counter, eyeing him. His long hands smoothed Sly's fur so the old cat purred his ecstasy, a long line of drool falling from one lip. Rich's hair was still damp from their shower together, and he'd shaved with a disposable ladies razor she'd had, so his skin was smooth and tempting to touch. She'd like to run her hands over that hard body again, maybe go with him to his place when he changed.

You're turning into a friggin' cougar, Hunter.

"You know I hardly know you."

It came out before she could stop it. Thinking of his place had made her realize she didn't even know where he lived. In fact she knew nothing about him anymore, or about the life he'd lived between their meetings. That left her feeling a little vulnerable and that the fact she'd slept with him was just a little tawdry. Not too much feminine mystique left now.

Rich put his toast down and leaned back in his chair with his thumbs hitched in his belt loops.

"Well I don't know about that, Ma'am. Seems to me you got a handle on what I need."

She batted his arm, sat down in another of the kitchen chairs. God he made her feel sexy and desired. She wasn't used to it.

"I don't even know where you live."

In answer he grabbed her hand, kissed the palm. "I'll show you. We've got all the time in the world, this time."

His blue eyes were so certain, she could almost believe, but Blake had seemed certain when he'd told her he loved her. Ravi had seemed sincere when he said his marriage was over. She couldn't let herself believe. Things were unsafe enough in her life. Like the truck yesterday.

Maybe she *should* tell him about it.

His pager went off and he released her to scoop it off the table. Reading it, all the warmth went out of his face and Deena was sure if she touched him, he'd brush her away.

"I gotta go." The cold way he said it sent a shiver up her back.

"Something with work?"

He shook his head, glanced at her, but his thoughts were clearly elsewhere.

Deena suddenly felt stupid. Here she'd been mooning over him when he wasn't letting her in anymore than she was letting him in. He had slept with her without ever telling her anything about himself. She'd just presumed he was exactly the same person she'd wanted eighteen years ago.

But she had no idea who he was now. Hell, she was an idiot—an infatuated old fool—falling into bed like she had.

Sighing, Rich stood, caught her by the hand and pulled her into him in a way she could grow to love—if she was foolish enough. She couldn't allow herself to be vulnerable even if something in his eyes sent all her doubts skittering away.

"Okay if I come by after work?" His voice was soft with desire, and she was just stupid enough to want to see him again.

Damnation, Hunter, get a grip.

But she said, "Hell, yes." Then leaned up for his kiss. "Hopefully I'll have some information by then."

Maybe she'd tell him about the truck then.

"I thought this was your day off?"

"It is, but with what you told me, I've got some follow-up."

"You'll be careful, right? If my partner's information is correct and these guys catch on to what you're doing, this could go very bad."

She avoided his gaze. "You think I don't know that? Besides, I need to warn Heywood and Underhill. I think Anita's on shift."

The concern didn't leave his eyes, but he nodded and led her to the door, his arm still around her waist. There he planted one last kiss on her lips before she watched him down the stairs. The way he paused at the bottom to wink up at her made her heart feel too big for her own good.

She scanned the town, laden in its early morning Fraser River mist. The Lougheed Highway traffic rumbled unseen down the hill and the air had that sweet-sour smell of leaf-fall that she loved. She listened for the rumble of Rich's SUV, and the sound of it pulling away, feeling the twinge of sadness that he was gone.

"You're out of control, Hunter," she murmured as she went inside.

Sly greeted her with a querulous meow, from his place by his bowl.

"Alright already. I get the message. Let's get you fed."

She went to the fridge, but a sound stopped her. Sly, gagging, vomiting white foam onto the floor.

"Sly!" She scooped him up, cradled him against her and ran for paper towels to clean up. What was the matter with him. He'd been sick too often—not something Julie had said she should expect with the diabetes. And his litter box hadn't gotten any better either since she started the insulin. He was still filling his litter box with pee.

What was taking so long with those tests Julie had ordered? Maybe she wasn't doing the needles right. Maybe it wasn't the right treatment at all. But she had to think she was helping, that she was doing the right thing.

Like she was doing the right thing not telling Rich about the near miss. Like sleeping with him was right? Or her investigation?

"Darn it, why is it I finally get to sleep with the man of my dreams and I obsess over whether it was the right thing to do? Am I stupid or what, Sly?"

He turned those gold eyes on her and she could have sworn he agreed with her.

"Don't you be getting smart-mouthed, Mister. Eat your breakfast." She set him down with a filled bowl and waited as he ate.

Then he threw up all over again and sat there dry heaving at her feet.

She didn't know what to do. Clean up of course. Fight back the urge to cry, and the feeling of panic because she couldn't make this better.

Well, she would do something. Maybe this was an allergic reaction. The vet had changed his food. That was probably it. She'd whip him in to see Julie first thing and then she'd deal with the stuff at the Hat.

She cleaned up and fed him again—this time from one of the old tins. Prayed he'd keep it down.

He didn't and she felt like ice had crept into her spine.

"You have to keep your strength up, buddy. You can't throw everything up." But as usual Sly had his cat-way and just looked at her and walked away to curl up in a pool of sunshine.

Feeling helpless and frustrated, she pulled on jeans and a fresh pink t-shirt, then loaded her little friend into his carry box. He started crying immediately.

"I know you hate the box. Heck, I hate putting you in the box. But we need to get you to the vet." Grabbing her purse, she let herself out, and carried Sly down to the Camry and headed for Mission Slopes Vet Clinic. Julie was always there early. She'd let them in.

Deena was surprised to see cars parked outside, even though the front door was still locked. She rang the buzzer, then waited until a tired-looking Julie finally opened the door.

"Deena? What are you doing here?" her voice was abrupt, professional, as if Deena had interrupted something. The strong scent of ammonia blew past Julie and almost set Deena back a pace.

"Sorry about the stink. We had an accident with one of the big dogs. Didn't get out enough, I guess. I was just trying to clean the mess up. How's my patient?" She peered down at Sly, who still mewed plaintively.

"Not well. He's been throwing up whatever he eats. I wanted to check in case it's an allergy to the food or something." Deena felt her carefully contained panic well up in the face of his doctor. Julie would sort this out.

She must have seen, because she finally nodded, stepped back to allow Deena access to the place, then led her to an examining room where she closed the door to the back.

"Whew, that smell's enough to peel paint." Deena set the cage on the examining table and opening the door. Sly was out in a flash, purring and alternating head-butts between Julie and Deena. "I think he's apologizing for screaming all the way here. Whatever's wrong hasn't affected his lungs any."

Julie just picked up Sly and chucked him under the chin, her gaze on Deena.

"We got the results of those tests." She said it softly, matter-of-factly and that made it dangerous.

All Deena's fear rushed in. Julie was as gentle and thoughtful with her owners as she was with her patients—all the things Deena appreciated in a vet. Finally Julie ruffled Sly's fur, chucked him under the chin and set him down.

"What you're describing isn't an allergy, Deena. The tests say it's CRF—Chronic Renal Failure."

Deena mouthed the words, not clear what they meant. "But…"

Julie caught her hand, urged her to the lone chair in the room and Sly leapt over to get comfortable on her lap.

"The tests are conclusive. It's not something that happens overnight and it's something I see too much in older cats. The kidneys—well they just slowly deteriorate and then suddenly the cat's in crisis." Julie stroked Sly's back. "Like Sly, here."

"But… you said diabetes." The words Julie was saying weren't making any sense. Sure Sly was older, but he hadn't been having problems until this.

"Sly's unusual. He's got both conditions and that makes treating him tougher. It's not something you should take on lightly."

She'd said treatment. There was treatment. Deena held onto that like a life saver. Swallowed.

"So what do I have to do because I'll do anything for Sly? You know it."

Julie eased her hip up onto the edge of the examining table.

"There is a way to manage it, but I'm going to give you all your options. First, it's untreatable. He has it, it's not going away. Some vets recommend euthanasia because the condition probably makes the animal feel poorly."

"You mean he's in pain?" The darn tears were coming, because she wouldn't do that to her friend—leave him in pain—but the thought of losing him… "He's not in pain. He probably just feels—well—poorly. But the throwing up, not eating, etc. are pretty typical. Symptoms can range all the way up to convulsions—which aren't a good sign. The condition isn't easy to deal with, but if you're prepared to try, there are things you can do."

"Like what?" Hold on Deena. Hold on and take hold. Sly needs you. But her mind had stopped at when Julie said euthanasia.

"He'll need fluids subcutaneously. It requires you to give him IV fluids every day. I've heard tell of kidney transplants, but I'm not aware of anyone local doing it. The fluids are about all you can do—and control his food, which is going to be a problem given his diabetes."

Euthanasia. Deena felt the whole world, her breath, seep away except for the softness of Sly's fur under her hands. Lose Sly?

"Deena." Julie knelt in front of her. "It's all we can do. I'm sorry. You have to make the decision whether you can provide the kind of care he needs. He's an old cat."

The choking feeling built, made it hard to move. She managed a slight jerk of her head, yes.

Julie stroked Sly's head and got an appreciative head butt. "Then you better let me show you how to do this and then take him home. Give him fluids when you get home—I'll write down a schedule—and keep him as comfortable as you have and you could have months or years left. Who knows?"

"Who knows?" Oh God she didn't want to have to deal with this. But she nodded, paid attention as Julie demonstrated and wrote down what Deena should do.

"How much do I owe you?"

"Nada."

"But..."

"Would you just get out of here and let me clean up this stink? I open in a minute and I don't want the rest of the world to think I run a shoddy shop."

The words almost came out cross, so Deena didn't push it. She let Julie lock the door behind her and went home, wondering how she was going to deal with Sly and the Stickley investigation. At least the relationship with Rich was going well.

"Keep telling yourself that, Hunter. Because that's what you always think—just

before they blow up in your face."

Chapter 29

RICH PHONED IN THAT HE'D BE late, then drove like a madman to the duplex he'd rented in the low-rent area of Mission called Birdland after the names of the streets. The run down little place was about all he could afford what with carrying the mortgage on Ivy's house, and the owner had seemed to figure that having a cop for a tenant would help keep his other tenant in order. So far it had worked.

He ducked inside to faded yellow walls and the couch cluttered with magazines that he used to keep himself occupied. Down the hall to the dingy bedroom that he *never* wanted Dee to see, quickly changed clothes, then aimed his truck over the Mission Bridge over the Fraser River toward Ivy's house by the U.S. border. The morning was one of those fine, hazy days where the light seemed half-liquid and the massive mountain loomed like a ghost to the southeast. The powerful scent of oncoming fall couldn't dislodge Deena's intoxicating scent from his nose.

This was the first time he'd experienced his eyes involuntarily closing each time he caught her scent on his fingers, his clothes. But it was something to hold onto when he faced off with Ivy.

The darn woman had left fifteen—count 'em—messages on his cell phone before she managed to get the office to page him. He'd been furious when he called Ivy as he was leaving Deena's. He was damn well going to stop it.

He pulled up in front of the house a little and stomped up to the door. He didn't bother to knock. She didn't deserve that courtesy until she set boundaries around her life. Of course maybe he was the one who should be helping her a little around that. This morning he would.

"Ivy! Where the hell are you?"

"Up here." Her thin voice came from upstairs and he took the risers two at a time.

"I need to get to work," he said roughly as he came into the room.

Ivy sat ensconced on her bed like it was a throne. Her hair was brushed. It gleamed on her naked shoulders. She had the covers pulled up to her waist, the rest of her boney form barely concealed in a thin, silken nightgown.

"Jeezus, Ivy, cover yourself."

"Why? You've seen me before. You loved me before." There was a wistful look in her eyes that once would have raised his guilt. But not anymore.

"Damn it, Ivy. It's been over for five years. Can't you understand that?" He crossed to the bed, yanked the covers up to her chin, then realized he'd placed himself in a position far more intimate than he wished it to be. He backed off.

"Now what was so damn important that you had to have work page me?"

She hesitated and he headed to the door. "You've got ten minutes and I'm leaving. I won't be coming back."

"Rich!" Her voice was almost a wail as he stomped down the stairs, angry that she'd called him and furious that he had come. Well it was over. Over and done.

Ivy's pathetic attempts to hold him in her life, and his more pathetic rescue attempts, couldn't go on.

He paced the kitchen. The counters were surprisingly clear; no dishes were piled in the sink either. The fridge still looked fresh inside.

So she had done some things herself. That was something, because he was about to take a tough love approach that Ivy wasn't going to like.

Beyond the kitchen window Majority Report loafed in the pasture, the angled morning sunlight showing off his ribs. Ivy should sell the damn animal and be done with it. She was never going to ride. It was another one of her pipe dreams, just like keeping him on the hook. Well this fish was getting away.

He turned back when he heard her enter. She stood in the shadow of the hallway door, dressed in a pair of jeans that looked like they would fall off of her, and a man's dress shirt he recognized as something he had left behind. That sent a sad twisted feeling into his gut.

"So. What's so urgent?"

She wouldn't look at him. Just ducked past and went to the cupboard. "The least I can do is offer you coffee."

"I don't need coffee. I need to go to work. You remember work? The thing you do to pay the bills instead of living off your parents?"

He saw her flinch and hated himself, but he had to do this. Her hands shook as she went through the motions of scooping grounds and pouring water.

"I had an emergency, not that you care." Her voice was icy. "You never were there for me, were you? Never were through the entire marriage. Your head was elsewhere from before we got married." She turned back to him her gaze shiny with contained tears. "You never thought I knew, did you?"

He didn't know what to say. He had never admitted it, but how could she not have? The way he felt like he was only going through the motions—even on their bloody wedding night. Even though she had waited for him and he realized the gift she was giving him.

"I've done nothing but be here for you. Now what was the emergency and what do you need now?"

She lifted her chin. "Where were you last night? I called and called and called and you weren't home. You didn't answer your cell, either."

She had no right to know and yet he felt guilty for the night he'd had, the joy he felt even facing Ivy. He felt the heat in his face, and knew she caught it by the way her lips pressed into a line.

"So. Another of your women. Was she a good screw, Rich? Better than me? Can *she* keep you happy?"

He headed for the door, not prepared to cheapen what he had with Deena by bringing her into it, but Ivy caught his arm. Her fingers clung with a surprising strength.

"I nearly lost Majority Report last night. I looked out my window and saw him standing funny, biting at his side. I went out and he was sweating, and his eyes were funny. I didn't know what to do."

He yanked loose. "So you call a vet, you don't call me."

"I didn't know a good one. I called you for help."

"And how the hell am I supposed to know a good vet? I haven't got a horse? Hell I haven't even got a cat!"

"But you always know what to do." Her gaze veiled with lashes, she caught his hand, brought it to her lips.

Rich hauled on his fury to deal with this pathetic little scene. He jerked away. He'd been gentle too long.

"Ivy, you're right. I wasn't fair when I married you. I thought I was doing the right thing because I'd proposed, but I knew it wasn't the right marriage even though I went through with it. I'm sorry. I'm sorry I can't give you back the years." He drew in a long breath. "But I can't do this any-more. I've helped you since we split because I felt guilty, but now I'm moving on. I'm filing for divorce."

He read her shock in the way she seemed to sag, then catch herself. Fear blossomed in her eyes. "But..."

He was struck by how thin she was, knew the fact that he hadn't filed for divorce might have been misconstrued as him not wanting out of the marriage.

"No buts. It's over and you know it. You just haven't let go. You have to. You can manage on your own. You're a skilled professional and I hear they need nurses around here. You can get a job. You can make new friends, meet new men. You're still young. You can have a life."

"Not without you."

"You know I don't love you and you can say that? You deserve better than that. Better than me."

"You've found someone new, haven't you? That's where you were last night." There was venom in her voice and the strength of her anger was actually refreshing.

"That's no business of yours. Your own life is. Get on with it. You dealt with Majority Report."

"I called around to a few of the neighbors. They recommended someone. The vet was pretty impressed with Major. She thought she might even be interested in leasing him."

"See, you dealt with it yourself. You didn't need me."

"I needed you to run a check on her to make sure she's alright before I do the lease thing. You always said it was good to check people out."

"You got recommendations from your neighbors, right?" A little light seemed to go on in her eyes.

"I did, didn't I?" It came out with a little bit of wonder.

He motioned around the room. "You're doing great. Just keep it up."

He checked his watch and swore. He was seriously late—again. But this would be the last time it would be due to Ivy.

"I've got to go. I'm not going to be at your beck and call anymore. Your life is yours now and I'm not going to be in it."

He saw the panic flare in her eyes, and again felt that damn responsibility for her.

"I'll make you a deal. I'll take calls from you between noon and one o'clock pm, so if you really need my help, I'll be available. But think hard before you call because I'll say no if you can take care of it yourself. Otherwise don't call, because I won't answer. Period. You got that?"

The panic was slowly being replaced by anger, but that was good. It would fuel her, move her forward out of depression and let her get on with her life. He could deal with being the bastard who'd left her. He just couldn't deal with being the bastard who ruined her life.

"You fucking asshole."

"That's me. You don't need or want me around."

"Get the fuck out of my house, you philandering prick! I was going to take you back. I was going to put up with your shit! But I realize I'm too good for you."

"That just might be the truth."

She slapped him and he nodded.

It just made her madder. She punched him in the chest, kicked at him and he let her. Let her go on swearing at him, her voice rising to a screech as he went for the front door.

She slammed it behind him, but the sting on his cheek, the rage behind him, all seemed to place a new buoyancy in his step.

He was free and Deena was waiting.

Chapter 30

AFTER PARKING IN HER DRIVEWAY, Deena hauled Sly out of the car into the silence of the still-misty morning. She'd let Sly down. He was on borrowed time, now, and she wished she could lend him some of hers, because, darn it, she was supposed to be able to master just about everything.

Of course she hadn't been able to save her mother, either. She fought back the haunting helplessness and steadied herself against the cold steel of the car. Didn't work. The lawn might still be overgrown and lush green. There might still be Lana's toys scattered on the grass, but the world felt unsteady this morning

Sly would die, just like any of them could any time the maker decided. Like Lana or she could have died yesterday.

She shivered and looked at the road. Not even skid marks on the road. The guy hadn't even tried to brake.

She wasn't just imagining things, that knowing part of her said.

She crossed the dew-covered yard dodging Lana's toys and was just about to head up the stairs when Suz caught her with a hand on her arm.

"Morning, sunshine. You walking the cat, now?" Suz's voice was all light and friendly, but there was concern in her eyes that Deena really didn't need right now. She needed to be alone, but, sighing, she turned back. She should tell Suz to keep a closer eye on Lana.

But Suz looked, well, haggard. Black circled the space between her large eyes and high cheekbones. She was dressed in a T-shirt Deena was sure she'd seen her in yesterday. Not good.

"Have you even been to bed?"

"I'd ask you the same thing, but I think the better question is have you slept lately?" Suz's grin brought what Deena was sure was a brilliant flush to her cheeks.

"So you heard."

"Hey, it's an old house. I can live vicariously." Suz did a leering lift of her brows, but it didn't do away with the fact that Deena's bedroom gymnastics had kept Suz awake.

"Oh, god, Suz. I'm so sorry. I didn't mean to keep you up. It won't happen again."

"Hold on a moment. I was awake anyway, planning my course of action for the fabric and getting all the patterns ready for your designs. I'm going to sew like a madwoman all weekend and we might just have everything pressed and ready for the show." Her eager eyes made Deena feel a little better. "You got time for a cup of coffee? I got something I need to talk to you about?"

"Now? This moment? 'Cause I was going to head up to the Hat after I dropped Sly off and did this subcutaneous drip thing the vet prescribed. I wanted to check a few things, talk to a couple of staff."

The look in Suz's eyes said it had to be now and for a moment Deena resented all the connections she had to people, all the responsibility she felt. For once she'd just like to do what she needed.

And just what do you call a night of mindless sex, she reminded herself. Totally irresponsible.

"Just let me get Sly settled then, and I'll be down."

"I'll put the coffee on. Should be ready when you are."

Deena trudged up the stairs, wishing the mist would just thicken and send the rest of the world away.

Thirty minutes later, with hands still shaking from having to insert the needle, then holding Sly down while the liquid dripped under his skin, she knocked on Suz's door, just as a van pulled up. The driver, obviously a delivery guy, leapt out and hauled five bolts of plastic and bubble-wrapped cloth out of the back and jogged up the front walkway.

"Hey," he said and looked down at his electronic tablet. "Rush delivery for S. Miller. This the place?"

"Sure." She signed for the bolts, then hefted them inside. The place was quiet for a change, Lana obviously still in bed. It would be even quieter if Deena hadn't reacted quickly yesterday. A chill ran up her spine.

That the precious little girl could be at risk...She had to talk to Suz.

"I come bearing gifts," she said as she entered the kitchen where she was met by the scent of coffee and fresh sticky buns.

Suz squealed with delight, grabbed the bolts and tore them open to reveal a crisp, pale-blue cotton/poly fabric, a heavy blue wool that was intended for trousers and dress jackets, a sturdy grey-blue gortex and some softer fabrics good for sweaters and snappy looking t-shirts.

Deena was too worried by her thoughts and what she saw on the counters to really take notice. Most were covered in flour. The floor carried a nice dusting as well. The top of the stove was awash with muffin tins and bread loafs and the table was covered with cooling racks of muffins and fruit breads. A huge bowl with a tea towel covering by the fridge looked suspiciously like its contents were rising.

Not a good sign. Not good at all, because for as long as Deena had known Suz, baking had been her way of dealing with stress.

"Okay baking girl, what gives?" Deena hauled Suz back from her oohs and aahs over the fabric. "You're going to get flour all over that stuff if you're not careful. Let's put 'em in your sewing room." She grabbed the bolts, hauled them down to the front bedroom that served as their design studio and sewing room.

"So?" She said as she strolled into the kitchen.

Suz wouldn't meet her gaze. Deena motioned to the baking and took charge—like always.

"Something's got you wigged out enough you could supply Lana's entire kindergarten bake sale and I want to know what it is. Now pour the coffee and spill."

Suz obediently—wonder of wonders—went to the cupboard and poured two large Sesame Street mugs of black coffee, then brought them to the table.

"I thought you were a cream and sugar girl?"

"This is kind of a black morning."

That stopped Deena, because regardless of Sly's illness, and her concern for Lana, after the night she'd had and the look in Rich's eyes, it was actually a pretty bright kind of day.

Suz's gaze was on her, watchful.

"You *really* like this Rich guy, don't you?" She sipped her coffee.

"Let's just say I don't usually keep men in my bed that long." Deena tried a grin, but it didn't seem to infect Suz like usual. Instead she shook her head.

"I'm not talking about the sex. I'm talking about the heart and you know it. This guy is special."

And that was the trouble, because whenever Deena was with Rich she knew he just might be the one—a notion she'd given up on long ago. She nodded cautiously, afraid that acknowledging it made it even less refutable.

"I'm almost afraid of how I feel." It came out as a whisper.

She looked at Suz, saw the pain there and knew something was wrong. Really wrong. As wrong as the danger Lana might be in. She had to stop whatever Suz was going to say, because it might just be too much to deal with.

She held up her hand to change the subject.

"Suz I'm not sure what you want to tell me, but I've got something I need to discuss. It's about Lana. I think she might be in danger and it's my fault."

"What?" Suz almost dropped her coffee cup and Deena caught her hand, steadied her.

"I'm not sure, hon, but I need to tell you this. So you can be careful of Lana. So you can both be careful."

Suz's haggard face had paled. Lana was her world, her purpose. If anything happened to that little red-headed terror, it would kill Suz. Probably only a moment before Deena went, too.

"Tell me."

Deena didn't want to do this, felt bad she'd even blurted it out, but it was the right thing if it would keep Lana and Suz safe.

"You know I'm investigating an inmate death. Well it's looking like staff could have been involved. I'm looking into it and I think the staff might know. Yesterday, when I came home from my run, I think a truck followed me. Lana came out to greet me and, well, I think the truck might have run straight at Lana and me."

Whatever color she had, drained from Suz's alabaster skin.

"Someone tried to run over my baby? And you?"

Deena caught her hand. "I think they were after me, but you need to keep Lana in the yard. She'll be alright then. Okay?"

Suz had this thousand yard stare that made Deena want to hit whoever was responsible of the threat.

"My God, Dee. What kind of people do you work with?"

"Criminals. It seems more than I thought." She sighed and stood.

"Sorry to dump this on you like this, but I need to get up to the jail. If I can nab these guys then the threat'll be over. You won't need to worry." A quick hug for Suz and she headed to the door.

Suz was still immobilized at the table.

"He's married, Dee."

That stopped her. She felt the pit of her stomach petrify, but turned back.

"Was married. He told me, remember?" If that's what Suz was on about, then maybe things were okay with Rich.

Suz shook her head.

"Nope. I was working in the sewing room when he came down from your place this morning. He stopped long enough to make a call just outside my window. I think it was his office, and he was picking up a message because he said something like, 'My wife called? Damn her.' If she was an ex, wouldn't he call her his 'ex'? Most men do. After the call he stormed off to his truck as if he was pissed off he'd been found out. I mean maybe his wife is away right now or something, so when he met you again he thought it was an opportunity to hook up."

The old, sick feeling of betrayal welled to the surface. It made too much sense. The way he'd told her nothing about himself. Suz was right. If he was really divorced, he's have said ex. She shut her eyes against the heart-pain and felt only humiliation that she'd been taken in once more. Willingly. He must have been killing himself laughing when she was going on about what a slime Ravi Sandhar was.

She sagged against the doorframe, then caught herself. Found the steel inside.

"So. I was wrong. Again. Another write-off." Forced a smile. "You okay about Lana, cause I really need to get up to the Hat."

"Dee? Are you alright?" Suz came to her, but Deena shook her off.

"Fine. I need to head." And she did, rushing out the door. Out to the mist and the day, and hoping to escape feeling so tired and old and foolish.

Escape the way all the places Rich had touched her felt soiled, but most of all her heart.

Like a forty-year-old woman could find love.

Chapter 31

THE BETRAYAL LEFT A PART OF Deena broken inside, but that didn't mean she wasn't going to deal. She held onto the steering wheel for dear life as she drove through traffic she barely saw. She was so going to get over him. She pulled around a slow-moving Chevy Van and yanked her car back to her lane just in time to miss a fully-loaded, long-haul trucker. No worries. She knew what she was doing—not. The road was straight here, but steep ditches filled with water to either side, lazy looking herons fishing for breakfast in the deep water, but reckless drivers had drowned there. A 'V' of Canada geese split the sky and boy-o-boy she should just be headed out southward right after them. Maybe go visit that mountain she loved. Get herself a cold heart, just like Rich. At Hatzic Road she turned off into what was once farmland for the drive up to the Hat.

So Rich had used her. Other men had and she'd always dealt. Her job had taught her to push away the emotions and to focus on the tasks at hand. Her job was what mattered now. Mist still clung to Hatzic Lake and the bevy of cabins and houses along its weedy shore.

Her job and Lana's safety.

But she'd pined for him for so long.

He'd been like a ghost hanging over her all through her marriage. It had always made her wonder whether Blake was right—that she just never committed to their union. She'd always wondered what life with Rich Webster would have been like.

"Well now you know."

She'd laid herself bare to him.

"And the frigging jerk just left me raw."

The Camry roared up the winding road into the mountain valley and she slammed it into her usual parking spot. She sat there, engine ticking, and stared down the slope at the Hat. She had to calm down before she went in. People took advantage of individuals who didn't have their head on straight. And with the threat yesterday she needed to be doubly on her game.

Deep breath and out of the car. She heard the whir of camera motors as surveillance tuned her in. The Control C.O.s would be wondering what the hell brought the Bitch-Goddess to their shift.

"And you should be worried. Because Deena Hunter is hunting your ass."

She strode down to the Center. She wasn't in uniform, but she knew her height could make her intimidating even in jeans.

Mavis, the blonde receptionist, nodded and Deena managed something probably closer to a snarl. Threaten her god-daughter would they? She waved to the mirrored control center windows to demand access to the ADW office. The door clicked and she strode through, knowing her presence would be telegraphed like the speed of sound across the Center.

It gave her a little sense of satisfaction that they'd be concerned. Her authority preceded her, and if the staff were really responsible for the death and the truck, then fine and dandy. Let them be nervous, because they were going down. She just had to keep her cool, do her investigation, and then heads would roll.

She knocked once on the ADW door and stuck her head in. Franklin Vanier, the other day shift supervisor, was poised behind his desk like a bird about to take flight. His thin hands fluttered above the papers on his desk. Not much of a leader, but Frank was a good administrator.

"Howdy, Frank. Mind if I come in?"

He twisted his head toward the lone chair.

"To what do we owe the honor of your presence?" There was enough sarcasm in his voice to make her reconsider her assessment of him as a decent enough guy.

"I had a few things I needed to follow-up on, and I wanted to touch base with Underhill. I understand she's working today?" Frank's rheumy eyes stayed locked on her. He nodded.

"She one of your protégés or something?"

"Nah. Just she was having trouble the other day. I rode her ass hard and I wanted to make sure I didn't beat her up too bad." Frank just raised his grizzled brows.

"A little extreme, isn't it? Coming in to apologize?"

"Not apologize. She strikes me as having potential. I don't want me going off half-cocked destroying her potential."

His disbelief was on his face.

"Sort of unusual, the Goddess of day shift admitting she's fallible."

That was enough. She expected a tough time from the line, but not the other ADW. They were supposed to model professional courtesy and respect. Well two could play at that game. She placed her elbows on his desk, her face closer to his than she liked.

"I believe the term is Bitch-Goddess and I'm quite prepared to play the part. Now how's Underhill doing and when's she taking her break?" She managed to keep her voice sweet, even if the words weren't. Frank shrugged, reached behind him to the bank of portable radios and jabbed in the call button.

"Underhill, Vanier."

"Underhill, here."

"Get your ass down to my office? You got a visitor." He lifted his finger from the radio and glared at her. "Anything else I can do for you?"

It wasn't supposed to be like this.

"Damn it, Franklin, what's gotten up your ass, and don't say me? I came in to get my work done, that's all, so why are you giving me a hard time?

Franklin eyed her a moment, then reached into her mail slot, handed her a slip of folded paper.

"Found this in the ADW locker today. Addressed to you. You need to think long and hard about whatever the hell you're doing, Deena, because we all need to stick together."

When she opened the page it exposed a crude drawing of a rat and a bullet, the rat obviously dead. She knew what it meant. Usually it would be inmates who made such a threat. But inmates didn't have access to her locker.

"You're telling me you think I'm ratting out staff." It was hard given how this confirmed the speeding truck yesterday, but she managed to keep her voice calm. Everything inside her was on high alert.

"Someone does. Are you?"

Deena stood up. "I'm trying to do my job. That's all any of us can do. What we're expected to do."

"Word is, you're getting cozy with the police. Maybe you think you're still one of them?"

That chilled her. Were they watching her?

She planted her hands in the middle of Frank's papers, leaned over until she could smell the peppermint gum he always chewed against constant halitosis. "I've been a good officer at this institution since I started. I do my job and I run a tight shift. If I do anything, it's set high expectations. For the good of the Hat. My personal life, such as it is, means nothing." Was nothing, more like.

She was officially finished with her Rich Webster infatuation. Suz's story had cured her cold turkey.

Regardless of the blinding hurt. She had no time for it.

A knock came at the door. Franklin looked like someone had ruffled his crown feathers and he didn't know quite what to do about it. She—well, she didn't care what Franklin Vanier thought.

She yanked back from his desk and the two of them growled come-in together.

Anita Underhill poked her head around the door, her gaze flashing to Deena and all the color drained from her face. She looked back to Franklin.

"You called me, Sir?"

He heaved himself up from his chair. "She wants to see you. I'm going to find a coffee."

He slammed the door a little harder than necessary, and Deena slipped down on the corner of the desk and motioned Anita into the chair.

"Thanks for coming," she smiled, but Anita didn't pick up the smile. Instead she wouldn't meet Deena's eyes. "I wanted to talk about yesterday. I rode you pretty hard."

Anita's gaze snapped up to her. The flash of Deena's Little Sister was quickly masked by animosity.

"Yeah. You did. You made a fool of me in front of everyone and then you held me back at end of shift so it was pretty obvious you were going to ream me out. So much for building me up with the shift."

Deena closed her eyes because it was true and because, it brought home the fact that working in a correctional center had skewed how she related to everyone around her—just like when she'd gone all masculine as a police officer.

She wasn't quite as in control as she thought. She opened her eyes.

"You're right. That's why I'm here. I shouldn't have treated you that way. It's the way things are done here, but it doesn't make it right. I'm a good enough supervisor I should know that."

The surprise in Anita's eyes was enough to make Deena smile. "Didn't think I had it in me, did you?"

"No. I mean...well, no...Ma'am."

"So I won't treat you that way again, but don't you dare tell my shift I apologized or it'll destroy my rep. I had to work hard for the Bitch-Goddess name."

"So you know." Anita looked a little uncertain.

"How could I not? It helps to have a rep around here." Deena inhaled and looked down at the little blonde, still not sure things were right between them, but knowing there really wasn't much more she could do at the moment.

"Listen, apologizing isn't the only reason I wanted to talk to you. You recall that help I asked you for? Something happened yesterday that tells me it's dangerous to be involved. I want to give you the option of changing your mind about helping with the ISI. If you decide to stay involved, you need to be extremely careful."

She waited for the news to sink in, waited for the bloom of fear on Anita's face, but it didn't come. There was concern. There was consideration, but no fear. There was even a little calculation that gave Deena something to think about, but finally Anita met Deena's gaze.

"I'll help, but I can't investigate other staff."

There it was again. Just how had the word leaked into the Center already? The only people who knew about the investigation were her and Heywood and Underhill. And Ravi. That thought made her skin go cold. If it was South Asian gangs, he could be the link.

"I'm not asking you to investigate anything. I only want you to report what you see or hear. And I don't want you mentioning this to anyone. As a matter of fact, I only want you to report to me outside. You can call me at home or come by. That way we can keep everything like a simple CO-ADW relationship here."

"You're making this sound pretty serious."

"It is. Someone tried to run me and my god-daughter down. I believe they might have killed Stickley. I don't want anything happening to you. Understand?"

An uncertain nod.

"So, have you changed your mind?"

Anita pursed her lips. "Just report what I see or hear. And if I hear or see nothing? That's it, right?"

"That's it." Deena held her breath almost hoping Anita would opt out so she wouldn't have to worry about her. The note made the threat even more clear.

"I guess I'm in—Ma'am." Anita shrugged, stood. "And now I better get back to rounds or I'm going to be so late someone'll probably fire my ass."

Deena took the not-so-gentle rebuke and considered Anita as the door shut behind her. In the space of a week at the Center she'd changed. Deena wondered if the toughness was for the better.

Of course toughening the skin was what life demanded. She was doing it right now, to deal with Rich. Had been trained in it by Blake and Ravi.

"Third time's a charm," she said, as she turned her mind to interviewing Jim Henry. She punched one of the portable talk buttons.

"Control, ADW Hunter. Can you have a movements officer bring Inmate Henry to one of the interview rooms, please."

She waited for what seemed like an extremely long time. Must be busy in Control.

"Hunter, Control. Roger that. Might take a few minutes though. Sheriff's van just arrived."

"Call me when he's there. Hunter out."

Chapter 32

DEENA SLUMPED IN HER CHAIR in the SCO office, listening to the hum of institutional conversations over the radio and considering just how ugly and small the room seemed from the other side of the desk. It was like all the air was sucked out of this part of the office and shipped to the SCO side of the desk. Her side. The power side, but right now she didn't feel it. It felt, well, small, and mean and no place she'd ever imagined herself being. Over the radio, Control opened and closed doors for inmate movements to programs. C.O.s called in issues or made arrangements to meet for coffee. The recycled air hung stagnant against her skin.

But no call came. Hell, there was no call for Henry to be brought down.

Franklin came back; looked more than a little disappointed when he saw she was still here. He ignored her and sat down, busying himself in paper work.

"I requested Henry be brought down. I haven't heard them radio a request yet."

Franklin barely glanced up. "They must be busy."

She stood up, finally letting her frustration come through.

"Maybe they told Movements in person. Or you missed the call." Franklin didn't even look up from his papers, and it was just about the last straw because too many things weren't working out today. She was tired of it.

"If Mohammed won't come to the mountain, let the mountain come to Mohammed. Where is he?"

Franklin looked up this time, his pique at her presence showing in the pinched line of his mouth. No ADW liked being bothered by another, but his lack of hospitality was beginning to bug her like ruffling Sly's fur the wrong way.

"Who?"

"Henry, damn it. Which unit is Jim Henry on?"

Franklin twisted in his chair to grab the Unit assignment, but Deena was too fast, she grabbed it and cocked a hip on his desk, scanned the list.

"Still East 1." She grabbed the phone, dialed the local. The unit officer picked up. "ADW Hunter here. You got Jim Hunter on that unit?"

"Yeah, but he's in programs now. Should be coming back for lunch soon."

Deena checked her watch. He was right. The inmates would be moving back through the Center soon enough. She could catch him still in the hall and sidetrack him to the interview room if she was fast enough.

"Thanks." She plunked the phone down, aware of Franklin's gaze and the clear dislike in his eyes. "Don't worry, I'll get out of your hair now. But I need to borrow one of these." She grabbed a portable from the rack. Checked it and it squawked.

"And one of these." She reached over the desk and slid open the middle drawer for one of the electronic cards that would open institutional doors. "Do me a favor and call the card into Control so they can track me, would you?"

Franklin gave her a stony gaze.

"You're not in uniform. You're supposed to be in uniform if you're inside."

"Contractors do it all the time," she said sweetly and let the door click behind her, shutting off his protests.

And she was striding toward Programs.

If the love note left in her inbox was any indication, she had to move fast. The evidence in this case was going to dry up pretty quick. That meant Henry might end up as another victim if she wasn't faster.

Programs all operated out of the north wing of the Hat, with classrooms on the second floor and machine and fiberglass shops on ground floor. By what she'd seen of Henry, she didn't figure him for a classroom kinda guy.

She buzzed herself through the doors into the program wing as a group of classroom inmates came through to their units. Probably one of the A.A./N.A. groups, judging by the strung out look of them. They herded through the door and into the hallway she'd just vacated. She card-called the elevator and watched them saunter down the hall like so many sheep driven by the uniformed officer behind them. The broad shoulders of one of the men reminded her too much of a certain cop.

Get over it, Hunter. You've got work to do.

"This is Hunter," she radioed. "Advise the shop instructors I'm coming down for Henry."

"Ten-four, Hunter." She listened to the call. The elevator dinged beside her, slid open and she turned.

A fist slammed into her jaw and threw her into the wall.

Something cracked. Stars. Black and white stars popping in her brain. What the...She shook her head, trying to focus through the stunned daze, her fists coming up.

Two muscle-bound forms. She swung, but she couldn't see.

Another fist found her gut. Another. Too fast. Slam of pain. They weren't fooling around.

She went down. On her knees. Breath gone.

Adrenaline kicked in and she scrambled sideways, fighting for breath. Rolled. Slammed her hand for the panic button on her belt. *On her uniform.*

Not here. Idiot!

A boot caught her in her side, sent the radio sailing across the floor. Pain.

She rolled, lashed out with her feet, her fists and knew she connected. Heard a grunt of pain.

Rolled again and almost made it up but the boots were too fast. One of the two bruisers grabbed her arm, twisted it behind her and dragged her up before she could get her body working. Forced her to her knees.

Struggling. Helpless. Hair blinding her.

"They catch you, you'll pay." It came out in a croak and she tasted copper. Split lip. Or broken jaw. Pain radiated up through her shoulder. Her side.

Stale breath as one of them leaned down to her. "This's what happens to female rats." Arm twisted so she couldn't move.

But they could.

A hand groped her breasts. A knee battered her face, her gut, and cut off her groan. Bright colors flashed warning. Too late.

"Fucking Bitch. Let this be a lesson."

A fist caught her temple. Warm blood on her brow. And laughter. When they released her, cool linoleum rushed to meet her.

And then darkness.

§

Down the antiseptic cream walls, Anita felt like she spent her life running. Her footfall echoed hollowly behind her. Hard fluorescent light glared into her eyes. Her card beeped her into Observation and she rammed the reader into the waiting wall clock, then was out the door without a word to the unit officer and running again.

ADW Vanier had placed her on prowl—again. He'd said it was because she knew the job, and darn it, she was going to prove to herself she could do it right. But it was a damn battle and she had this horrible feeling she was losing—also again.

More so since Dee—ADW Hunter had called her to the office. Weird little scene that had been. Hunter making all nicey-nice—as if that could undo what she'd put Anita through. Deena didn't have a clue, judging by that little display of concerned friendship. Chad had said she might do something like that—try to win Anita back.

Well, forewarned is fore-armed, they say.

She'd been prepared to say whatever it took to get out of that office. It had been interesting though. Hunter had seemed really concerned about Anita's safety. Almost like the Dee Anita remembered. But what did she need with Dee Hunter when the Correctional Officers were solid behind her?

She buzzed herself into West 2, nodded at Jim Richmond, the living unit officer, rammed her reader at the clock on the wall and bugged out of there already running for the next unit. At least she knew she was getting her exercise. Heck, at this rate she might even make it back on schedule. She slid around the corner toward East 1 and heard Dee radio she was going to Programs.

Then the conversations went silent. Anita clicked the mike, heard the familiar static that said it was working. Weird silence. Like the Center was holding its breath.

She was at the door to E1 when the call came.

"Control, shift. Seems we might have an officer in need of assistance. Program elevator, level two."

The silence breathed. Anita hesitated in carding the door, recalled the response to the Stickley suicide. In training they'd said that an officer down rated full response. Even unit officers left their posts for those calls.

But there was *nothing*.

"E2, Control. I can't copy that. Repeat, please. You're breaking up."

But Control wasn't breaking up. Radio transmission was clear as day. And where was everyone else?

Anita gave up on East 1 and ran. She smacked the mike on her shoulder as she bolted along the corridor because something was definitely horribly wrong.

"Prowl, Control. Responding."

She waved her card at the first door panel, heard it click and rammed through. The next. Slammed past. Programs ahead. Door buzz and stopped. Blood. Blood spatter everywhere, but most of all on the person on the floor. The elevator door just sliding shut on two inmates.

"Oh shit!" She didn't care that her hand was still on the mike. She was on her knees. "Dee! Dee! Shit. Control, she might be dead!"

She released the mike to roll Dee over. The hallway reeked of the copper scent of blood. It was on Dee's hands, covered her face, the t-shirt she'd worn, her jeans. The floor. The wall. It still flowed from a cut on Dee's temple, a bloodied nose, crooked sideways on her face. Anita hadn't known there was so much blood in a human body.

Remembering her first aid she swore at herself for moving Dee. If her neck was broken, Anita might have crippled her for life.

"Oh God, oh God, oh God." She couldn't get herself to stop saying it as she used shaking hands to check for a pulse. Couldn't feel one. Oh God, Dee was dead. It was all her fault. All her fault. She'd been so angry.

Dee's brown eyes fluttered open, glazed, blind.

"Dee, it's me!"

Then hands hauled Anita away. A white clad figure—institutional nurse—was on the floor in the blood, checking pulse, checking airways with gloved hands. The damned hands on Anita were trying to pull her away, but she jerked out of them, rounded on whoever it was. One of the living unit officers whose name she couldn't remember.

"Get the hell away from me." Then she was back on her knees beside Dee. "Come on Dee. Come on." To the nurse. "How is she?"

Dee was trying to sit up. Did, barely, with the nurse's assistance, but there was a terrifying vacancy in Dee's expression. An absence of understanding.

And then there were ambulance attendants and they were lifting Dee up, taking her away and the other staff were gone, faded back to their regular duties and Anita was there, with the Hat's ticking time checks and Dee's blood on her hands.

It was just about noon.

Chapter 33

RICH HAD HAD SPENT A GOOD part of the morning just driving around, just trying to get his head on straight. He'd called in that he'd be late. Heck he put in enough overtime, he could play hooky this once.

The morning's events made thinking difficult. First there'd been waking with Deena Hunt in his arms. How many times had he dreamed that particular dream? The reality was a whole lot better.

"Like real, range-fed filet mignon, compared to lot-fattened chuck."

He rolled his eyes. Spoken like an Alberta boy. Deena would not be particularly flattered by being compared to a piece of meat.

Well he was going to see that she was. Flattered and made to feel just as special as she was. She'd been burned before, and he was going to make sure any doubts she had about the two of them just plain disappeared from her brain.

Rich shook his head. Chuck Kozloff was gonna laugh his head off.

He drove across the Mission Bridge from Abbotsford as an Ambulance roared past, Abbotsford bound, lights flashing, siren wailing. Another bit of unhappiness in the world.

Well *he* was happy and Chuck's ridicule wasn't going to stop it. And aside from the blow-the-top-of-your-head-off sex, and the feelings he had for Deena, he'd finally, finally, put the thing with Ivy to rest. The guilty ache in his chest wasn't there anymore.

It left him almost giddy. Hell, he'd been driving around with his windows down and the radio blaring for the past two hours, feeling like a kid again.

He flicked off the radio as he turned into the detachment parking lot. When he got out, he had this stupid urge to just go stand at the top of the bluff and holler, but instead he sauntered casually to his office, sank behind his desk and tried to look purposeful. When he caught Chuck's eye, he knew he hadn't quite succeeded.

"Big night last night?" Chuck looked back to his computer screen scanning some database.

Rich leaned back in his chair, realizing regardless of his euphoria, he was bone tired. The forty-five-year-old body couldn't quite pull off an all-nighter the way a twenty-two year old body might.

"I think this might work out."

He was about to put his boots up on the desk, when Inspector Reeves walked in looking unusually shiny in a pressed uniform. Rich clunked his chair back to the floor, feeling just a tad too rumpled in the face of all that splendor. He forced the self-satisfied grin off his face.

"What might work?"

"A little project Webster has going," Chuck jumped to fill the breach while Rich tried to focus on work. "What can we do for you?"

"Just wanted to follow-up on that Corrections case. I got a call from some union guy inquiring whether there was an investigation going on in the Hat. He offered to assist. I told him squat, but I thought you should know."

"And who was this helpful soul?" Reeves had caught Chuck's attention, and Rich's cop blood swept his infatuation aside—for the moment.

"Fellow named Roberts. Works at Fraser Correctional Center. He's tied in to us through some kind of internal investigation team that collects intelligence about drugs coming into correctional centers. Thought he might be an asset to you." He gave them Robert's number, cast a hard look at Rich that seemed to say he'd better get his act together, and then he wandered back to his office.

"Reeves got a wedding or something?" Rich asked.

"I think it's a talk with the Rotary Club."

Rich picked up the paper. "You gonna call him?"

Chuck shrugged. "You trust one of these guys? The more I read about the Independence Army, the more I figure everyone's compromised in those centers."

"I hear you. Lucky Deena can get inside information. People talk to her. I'll check this guy out." He scooped up the paper.

Chuck only nodded and returned to scanning his computer screen, leaving Rich to review the staff background reports Chuck had prepared.

As usual Chuck was thorough. What quickly became clear were the family connections that were a complex web between many of the Hat's employees. The question was whether they also connected up to any of the known members of the Independence Army.

"You charted any of this?"

Chuck shrugged. "No time."

"Then I'll get started." Rich went to the white board covering one wall and listed staff names at the top, relatives below and drawing connections between. Chuck still didn't say much, and the silence was starting to get on Rich's nerves.

Rich stepped back to consider what he had so far. Connections across staff. Connections to convenience stores and other businesses— trucking, especially, as well as into the non-South Asian community through marriage and work associations.

"You know, I was expecting a hell of a lot more trouble from you, coming in this late." He didn't look at Chuck.

"I figure a man's gotta do, what a man's gotta do."

Rich glanced at his friend and partner. It wasn't that he wanted to talk about what had happened between him and Deena. He'd never been one for locker room tales. But he thought Chuck would want to tease him none-the-less.

"I laid down the law with Ivy. Told her I was filing for divorce. That's why I was late."

Chuck looked at him from the tops of his eyes.

"Alright it's part of why I was late. The other part is I was driving around like a school kid celebrating."

At this, Chuck pushed himself back from his computer.

"So this is serious." There was caution in Chuck's tone, just like Rich imagined a father would speak to his son about getting too involved with a first girlfriend.

"You think? She's everything I ever wanted and didn't have. I'm not letting her go again. Deena Hunter is mine, even if she doesn't realize it yet."

It came out sounding stupid and macho, but that was the fact. Even though he thought all that 'made for each other' stuff was a load of crap, that phrase was the only way he could describe it.

"So how well do you know her?"

The caution in the question reminded him of Deena's comment that morning—and how he'd answered it. Deena Hunter's skin under his hands, her athletic thighs around him and the dark passion that almost pulled him into her eyes as they made love. That was how well he knew her.

"She's an ex-cop I've known for years. She works at the Hat. She lives in an apartment in a big old house that was her parents, with a friend living downstairs. She has a cat she's had for what?—fifteen years. She was married. Isn't now. She's not too good with tools, but she makes a mean cornbread. And she's attracted to me enough to look past my flaws and consider a relationship." He glowered at Chuck. "Enough? Or were you hoping for the sex details, too?"

Chuck wouldn't meet his gaze and Rich found himself waffling between pissed off and concerned.

"Would you just tell me what's going on? You were all for this the other day."

Chuck's sigh was audible.

"You haven't finished your charting, have you?"

"No. Why?" Rich looked down at the sheaf of papers in his hand still with info to be added to the chart.

This time Chuck met his gaze and the pity there sent ice through Rich's veins. Chuck wasn't a man who did pity often or well.

"Do Sandhar's connections."

Rich flipped through the background documents, found Ravi Sandhar's and turned his back on Chuck as he started to list Ravi's relatives and known associations down the board. The usual connections—to a local coffee shop, owned by a cousin who was also a relative of Randy Johal. He drew a line of connection and paused, recalling a comment from one of the School Liaison Officers that the proprietor of a certain Café Crème Brûlée was suspected of being a drug pusher. Connections through marriage and a cousin of his wife to a figure high up in the Independence Army.

Rich stopped.

"This is promising. There's a direct connection. Shit, doesn't Corrections vet these guys?"

Chuck looked up from where he was biding his time behind the computer.

"They did it when Sandhar joined the service. He was single. No connections through direct family. They didn't check his wife when he got married or recheck him."

"One hell of a hole in their security."

"You haven't read the second page yet."

Rich flipped the page and continued adding names to the board. Then he stopped. Heard Chuck's chair squeak as he got up and came around the desk.

"I'm real sorry man. I'm going to go get us both a cup of coffee."

Then he left Rich. He couldn't move, could barely breathe as he read and reread the suspected associates. Deena Hunter was listed as having had a possible affair.

The information shouldn't bother him, but he felt like he'd been sucker-punched. He settled on the edge of the desk and silently accepted Chuck's offering of black coffee. Bitter as he expected.

"We've both got pasts."

Chuck settled back in his chair. "You'd be expected to, given your ages."

"She's not a nun. I wouldn't expect her to have been one." He couldn't think. Everything felt too jumbled inside.

"I'd say she's not a nun."

Rich turned on his partner, ready to fight, and Chuck must have seen because he held up his hands.

"I didn't mean anything like that. I meant she obviously pleased you a hell of a lot because I've never seen such an idiot grin in my life."

Rich scanned the paper again, a little pissed at Chuck's attitude because it wasn't that she 'had pleased him', but that he'd felt such a connection.

"It's not the affair, it's the connections that have you wigging out, isn't it?"

"You gotta be aware, Rich. If she's tight with the Warden and he's 'made' in the Army, then there's a good chance she's just as dirty as he is. Hell she could be doing this—leading you on to get intelligence—or keep you occupied. Or maybe she is trying to land you to get access to intelligence on a regular basis."

Rich glared at Chuck, denial ready. There was no damn way he pillow-talked about his investigations.

Chuck just took the glare.

"You said she was easy to talk to."

And she was. Chuck expressed what had left Rich unable to breathe. Maybe it was all too good to be true. A little too convenient. He looked down at the paper.

The suspected affair was within the past two years. They weren't sure if it was over. Maybe she'd come too easily to Rich's arms, even though there had been that little dance they played. Maybe it had been a set up all along.

But a skilled courtesan could do that, couldn't she? Spies like Mata Hari. Play coy to reel in the man she was after. But hadn't he pursued her?

"But it wasn't like that." The words came out too soft, unconvincing even to him. He wasn't sure how things had gone as far as they had. He needed the time to look at things objectively. Because one thing was for sure: just as surely as Deena Hunter had been his, now Deena Hunter was his problem.

Chapter 34

The HARSH WHITE LIGHT OF Emergency was too
bright; the blare of the ambulance still wound over and over
in her head so she couldn't think. She couldn't really see, either, except dark
figures hovering over her, inhale the stink of alcohol and copper blood and
someone had been ill. The way her mouth tasted it might have been her.

"I'm alright. I'm alright." Her voice sounded all mushy and the
pain in her jaw made her think she might lose some teeth, but Deena
pushed away the nurse and doctor. She fought to sit up, to prove to them
and to her, that she really was just fine.

Actually she felt like she'd been run over by a truck and almost as
weak. The nurse pushed her back onto the bed with one hand and she lay
their shivering. That couldn't be good. She wasn't sure she'd ever get warm
again.

"Young woman, how are we going to suture this cut if you keep
fighting us like this?" The doctor made sure the IV needle in the back of
her hand hadn't been displaced. A bag of liquid silently drip-drip-dripped
something into her veins.

She almost burst out laughing. Young woman, indeed. But she lay
back, flinched a bit as a needle bit her scalp and numbness spread. Her
whole body felt numb—over a blanket of pain. Whatever was in the IV
packed at least that much wallop, but she didn't like the fact she couldn't
remember how she got here or what had happened.

It was all a fog that she'd been fighting since she suddenly came-to
being rolled out of an ambulance. There'd been loud voices that had made
it hard to think and then too-bright lights. Then darkness again. Then this.

The doctor left the sutures to the nurse. A matronly sort with crisp grey-brown curls, she threaded the needle and leaned in close.

"Let's do this right, shall we? You stay very still and I promise I'll make nice neat stitches that should leave very little scar on that pretty face of yours."

Deena nodded, winced, because even just the slight nod made her brain hurt.

The nurse used her curved needles far too close to Deena's right eye, swiftly sewing and tying each suture off. When she was done Deena looked up at her warily.

"I sure hope you did a good job, cause my roommate's a seamstress and she'll come hunting you if you didn't."

The nurse quirked a grin as she cleaned up her equipment.

"I'll pass. And the ER doc did a good job on your nose. They said this happened at one of the correctional centers in Mission. You a visitor?"

Deena closed her eyes seeking back. Faint images of the Hat parking lot. Something about Programs—she was heading down to Programs—but the memory of what had happened still eluded her.

"Work there. I did a damn fool thing and went inside out of uniform. I don't remember much else."

The nurse's gaze narrowed. "Tell me."

Deena regretted her head shake. The front of her head just might explode. She couldn't breathe through her nose that seemed packed full of something. Great—she was a mouth-breather, now.

"I remember driving up to the Hat. I remember going into the ADW office and heading down to Programs, but after that's just a blank."

The nurse made a notation on her clipboard, then took her leave. Deena lay there, trying to find strength when she really didn't feel strong. She didn't like knowing she had a hole in her memory. She had a vague sense of something flying toward her face—which could explain the pain—but nothing else.

"Damn. Anita."

What if she hadn't warned her? What about Henry? She'd gone up there for a reason. What if she'd put them in danger?

Lana!

She had to get out of here, had to get a warning to Suz and the others. Heywood, too. Things were getting way too serious.

Struggling, she managed to push herself up, get her legs over the side of the bed and felt the whole emergency cubicle do a sideways roll like one of those darn-fool aviators at the Abbotsford Air Show. She held onto the edge of the bed, afraid it might buck her off and waited for the spinning to stop.

Gradually, it did, but when she tried to stand, her legs gave out, in her panic, she knocked a bed pan clattering to the floor and nearly upset the pole with its dripping bag of liquid.

"Shit."

"No...and it's a good thing that wasn't in use." She opened her eyes and found the same nurse standing there arms crossed. "Just where do you think you're going?"

"Home?"

The nurse grabbed her arm and got Deena settled on the bed again. Every part of her body screamed at the movement.

"You even know where home is?"

Deena recited her address.

"Any chance of making a phone call for a ride? You've got to have sicker people than me needing a bed."

"So you're one of those people who doesn't know when to give up? Like a cop. Run into things and never stop to think it might get them hurt." The nurse shook her head, but Deena thought of what was probably happening at the Hat.

"If I don't get home, if my roomy just gets a call from the institution, she's going to freak. I'd like to nip that in the bud. Okay? Please?" She tried on her best winning smile and hoped it would work because Suz really would freak.

"I'll see what I can do."

The nurse pushed her back against the pillow and Deena gave in. Sound and sight had this sick way of fading in and out. Finally she gave in to the pain and the wave of fatigue and whatever the heck they had dripping into her arm.

§

"Ohmygawd, Dee!"

Suz's voice clawed Deena back from darkness and she opened blurry eyes to see Suz standing there with her hands covering her mouth, horror in her eyes.

"I'm sorry. I didn't mean to wake you."

"'ts awright." Deena's jaw wasn't working right. The skin on her face felt painfully tight. She touched her cheek and nose and grimaced at the dried blood from around her nostrils, the wadding up her nose—no wonder she couldn't breathe through it. Swelling seemed to disfigure her. No wonder Suz's reaction looked like something from a horror movie.

"Lovely, huh?" Deena managed to push up onto her elbows – one thing that didn't seem to hurt, but her left forearm hurt like blazes. Must have caught it when they kicked her in her side.

The recollection brought a surge of satisfaction. She remembered that much. More would come, probably. And the way her knuckles hurt, she supposed she'd landed a couple of blows as well.

"What time?" It hurt to talk.

Suz came up beside the bed, caught her hand, still dirty from falling, Deena supposed. And dried blood, probably her own.

"About two thirty. The correctional center called me—some guy named Vanier. Said I was listed as next of kin and that just freaked me out. He'd only tell me you were in MSA Hospital and I might want to come here."

"Where's Lana?"

"Safe with neighbors. Deena—this is what you were talking about, isn't it? This is the danger."

Deena looked away, finally nodded.

"You see why I wanted you to take extra care."

"I told Mrs. Fenz to keep her close. The call just about freaked me out."

Sitting up just took too much energy and she settled back on the pillows, saw the fear in Suz's eyes.

"Vanier could have handled things a little better."

"Are you...are you hurt bad?" The question came out in a rush of fear.

Deena squeezed Suz's fingers. "I'll live long enough to get the bastards who did this, if I can just remember what they looked like."

Trouble was, she was just so darned tired.

"The nurse said they wanted you to stay overnight due to your memory loss. They're worried about concussion."

Deena almost shook her head, then thought better of it because she didn't want to aggravate the pile-drivers already trying to split her skull.

"I'm not staying here any longer than I have to. I've got work to do, and Sly needs me at home. As a matter of fact, I'd feel a whole lot happier just getting the hell out of here now."

She managed to sit up again, this time way more aware of the pain jolting her body. At least the world didn't spin quite so badly and the IV tube had been disconnected sometime while she slept.

"Give me a hand?"

Suz was at her side, the slim redhead showing she was way stronger than she looked when she let Deena lean on her shoulder.

"First stop's a bathroom because I gotta pee like a racehorse and I want to see the color I've got in my cheeks." Deena glanced at Suz's face. "I've got a feeling I'm not going to be able to deal with this using a cover pencil, am I?"

Suz gave a wan smile and helped her through the curtain and down the hall to a washroom. Thankfully some larger emergency seemed to have called most of the nursing staff away, so they reached the bathroom without a hitch.

The view in the mirror was worse than she'd expected. Sure, she'd seen worse, but…Two black eyes and the right side of her face was discolored a lovely deep blue. A white dressing on her temple must cover the line of sutures. The skin around it was swollen in a huge goose-egg. And her nose hadn't been in quite that position before.

"That's where one of them caught me with his knee," she said, pleased the memory had come back even if it brought a sense of helpless rage and pain. "I'll live."

Her jaw, where that first flying fist had caught her so unprepared she'd been like a rabbit to a hawk, that was also swollen and blue.

She washed the blood off, pulled the wadding from her nose, wincing when the water stung, but overall it felt good to get the blood off her hands and face and breathe through her nose again, even if it hurt like heck. She couldn't get rid of the stains on her shirt, but with Suz's help she got the worst of it out of her hair.

"Well ain't I a sight. And this was one of my favorite t-shirt's, too. The bastards."

"Who did it? Do you remember?"

"Not yet. I will." She hoped. Because what she did recall didn't seem to involve any face, only a sense of size. She didn't know whether it was that she hadn't seen any faces, or that the fog still prevented her from recalling them. She had to warn Anita and Heywood and try to get Henry out of harm's way.

Deena signed herself out—against the doctor's objections—and limped out to the parking lot. Suz hailed a cab because the only car between them was still parked up at the Hat.

At the house, between the cab driver and Suz, they got Deena into Suz's apartment because there was just no way Deena could face those red stairs at this moment.

Instead she settled herself on Suz's couch, gave Suz her keys, and sent her with the cabby up to retrieve the Camry. Deena struggled into a clean t-shirt and tried to figure out how she was going to get word to Anita. If Deena hadn't warned her, then Anita could be walking into a heap of trouble.

Lana, home from the neighbors, buzzed around Deena. She bandaged Deena's wrist, offering glasses of water and candy medicine and chattering so incessantly it would have been easy to scream at the child. But Lana was her goddaughter and sweetness incarnate, and Lana was safe—thank goodness.

Finally the little girl stopped her ministrations and studied Deena as she struggled to get to a phone. She'd get directory assistance to give her a number. There couldn't be that many Underhill's in the book. When her legs caved, Lana tapped a five year-old toe and looked far too much like her mother—all sweetness and steel.

"You don't look good, Aunty Dee. Maybe you need a nap, because Mommy says a good nap makes for a good day."

"She does, does she?" It was all Deena could do to deal with the pain and keep her eyes open. Maybe she'd wait until Suz got home to make the call. "It sounds like a good idea, but what are you going to do? Maybe you should go back to Lisa's."

It would let her have some peace. She would sleep then, she knew.

Lana considered.

"Nope. I'm going to stay here in case you need something but I'm going to go outside and play real quiet, okay?"

"That would be wonderful, honey, but there's one thing that will make me get better even quicker."

Lana's eyes widened. The kid was like a puppy eager to please and show just how responsible she was. It made Deena remember she had been like that once. Probably still was, always trying to please the higher ups with her dedication.

She tapped her left cheek with a forefinger. "I need a Lana kiss to make it all get better."

The little girl giggled and leaned in to place a smoochy kiss on Deena's cheek that might have hurt if it hadn't come from her favorite little person.

"I'm going to have that nap now, honey, but would you play inside? I like having you close." Keep her safe.

"Okay, Aunty Dee. But I'll be real quiet."

She sounded so old for her age. A typical only child. So damned responsible.

Of course she was only as quiet as a five year old.

Chapter 35

FOR ANITA END OF SHIFT TOOK forever to get there, even though it was only two o'clock. She went through the motions in a daze and carrying the dead weight of the radio on her hip and the incident report in her hands, she buzz-clicked out the heavy door that marked the perimeter of the most secure part of the institution and pushed into the SCO's office. There was so much to report. So much she needed to understand.

The thing was, it wasn't just some convict who got beaten up, or some name in the newspaper.

This was Dee! Dee, who had been there when her Dad was too busy keeping food on the table and a roof over their head. Dee, who had shown her how to dress for a date in a way that would turn a boy's head, but still get past her father's inspection. Dee, who had laughed with her, cried with her, and talked over dreams with her.

Dee, who Anita'd decided wasn't her friend.

Running the Hat today after the incident, getting the time checks done, she'd come to the realization she was wrong. ADW Hunter was just doing her job and making sure Anita learned hers.

The right way.

Which meant that maybe the other way was wrong regardless of what the other staff said?

She didn't know anymore, and that was the worst part as she came into shift change and handed ADW Vanier her tersely written sheaf of papers.

"What's this?" he asked, interrupting a conversation he was having with the one of the living unit officers.

"My report on the critical incident. I knew you'd need it, so I wrote it on my meal break. Don't worry, it's complete."

"Good for you. They gave you good accident training at the Justice Institute."

His voice was smooth, friendly even, but his eyes weren't. It left Anita with a little flutter of unease.

"It didn't seem like an accident, Sir."

"Well ain't that nice, crew? Nice to have the opinion of a staff who's still wet around the ears. From what I hear, you're wrong. A couple of inmates managed to swipe a staff's pass card and get into the elevator. Hunter was just in the wrong place at the right time."

He scanned the room. "Right, then. The rest of you get your reports in to me tomorrow morning at start of shift. Okay?"

There were grumbles, but nothing more. Anita frowned because in training they'd said the reports were to be done immediately after an incident and staff weren't to talk to each other about it. And now there was no offer of critical incident debriefing, just when Anita could really use someone to talk to because a part of her hadn't quit shaking since she'd seen Deena laying in all that blood.

"Good shift, everybody." Vanier checked his watch. "That's a wrap."

Vanier's shift filed out the office door, tossing hellos to the crew coming on. Anita wandered into the women's locker room and sank onto a bench. Her hands were shaking. Darn it, her knees were shaking. Nope, try the whole nine yards.

She forced herself to change and was just brushing out her hair when the locker room door pushed open a sliver.

"Underhill? You in there?" Chad's voice. Anita had never been so glad to hear a friend's voice before in her life.

"Hang on. I'll be right there."

She checked her face—paler than usual and tried to pinch some pink back into her cheeks, applied some lipstick and tried to force the stunned fear out of her eyes. It didn't work. If someone could do that to Deena, what chance did Anita Underhill have?

She found Chad seated on one of the tables, talking too quietly to a couple of the guys from Anita's shift. He stood when he saw her.

"You okay?"

She nodded, regretted that she couldn't look more confident about it.

"Hell of a thing. I was bringing in a leave application and heard what happened. I thought I'd hang and see how you were doing."

"Thanks." She just stood there, didn't know what to say or do until Chad caught her elbow.

"Let's blow this pop stand and go get a drink. You look like you could use it."

He led her out to his truck.

"I'm not leaving my car. I'll follow you."

Chad shook his head. "Stubborn independence is all well and good, but you're in no condition to drive. You're shaking, Underhill. And you're white as a ghost. You want to cause an accident?"

She didn't. But she didn't want to leave her car either. God, it was so hard to think. Chad caught her arms, pulled her into him lightly.

"I understand. Listen, you climb into my truck and I'll go in and see if I can wrangle someone to drive your car down to your place, okay? A couple of those guys drive together. Now give me your keys."

She did. She did all that he told her, climbing into the truck cab and feeling so darn cold that all she could think of was warm blankets and a fire.

"All taken care of," Chad said when he came back. Then he took a look at her and swore.

"Hold onto your hat, little lady, we're heading for a drink, priority one." He gunned it out the parking lot practically before she could put her seatbelt on, and then they were almost flying between the cedars and broad-leafed maples and pine that cloaked the mountain slopes down from the Hat. They came down onto Hatzic Prairie and motored west through Mission and avoided the usual Correction's hangouts for a pub/restaurant beside the RCMP detachment. Inside, he got them a booth and slipped in beside her.

"You're frigging freezing," he said, rubbing her arms, her hands as he ordered her an Irish coffee and himself a beer. "So talk. You got to talk about it or it's going to eat you up."

Where should she start? What should she say? It was all so mixed up inside and just thinking about it frightened her. Writing the report had been the most difficult thing she had ever done.

She took a sip of her coffee and almost didn't notice the heat of alcohol burning down her throat. She took another sip. Another, and finally felt heat. Maybe the shaking wasn't going to tear her apart. Chad waited patiently.

"Nobody answered the call, Chad. Nobody. Control called for backup and no one came. It was like the whole Center was gone at that moment."

Chad shook his head. "No, 'Nita. It couldn't have been like that. In an emergency everyone's time sense just goes all wonky. A moment takes forever. You're just imagining it. Really." He kept rubbing her hands, ordered her another coffee when she finished gulping the first one down.

But she was pretty sure it wasn't like that. She hadn't known what she was running to, so why would her mind telescope the time?

"It was like the guys on the shift were just ignoring it. Like they were going to let it happen. Heck, it could have happened to me, too, if I'd got there quicker. And I should have got there sooner. I froze, Chad. When the call went out, I just froze."

She looked at him, the fear pumping through her veins. She could have died or been hurt as badly as Dee had looked. And how maybe she could have stopped it—if she'd done her job properly and been faster in responding.

"I should have gone with Dee to the hospital."

Chad rolled his eyes, then must have seen something in her face because he pulled her into his side, his arm around her shoulders. His palm ran up and down her arm as if catching her need for heat, and she liked the way he was concerned for her.

"You are one heck of an officer to have watching your back. I'd be proud to have you watching mine."

"That's just it, Chad. Where was everyone? They were supposed to be watching Deena's back. How did those guys get into the elevator and who were they? I caught a glimpse of them. They didn't look like anyone I know. I don't think it was an accident."

Chad's gaze narrowed. "What are you talking about? You didn't say anything about seeing who did this."

She shook her head. She'd put it in her report, but thinking about it sent more shivers up her back. She took another long drink of the powerful coffee and felt the little numbness that came into her nose when she'd had too much to drink. But it didn't numb her fear.

"It was so fast. I keep running over it in my mind. I saw a flash of prison green so it had to be inmates, right? But the trouble is the faces. I'm real good with faces and I'm pretty sure these weren't guys I'd seen before."

"'Nita, you were in shock. You were focused on Hunter. How can you be sure of who you saw, or what happened."

A soft concern filled his face. His hand somehow found her cheek, cradled it in his palm.

"You've had a shock. That's all. It's pretty regular to feel shook up like you do."

Darn it, her eyes were filling up with tears. He was right. She had had a shock. It felt like little jolts of energy flashed across her skin. Her mind was the proverbial ping-pong ball in a bingo hopper.

"Dee was hurt so bad. She looked so bad. So vulnerable. It was hard to see her that way." She sniffed back tears, but one got away and she brushed it away hoping Chad hadn't seen.

He caught her hand and turned her to him. "'Nita, you've got to quit thinking about Hunter as your friend. You said yourself, she's only trying to make herself look good. That's what she was doing today, too. Grandstanding. Trying to look good by coming in on her day off. Checking up on staff, probably. She shouldn't be doing that."

That didn't make sense anymore than the story about time moving slowly.

"But if something's wrong, someone has to look into it, don't they?"

"Oh, God, Anita. I know you're shook up, but work with me here. If something's wrong with inmates, C.O.s look into it. But C.O.s don't investigate staff. We got to stick together. We watch each other's back because no one else will. Fucking management is always on our case, always trying to give us more to do and less to do it with. Your friggin' Hunter broke the cardinal rule."

She should be able to think this all through, darn it. She had a good head on her shoulders—all her professors told her that. So why was it so hard to follow what Chad was trying to say?

"Cardinal rule?"

"Damn it, Anita, think." The hardness of his voice shocked her, but then his voice went soft and he caught her hand, bent down so he could look at her almost eyes to eye. "How are you going to depend on a brother if you know that brother could rat you out anytime? We don't hold with rats in the Hat. Never have and never will. We've got a solid bunch of staff. Just like you're solid, right?"

Those darn dimples and all the hardness was gone from his eyes. He was looking out for her, trying to tell her something. Unfortunately, his lesson just left her feeling smaller and more confused and more caught up with forces she didn't understand.

The tears started to flow and she turned away so he wouldn't see.

"Stupid. I'm so stupid."

"Aw, 'nita. Don't cry." He pulled her into his warm chest, those strong arms coming around her and she felt a kiss on her hair, his hands trying to smooth away her hiccoughed sobs. Another kiss on her head and she raised her face, scrubbing at the tears.

"I'm sorry…"

"Don't be. It's natural. Like this." His lips followed the tear tracks down her face to her mouth and she was caught in the scent of him. Mint shower gel and power. His kiss reminded her she was alive, not lying in a hospital like Dee. She suddenly, desperately, needed that reminder.

Her lips parted, answered, and Chad made a small sound in his throat as the kiss deepened, as his hands pressed her more firmly to him. When he broke the kiss, he stared down at her, trapping her gaze with his.

"You working tomorrow?"

She shook her head.

"Good." He waved to the waitress, kept one large palm in the small of her back, holding her to him.

The shivers that ran through her weren't totally of fear anymore. Chad's touch was like fire in the night and desperately needed. He was alive. Something other than working in the Hat.

When he'd paid, he half lifted her out of the booth and Anita realized the coffee had done more than numb the edges.

"What was in those drinks?"

It was hard to see, harder to talk and she could feel herself sway under Chad's easy hand.

"Irish mist whiskey. Double shots."

"You trying to get me drunk?" She tried looking disapproving, but his dimples said she didn't quite pull it off.

"Mission accomplished."

"What the hell are you talking about?" He had her by the elbow again, was leading her through the parking lot in the fading day.

"Just that if I was trying to get you drunk, I'd have accomplished it. I'm going to drive you home."

"I am not drunk. Yeah, I can feel the booze a little, but I'm thinking quite clearly, thank you very much." She was careful to articulate. "Heck, I could have driven myself home, if you'd let me bring my car."

"And thank god for small mercies." He held the truck door open and aided her up, letting that warm hand of his slip down provocatively to her butt.

"You touch me there, you marry me," she said as she slipped into the seat and peered down at him.

Chad's brows rose. "That so?" He leaned in, caught her chin and pulled her face down to his. "This'll have to do for now."

When he released her, she was breathless and her heart was racing just a little bit too fast. Actually not a little bit. She knew a warm flush was spreading over her skin and that it meant she was seriously considering sleeping with this man.

Why not? He was good looking and the nearest thing she had to a friend these days. And frankly, getting naked with a hard body like that might be just the thing she needed to take her mind off of what had happened, remind her she was alive.

Chad slid in beside her and caught her hand. "So... shall we head?"

He leaned into her, not kissing, just letting their breath mingle as he ran his face beside hers, not touching. Not touching and damn it, she wanted him to. She turned her head, caught the edge of his mouth with her kiss, but he pulled back looking at her with such concern in his eyes it made her sure she was doing the right thing.

"I... I don't want to be alone right now." She swallowed. It was as forward as she'd even been.

His hand came up to cup her cheek again in a gesture so intimate and sexy it made her want him right there in the truck.

"Then we'll make sure you're not."

Chapter 36

$\mathbf{D}$EENA WOKE TO THE SOUND OF voices and opened her eyes on the comfortable clutter and worn overstuffed furniture of Suz's apartment. Peaceful sunlight filtered through the blue curtains and the comforting sound of Suz and Lana laughing came through the window from the front yard. Their feet clattered too loud up the front porch stairs.

The sound reminded her of her parents laughing as they came in from one of their 'dates'. The memory left sorrow in its wake. Her parents. Sly failing. The loss of trust of the men and women at the Hat. And Rich.

Don't go there.

She'd known things weren't good at the Hat when Stickley died, but the fact she'd been set up made it worse. The question was how they arranged it, when no one had known she was coming to the Hat and no one had known she was going to go see Henry.

But there'd been that delay.

"Shit," she swore into the silence.

"Mommy, Aunty Dee said a bad word."

Suz and Lana stood in the living room doorway, Suz with her arms crossed. "She did, didn't she? And what did we say about bad words?"

"Anyone who says a bad word has to get a punishment." Lana was shaking her head. "Aunty Dee, now you got to get a punishment. I don't like this anymore than you do."

Dee glanced up at Suz. "Let me guess. Yours?"

Suz shrugged. "Beats 'this is going to hurt me more than it is you.'"

Deena tried to sit but her whole body seemed to have seized up. Muscles she didn't remember having screamed as she forced her legs off the couch and then collapsed back into the pillows.

"So what's my punishment, honey?" She held out her arms for Lana and the little girl scrambled up on Deena's lap in a movement that today just about got a scream from Deena.

"Lana, honey, it might be better to sit beside Aunt Dee today, 'cause she'd got a bunch of hurty things all over."

Lana shook her head with the five-year-old assurance. "No she doesn't. She likes it when I sit on her knee. It makes her feel happy. She told me."

"It's alright. I'll live. Can you grab me a glass of water and some of those Tylenol?" Deena leaned back in the pillows and pulled Lana into her, the warmth of the little girl somehow helping with the pain. Safe. "So what do I get for punishment?"

Lana looked up from underneath that tangle of red curls, her blue eyes considering. "Maybe you can help me pick up all my toys."

It was hard to suppress her smile, but Deena managed to look upset. "Do I have to? That's a lot of toys."

"Well maybe next time you'll remember not to say a bad word."

"How right you are."

"You got your punishment, huh?" Suz held out a glass of water and the pills and Deena knocked them back.

"The worst kind. Wonder if picking up Lana's toys would work on some of the guys at the Hat."

"Aah, I'm thinking inmates as playmates is not exactly suitable for my daughter.

"I was talking about staff."

"Same diff. They let this happen to you." Suz met Deena's eyes, but her friend's gaze had gone dark, like steel. Deena hadn't seen that look before—protective like a mother bear.

"They didn't 'let'. I walked right into it. It was stupid going in on a day off and then rushing down to Henry. I should have played their game, but I let them play me like well-oiled flute." She almost swore but caught Lana eyeing her. "They know I'm investigating. Somehow they know."

"Gee, Deena Hunter asking questions. What a surprise. You have a history of worrying something until you figure things out. You think after all this time they don't know that?"

Deena thought about what she'd said. "So I'm not subtle."

"That'd be an understatement." Suz dropped down cross-legged in front of her. "The question is what do you do now? I don't want you to go back there, Deena. They hurt you bad. They could have killed you."

Deena just looked at her friend until finally Suz shook her head.

"What am I saying? This is Deena Hunter, superwoman."

"I'm not feeling too superwomanly right now. More foolish. They've played me from the start, I swear. You know, when I got into the institution the morning that inmate died, the staff had a birthday celebration for me. I think it was probably all a cover for what was going down. They used *me* as a cover for murder. Do you know how that sticks in my craw?"

It did. It made her feel worse than the beating. It made her question everything she thought she was. If she hadn't realized when she started acting masculine when she was young, maybe she was missing something now. Maybe she was fooling herself that she was a good officer and that law was her calling. It wasn't like it was a passion like music or acting or sports was for some people. She'd never felt like that about anything.

Except maybe Rich Webster and that was over now.

Suz grabbed her hand. "Lana, honey, why don't you go play upstairs for a little bit. Mommy wants to talk to Aunty Dee."

Lana lifted her head from Deena's chest, and slid off her lap, leaving a vacancy behind. Smiling fondly, Deena watched her scoot out the door.

"You love her like she was your own." Suz's simple observations brought a mist to Deena's eyes. God, she was turning into a total emotional sot. It had to be the pain and the drugs, because she was usually under control.

Like she controlled her life, her work, her relationships.

"Dee, I love you, but I have to be honest. You're looking scared, and that terrifies me."

Suz's concern left Deena feeling inadequate. She was the one Suz came to when things went wrong. It was Deena who rescued her. It was Deena's house, her career, her driven direction that kept everything running forward. Everything depended on Deena.

"And what have I got to be scared of?"

Suz's blue eyes were great blue pools, but Deena wasn't going to fall in. She didn't need Suz's sympathy. Truth be known, she didn't need anyone. *She* was helping Suz out.

Suz caught Deena's hands and brought them to her lap, tangling all their fingers together.

"Deena, you are the bravest, strongest, most together woman I've ever known and I love you like a sister, but you're scaring me big time. Knowing you, you're making plans to bring these guys down and I don't know if one woman can do that. I'm afraid you're fooling yourself. You need help. You need to push the police to investigate your beating."

Deena twisted her fingers free. "What happened at the Center is institutional business. They won't have any better luck investigating this than they have investigating murder. Besides, the Hat is Rich Webster's case and I'm just a tad off of dealing with Officer Webster."

It came out more bitter than she'd intended, from a spot in her chest she hadn't wanted to recognize was aching.

"You know, there isn't a damn thing in my life that's going well right now." She caught Suz's eye. "Present company excepted, of course."

A slow smile melted over Suz's face and she pushed herself to her knees.

"I might just be able to convince you otherwise. Maybe all this angst is because something better is on the way. Maybe it's a chance to clear away old stuff and move on. Wait here a moment."

As if Deena could move. Just thinking of moving was painful.

Suz left the room like a woman on a mission and Deena collapsed against the couch pillows. Nope. No matter Suz's attempt at hope, things were looking pretty dark right now. Deena wasn't sure what would put the lights on. The Hat was being overrun by disease just as surely as Sly was, and she didn't know if she could fix it, anymore than she could fix Sly.

It left her helpless and doubting herself, and if there were two things Deena Hunter did not do well, it was helplessness and self-doubt. Well laying here wasn't going to make things any better. Her muscles would just tighten up and hurt more.

She was trying to stand when Suz buzzed back into the room wearing a sleek little number of navy trousers and a white shirt with princess seams that showed her woman's body, but looked crisp and professional. The clothing was big on her frame, but the triumphant grin on her face telegraphed just how pleased she was with her efforts.

"Wow! Where the heck did all that come from?" Deena straightened, upright, and winced at the pain in her hips and legs. Amazing the damage a few kicks could administer.

"After you left this morning I got ambitious. I had all the patterns I'd made, so I decided to get busy with the cloth. I spent the morning on it and this is the result. I've got a dress jacket part way done, too."

"You speed-demon, you." Deena examined the clothing and Suz did a tip-toe pirouette that was clumsy enough Deena had to catch Suz's arm to right her.

"Sorry," Suz said when Deena winced.

"No worries. Not too many police or corrections types are going to be pirouetting."

The clothing was darn fine. The trouser had a small pleat in the front that would ease nicely over a woman's hips. That had been something Deena had demanded because she despised the tight-butted trousers she saw far too often at work. The shirt was somehow feminine and yet professional— the seaming she'd planned doing its job. She fingered the fabric.

"It's got a bit of lycra in it, but otherwise it's cotton. Holds a crease and hardly wrinkles and it breathes. It's exactly what we were looking for." She did a more cautious pirouette this time. "So?"

"It's a bit big," Deena said critically, hefting the hanging shoulder seams.

"They should be. This is your uniform. Mine's still in pieces."

"Yours."

"Well if we're going to do a display at Police Expo I have to wear something and it might as well be another uniform. It's a good way to show them off. Besides, if I don't put stripes up the sides of the legs I'll have a really nice set of dress pants to wear."

She waggled the slight drape of the trouser over her leg, a look of hope in her eyes. Deena knew Suz needed to hear her assessment because Suz had been down so many times and never really recognized just how talented she was.

"You are good, woman. They look—well they look better than anything I've ever worn for work. Almost like expensive dress pants, but not wide enough to get in the way. Comfortable enough to move in and look good doing it. Now we just have to deal with short and long-waisted issues and we're laughing. No one will have a line like this."

"So you really like them?"

Deena caught Suz in a hug, winced big-time, but didn't care. "Suz, they're going to eat this up. No one has done a good job of women's uniforms. We're going to fill that niche – just you wait and see."

So maybe one good thing was happening in her life. Actually three, because she had Suz and Lana and they were the real deal. Friends, she hadn't known she needed in her life until she'd asked them to move in.

Speaking of which...Voices from the front.

"I thought Lana was upstairs."

Both of them looked to the door, instantly on their guard. Suz bolted for the open front door, but Lana's voice and heavy treads on the porch reached them first.

"Mom! There's a man here for Aunty Dee!"

Rich Webster appeared in the open door.

Chapter 37

RICH HAD TO FIGHT CONFLICTING emotions when he saw the two women. He forgot the anger and suspicion he'd built into an indignant rage, because the bruises on Deena's face overwhelmed him with doubt at his suspicions—and the need to protect.

He shifted his gaze to the redhead he'd talked to briefly the other morning. In the baggy uniform she still wasn't bad looking. A little winsome for his taste, but not bad.

Deena Hunter, however. The swelling and discoloration on her face...the way she stood, looked incredibly painful and he wanted to stop it.

Then a small red-headed tornado came bursting in around his legs, holding up a red truck, offering to play. All he could see was the bandage on Deena's temple, the way when she straightened at the sight of him, her face winced with pain – and something more guarded.

"What the...?"

"Hold it!" Deena held up a hand to stop him, her gaze still less than friendly. "We've got language police present." She nodded at the little girl, who looked up at him with narrowed blue eyes as if she knew what was going to come out of his mouth.

"What happened to you?" He said, as he knelt down to accept the truck from the girl. "Hi. What's your name?"

She glanced over her shoulder to her mother and caught the light nod. "Lana. Who are you?"

"My name's Rich. I'm a policeman."

Her big blue eyes got bigger.

"Really? My Aunty Dee used to be a policeman, too. She bought me a police car. I'll go find it."

She abandoned him with the red truck and the soft scent of child's shampoo, and scooted up the stairs. Rich stood.

"So? What the he-," he stopped himself with a glance at the stairs. "–Heck happened?"

The red-headed woman stayed guarding Deena's side. By the look of Deena—the way she didn't move—the bruising covered more than her face and it wasn't the kind of bruising you got from a car accident. Nope, the slight bend in her swollen nose and the two black eyes were the kind of things that came from a fist or other beating implements and he felt his hands curl with the need to hurt whoever had done this.

"Happened?" Deena's voice was cool enough it stopped him, when all his instincts said he should go to her—which wasn't particularly wise, given what he'd learned about Ms. Deena Hunter.

"What happened to you?" He leaned against the door frame, congratulating himself on keeping cool. "You didn't get to look like that by falling out of bed. I remember."

Deena turned, tried to stride to the couch, but it wasn't much more than a shuffle. She sank down into cushions that showed she'd been laying there. Probably daunted by the stairs to her apartment.

She still wouldn't meet his gaze and every move she made shouted tightly controlled pain.

"I had a little problem at the Hat. Got taken by surprise by a couple of guys." She shrugged, winced and quickly smoothed the pain away. "What brings you here?"

God she was cool. Cold as ice, actually, which made it a hell of a lot easier to keep his distance, when his tendency to rescue was struggling to get out. This was Deena. His Deena.

Ravi Sandhar's Deena. Remember that.

Trouble was, he couldn't frigging well forget it and he hated the way jealousy surged through him when he thought of it. That and the anger at her potential betrayal.

Hold onto the anger and keep this professional.

"You call it in?"

Her gaze snapped to him. "And what good would that do?"

"For Chris'ssake, it'll start an investigation. It might catch the inmates who did it. It might get a conviction."

She was friggin' shaking her head and looking so damned tired behind her façade of bravado he wanted to just sweep her up and get her up to her bed and make all the pain go away.

But he wouldn't do something that stupid. Not even when she closed her eyes in exhaustion.

"It was a set-up. It was all a set-up right from the start, Rich. I was wrong about my staff and you were right. They used my reputation against me by murdering Stickley right under my nose. They knew I'd blame myself for his death, but they figured I'd just tuck my tail between my legs and try to cover my ass. It's what they would have done. They didn't figure I'd start asking questions. Now that I have, they've got to do something about me."

Her gaze when she looked at him, was so bleak it took his breath away. She nodded and he knew.

"You're not going to stop."

"If I stop, they win."

"Deena, you can't mean that," the redhead interrupted, went to the couch to stand between Deena and himself.

"Rich, meet Suz, my best friend and seamstress extraordinaire, and apparently my bodyguard."

Her voice was tired, sounded like all she really wanted to do was collapse, but typical of his Deena, she was too much a fighter for that. It was what he loved about her.

Chuck would call him a fool, but there was no way in hell their suspicions could be true.

He went to her, stood shoulder to shoulder with Suz. "She's got a point. You look like hell."

"Just what a woman wants to hear, you sweet talker, you."

At least her sarcasm was working.

"You know damn well it makes sense. They've hurt you—badly by the look of it. I'm surprised you're not in the hospital."

"She signed herself out—against doctor's orders."

"What?" He looked from Suz, to Deena and saw this was already a point of friction between them. Knowing Deena, she'd won the argument and would continue to do so unless someone strong enough put their foot down.

"What the hell are you trying to do, get yourself killed?"

"Mommy, he said a bad word."

Rich strangled back the rest of what he wanted to say, and looked at the little girl standing at the door with a well-used plastic police car in her hand.

"He did, didn't he, honey. What should his punishment be?" Deena was way too quick to jump on punishing him. She smiled up at him with a venom he didn't understand. "Maybe he should just leave. Wouldn't that be a good punishment? Then he couldn't have any of your mommy's wonderful muffins and Aunty Dee could get some rest."

Lana cocked her head. She looked at him, then at Deena, then at her mother as if she was reading all the undercurrents in the room.

"Nooo. I think maybe he should help Aunty Dee with my toys, don't you, Mommy? They should clean up the whole yard like you were talking about and I could relax." The triumphant, gap-toothed smile she gave him could just about steal a man's heart already. When she was grown she was going to be a man-magnet like her mom, he supposed.

Deena looked like she was going to protest, but Suz just nodded. Then she looked at him coldly.

"Sounds like a fine punishment, honey, but I think Mr. police officer here is just leaving. Aren't you?"

Something was definitely going on. There was no friendship in Suz's big eyes, even though he'd aligned himself with her against Deena's foolish determination.

"I have some things I need to talk to Deena about."

"And I think Deena needs to rest and not to think about anything but getting better. I'm sure you understand."

She might be small, but this little person had a mettle he hadn't often seen. Probably something that she picked up from Deena—or that certain something mothers had when protecting their young.

"I'm sure she does," he said, his gaze meeting Deena's. "It would probably be better if she was in her own apartment and could rest in peace. Maybe I can be of assistance."

Ignoring the protests, he swooped in on Deena and scooped her up. He already knew she wasn't that heavy. She might be tallish but she was reed-thin with long muscles he knew well and would like to know better. In his arms she felt like a tight mass of knotted rope under a skin of velvet flesh—a tight mass that would normally explode. He shook his head to stop her protest.

"Now you can be quiet and let me carry you up to your place, or you can fight. And believe me, fighting will hurt you a hell of a lot more than it'll hurt me."

She glared at him. Positively glared a dislike so vitriolic that he almost considered putting her down.

"What mosquito's got up your butt?" He said softly, hoping he hadn't broken the language rules again.

"Just get me upstairs," Deena said through clenched teeth.

Rich glanced at Suz. "I won't be long. I promise. But she might need some help with things up there."

"I'm here. Deena, are you sure you want to do this?"

"If it'll get me home and this guy outta here, it's fine by me." She turned back to him with a poisoned smile. "So get moving there, Mr. Toolbox." It came out almost a snarl.

Rich moved, Lana following him to the base of the stairs, chattering away about her police car until Suz hauled her back, and the two of them stood silently watching as Rich fumbled Deena's keys and let them in.

When he shouldered the door shut behind them, she hauled off and belted him in the chest.

"Put me down, damn you. It's bad enough I can't help myself, let alone getting you to help me."

Rich gently settled her feet to the floor, but she yanked away, almost fell before she caught herself, but somehow managed to avoid his touch. She limped over to the couch and Sly came padding out of the bedroom meowing at the top of his lungs.

"I'm right here, Sly. Come on, buddy. You're the kind of fella a woman wants, aren't you. The dependable kind." She scooped Sly onto her lap, groaned, and threw a hateful look in Rich's direction.

Okay. Something wasn't right, because he sure enough knew he hadn't done a darn thing wrong. As a matter of fact, carrying her up to her apartment sort of went above and beyond the call of duty.

He leaned against the kitchen wall and considered.

"So mind filling me in on what I've done?"

"As if you didn't know. I've got no use for men like you. I've been burned once too often and I'm not doing it again."

"What the hell are you talking about?"

She went to get up, but a wave of pain crossed her face and her legs didn't seem to obey. Frustration filled her face and two silver tears ran down her cheeks—to be swiftly palmed away. His first inclination was to help her, but her expression stopped him. Even through her tears he could read her distrust.

"You know what? Suz was right. This really isn't a good time. I don't care what you've got to talk to me about; I don't think I can deal with it right now."

Pain, physical and mental, radiated from her, leaving him feeling so bloody helpless. He crossed to her, but she waved him off.

"I don't need or want your attention, Rich. Now I'd like to get some sleep, so please, just go. Better yet, take your tools with you."

She closed her eyes and it was like a light went out. Whatever had happened was serious. By her expression she was tossing him out of her life and no matter how hard he'd tried to make himself angry, he hadn't been prepared for that. He'd had suspicions about her, true, But he hadn't wanted to. And one look at the bruises on her face said those suspicions weren't worth the spit they'd been spoken with. Her injuries also said this wasn't the time to discuss whatever had her upset.

Nope, better to leave that for another day.

He retrieved the red toolbox and returned to the living room. She hadn't moved. Damn it, this wasn't the way it was supposed to be, and he wasn't just going to walk away. He dumped the tools by the door and went to her.

Her gaze flicked open, shocked by his palm on her head, fingers stroked through her hair. He wanted to kiss her, to make the pain go away. To see the woman of the day before look back at him. But there was none of that softness in Deena's gaze today.

"I'm going, but I'll be back tomorrow to check on you." His fingers slid down to cup her swollen cheek, her injured jaw. He was going to get whoever had done this to her. He would make them pay. "Whatever it is that's got your knickers in a twist—we're going to have it out, Deena."

She twisted away from his hand, her stare cold and distant as that damn mountain across the valley.

"The only thing I want out is you."

Chapter 38

IN THE IMMACULATE WHITE MARBLE bathroom with the ultramodern faucets Anita's shower in the oversized glassed in shower cabinet ran warm and thick with lather. The alcohol glow had faded some, to leave doubts about falling into bed with Chad.

But at least she felt alive again. Like a woman again. A woman who a man had wanted, and she had wanted him, too.

It was simple as that. She began rinsing the mint-scented shampoo out of her hair. Two people with needs had made choices. Heck, maybe it would lead to even more than that. Chad really seemed to like her. He paid attention to her. She had a quiet little suspicion that he'd known she was on shift and had come to see how she was doing.

Her heart did a little *fillip*, and as she finished rinsing and turned off the water she knew her feelings were kind of stupid given she'd only known Chad for a week. She looked down at her body, still tender from sex, and grinned.

A lot could happen in a week.

Not bad. Not bad at all. She'd found a place in Corrections—she just hadn't imagined it would be under Chad Preston. Well under, on top, and a few other places she could almost be embarrassed about.

She toweled off, stepped over the pieces of clothing Chad left discarded in his bathroom and padded out to the bedroom and her purse. She needed her comb to tame her mane back into place, but it wouldn't take much. Thankfully she'd been gifted with the grace not to require much fussing in the morning. Her friends always marveled at how quickly she could get ready.

Comb through the hair. Pulling on clothes she'd yanked off only a few hours ago. Heck, the last light of day was still fading through the window and she felt, well, ready to go do something. Everything sort of tingled with new energy.

Heck, maybe she could even talk Chad back into bed because then she wouldn't have to think about everything that had happened today.

All that blood.

She yanked her thoughts back.

Yes, try to get Chad back in bed. A last glance at the tousled sheets and she headed downstairs to where Chad was making some phone calls. She'd see what she could do to seduce him away.

Her body warmed in anticipation of what he would do to her, how she could get lost in sensation and what she would do to please him. She reached the round foyer at the bottom of the curved stairs.

Chad's house was way bigger than she'd expected. Five bedrooms, high ceilings, huge marble fireplace and an almost non-existent yard in one of the expensive new subdivisions springing up all over Mission. The interior was painted a deep, luxurious green, but the furniture didn't fit.

The foyer was empty except for a litter of shoes. The living room held two battered couches, a big screen T.V., accompanied by an expensive-looking sound system, an open beer case full of empties and a few empty pizza boxes. So much for decorating. Not that her place had a lot, but heck, this was a great house and it didn't even have pictures on the wall.

From the back of the house—the kitchen—came the sound of Chad's voice. Anita checked herself out in double glass doors into what was supposed to be a formal dining room. Boxes filled the space like a shipping depot. She didn't look half bad as she shook her damp hair around her shoulders and threw her shoulders back. The baby-t rode up just enough to allow glimpses of smooth skin at the top of her jeans.

"Watch out, Chad, cause here I come."

Girded, she headed for the kitchen, pushed through the swinging door and saw him, back to her, phone at his ear as he stared out the kitchen window. He took a swig from a beer bottle and shook his head.

"Like I said. There's not going to be a problem. She was shaken, but I dealt with it. She kept on about how no one responded, but I told her it was all in her mind." A small chuckle.

Anita froze. He was talking about her—and laughing!

She eased back through the door, let it close not knowing what to do. Cold. The hallway had the temperature of a freezer and the shakes returned to her hands. Run? Listen? Go back upstairs?

He was probably just talking to some of his buddies who were concerned about her.

She looked back at the door. That was it.

But he'd *laughed*. Not a friendly laugh. Derisive. Goose pimples peppered her flesh and she looked up the stairs. Wished she was still upstairs blithely planning a seduction. Better still, that she wasn't here at all.

But if she left he'd know something was the matter, and suddenly it was really important that he didn't.

She stayed, listening, where she was.

"Listen I can only do what I do best, but you better tell the boss this has gotta get dealt with. It was stupid doing it today. Sure you had the opportunity, but Anita almost fucking saw our guys. It's one thing to ease her into this, but that takes time and Anita's not stupid."

Anita gritted her teeth and felt anger light a fire against the fear. Small mercies. He didn't think she was stupid. She was tempted to slam through the door and tell him just how smart she was.

Because it sounded seriously like Chad Preston was confirming her suspicions about what had happened to Dee. It hadn't been an accident.

"Would you listen to me?" Chad's voice got louder, then softened so she had to strain to hear. "She's planning on fucking law school, for chrissake. She's not just some bimbo. I've got to take my time if this is going to work." A silence, then a sigh. "Yeah I know. Well I'm keeping my fingers crossed I can deal with her this way. She's cute. Not a bad lay."

Anita's breath came in tight little gasps as Chad signed off and began moving around the kitchen. He couldn't find her here. Couldn't know what she'd overheard. If Chad was 'taking his time' so he could 'deal with her', she probably wouldn't like the alternative. Fear strangled all heat from her. She should have listened to Dee.

She backed up, backed up until her heels hit the first stair riser. So cold, she was almost numb. She couldn't feel her feet, her face, her fingers. Her blood pounded so loud in her ears she was surprised it didn't echo in the high ceiling.

Every part of her said run, but she wasn't going to. She was going to be like Dee. She was going to do what Dee would do. Do what Dee had asked and get information. Be the officer Dee expected, not like the others who let Dee down.

She swallowed, threw her shoulders back and prayed she wasn't as pale as she felt, just as Chad pushed through the kitchen door.

"Hey! I was just going to call you." The smile on his face made her almost cringe.

She forced her mouth into something she hoped resembled a grin and felt ill as she walked into his arms. Would he feel her shaking?

"I was hoping you'd come back up." She forced herself to press into him.

"Geeze, 'nita. You're like ice." He ran his hands up under her shirt in a caress that had previous made her quiver with desire. Now it just made her shiver as his lips lowered and took.

It took everything she had to answer, because maybe if she could do this, it would put him at ease, make him talk more. She had to keep him feeling sure of her. But she felt dirty doing it. Filthy because his hands had been all over her, knew her.

Women had been using their bodies for centuries to get information. She could do this.

She moaned and he pulled back, grinned down at her.

"You like getting guys all hot and bothered? That why you work in a jail?"

She play-punched his chest.

"I could get seriously offended by that."

She pulled back, knew she pouted prettily by the way Chad got all contrite.

"I'm sorry, baby. I know this is something kinda special." He pulled her back to him, ran his hands up and down her back.

Like hell it is. Bastard, was what she wanted to call him. Fucking murderous bastard. Instead she laid her head against his chest.

"I'm going to say something you're going to think is pretty stupid, but I think I really need you, Chad. You make things make sense."

He stiffened in a typical male response to a relationship that was moving too fast and she had to stifle the urge to laugh. There, you Bastard.

"I was talking pretty foolish, wasn't I? After, I mean. What happened had to be an accident, didn't it? Because staff stick together. We're like family. Like blood."

His tension eased and he kissed her hair, ran his too-warm hands under her shirt and cupped her breasts, so she knew she was going to want to shower for a week. She only hoped she could get rid of the feel of him.

She pulled back, because she really didn't want to have sex with this man again.

"So what do you want to do tonight?"

A little flutter of her eyelashes—and just where did she learn to flirt so outrageously—she placed her hands on his chest, pressed her fingertips into his pecs.

"Cause I was thinking maybe we should get to know each other better. Maybe I could buy you dinner to thank you for—well—everything?" Another flutter and she cocked her hip, trailed her fingers down his chest and felt the little spasm tighten his belly. Wanted to kick him right where it would hurt. She looked at him from the tops of her eyes. "Then maybe we could go back to my place."

"I could only wish, baby." There was regret in his voice and she could only think Chad was putting in an academy award quality performance. But then, so was she.

"I've got a place I gotta be, 'nita. But maybe I could come back to your place later?"

She nodded, pressed into him so he wouldn't see her relief and her fear. No way was she letting Chad Preston into her apartment. Her basement suite was in her father's home and the last thing she wanted to do was bring a man like Chad under her father's watchful eye.

"I guess that'll have to do."

He packed her out of the house a little too quickly and helped her up into his truck.

"This's sure a nice truck," she said, stroking the leather bucket seat.

"Ain't it though? I bought it new three months ago. It's the first time I've ever been able to afford a new car."

The pride of ownership shone in his face, reminding her of boys and toys.

"Must be hard with the payments, what with the mortgage on your house and all. I figure by the time I pay off student loans I should be eighty before I can afford something that fancy."

She shook her head with feigned regret and he caught her hand and pulled her to him across the space between the seats. Kissed her.

"Stick with me kid. I've made some good investments and they're paying off—thus the truck. Maybe I can get you involved as well."

She could smell their sex on his skin and her stomach turned over, but: "What kind of investments?"

"High risk, high pay-off. Call it the International Investment Fund, but you won't find it on any mutual fund listing. It's small and private, but it's worked for me."

He drove expertly, easily threading through the Mission neighbourhoods even with her distractions, and then they were in front of her house and she suddenly didn't really like that he knew where she lived. He pulled up behind her car and gave her a long, hard kiss that only made her want to shudder. What kind of man was this, who could use a woman like this? Then he checked the clock in his dash.

"Sorry, baby." His endearment made her skin crawl. "I got to get a move on. I'm going to be late as it is."

"So where are you headed?"

His gaze slipped away, then back to her and she knew she might not be a lawyer yet, but she had enough skills to recognize a lie was coming.

"Out with the boys. Guys' night out. That sort of thing."

She reached over to touch him in a way she hoped would show desire, running her fingers down his face.

"You come back soon, okay?"

He caught her hand, mouthed her fingertips. "Count on it."

And then she was out of the truck, waving good bye and noting his license number. When he turned the corner she sprinted for her father's plain brown two-story house with its perfectly groomed lawn and its lonely rhododendron that was all that passed for a garden and her bedroom over the two-car garage. She was up the three steps to the front door and inside.

"Dad!" Her father came out of the kitchen wiping his hands. He was a small neat, bright-eyed man bowed at the shoulders from years pouring over account sheets.

Anita? I wasn't expecting you."

She scribbled down Chad's license number and stuffed it into her Dad's hand.

"No questions, Dad. Just if anything happens to me, give that to the cops. Tell them I was with him."

Then she was out the door to her car and yes—thank god—the guys from work had left her keys under the front seat. She spun the car away from the curb and not knowing where she was going, but she sure enough was going to find out.

Deena deserved that much.

Chapter 39

DEENA HAD TO SAVE THEM ALL.

The world pitched under her. The huge bulk of Mount Baker pitched and rolled against the sullen sunrise, while existence shattered around her. The air reeked of brimstone as buildings collapsed. People screamed, ran, and she was running, running so hard to outrun the huge cracks in the earth, but they were hard on her heels. Hard on the heels of the man pounding beside her.

Rich. He was carrying Lana. Suz was long lost and Deena's tears clogged her eyes, just as blinding as the ash that filled the air, that blanketed the earth, the trees, the houses. Moss on cedar shingles acted as a wick to flames on the huge, old house her father built. The structure blazed, taking everything Deena ran for, all of her history, everything she was.

She stopped, ash stealing her breath, clogging her mouth.

"No," she sobbed. "No."

The ground rumbled and shook until she couldn't stand, until Rich stumbled and fell towards the huge crack in the earth. The mountain exploded, and he and Lana tumbled into the crevasse. Deena screamed. Screamed as the crack spread under her. As the mountain rained darkness around her.

Falling.

As she was.

But the world continued to shake.

She woke up and almost screamed because her world still shook. The bed under her. The small back body rigid against her chest.

"No!" She bolted upright into semi-darkness and realized the rest of the room was as still as when she'd collapsed on the bed at five o'clock. Sly jerked, spasmed, convulsed and so the bed shook.

"Oh God, no."

She scrambled for the bedside lamp, ignoring the scream of her muscles, the pain in her face. The digital alarm read six thirty as she knocked it to the floor. Something was horribly wrong and her darn fingers couldn't get the damn light to work.

Finally a pool of amber light filled the side of the bed. Sly lay on his side, his body flopping, legs rigid, his pink tongue protruding and his golden eyes rolled back.

"Sly! Sly, buddy." She picked him up, snuggled him into her chin. "Oh God, no!"

And the tears caught in her dream swelled in her chest because Julie had told her what this meant. The damn disease was getting worse.

Slowly, the convulsion stopped and his body went limp. Sly opened his eyes, but hung in her hands. His whole body trembled, just as hers did from fear.

"This isn't supposed to happen, buddy. You're supposed to live forever."

She lay down on the bed, pulling him into her, holding him safe against his fear and what was to come and stroking that plush fur until slowly, slowly, his great-hearted purr sent them both to sleep.

Chapter 40

THE WHEELS OF ANITA'S LITTLE RED car spun out on the pavement as she accelerated, down the hill from her father's house trying to catch up to Chad. Well not quite catch up. She just needed to spot the truck and then she'd follow at a cautious distance because given what she'd heard, just following him was a pretty big risk.

Across the river, the mountains faded away in shades of blue that lifted in layers like crinoline skirts towards the granddaddy of mountains. The air had definitely turned towards fall with a mist turning everything golden. Even the damned red truck.

"This is way stupid, Underhill." She could hear Dee's voice, but this was the kind of thing Dee would do. Take charge and get the information because no one else could. She wove through the late afternoon traffic until she spotted the big red four-by-four cruising about ten cars up. Settled back and drove.

Besides, Chad had used her and she wanted her revenge. He'd been trying to convince her she couldn't believe her own eyes. The fact he'd wanted her to doubt herself tightened her hands on the steering wheel.

It had been an act from the start. He'd played the nice guy. Been kind to her. Taking time for her. Making sure she got home that first night. A perfect gentleman, and a great lover.

"Bastard."

She cranked the heater up against her cold fury. The stoplight up ahead turned amber, and the big red truck accelerated and cranked a left onto Stave Lake Road, nearly cutting off oncoming traffic. The vehicle disappeared up the hill and Anita swore.

She wasn't going to lose him. There was a reasonable chance he was headed to the Heritage Pub. Darn it, wasn't it *ever* going to be her turn. Finally the light changed.

She made a dangerous turn, narrowly missing a logging truck, and sped up the hill. If he wasn't at the pub, she'd cruise the side streets because she wasn't letting Chad Preston get away with what he'd done. She was going to bring the guy down.

The pub sat on a bluff near Heritage Park, where Mission held its annual folk festival and community fairs. Broad expanses of lawn and shade trees overlooked the Fraser River and the bulk of Mount Baker beyond. The mountain's forbidding blue shadows added to her chill.

The Heritage Pub sat amid a stand of cedars, with large glass windows and a verandah. Of course inside the log walls and small side rooms allowed patrons to drink in shadows. She drove up the curved drive but stopped when she spotted the distinctive red truck. There was no sign of Chad.

She left the pub and parked out on the street. Maybe he *was* just getting together with the boys. Maybe it wasn't as bad as she'd thought. A good lawyer probably shouldn't let herself go to wild with speculations.

Focus on the facts and the law. That was what they taught in Criminology and Law. The facts were the bottom line—the evidence to connect the dots of the case. The law's elements that had either been broken or not.

Consider: Deena was investigating staff on the Stickley death because this whole thing started after the inmate died. Deena was beaten badly. When Anita had arrived on scene the elevator door had just been closing. What had she seen?

Dee's body sprawled like she was dead. Two large men in prison coveralls.

She'd heard voices. Laughter that jarred because of all the blood on the floor. But there was something about the guys and that was what she had tried to explain to Chad.

It was also what he kept deflecting her from.

She closed her eyes, focused. It had happened like this.

Breathless from running, she pushed the door open. Heard something. Deena on the floor. Laughter. Something caught her eye as she ran to Deena. She half-turned. Door sliding, covering two men. Big. Muscular like weight-lifters. Shortish hair. Clean shaven. Unfamiliar. Prison greens. Her gaze slid down to the floor because she'd been going down onto her knees beside Dee.

The men's shoes before they're hidden. Not institutional runners. Not even the worn, steel-toed boots some of the inmates wore when they were working in the shops.

These were heavy boots. Black. Thick treaded. Glossy toed.

She almost didn't hear the truck rumble past, as she struggled to breathe, because it wasn't just that Dee had been set-up; staff had beaten her, and she, Anita, wasn't supposed to have seen.

If they knew, she knew she was sure to meet a fate worse than Dee's.

She suddenly realized it was Chad's truck turning onto the road, followed by another truck driven by Randy Johal.

So Chad could still be going out with the boys, but everything told her it was more than that. She started her car when the two trucks were a block down the road. Followed behind them, trying to work things through.

Dee had worked at the Hat for a long time and she'd been ADW for awhile, too. So why take a chance on beating her, now?

Anita had worked in the Center long enough to understand the concept of needing your co-workers to cover your back, and she'd heard talk of staff who had gotten into a jam with an inmate and the rest of the staff just happened to not have radios that worked, or were slow in responding so the correctional officer got beaten. A tuning, they called it, because the officer in question had provided evidence in the beating of an inmate or on some other disciplinary matter. As if the officer needed to be re-tuned to the same frequency as the rest of the staff.

The trucks turned west on the Lougheed Highway and then south to the bridge over the river to Abbotsford. The broad sweep of the late summer corn fields shielded the farm houses beyond the road. The trucks sped up and Anita kept pace, a few cars between her and Johal's vehicle. It was tougher than she'd thought to follow discreetly, because she had to make sure she made it through the stoplights with them.

Ahead, the trucks took the turn that would lead them along Highway 11 to the U.S. and the numerous farms and hobby acreages that covered the fertile Fraser Valley right down to the border. There weren't any pubs or anything down here, so maybe they were going to a friend's place.

"You really are trying to give him the benefit of the doubt, aren't you?"

And it was the truth, because she didn't want to believe this was happening, that she was doing this, that she had slept with someone capable of aiding and abetting Dee's beating, and that she had played a part in it.

Because the only thing that seemed to make sense was that Dee's Internal Security Initiative and her investigation into the inmate death was what had gotten Dee beaten. Which meant the staff must be involved.

And she had told Chad about the ISI.

Feeling sick, she gripped the steering wheel as the two trucks turned west onto Zero Avenue and followed along the low hills of border. The light was failing, just as she had failed Dee. She'd been the cause of the beating and, oh God, she had to find a way to make amends.

She slowed, as the traffic disappeared between her and the two vehicles. The light faded from the sky, staining Mt. Baker apricot in her rearview mirror. It was a lovely evening, cloudless and cool, but not cool enough to explain the shivers she felt.

She had been an idiot, dewy-eyed, idealist when she walked through the doors of the Hat for that first shift. Dee had tried to help her, and she had tossed it right back in Dee's face, because Anita'd been charmed by Chad and filled with the need to show she was tough enough to belong to the crew.

All she'd done was royally mess up.

Like Dee had said, Anita had been so busy becoming whatever it was that would fit in at the Hat, she'd almost forgotten who and what she was.

Not going to happen again. She'd remembered and she was going to hold on tight. She wanted to be a lawyer—a good one who fought for the law—not some sleaze.

The truck taillights flared ahead and she slowed, drove past as the two vehicles bumped up a long driveway screened with cedars to a barn set back behind a two story house. A couple of cars were parked by the barn. The place was one of those spiffy, country-estate type places, with white fences around pasture and matching white trim on the blue barn and house, but this place looked a little rundown. Judging by the state of sunburned lawn and the thick stand of seeded dandelions in the ditch, definitely less cared for.

She drove up a few blocks and pulled a u-turn, then drove slowly back with her lights off and parked at the side of the road where she hoped her car looked like she might just be visiting another of the hobby farms. She still had a pretty good view of the barn from here.

Johal had backed his truck up to the barn but had to move it so another pickup could pull out. Then he backed in and the barn door rolled closed. The driver of the third vehicle stopped long enough to talk to Chad, who was finishing a smoke. Then the truck drove towards her and she ducked down. She managed to catch a couple of numbers on his license plate in her rearview mirror.

Just sitting here wasn't going to get her any information. In the failing light it was harder to see. She waited until Chad finished his cigarette and entered the barn, then got out of her car and inhaled the cool air, heavy with hay-scent. Mist had started to condense over the fields.

She crossed the road in three strides. At least there were trees next to the barn. The poplar and spruce trees and the cedars along the drive would give her cover.

Scrambling up the far bank of the ditch, she swore oaths at the mud caking her runners, and entered the line of trees. A whoosh over her head nearly made her scream.

A bat. Only a bat, you ninny.

But she shouldn't be doing this. She should have called the police. If there was something going on and she was caught, she'd be in serious doo-doo.

But she had to know. It would useless if all she could bring Dee was that Chad and a bunch of other staff had met at a barn in Abbotsford.

For all she knew, they could be starting a business together. Chad *had* mentioned International Investments or something.

She came even with the barn and took a moment to commit the vehicle license plates to memory, then crept through the trees, keeping an eye on the door. Light poured through grimy windows set over her head on the sides of the barn. Through tall grass gone to seed, she eased up to the wall.

Her path would leave a trail. All she could hope was that no one bothered to check. Close up, she heard voices.

"Shit, I hate this." Chad's voice. "I didn't sign on to be a fucking coal miner."

Anita went up on her toes, swearing at her height deficiency, grabbed the window sill, her toes scrabbling for purchase on the barn siding, and managed to haul herself up slightly so she could see inside.

"What was that?" A voice she didn't know, from a man she didn't recognize. Chad faced him, looking a little foolish and whole lot pissed as he slid a silly miner's headlight cap on his head and picked up a shovel. Both men turned toward Anita's vantage.

Chad's headlight slid across the window. Anita fell back, landed on her butt on the ground. If they hadn't seen her, it had been damn close, and she wasn't going to wait around to find out. She was up and running back through the trees, heard the grind of the barn door, and increased her speed.

They'd hear her because she wasn't taking any care to be quiet. Just get out of here and get someplace safe, otherwise that paper she'd left with her dad was her only legacy. That and the fact that from what she had seen, Dee was seriously in danger.

Chapter 41

BUNDLING SLY INTO THE CAT CARRIER was almost the toughest thing Deena had ever done. It was made tougher by the mass of aches and pains and creaky joints that told her she really was forty years old—going on a hundred and forty.

All she really wanted was to stay in bed with Sly snuggled next to her, but she couldn't do that to him.

That would be for her. But through the night she'd spent a lot of time thinking. And crying. And feeling sorry for herself. And trying to make deals with life and death.

None of it helped deny the fact that Sly was seriously sick—perhaps even beyond help. She'd been fooling herself that the insulin was going to save him. With all his vomiting, the poor little guy must be hungry all the time, must wonder why she wasn't taking care of him. That was what broke her heart.

That and knowing how terrified he'd been after the seizure. It couldn't go on. If she let it, it would only be selfish on her part. Sly would continue to fail and she couldn't stand to see him go through that. Did she want him to lose all dignity?

She peered into Sly's golden eyes. "Hey, buddy. Aren't we a couple of good looking old codgers?"

His little pink tongue was poked out at her and drool spooled onto his paws. As for her, well when she'd checked in the mirror this morning, the swelling on her temple was like a firm goose egg swathed in the dressing, while the bruising over her nose had shifted into the soft tissue around her eyes so she was sporting two extreme shiners.

Sly's gargled mew of agreement brought the tears she'd sworn she wasn't going to cry.

This was one of those moments she could use a hug, but it wasn't going to happen. It was still early, the sun painting the darn mountain fiery pink. At least it wasn't the color of the mountain in her dreams. At least she wasn't running for her life and having to watch Rich and Lana die.

No, Lana was sleeping peacefully downstairs as was her mother, and Rich, well she didn't give a damn where he was.

Married, bastard.

No, she'd take care of Sly, just as she had taken care of herself—alone. That was how you came into the world and that was how you went out of it and she was living proof. You get close to someone, love someone, and all you can look forward to is hurt and disappointment and betrayal and death.

Hefting Sly's cage, she left the apartment and started down the stairs. Not good. Really not good when one of her legs almost buckled with the pain. She sank down on the step with Sly on her lap, fighting back tears of frustration.

She had started to bum-bump down the flight, when she saw the black SUV pull in at the curb.

Her stomach did a wobbling fall.

Damn it, why was everything happening like this? Because Rich Webster was about the last thing she needed at this particular moment.

Chapter 42

IN THE MISTS OF MORNING, RICH found her looking pained and angry, halfway down the flight of red stairs. Above her the sky was still watery blue and with thin cloud that the morning sun would soon rip away, but beside the house was in shadows. Her shoulders slumped, she'd rested her head against the wall of the house, the cat carry case balanced in her lap and she looked like she might have been crying.

He hadn't planned to come by so early, but something had got him out of bed. Maybe it was the fact he'd been awake all night trying to figure out what he'd done to wreck things and how the hell he could fix it. Because regardless of Chuck's suspicions, Rich couldn't leave things like this with Deena. Besides, fixing things was what he did.

"So this is a different method of getting down stairs. Use it often?" He leaned against the side of the house—it could use a little paint—and watched the emotions flow over her face. A little pissed. A lot of fatigue. Pain she was working hard to control.

"I need to get Sly to the vet."

Her lips closed around the words as if she was afraid of something else getting out and it brought him upright, concerned. She bum-bumped down another stair.

"Let me give you a hand." He was up the stairs in a few easy strides, but she shook her head, shoved him back and he didn't like it. "Damn it, I'm just trying to help, here."

"And I don't need your help." She grabbed the stair rail with one hand, hefted Sly's cage with the other though he could see it cost her. She limped down a stair, her face starkest white, her lips pressed into a line.

Held upright by force of will alone. When she tried to push past him, he blocked her way.

"Deena. What's happened?" He kept his voice gentle, knew a soft voice might help to de-escalate something that so easily could get out of hand. "I thought we were good together—that we had a chance this time 'round."

Her brown gaze held his for a moment, dark, but with a glow concealed inside like curtained light in the middle of the night. Sly mewed, his black paw reaching through the wire mesh door, and that seemed to break the spell of her eyes. The light disappeared.

"I'm sorry. I can't do this now. I thought I might today, but I just need to take care of Sly. He's very sick."

"Then let me help." He knew how important the darn cat was. He grabbed the cage from her through her protests, caught her hand, and saw her fight back an urge to pull free. So there was hope. Maybe.

Deena dug in her heels in front of her car. "I can take it from here."

"Like hell. You're in no shape to drive. Or anything else."

She stuck her chin out and crossed her arms so she looked like a defiant child—if not for the bruises across her face. And then there were those most kissable lips—even if they were set in a line that he knew meant she was one moment from exploding.

In her condition she couldn't do much damage.

"He's my cat and I'll drive him. This is private."

"Private. Taking a cat to the vet is private."

"It is." She held out her hands for the cage but he wasn't giving up, because there was something about her eyes—something so shiny-vulnerable that he couldn't let her go. Not yet. He had to keep trying.

"Tell you what. I'll drive, because I know you've got to be in pain, and frankly I'm concerned about you driving—reaction times and all that. You could be a menace on the road." He dug for some other excuse, but that was all he could come up with. "When we get there, I'll wait in the car."

Her gaze narrowed as he tried to look innocently helpful.

"Come on, give me a break."

All the strength seemed to run out of her and she sagged a little.

"Okay. But I warn you, he doesn't like to travel."

"How bad can it be? It's only to the vet's."

The smirk on her face should have warned him.

It was bad. Cat screams echoed in the SUV. The darn animal released hair like a porcupine was supposed to loose quills. Hair floated everywhere, and all the time Deena talked gently, tried to ease the little feline, until finally they arrived at the vets. As soon as the engine stopped, Sly stopped.

"Why the hell does he do that?"

Deena turned a pale gaze to him. "Why do any of us do anything. Fear? Pain? The need to communicate it?" She looked at the vet's and took a deep breath. "I—we—won't be long."

She climbed out of the truck and limped toward the entrance, clutching the cage like her life depended on it. Through the glass front he watched her go to the counter, saw the slump to her shoulders, watched her take Sly out of his cage and sit huddled with him on her lap. It wasn't like Deena. He didn't like to see her that way.

A woman, maybe the vet, took Deena and the cat into another room and Rich climbed out of his truck and went inside to the woman at the counter.

"Hi." He smiled his most winning smile. "I was supposed to meet Deena Hunter here."

The woman looked up him. "She's just gone inside."

"So how's the little guy doing?"

"As good as can be expected, I suppose. Renal failure and diabetes are never good. Deena's tried to manage it, but I guess it's getting away. He had a seizure, poor thing. She doesn't want to cause him pain."

The knowledge of what she was dealing with, of what she must be going through, left him feeling sick. He didn't think, just entered the examining room, because he knew she needed someone with her and it was damn-well going to be him. He found the vet and Deena with Sly on the examining table.

Deena brushed away tears and rounded on him.

"You said you'd wait in the truck."

"I lied. You need someone here with you." He put his arm around her shoulders and she shrugged him off.

"Just stay out of the way." She went down beside the cat, running her hands through his fur. "Hey, little buddy. What are we going to do with you?"

The vet stroked Sly's fur and he lay there, looking like he'd collapsed, but purring. A comforting sound, but the look of the animal wasn't comforting and Deena wasn't. Small shudders ran through her.

"It's a tough call, Deena. I told you diabetes required close monitoring until he's stabilized, but the addition of the renal failure makes treatment—especially home treatment difficult."

"You know I'll do anything. I've been giving him his insulin like you said."

"Has he been eating?"

"He tries. But he throws up a lot."

The vet pulled up the scruff of Sly's neck and released it. The loose skin slowly returned to its place and the vet shook her head.

"He's very dehydrated."

Deena looked like she was going to collapse and he caught her arm to steady her. Felt her tense, then relax, a defeated slope coming to her shoulders.

"I tried. I really tried." She managed to choke out. She straightened, took a deep breath, being strong as only Deena Hunter could be, and he loved her for it. Loved the way she wanted to ease her pet even though just standing had to be painful as heck. "What can we do?"

"Well..." The vet tested Sly's loose skin again. "I can give him IV fluids and try to stabilize him again, then we'll see how it goes. He may come back enough to keep him going but..."

"But what?"

The vet gripped the edge of the examining table and looked Deena so hard in the eyes that Rich wanted to intervene.

"But he had a seizure. That's bad. Very bad. And keeping him going is going to take a heck of a lot of work what with his diabetes and the need for fluids. I know I gave you the fluids before, but I don't actually believe in owners doing it."

"Why?" The small shivers were increasing, rushing through Deena's body, gooseflesh covering her arm. Rich slid his arm around her, wished he had a jacket to throw over her shoulders.

She immediately shrugged him off, to face off with the vet. "Julie? Tell me?"

"Because owners don't take this seriously. They don't do things properly because they're afraid they're hurting their pet by giving a needle. They get squeamish when actually they're saving the animal's life. I know you're trying, but this is serious. It's more work and the animals often object."

Deena was already shaking her head. "I can do it. I can." Then she almost went to her knees, caught herself on the examining table. "Oh

God, this is my fault. Yesterday he struggled so I let him off with only half the liquid. I didn't understand. Oh God. Sly I'm so sorry. Anything, Julie. Anything if it will help Sly. I don't want to see him like this. I don't want him to die."

She ran her fingers through Sly's fur and he turned that golden gaze on her and chirruped so it near broke Rich's heart. He touched her shoulder, stepped close once more.

"Deena, why don't you have her give the fluids now and make him comfortable. If he comes back, well then you can decide."

She was shivering under his hands as she nodded. Julie looked from him to Deena and nodded. The vet left the room and Deena turned on him, shook loose.

"I said I didn't need you here." Her gaze flashed with anger, but he could tell she had difficulty sustaining it. Fatigue radiated from her even more than the pain.

"You were wrong." He caught her arms, ran his hands lightly up them and saw her wince at his touch. "You're exhausted, you're in pain and you're dealing with something emotionally traumatic. You need someone."

"Not you."

"Well I'm who you've got. Deal with it." He put his arm around her shoulder as the vet returned. This time Deena didn't pull away, even if she was stiff. He'd wait for her to melt. It would come.

It had to.

Deena brushed her eyes as the cat pawed her and chirruped as if he knew she was upset and didn't want her to be. The darn cat purred as the vet hung a bag of fluids above the table, and inserted the needle in the loose flesh behind his neck. Then Deena had him in her arms, was cuddling him as the vet set the fluids running.

Rich saw the shudder run through Deena as she kissed the black fur. The vet checked the fluid flow, caressed Sly's head.

"If only they were all this good about it. But you should stand back. Sometimes the feel of the fluid can make them fight." Julie eased Deena up, away.

He was there when she turned, devastation on her face as he caught her in his arms and pulled her into his chest, scenting the wild roses of her hair. Something caught in her throat, and then soft sobs started, came in earnest, wrenching through her body.

"I did this. I made him go through this. Everything at the jail got in the way. I should have made sure...I should have brought him in sooner."

"Deena, it's okay. He's here now." He stroked her hair, loving its silk, loving the way she loved the cat so fiercely.

"Stop it. Go away." She pulled back, tried to pull free of him and he saw the vet raise her brows. Rich shook his head and the vet focused on Sly.

"This is hard. You need someone and I'm not going anywhere." Finally her weariness seemed to win. He eased her back against him, but she was still stiff in his arms.

"He's a good cat." It came out choked and simple, an attempt to explain the grief.

"I saw that. A good friend."

"Someone I can trust." That came out sharp and he knew the arrow was aimed at him. Somehow he'd damaged her trust. He couldn't think how, but now was not the time.

On the table, Sly rolled over, tried to get up, but the vet held him in place. Sly just chirruped and purred.

"You are a good little fellow, aren't you?" The vet asked, rubbing his belly. "Just a couple more minutes."

Sly seemed to accept her ministrations and if anything his purr grew until it filled the room. Deena turned in his arms to see, but didn't try to escape. He inhaled the scent of her hair, knowing he'd always be there for her, knew things had to work out between them, because this was meant to be. Why else would he have found her again?

Now. When they were both free.

Another five minutes and the vet removed the needle. Sly sat up, chirruped and pawed the air as if to demand acknowledgement that he'd done something momentous.

"Well look at that." A little amazement from the vet.

Rich released Deena and she went to her pet. Petted him and finally hefted him in a hug. "He seems better."

"He is. Fluids help."

"So is he okay to come home?"

"I think I should keep him here a while to run some tests. It'll help us figure out what the best course of treatment is. But Deena..." The vet laid her hand on Deena's arm. "He isn't cured. You need to understand he'll never be cured. The best you can do it help him survive as long as possible. It's going to be work."

Deena swallowed, the fine column of her neck working as she buried her face in Sly's fur. God, he wanted to hold her, take her pain for her, but he supposed it was something he'd have to get used to. Deena Hunter bore her own pain. He couldn't rescue all the time. He stayed back, though it was painfully hard.

"Will he be in pain? I don't want him to be in pain."

"No. Just as we discussed before. And the fluids help him feel better as you can see."

"Then I'll do whatever it takes."

They left Sly there for his tests and so the vet could monitor him for the day. Rich offered Deena a tissue from the vet's counter and she dabbed her eyes, looked up at him.

"I'm sorry. You're really getting to see me at my very best."

"You look good to me."

"Liar." She turned away, all her guards snapped into place again. Rich stepped back to give her space.

"Just take me home."

At the SUV he didn't help her inside because he knew this was all something Deena had to do herself.

The drive home was silent—strange after the raucous noise of the trip the other way. It was like a reminder of the absence she must be feeling. Of what she was afraid of.

At the house he was around the truck to help her, because he could see her fatigue and it worried him. He wanted to hold her, to carry her up the stairs, but this wasn't Ivy. This was a woman intent on caring for herself. Deena wouldn't collapse until the world itself took her down. He wanted to make sure that didn't happen.

He offered her his arm and her hard, calculating look was the one he remembered her using on suspects who lied. She limped past him, around the toys littering the yard and to the stairs. She white knuckled the railing and started up with him at her heels, so when she had to stop, he was there.

"Here." He offered her his arm again. "Nothing more than a hand, I promise."

Her baleful look was enough rebuke. "You lied before."

"And look what it got you: a hug when you needed it."

Grimacing she accepted his arm and they made it to her door together. She unlocked it and stepped inside, then turned and gave him a bleak look.

"Thank you. It helped to have you there. I appreciate it, though it shouldn't give you any ideas."

She was shutting him out, damn it. Shutting him out and there was no way in hell he was going to accept that.

"Deena, you haven't told me what's caused this. It's like suddenly there's more than geography separating us."

She was shaking her head even before he finished and that just plain pissed him off because she wasn't listening.

"Damn it, talk to me!" He reached for her, but she stepped back and her gaze met his and a world of hurt came through as she swung the door almost closed until only her pale face peered out at him.

"I would have once, but I've learned a lot of lessons in this life. One of them is about the price you pay when you do something stupid. I'm not getting involved with a married man again."

The door clicked shut before he could protest. He stood stunned, wanting to pound on the door, wanting to yell she was wrong, wanting to break down the door to tell her. He ground his teeth in frustration because this wasn't the time. She was too hurt and too torn up with other things.

And—at least technically—she was right.

Chapter 43

CLOSING THAT DOOR ON RICH had been almost as bad as taking Sly into that room, and the emotional roller coaster left her weak and almost unable to move. She stood there in the suddenly venomous light and considered sliding down the wall to the shag carpeted floor and just crying. But that was the coward, the weakling's way out.

Well she wouldn't do that. She had other things to fill her life than a man.

Like getting her cat home. Taking care of Sly was a whole lot more important than grieving the loss of Rich Webster. Sly had been part of her life for a whole lot longer.

Leaning her shoulder on the wall for balance and to protect her injured side, she went out to the verandah where the kitchen table still waited in pieces. In the street, the black SUV still waited so Rich hadn't quite left yet. In the distance, clouds masked the bulk of Mount Baker this morning. Just as well, given her bad dreams last night.

Overhead the sky was bluing and the river ran like a thick blue vein down the broad valley. The air smelled like leaf fall and burning and the last hay cut of the season and a haze hung low over the water. The farmers on Sumas Prairie would be out early in case the clouds to the south presaged rain.

She ignored the black vehicle and the ache in her body, and ran her fingers over the wounds in the table. Well, she could get started with sanding this morning and let her mind work over the case at the Hat. At least her memory had returned since yesterday—a bit patchy, but there.

At least she'd warned Anita. There was still Heywood to talk to and she would do that today. And there was Henry, and she needed to review the video tapes and computer logs from the Center. Maybe, if she kept moving, her body would loosen a little.

She limped into the kitchen to retrieve the sandpaper she'd bought, and almost jumped when she thought she saw a little black shape out of the corner of her eye. Of course there was nothing there, but the thought of how close she'd come to losing him brought a fresh stab of grief.

The tears started to flow again, leaving her weak and leaning against the counter. His bowls were there, and she grabbed them, slopped water over the floor in the process and that just sent her to pieces, so she slid down the cupboard to sit crying.

Stupid. Stupid. Stupid. He wasn't dead. She'd keep him alive for a lot longer. But the thought of losing him hurt so much even if he was only a cat. As if Sly could ever be *only*. But if Sly's loss hurt this much, then she didn't want to take a chance with anything or anyone else. She was better off alone. Even Suz and Lana were dangerous.

A knock came at the door and that forced her to her feet. Open it when she was such a wreck? It might be Rich and she didn't know if she was strong enough to send him away again. She scrubbed her cheeks free of tears and unlatched the door.

Thankfully, not Rich.

Anita Underhill stood there looking a tad rumpled and a whole lot afraid, judging by the way she kept checking the street over her shoulder.

"Dee! Thank god!" Another check over the shoulder. "Can I come in? You said I should come to you here, right?"

Deena remembered herself and after sweeping the street once herself—thankfully the black SUV was finally gone—she stepped back.

In the center of the living room, Anita turned to her. "I'm so sorry about what happened. I got there as fast as I could. Are you alright? You look like you've been crying."

Deena choked back a laugh. "You can tell through all the bruising? Sorry. I was just feeling sorry for myself. My cat's sick." She tried to say it matter-of-factly, but ended up hating the way her voice got thick with emotion.

"Aww, Dee. I'm sorry. Not that on top of everything else." Anita looked like she was considering a hug, but sympathy would only make the whole thing worse.

"So, what can I do for you? Do you want a cup of coffee? Tea?"

"Tea, please. I think I rotted my gut with coffee last night."

Deena left her to put the kettle on, heard Anita shifting around the room. Probably looking at the collection of books on the shelves, the photos on the walls. There was one of Deena at her graduation from police training and one of Anita and Deena when Anita was a kid. There was also one of her and her first training officer in Morinville—one she was probably going to take down, now.

"So was that the cop investigating the Stickley murder?"

The question almost made Deena drop the kettle. Had she seen the photos?

"I thought I saw him sitting in a big black SUV out front. He was talking on his cell, but he drove off so I didn't get a good look." Anita came into the kitchen.

Not the photo, then; but Deena really did need to take it down. Hands shaking, she shifted the full kettle to the stove, then leaned on the counter.

"Yeah. Him."

"So he's still investigating, right?" Deena looked up at the urgency in Anita's voice.

"We both are." Deena fished the teapot out of the cupboard and placed some cranberry herbal tea bags in it.
She saw the little lift of Anita's brows. "You look surprised."

"It's just—well you got pretty banged up. I thought maybe you'd back off."

Deena looked sideways at her, caught the slow bloom of a smile.

"I know. I should have known better. This is Deena Hunter we're talking about."

"Damn straight." Deena hauled herself upright against the pain. The kid was right. Deena had a reputation to uphold. It was a point of honor that she wouldn't let things like a stupid beating, stop her. "It's a hold-over from my RCMP days. Always get your man."

She ignored the potential double meaning, poured boiling water over tea bags in the teapot, then poured two cups and led Anita back into the living room because all the aches and pains said Deena had pushed things today and the day was young yet.

"So what did you want to talk to me about?" She settled in the chair and appreciated just how good it felt to simply not move.

Anita's chewed lip said something hard was coming out.

"I guess I should start by apologizing because everything you've said and done has been for my own good and I was just too thick to see." Anita's gaze flicked towards Deena's, held for a moment and fled. Still not everything.

"There's nothing to apologize for. I asked you to do something that could put you in danger. I shouldn't have done that."

Anita stood and started pacing as if trying to build up momentum to get out what she wanted to say. It left Deena tense and expecting the worst, even though she didn't know what the worst was.

"That's not what I'm talking about, and I wish you'd quit trying to be gracious." Anita turned, her face stark.

"You need to know, Dee. I'm the one that set you up for your beating."

Chapter 44

THE STORY CAME OUT IN A RUSH, like pus from a boil. That was the only way Anita could get it out even though she felt like she was going to be sick every time she glanced at Dee's face and saw the look of shock and revulsion.

Dee would hate her after this and Anita deserved that hate. If only there was some way she could make it up to this woman who had once meant the world to her. Keeping Dee in her life was more important than ever.

Anita told about how she'd felt when she started at the Hat, how she'd wanted to fit in, how she'd been angry when Dee rode her, and how Chad and the others had accepted her, had even seemed to encourage her to let things slide a little, and how things had progressed far out of her control. And how she'd betrayed Dee by telling about the Internal Security Initiative."

Then she collapsed back on the couch awaiting the full brunt of Dee's hate.

"I'm sorry. I was mad at you. You were after me to do a good job, to do my job the way it was supposed to be done, and all I thought was you were being a bitch. I'm not trying to cast blame, but I think they fed that feeling — Chad and the others. The fact remains, I was still willing to eat it up."

Dee sat there looking brave and beaten and didn't say a word. That was the worst thing of all. The guilt was a leaden weight on Anita' shoulders.

"It shouldn't have happened. I should have known better, but I was a fool."

Dee sat as inanimate as a statue, then drew in a long audible breath and moved onto the couch beside Anita. The compassion in Dee's face wasn't expected.

"You were new. You hadn't worked in a place like the Hat before. You wanted to fit in and got overwhelmed by all of it. You weren't a fool."

"Don't make excuses for me. I don't deserve it."

"And that sounds like martyrdom." That brought Anita's gaze up to Dee's, but she was smiling as she shook her head. "I told you. We all make mistakes. We need to learn from them and move on and not repeat them. We can't undo them – so what other choice do we have? Going through life with regret is no way to live."

For a moment Dee looked shaken and lost in thought. Then she focused on Anita.

"There's more, isn't there."

God she was an admirable woman. Even sitting there all bruised and battered-looking, there was an authority, an integrity and a force of intelligence and will that Anita could only hope to develop. She nodded.

"Yesterday—after—I was pretty shaken up."

Dee's gaze narrowed. "You were there. You—you found me."

That was a relief. "You were so out of it when I did. Unconscious, and then you didn't seem to recognize anything. I thought-" Darn it, she wasn't going to choke up here. She was going to do this like a professional and take her lead from Dee. "- well I thought you might be dead at first. Then I thought you might be brain injured."

"I'm not." Dee caught Anita's hand. "Thanks for responding. I get the feeling they might have left me there, otherwise." Dee's voice and her hand were both warm and dry, and there was grimness in her gaze. "No backup. Typical."

"You don't know the half of it, Dee. When Control put out the call that there was an officer down, no one answered. Absolutely no one— until I did. I got there and I saw you, but I also saw the men who did it." Anita squeezed Dee's fingers because this was the hard part. Well, the start of it.

"They were dressed in prison coveralls, but they weren't inmates. I saw their faces and I didn't know them, but it was their shoes that really gave them away."

She told, and saw Dee's gaze widen. It widened further when she told about Chad's phone call, even though it was hard to meet Dee's eyes.

"So he dropped me off and I followed him."

"You what?" Anita had to pull her hand back to stop Dee from hurting her, Dee was that upset. "Are you nuts? They could have killed you."

"I sort of thought of that after I was committed to action. But I had to know what was going on. Heck, Dee, I had to do something to redeem myself. You would have."

Dee sank back against the couch and closed her eyes. When she opened them she shook her head.

"I was one hell of a bad influence on you."

"No. Well, maybe an influence—but not bad. Never bad." She had to get Dee to see. "You were beaten and maybe dying, and I wasn't going to let whoever did it get away with it. If it had been me beaten, you would have followed Chad, too."

Dee still shook her head. "Hell of a bad influence. Whatever made me think I could influence a young girl for the better?"

Anita stood, hands on hips because Dee's doubts were about the last thing she wanted to hear.

"Would you stop? You were a great Big Sister. You gave me backbone and taught me women could do anything. That was a good thing. Between you and my Dad, you gave me a lot of good stuff—stuff I still use now. Stuff that helped me to realize—like you did—that I was selling myself out. So I followed Randy Johal and Chad to a place down by the border. There were other guys there, too, that I didn't know, but they had that look of Corrections about them—the short hair and so on. I managed to get a look in the barn and they were digging something. I didn't get a chance to see more because they saw me. I shot out of there like a bat outta hell, but I was afraid to go home."

"So you spent last night where? A friend's? Some diner?" Concern in Dee's voice.

"Denny's in Coquitlam. I figured that was far enough away."

Dee collapsed back into the couch again, concern and relief battling on her face. "My God you took a risk."

She was shaking her head like a parent whose kid had done something perilously stupid, and that pissed Anita off. She wasn't a kid anymore. She was a woman as capable as Dee and right now she was a heck of a lot more physically able. She plunked back down on the couch.

"So I came to tell you and to ask what I need to do next."

"Go home. Tell your Dad and stay inside. You were worried they were watching for you here, weren't you?" Anita hesitated. "I saw you checking when you arrived. Seeing the black SUV must have freaked you out."

"I nearly drove by." It left her a little ashamed.

"But you didn't. You took a chance to come in." Dee stood, putting her hands on her hips, looking battered and proud like a warrior queen. "I hope you know you're one hell of a woman, Anita Underhill."

It was more than Anita had hoped for, more than she deserved. All she could do was blush a little and look away. "I don't want to go home yet. There's still stuff to be done."

"You're right. But you've done you're part. The rest is up to me." Dee paced the floor, her limp fading as if she forced the pain away. It didn't quite work and that had Anita up and to her side.

"No way. You're hurt." She tried to catch Dee's hands, to make her admit it, but Dee was already at the closet, grabbing a jacket.

"If you want to help, you'll stay here and be safe. Otherwise I'll worry about you. I'm going to the Hat. Knowing Ravi, he'll be there. I'll let him know what's happening and I'll interview Henry. That should get enough evidence so management can decide whether to call in the police."

"But I want to help." Dammit, Dee wasn't listening any better than she had in the past. She was still treating Anita like a kid.

Dee stopped at the apartment door. Turned back. "You want to help?"

Anita nodded. "Anything."

Dee lifted her chin towards the verandah and grinned evilly.

"There's a table out there that needs sanding. See what you can do."

Chapter 45

THE CLOUDS OVER THE MOUNTAINS looked heavy with rain, the air at the Hat filled with fine mist and the scent of old leaves. It was going to be an early fall. During the bad rains, the parking lot ran like a river. Right now it was mostly empty, just staff and Ravi's lone midnight-blue BMW in the management parking area.

Deena groaned and glanced at herself in the rearview mirror. A bigger groan.

She looked like hell. Not just the bruises, but she had no makeup on and her hair was loose and tangled around her shoulders. Her t-shirt and faded jeans were the most worn, but most comfortable clothing she owned. Not too authoritative. Her reputation would just have to do.

She had fought back the pain and double-vision to make it down the stairs at home with only one slight stumble. It was easier when all she was carrying was grief—for Sly, for the Hat, for something crushed before it could become a relationship. But this was how you dealt with painful emotions—you threw yourself into work-mode and got busy.

It had worked for her before. Had even advanced her career. So what if it left pain unresolved. So what if she was alone.

Deena Hunter was a career peace officer. They'd put it on her gravestone someday.

If there was anyone who cared enough to put up a gravestone.

She pushed away the pain and the grim thoughts. A practical part of her said to call Rich Webster for help, but Rich was the enemy right now. Maybe not THE enemy, but definitely not someone she wanted to deal with.

Besides, she was just going to talk to a couple of people in the Hat and then the police could take over. She wasn't a cowboy. She knew the limits of her mandate. She wasn't a police officer anymore.

It took everything she had to stride tall and straight, through the Hat's door when her muscles screamed and her cracked ribs made it hard to breathe. The antiseptic smell of recycled air made her throat tighten. Her body remembered where she'd been injured.

She nodded at the weekend receptionist, ignored the quickly hidden shock at Deena's visible injuries, and went to the door into the Center.

It took a moment, but the familiar buzz unlocked the door. She imagined the radio traffic was off the charts with news of her presence. Vanier would not be pleased.

Well, Vanier could go to hell, because Deena Hunter was back in business and it would take a lot more than Vanier and his thugs to put her down.

She didn't bother knocking on the ADW door, just entered and found him waiting. He winced when he saw her.

"This is probably the stupidest thing I've seen you do, Hunter." He leaned back in his chair, arms crossed and looking so bloody pompous she could strangle him with his puny, clip-on tie.

"And I'd say the stupidest thing you've done was arranging to have me beaten on your watch."

She sat down on the edge of the desk, winced a little, and knew he saw it. A smirk found his lips.

"Not quite right as rain, I see."

"You see nothing. You and your pals and your little venture down by the border. I'm taking you down, Vanier. It's a *fait accompli*." Damn him, he was dragging the Center down with him, telling his staff to set her up.

That got his attention, the jovial gloating melting away. The chair groaned as he shifted position. Good. She wanted him unbalanced, because that probably meant it would unbalance the whole shift.

"You think that's going to end your problems? If you do, you're stupider than I thought." He leaned forward to resume reading, but she caught his wrist. Let him know she had him. She wasn't going to let a ringleader off easy.

"From where I'm sitting, I don't have any problems. Unless maybe it's getting your staff off their asses to bring Inmate Henry down here. You think you can do that for me? Get Henry down here? Still healthy?" She smiled sweetly, while her fingers drilled into his flesh. Her side screamed at the effort.

He twisted his arm free.

"Actually, there is a bit of a problem. Inmate Henry isn't here. Seems last night he got into a fight with another inmate. The other inmate had a shiv. They took Henry to the hospital and were trying to get the shiv out of his gut. Last I heard he was touch and go."

The coldness of his tone told the tale. Another set-up. Another thing she couldn't prove.

"Just like Stickley. Only this time you got an inmate to help. Or were these 'inmates' like the kind who beat me?"

She watched his eyes, saw the flicker confirming Anita's story. On a hunch she said: "Bringing in outside help, now."

A little shock in the eyes this time.

Vanier wasn't a good liar, at least not as good as the cons. So whatever was going on was wider than the Hat and that brought a little shiver to her. She didn't like that her organization was seriously compromised.

She eased herself off the desk and stood. "Guess that leaves you off the hook. I'll pay Henry a visit at the hospital."

She left him without a word, knowing he was probably already on the telephone as she marched out to administration. She might not have all the details, but she had enough to get Ravi doing something.

The administration area was dead; to be expected on a Sunday. The light from Ravi's office flooded out through is door, illuminating the corner of the larger room. She circled through the cubicles, already smelling Ravi's florid aftershave, and paused just outside of the spill of light.

For all his faults, Ravi Sandhar was a committed officer. He was pouring over the quarterly budget printouts, making notations in the columns that she knew would lead to concise variance reports. During their six-month affair he'd often finished his work at the little apartment where they met.

When she cleared her throat he startled, then smiled as he recognized her.

The smile faded when she stepped into the light.

"My God, Deena." He was up and around his desk faster than she would have expected. She didn't want or need his help, but he grabbed her arm, eased her into a chair as if she was a broken thing.

"Your face. Oh, God, your beautiful face."

For a moment she almost appreciated that he'd thought she was beautiful. But that didn't excuse his dishonesty to her or to his wife. Not cool at all, despite him making her feel like a desirable woman after Blake had left her certain she wasn't worthy of any man.

"I'm fine, Ravi."

She held up her hand to stop his gush of sympathy, his assurances they'd find the perpetrator.

"I already know who did it and that's why I'm here. I'm way over my head and I want to hand things off. To you."

That stopped him because they both knew Deena Hunter never backed down. Slowly, he nodded.

"So fill me in."

She did. Everything from Anita Underhill's observation of the faux inmates' shoes, to the place along the border, to the police suspicion that South Asian gangs were making inroads into the Center.

"They don't have to be South Asian to be working with them," she ended. "It could be anyone on staff."

"But more likely South Asians. Like me," he said. "Why are you trusting me?"

In truth she didn't know why. Rich had thrown the veil of suspicion over Ravi, but she couldn't believe he'd do it.

"Because I think you have something to prove. You want to succeed too badly. You might not have the ethics I think you should have, but you want to get ahead more or less the right way." It was the best she could do and it wasn't exactly a glowing endorsement.

"Guess that's all I deserve." But he didn't like it.

"Guess it is." She stood.

"So I'm going to go talk to Henry and hopefully he can fill me in, but I think you need to get in touch with the big boss and decide the best way to deal, because there's a serious house-cleaning needed."

"I'll try." His voice was soft.

"You better do better than that." Hers was hard as nails.

Ravi gave her a smile that would have melted butter and a few lesser women.

"I remember you saying that to me before."

It no longer worked on her. She turned and left the office and the letch she worked for. Limping, she headed for her car.

There was Henry. There was getting the information back to Ravi, and then she could rest.

She just hoped she could keep going that long.

Chapter 46

RICH STOPPED IN AT THE OFFICE because he couldn't bring himself to face the depressing space he called his home. He needed to strategize the best way to deal with Deena and her belief that he was married. His best thinking went on in his office or staring out over the river.

Either way, he was standing there, staring at the cloud-shrouded mountain and letting his mind range the gamut of options, which weren't quite as many as he'd have liked.

"Penny." Chuck's familiar voice came from behind him.

"Just stuff. Deena. The case. I don't think she's involved with Sandhar anymore."

"What gives you that idea?" Chuck moved up beside him, joined him watching a fishing boat trawl vainly up the river after salmon that had simply failed to appear. The put-put-put of the boat's engine seemed to echo all Rich's hopelessness.

"Because she turfed me out because I'm still married. Didn't even give me a chance to explain."

"You mean you hadn't already?"

Rich turned and met Chuck's gaze. He shook his head.

"Why me, lord? Why are you visiting me with a man who seems destined to make bad decisions about women?"

"Hey! I'm standing right here! My decisions haven't been bad; I just didn't have the opportunity to bring up the fact Ivy and I never bothered getting divorced."

"You found time to sleep with her."

The way Chuck continued to shake his head it was pretty clear just what a sorry piece of manhood he thought Rich was.

"You even found time to fix her kitchen cupboards. But you didn't have the time to tell her about the sorry son-of-a-bitch you've been while you waited for her to come rescue you?"

The last was just a little too close to the bone. "I don't have to take this."

"Truth hurts, doesn't it?"

Chuck tossed it over his shoulder as Rich crossed the parking lot, because if he stayed he might just clean Chuck Kozloff's clock.

Chuck wasn't right. He couldn't be right. Rich hadn't been waiting around for Deena Hunter. He'd dated. He'd had women in his bed. He'd had plenty of women in his life—all while he was taking care of Ivy.

It meant nothing that he'd finally laid down the law and asked Ivy for the divorce only after he'd found Deena again. He slowed.

Or else he might have to admit Chuck was right.

He turned around to apologize and found Chuck was right there a knowing look on his face, not waiting at the edge of the parking lot. He motioned to their offices.

"Your life is your problem, but if you ask me, you should have that talk with her and come clean. But that's not why I came down here. I tried calling and your cell phone was off, so I took a chance you'd be here. I got news."

Rich followed the older man inside. In their office, Chuck closed the door.

"When was the last time you saw Deena?"

Rich shook his head. "Early this morning. I thought we were finished with that topic."

"We are and we aren't." Chuck settled himself in his chair, leaned back and put his feet up while he waited for Rich to take a seat. "Reason I ask is that there's news from the undercover cop in the Independent Army. Seems something's happened out this way. He's not sure what, but it has people worried. Something about supply lines and weapons. You got anything from the lovely ADW Hunter that might fill in the blanks?"

The information brought a chill to Rich.

"She got ambushed in the jail yesterday. They hurt her pretty bad. Somebody's gunning for her and they put her in the hospital. It tells me she's on to something solid—and that she's not involved."

"Spoken like a man in love."

"Go fuck yourself."

"Let me rephrase. Spoken like a stupid man in love."

Meeting Chuck's gaze, Rich couldn't help the slow smile that formed first of all in his chest.

"So I might love her. Fat lot of good it's doing."

"Again, not my problem, but you'd better let her know something big is coming down and to lay low for a while."

That brought a sick laugh from Rich.

"Like she'll listen to me? Hell, she's not even talking to me."

But he was already moving toward the office door because he knew Chuck was right. If something big was coming down there was too good a chance Deena'd be in the thick of it. He stopped at the office door.

"Thanks. You and Greta are lifesavers."

"Just sort things out with Deena and make us both happy grandparents, will you?" He waved Rich out the door.

By the time he reached the parking lot, Rich was almost running because something in his gut told him whatever it was, it was coming down now.

Chapter 47

EVEN STANDING IN THE CALMING apartment that was Dee's private refuge Anita couldn't get rid of the tension she felt. She shouldn't have let Dee go off alone. She *should* have driven Dee wherever she thought she needed to go. She paced the green carpet, doddled over the table Dee had asked her to sand and had finally found herself here at the window, staring past the spider plants and philodendron at the cool bulk of the distant mountain. She suspected there was trouble as soon as she saw the van. It was a windowless, blue panel van with a high-gloss paint job and tinted side windows so you couldn't see the driver unless you were in front of him. John Jeffries and Janet Lefevre climbed out.

Here to pay their respects, maybe. John, she knew, was an old friend of Deena's.

They'd have heard Deena was beaten. But the way the buxom, redheaded control officer swaggered up the driveway it left Anita feeling that something bad was coming down.

She'd been half-heartedly sanding Deena's kitchen table for lack of something better to do, but ducked inside and went to the door leading out to Dee's stairs. No sound there, but through the floor came the sound of voices. A child shrieked—Anita had spoken to the little girl last time she'd dropped by—a mother yelled. A crash had Anita half out the door before the downstairs front door slammed shut. The angry voices froze her and by the time she'd decided to find out what was going on, the van pulled away.

Forgetting Dee's instructions, she was down the stairs in a flash. Please don't let what she suspected be true. Please not that.

She banged on the front door, but no one answered. When she tried the doorknob, it turned. She pushed inside into the scent of something baking.

"Hello? Anyone here? I'm a friend of Dee's. I saw those people and wanted to make sure you're alright."

Only silence.

She left the door open in case she needed to make a run for it and entered the living room. Toys covered the floor like a disaster had struck, but that could be normal.

Then she saw the fallen cup of tea and that wasn't so normal.

An insistent dinging almost made her leapt out of her skin. She followed it into the kitchen and it was only the stove timer. She checked the oven.

Cupcakes left unattended. Definitely not so normal.

She'd grabbed a tea-towel and was just hauling them out of the oven when a man's shadowed form filled the doorway. She nearly threw the cupcake pan before she recognized him.

"You're the cop investigating the inmate death, right? You interviewed me. Corporal Webster?" He frowned, then his face smoothed into that emotionless look that all cops have.

"Where is she?"

"Deena? She went up to the Hat."

"I just called there and they tell me she left a half hour ago."

Anita's legs went a little mushy. If something had happened to Dee...She hauled out a chair and sat down.

"It doesn't take a half an hour to get to Mission from the Hat."

"Don't I know it." He looked around the room, looked at her as if seeing her for the first time. "Underhill, right?"

Anita nodded. "I—I think there's a problem. A couple of staff from the Hat came here. I think they took the little girl and her mother who live here. I don't think they went by choice."

The news seemed to take him back a bit.

"You sure?"

"I was upstairs. I saw. The people arrived and I heard what sounded like a fight. Did you see the..."

"The tea cup? I saw."

His gaze went distant a moment, then he was headed to the door. Anita dumped the tea towel and ran after him.

"If this is tied up in Deena's investigation, I think I know where they've taken them. And I know who took them, too."

He gave a nod and she had to run to keep up as he strode out to his black SUV. Overhead the day dimmed toward the twilight and gilded the edges of rain-heavy clouds that were always more common with the fall. He was already hauling out his cell phone.

"Chuck? It's coming down. They just grabbed Deena's best friend and her daughter. I'm thinking they're trying to shut her down. Now I'm putting someone on with a description of the suspect vehicle."

He almost threw the phone at her as he cranked the ignition.

"Where?" His voice was a dangerous growl and Anita was glad he was on her side because the look in his eyes said he was ready to kill.

"Zero Avenue." She said, naming the location ten miles away as a flash of sunlight through the clouds almost blinded her.

Then she focused on the phone and went through her description.

Chapter 48

MSA HOSPITAL WAS A HOPELESSLY small, hopelessly outdated, small town hospital that was trying valiantly to cope with the massive population growth that had occurred in Abbotsford. Its faded pink, circular, eight-story tower protruded out of the middle of a parking lot that sat in the middle of a working class neighborhood so the hospital looked like nothing so much as disembodied penis. The Provincial Government was building a new hospital, which meant that absolutely no new money was going into MSA. So MSA got dowdier and more run-down. A dick down on its luck.

Deena snorted—and regretted it—as she climbed out of her car and into a momentary rain shower that pelted the parking lot. Fighting pain, she steadied herself against the car. The rain was just preparatory to the usual fall and winter deluge. The pain and fatigue however, were taking their toll, and the fact everything inside was vibrating with loss didn't help either.

But she hadn't lost Sly yet, so what was she grieving?

Set it aside. She marched into the hospital or convinced herself she did. It was actually more of a stumble and limp, but she got Henry's room number, then rode the frustratingly slow elevator the four floors up. It was easy to spot Henry's room, because a correctional officer cooled his heels at the door. Beckett or something was his name—one of the on-call staff like Anita, which meant he might be less of a problem.

She nodded, asked him how he was doing and then entered.

Jim Henry's bulk seemed diminished in the hospital bed. The man was as pale as the sheets he lay in and the sickening smell of feces hung around him—the product, she suspected—of being gut-stabbed. Chance of peritonitis and all that good stuff.

He turned a weary eye to her and that same sardonic grin she remembered from her office flashed across his face.

"Come to finish the job?"

"My interview? Hell, yes. You never did tell me what I wanted to know. I thought you might be more forthcoming now."

A slight chuckle and he winced.

"Hurts some does it."

"Only when I breathe, which pretty much means all the time." He studied her. "Looks like you got a little tuning yourself. And now you want me to take a bigger risk?"

She hitched over a chair and sort of collapsed in it trying to hide the pain

"I need to know what happened the morning Stickley died. It doesn't matter what you've told me—they know you saw something so they're gunning for you. If you help, I might be able to get you some place safe."

Again that chuckle. He closed his eyes against what must have been searing pain because his pale face blanched even further. When he opened his eyes, they held on her, calculating.

"I want out of the Hat. As a matter of fact I want out of any B.C. Corrections jail."

That was a shocker.

"It's that bad? It's gone that far?"

"Hell if I know, but I'm not taking chances. I want out. I want to do my time and live to tell about it. I got a wife, you know. And kids."

"That'll take some arranging. I'll see what I can do. That's all I can promise."

She held his gaze. There was a time not too long ago she was known as a solid officer. Inmates and staff alike had trusted her. Or so she'd thought. But it was the only tender she had to trade right now.

Henry closed his eyes and nodded.

"There were two of them that morning. They came in together. I'm not sure who the first man was—the leader—but he was older. The other one was Amarjit Sandhu. I heard the door to Stickley's cell get cracked and the two of them went in. There was a struggle and I heard Stickley pounding the wall. Then the guy I didn't know came out and went downstairs. Sandhu radio'd in for backup and I heard Preston come in. That must have been how the other guy left. The rest you know."

Deena leaned forward and caught Henry's hand. "You'd testify to that?"

He nodded, pain gripping his face.

"Could you identify the other man if you saw him?"

"Maybe. Listen, I really need sleep."

She stood and thanked him.

"I'll do my best to get you out of the Hat."

"Knew you would." His eyes closed and she wished for a moment she could get herself out of the Hat as well.

"Deena Hunter please report to the nearest nursing station."

The page came just as she was heading out of the room. She stopped, wondering who could be calling. Ravi? Vanier?

They were the only ones who knew she was heading here. A trickle of cold ran into her gut as she headed for the nurse's station. She had to go back to the Hat and view the Center videotapes, because they might show the unknown officer.

She introduced herself at the nursing station and was provided with a phone. The hospital operator gave her a number and advised that the matter was urgent.

Deena hung up, the trickle of cold increasing. The number was none she knew. She went down to her car, a bank of black clouds swallowing the last of the day's sunshine as she collapsed in the driver's seat and hauled out the cell she never kept turned on. A whole lotta messages left on voice mail by the look of it, but they would have to wait.

She keyed in the number and watched the rain drops splatter themselves against her windshield.

"Hunter?" Man's voice, muffled but familiar. She couldn't place it based on just one word.

"This is Hunter. I was paged at MSA hospital."

The phone went silent and then there was a childish squeal of pain and a voice she knew too well came on. "Aunty Dee? Aunty Dee? They hurt Mommy, Aunty Dee!"

"Lana? Who hurt Mommy? Where are you honey?" Outside the rain began to drum the roof, the inside of the car suddenly frigid.

Another little squeal.

"Lana!"

"Aunty Dee!" Lana's voice faded as the phone was pulled away from her. Male and female voices in the background, and then:

"You want to hear that voice again, you'll follow these instructions."

Icicles in her blood at the different voice, one she wasn't sure of at all, but that was loud and clear above the rain's drumming.

"I'm not following any instructions until I talk to Suz – Lana's mother."

"I'm afraid Ms. Miller is a little under the weather right now. Here are your directions. Whether you follow them will determine if Ms. Miller's situation improves."

She listened to the chill precision of the instruction. No phone calls. They had someone watching her. Follow directions and the admonition to come alone and leave the police out of it.

She had twenty minutes to do as she was told or the deal was off.

The line went dead, the buzz drilling into her head. Lana and Suz. Lana and Suz.

They were the most valuable things in her life and she was on the verge of losing them, too.

Chapter 49

LANA AND SUZ'S LIVES DEPENDED on doing what she was told.

The parking lot reflected the hard metal light of the clouds, but the lot and the road beyond boiled with raindrops. Vehicles on the street raised huge sheets of water. She started the Camry's engine, gunned it across the soaked parking lot, and careened onto the street, headed south. Where she was going wasn't all that distant, but the traffic was heavy at this time of day. In the rain it would take her the full twenty minutes to get there.

She eyed the cell phone, tempted to call Rich, but if someone was following her, they'd see her make the call. Better not to.

McCallum Road was slippery with water as she roared over the highway overpass and headed south for the border. She got stopped at King Road by heavy traffic from the University-College and swore at an old woman who hesitated too long to turn.

The rain drummed on her roof. Her clothes steamed in the heat she'd cranked up, but she couldn't get warm. Time was wasting. If she didn't get there in time who knew what would happen to Suz.

To Lana. She fought to control the helpless hysterics she felt.

If they did *anything* to Lana there'd be hell to pay, and Deena Hunter was the one who'd be taking the payment.

The road ran straight and steeply downhill towards the border. She reached Zero Avenue with only a few minutes to spare, roared down the road until she spotted the blue house and barn, just as she'd been instructed. Just as Anita had described.

At least Anita was out there. She might even be able to tell the tale if something happened to Deena and the others.

Grimly, she wheeled the Camry onto the pot-holed driveway. Winced as the car bumped along.

Nothing was going to happen to anyone. She was going to make sure of it, even if she no longer had a service revolver at her side.

She pulled in front of the barn as the clouds opened. Typical, west-coast rain pummeled her car and the two pickups that were on either side. Huge puddles leapt and jumped under the barrage of drops.

She climbed out, ignored the pain, and stared at the barn. Randy Johal came to the door.

"Get your ass in here."

She got.

"And I thought you were a good officer," she said as she passed him, edging around a pickup backed into the barn. Its bed was filled with mud-scented earth. "Shows what I know."

"Shows how little you know, you mean." A voice she recognized, but all her attention was on a woman with red hair slumped in a dark corner and the little girl crouched sobbing, beside her.

"Lana, honey!" Deena was across the room in a few quick strides and down on her knees to catch Lana's hug. Her mass of curls fell around wide, terrified eyes and the ammonia scent of fear overwhelmed her little girl scent.

"Aunty Dee. Aunty Dee. I want Mommy better. I want to go home."

"Your Mom's going to be just fine, baby." Deena kept one arm around Lana as she checked Suz over. She was breathing, but her pale face and the blood on her forehead spoke of a blow.

"What happened to her?"

"She fought. We hit her." That familiar voice again, but colder, and this time Deena looked up.

A flash of light through one of the high-set windows illuminated the shadows cast by the barn's lone light and caught the cherubic face of Mitchell Digneault, leaving Deena feeling like the thunder that followed was all in her head.

He wore a wind breaker and jeans over his round little body, but tucked into his waist was the handle of what looked like an old police special.

"Mitch?" She stood up, feeling the whole world was unsteady, but somehow holding Lana in her arms. "What's this all about?"

"Money. Power. Getting what you deserve. What else? Isn't it always about that?"

Deena shook her head.

"That's not computing for me, I'm afraid. You're a good officer. You run the jail. You earn a good wage. What the hell are you doing here? With this?" She scanned the barn interior, taking in what she hadn't before. Wooden scaffolding had been built around the lip of a large hole in the floor, debris from the structure piled along the walls. The hole had a sturdy frame built inside it—probably to stop earth from slipping back down. A tunnel. Had to be.

"I guess we know what she thinks of the rest of us. She always was kiss-ass for management."

Blake Roberts swaggering into the light, and the sight of her ex-husband just about made Deena's knees give. For all she'd loved him once, Blake was a hard man. An unforgiving one, she'd learned. One who had seriously tried to ruin her rep in Corrections after their split. If he was involved it meant there wasn't much mercy here.

She faced him, Lana clinging to her, the light glinting off his steel-grey hair. Once the hard lines of his body had made her think he was the sexiest man in Corrections. Now he just looked mean.

A swell of agreement came from others she'd trusted. Chad Preston. Amarjit Sandhu. Janet Lefevre. She turned back to Blake.

"I should have known. I guess I should have figured about you, too, Mitch, now that I think about it. You warned me off, didn't you? You told me not to investigate staff. It must have just about killed you to know I was going to be looking into things and you couldn't order me not to."

He shrugged. "It all comes out in the wash. With your disappearance there'll be no one to push this and no evidence. So I really will run the jail—not that idiot Sandhar. I already took care of the video tape. Seems someone went too close to it with a magnet. There's nothing to disagree with the amended computer printouts of staff's movements. We get rid of you and everything goes back to normal."

"Normal?" She made it a little bit of a question because she wanted confirmation of what was going on with a tunnel that looked large enough for a Shetland pony. "Oh my God. It *is* the Independence Army. They financed this. You've got a tunnel right under the noses of the Canadian and US border patrols. You're what? Trading drugs for weapons?"

"Well we do seem to have a lot of one and not much of the other, unlike our friends to the south."

The size of the operation left her almost speechless. She'd figured drugs in the jail. That was within her scope.

But this—they were involved in something so far beyond what she'd thought was going on there was no way they could let her or Suz or Lana live.

Adrenaline surged at the knowledge. It numbed the pain. She set Lana down, pushed her behind her, and Mitch's lips curved in a smile that left her stomach a solid mass of stone.

"That's not really going to help." He said softly. Then he turned to the others as if she was a problem no longer worth considering. "Let's get this finished, people. Get the cave-in cleared and we can use it to clear out the—debris."

He glanced in her direction and she thought of what she knew of the man. He had been passed over. It must have caused a bitterness she couldn't even fathom. He'd probably promoted her as a way to cover his tracks. After all, who would push for a cop to be in charge when they were working outside the law?

It made everything she'd believed about herself a sham. Even with the adrenaline, she sat down hard. God, she was cold—even in the warm, hay and manure-scented air.

"Is Mommy going to be alright?" Lana's little-girl warmth pressed into her.

"Let's see, shall we?" Deena turned to Suz, making a game of showing Lana how to check her breathing—thankfully steady. Her heart— slow but steady. Her pulse seemed a little thready, but then what did Deena know? She wasn't an EMT.

"We got company at the house," Johal said from his observation post by the door. The rest of the people went still. Buckets stopped brigading mud from the tunnel into the pickup. "Big SUV. Black. I've seen it before. The drunk's ex."

"The cop you mean."

That got Deena's attention.

A black SUV and a cop. They could only be describing Rich Webster and that meant if she could create a diversion—if she could somehow get Lana and Suz out of here—they might stand a chance.

Chapter 50

THE BLUE HOUSE LOOKED LONELY and run down in the rain. Beyond it, the fields were a mangy looking brown and the horse stood alone, head down in the sheeting downpour. He'd seen this place so many times, had spent so many hours lovingly building everything in the scene, from the white fences to the barn to the stone retaining wall that was a continuation of the stone-built fireplace inside. Yes, he knew the place like it was branded on his brain, but he felt like everything he knew had been seared right out of him when, at Anita's direction, he pulled up in front of Ivy's house. It just wasn't possible, and yet the presence of Deena's Camry by the barn was all the confirmation he needed. How many times had he been here?

Hell, he'd even been out by the barn the other day when he'd helped Majority Report. He'd been going to go into the barn to get tools to fix the water, but sheer laziness had stopped him. How long had this been going on right under his nose?

"Tell me again what you saw?" he said to the petite woman beside him. Underhill was small, yes. A neat little package of a thing, but with eyes that reminded him a lot of Deena, the way they were thoughtful and determined and the way she took care with what she said.

She told him, carefully describing the interior of the barn from what she remembered, but with his knowledge from having built the darn thing, it gave him a pretty good lay of the land.

"They're smuggling."

"What?"

"They've got a tunnel or are building one under the border. They caught one a year or so ago. This must have been their fallback position. Probably a pretty good one given the land is owned by a cop."

Anita only looked confused as he shook his head.

"You're wondering how I know. Simple. I own the place jointly with my ex-wife. She lives here. We've been split for about five years, but we just haven't done anything legal about it."

No matter how matter-of-factly he said it, he knew it just sounded lame. No wonder Chuck gave him a hard time. Deena probably wouldn't understand even if he explained, but that was the least of his worries at the moment. His first order of business was getting her and Suz and little Lana out of that barn alive.

"Come on. If we sit here too long they're going to figure there's a problem." He climbed out of the truck into the downpour and waited for Anita to follow him up to the house. They were both soaked by the time they stomped onto the porch.

He knocked once, then opened the door and walked in. "Ivy? You here?"

"Back here." It came from the kitchen, which was a good sign. Dripping, Rich led Anita back through the house, aware of the unkempt state of the place. But it wasn't quite as bad as the last time he was here.

In the kitchen he inhaled the sweet-steamy scent of peaches and sugar. Ivy turned from stirring a hug pot on the stove and smiled at him shyly. Then her gaze slid over to Anita and he could see her certainty flicker.

"I decided I was going to make peach jam. You remember how I used to love it." Forced smile. "Who's this?"

"Ivy, meet Anita Underhill. She works at a Correctional Center I'm investigating. She's helping me." Ivy's face cleared a little, but there was still suspicion.

"So why bring her here?"

Because the woman I love is caught in your barn. You remember — the officer I was training and couldn't quit talking about.

Rich stepped to the side of the window and peered out. With the rain and the falling darkness it was hard to see anything beyond light streaming from the barn's partially open door.

"Your barn seems to figure into the investigation." He turned back to her. "You told me you leased it. Who'd you lease it to?"

"It was just a man. He said he needed a barn to store stuff in." Ivy said it so simply that it almost left him breathless. It was that simple—rent a barn and do what they wanted.

"A lot of activity for just storage. How long have they been coming out to the barn?"

She looked outside into the rain and back at him. "I don't know. Is it important? Maybe, oh, eight months?"

Her dark eyes were almost the eyes of the woman he remembered marrying, but they no longer filled him with guilt.

"They could move a lot of dirt in that time," Anita broke in and Rich nodded.

"They could have had the tunnel finished and moved a lot of other things, too. I'll bet they've had a little cave in and that's where their trouble started. Stickley must have learned something about it and been going to tell Deena. She's been more than they could manage so they're going to do something about it." His chest tightened at the thought, at the need to just go, guns blazing to the rescue. "We need back up."

He saw Anita shiver, thought of what had happened to Deena.

"My kind of backup."

He flipped open his cell and dialed Chuck. When he picked up, Rich interrupted his hello.

"It's coming down tonight. We need back-up big time and you might want to get Canada and US border services in the loop. We've got a little underground cross-border shopping going on."

"Where're you at?"

Rich told and heard Chuck's low whistle.

"A little too close for comfort, I'm thinking."

"I'm standing here and you don't know the half of it. By my count there're at least four vehicles outside the barn and there might be one inside. If there're two people per vehicle you see what we've got. And three hostages – alive, I'm hoping—Deena being one of them."

He saw Anita twitch, felt Ivy's gaze lock on him. He had to treat this like a job, no matter what he felt.

"How fast can you get someone here?"

"You know as well as me Emergency Response takes time, but we'll be there. Hold tight. If your girl is anything close to the woman you've described, she'll keep them alive."

Chuck signed off and Rich snapped the phone closed and peered out to the night. Then he handed the cell to Anita.

"Stay here. If anyone calls, I've gone to scope out the barn. Tell them whatever they need to know." He headed for the door, then stopped. "And stay away from the windows. You hang around there and they'll know something's amiss."

Then he headed out the front door, slipped around the side of the house where the gathering darkness would screen his actions and the glint off his Beretta.

Chapter 51

THE COMFORTING RUSTLE OF THE hay was a weird counterpoint to the sounds of the shovels and the sharp-edged voices of the men and women around her. The rain pounded the metal roof like thunder and the air stank of mud and sweat and fear and little girl piss from Lana's accident. The little girl's whimpering set a fury in Deena's veins she hadn't known she had. This shouldn't be happening. Not to her little girl. Not to her friend.

Lana had been willing to play the doctor game to help her mother, but when Suz had finally come-to and immediately had fallen to pieces, it had left Deena with two to worry about, not one.

Still, Deena did the best she could to shield mother and child while keeping track of the hurried movements of the tunnelers. It was hard to hear what they said over the roar of the rain, but she knew Mitch and Blake discussed her by the way they glanced in her direction.

Not friendly. None of the others were either, though there were few that held a small margin of regret. Not enough to help, though.

It was up to her and that was the way it always was. Her problem. Her solution. That was the way things worked even if she wouldn't mind a little assistance.

If only there was a little diversion, something to take their captor's attention. Otherwise the adrenaline pinging through her was just going to waste while the pain and fatigue were seeping back. Her mouth tasted like copper.

Then Chad Preston came up from the tunnel, his face covered in mud, his half-naked body filthy as he climbed up to face Mitch Digneault by the tunnel edge.

"We've got it. The last of the mud is going out the other end and we've got the new shoring in place. Given the water pouring in right now, if it's holding through this, it should hold through pretty much anything." He glanced in her direction. "So?"

Mitch turned him away but she figured she knew what they were saying.

A murder conviction would rate a lot lower sentence in Canada than it would in the U.S. No capital punishment. They'd be better off doing the deed here. That meant she was running out of time.

A flash of lightening lit the barn as they rolled the doors. Janet Lafevre climbed behind the truck's wheel. The barn door would shut after the truck was out, probably permanently on the three of them. Deena eased back beside Suz and Lana.

"Do you think you can be very brave?"

Suz just looked at her, unspeakable fear in her eyes. Lana had that glazed look of a cornered animal.

"I'm not kidding. This might be your only chance. Understand?"

Suz nodded and Deena caught her hand and squeezed until Suz tried to pull loose. Okay. She was awake. Deena leaned in close. Behind there was swearing as one of the barn doors stuck.

"They're going to drive the truck out. To do that they're going to open the door wide. I'm going to cause a diversion and I want you and Lana to run for the door, understand?"

"But what about..."

"Shh!"

There was no time for debate. No time to think of another plan. It was two of them free or none of them. If it cost her, what did it matter? She had nothing much to lose. Not like Suz did.

"On my count of three."

Suz pulled her feet under her as door gave and the truck roared to life. Deena crouched, ready for action, as Suz pulled Lana into her, tickled her until the little girl seemed to wake up.

The barn door rolled and Deena started counting.
One.
The barn door opened to its widest.
Two.
The truck's engine dropped in gear and the vehicle started forward. The driver and the others in the barn would be blind in the night.

Three.

Deena catapulted herself at Mitch Digneault and his gun. Suz grabbed Lana and bolted for the door.

Deena was almost on him, when Chad Preston tackled her. She went down, scrambled up. His boot found her injured side. She felt a rib break, take her breath with it.

No time to feel pain.

She rolled, rolled again and saw Mitch going for the gun.

Thankfully the man was awkward, not trained like police in shoot-don't-shoot decisions and years away from any training in martial arts. She was up and leaping again even as Mitch finally got his gun free. Chad slammed into her once more, caught her t-shirt, tried to swing her around.

She drove the heel of her hand into his nose. Spun as he went down and found herself face to face with Digneault's gun.

She froze, but the yells behind her were all she needed to hear. At least now—this moment—Lana and Suz were free. If they could make the road someone would help them. For that it was all worth it.

"I think you better drop that gun." A soft voice and one that rippled right into her core.

"Rich?" He'd come for them. She spun—just in time to see Johal step out of a dark corner. Bring a two by four down on Rich's head.

He went down hard and Deena almost screamed. Instead she took the chance and leapt.

Slammed her hand inside Digneault's gun hand. Forcing him back. The weapon jerked sideways, going off as Digneault lost his balance and fell—straight into the tunnel opening. The explosion filled the barn worse than thunder. She dove for the gun, but Blake Roberts grabbed her first.

She grappled with him, but he was no soft Mitch Digneault. And size and bulk were on his side.

She tried to twist, to dance away, but her leg gave. She sprawled into the pile of implements where the gun had fallen.

She rolled. Found the gun just as Blake flattened her, grabbed her hand for the weapon. Slammed it into the ground. More pain. Broken knuckles.

She was almost spent. Her head buzzed. Adrenaline only worked so long. She could hardly breathe as his knee held down her gun hand and his hands closed around her throat.

No air. No life. It was like an equation. Dark-edged vision. Sounds telescoped weirdly.

And then suddenly Blake went flying and there was only Rich above her.

Rich caught in revolving red and blue light.

And then pain and darkness like the tunnel to fall into.

Chapter 52

FADE IN FROM DARKNESS TO DIM light through eyelids. She came-to the first time to the scent of antiseptic and the sound of whispers close by her side. They were little girl and big girl whispers and they reminded her of a time long ago when she had a Little Sister and was so sure of her own way in the world that she was confident sharing it with others. When she opened her eyes there were two red heads bent together over a bouquet of flowers.

She slept then, knowing they were safe.

When she came around the second time she wrinkled her nose at the antiseptic air, but found a man slumbered in a chair beside her, dark haired and face shadowed with beard. The man who had dwelt in her heart for far too many years. She reached out but couldn't touch him, and knew that she dreamed.

The third time she woke Anita and Suz were seated on either side of her bed. They were talking over her, telling stories, she realized. Stories about her.

"Excuse me, but I think all my little indiscretions should be mine to share. Not yours." Her voice came out in a croak.

"You're awake!" Anita squealed. Both women leaned forward, caught her hands.

"About bloody well time," Suz complained. "Just like you to go get yourself hurt so I'm left to go to Police Expo alone."

That brought Deena fully awake because no matter how she computed it, Police Expo had been scheduled for Labor Day and it was only the third week in August when she went after Suz and Lana. She looked from Suz to Anita.

"Explain, please, 'cause I seem to be missing some days."

"Not surprising," Suz said, looking down at her hands. When she looked back at Deena there were tears in Suz's eyes.

"We almost lost you, Deena. When that gun went off, it nicked an artery in your leg. They nearly didn't get to you in time, and by the time they got you in here you'd lost so much blood. What with emergency surgery and transfusions and then surgery on that crushed rib..."

Her voice trailed off.

"Well I guess that would explain why I feel like I've been run over by a Mac truck—twice. So how's Lana?"

Suz's smile could light up an area a hell of a lot bigger than the private room Deena occupied.

"She's fine. You know kids and resilience. She wants to know what happened to the bad men and she's asking about you all the time and wanting to know when you're coming home."

"Soon, I hope." A sudden thought came to her. "Sly! I left him at the vet's."

"Don't worry. He's getting the best of care." Suz looked at Anita conspiratorially.

Deena tried to sit up, and found she was weaker than she liked to be. The need to sleep was overwhelming, but she forced her attention to Anita.

"I assume it's you I have to thank for the cavalry?"

"Me and Rich. Who wanted to be here, by the way, but he had this court appearance he couldn't miss."

Rich. The name seemed to hang like an entity in the air. Like that mountain she could see hanging above Suz's head through the window. So near and yet so far and she was never going near him again even if he had come through.

"Just as well," Deena said and suddenly felt that loss again. She caught Anita's worried gaze.

"Anita, something you should know—it wasn't you who betrayed me to the staff—it was Mitch Digneault." She closed her eyes, exhaustion sapping her. "Listen guys, I need to sleep a while, okay?"

Anita squeezed her hand. "Thanks for telling me, Dee. Not that it's going to make any difference. I've decided life'll be a lot safer outside of corrections. Rich has offered to recommend me for a Supernumerary Special Constable position with Mission RCMP."

With that, they excused themselves and it left her alone with her thoughts of the Hat and Rich Webster. It had all been a dream, hadn't it—Rich coming to the rescue, him in the chair beside her bed.

Then the nurse came in. She was a lovely South Asian woman with the deepest, kindest brown eyes Deena thought she had ever seen.

"Look at you, all awake and chipper. Doctor said if you woke today we'd give you a try on your crutches and if you can manage then we'll spring you tomorrow. Sound good?"

"Sounds fine to me. Bring 'em on." But her voice sounded tired, even to her.

The nurse's brows twitched with a smile. "Somehow that response doesn't surprise me, but maybe we'll let you rest a bit, first," the nurse tugged up the blankets, tucked them around Deena. "You're something of a celebrity, you know."

"A celebrity."

"Your picture's been on the news—the woman who brought down a major smuggling operation."

"Me?"

"There's nobody else in the room, is there?"

Deena sank back into her pillows. Just what she needed, because somehow while she'd been sleeping she'd decided what she had to do. Sure the law might be her life, but it wasn't enough anymore. She wanted people in her life, and relationships that went beyond work, because maybe that was the only way you had a chance of figuring out who you were and being something more than your work.

She fell asleep on that thought.

After the nap, that afternoon she successfully navigated crutches under the watchful eyes of the physiotherapist, and even demonstrated prowess going up and down a set of stairs, though the effort left her exhausted. The physio pronounced her crutch-worthy and Deena fell asleep knowing she could go home.

It was Suz and Lana who picked her up in Deena's Camry. Suz was mother-hen incarnate and Lana a miniature fuss-budget that would have driven Deena crazy if the little girl hadn't been so endearingly intent on caring for her. When they had Deena in the car, Lana chattered on and on about all the things she'd been helping with at home.

It was the mention of tools that got Deena's attention.

"Tools?"

"Yes, uh huh. And I've got my very own hammer and nails and a saw and a driver-thingy and a wrench, and... and..." Lana got lost trying to remember all the names as Deena turned her attention on Suz.

"Tools, Suz?"

"Well, uh huh. What do you expect? Wasn't it you who said a woman should know how to take care of herself? A woman's got to have tools you know."

She managed to evade Deena's glare in the rearview mirror.

"You never know when you might need a good hammer or..."

"A good screw."

"Well now that you mention it, yeah." Suz was all innocence as she turned them into the driveway. Deena scanned the area. No black SUV and for a moment she was almost a little sorry. A very little, she told herself. A married Rich Webster just meant trouble.

Between Lana being an able cheering section, and Suz carrying Deena's bag and providing a steadying hand, Deena managed to climb the horrendously long set of stairs to her apartment.

When she went inside she understood the tools. The kitchen table sat in its place, the wood grain glowing with a rich patina. The lower cupboards had all been rehung and relatched in a way she recognized. As a matter of fact a certain red tool box still filled a corner of her kitchen counter.

"Don't even try to tell me you did this."

Suz pouted. "I might have."

"You're not that good."

"A woodworker?"

"A liar." Deena inspected the work. "So, you and Rich got something going now?"

Suz leaned against the counter and shook her head. "Is it really you don't get it, or are you just choosing to be obtuse?"

"So I'm obtuse now. As well as a slacker for not going to Police Expo with you."

"Well I did manage to find someone to fill in, and Anita and I seemed to do well enough even in your absence. Of course it probably helped that we could play a videotape at the kiosk of the news item with you."

"You didn't!"

"Didn't I? I want to make this business a going concern and judging by the orders that have come in, we might just have done it—if you can get out of bed and help a little by being available for publicity photos and the like. Maybe even do a little bit of work like designing some Kevlar vests for women, instead of slacking off?"

Deena swung her crutch like a club, but Suz ducked out of the way, just as a tall, very male person entered the room and hefted a little red-haired terror into his arms.

"And how's my best girl, today?"

"Shh, Uncle Rich. You'll make Aunty Dee all jealous."

"He will, huh?" Deena hopped around to face him, thinking she was going a little crazy because she could swear she heard Sly crying, but the cat was nowhere to be seen.

Rich set Lana down, then Suz and Lana were saying their goodbyes and suddenly Deena was alone with Rich. The haggard look on his face told her maybe her hazy memory of him at the hospital wasn't a dream.

It brought home the emptiness of the apartment. The fact she'd neglected to ask about Sly. And how much Deena really wanted Rich Webster in her life. But she couldn't let it happen. Again came the Sly sound and she opened her mouth to ask him about it.

His raised hand stopped her.

"Listen, I'm sorry I didn't visit yesterday but I had this thing I had to do and it turned out to take all day."

"I heard. Court. Tough case?"

He shrugged and took a step towards her and all her guards went up. Rich stopped as if he knew and pulled a folded piece of paper out of his vest pocket.

"Here. Consider it a peace offering so maybe we can start again. You wouldn't believe the strings I had to pull to get this done. Of course with Ivy's consent it made things a hell of a lot easier and having it involve a celebrity kind of helped, too."

Whatever he was talking about, it made no sense. She unfolded the paper and read.

'*Decree Nisi*,' in official court script.

A divorce. The paper slipped from her numb fingers as he closed the distance between them and caught her in his arms.

"Course we still have to wait a year for the Decree Absolute, but the worst of it is done. Ivy's got the place by the border, but I'm not paying support anymore. I can get on with my life."

She looked up at him, not sure what to say, what to do.

"I'm quitting Corrections."

His hand smoothed her hair, cupped the back of her head and he dipped his lips toward hers. Tasted and it was like wine that went right to her head.

"Nothing would make me happier," he said. "Unless it was that my tools and your tools could sort of hang around together."

"I don't have any tools." He was kissing her face now, working his way down to her throat.

"Well then maybe we'll just have to share. If I remember, we share pretty well together." He almost hummed it into the cleft of her shoulder and she felt the tingle of lust soften all of her resolve and loosen the pain. She wondered whether she could make things work, what with all of the dressings still on her body. She wouldn't mind trying.

"We do, don't we," she whispered.

He lifted his head and smiled down at her. "And I have this feeling that we'll share other things pretty well, too. Because we both know who we are. Are strong enough. We can build something together."

That made her smile.

"I'm a bit of a work in progress at the moment."

Again that cry and he must have seen the puzzlement in her face because he gave her that look she'd never forgotten all the years they'd been apart.

A little bit man, a little bit mischievous boy.

He left her and went to the apartment door and brought in a certain travel cage. When he opened it Sly scooted out and across the floor to twine around Deena's legs.

"Sly? Sly? You're okay, buddy?"

Rich came back to her, picked up the cat and the room filled with a contented purr.

"We've been roomies for the past week and have had to learn to put up with each other." Rich mussed his fur in a way that Deena knew Sly hated, but the cat just head-butted Rich's hand for more. "The subcutaneous liquids seem to be working. He hasn't been sick and he's taking food. I thought we might share this, too."

His gaze was locked on hers, the desire, the love and determination almost leaving her breathless. She accepted Sly from him, cradling her old friend at her chest, feeling the rumbling purr. She couldn't take her eyes from Rich's.

"I was terrified when I thought I'd lost you." His voice came out in a soft growl.

She wondered if her own eyes looked the same—deep, vulnerable, and filled with questions.

"I felt the same when I saw you get hit over the head. I think that's why I fought so hard. I wasn't going to let them mess with you." It was true. As true as anything she'd ever said or felt.

"Guess we're even."

"Guess so."

Right now it was enough.

ABOUT THE AUTHOR

When she isn't writing, Karen L. Abrahamson explores other cultures and countries around the world. She spent seventeen years working in Corrections before escaping to pursue writing. She is the author of literary, romantic and fantasy fiction, including the highly regarded Cartographer Universe series. She lives on the west coast of Canada with two Bengal cats that aren't quite as well traveled as she is.

If you'd like to learn more about her, visit her at www.karenlmckee.com.

BOOKS BY THE AUTHOR

Ashes and Light
Shades of Moonlight
Judas Kiss
Second Spring
A Different Nightmusic
Shadow Play
Mutable Things
Surviving Safe Harbor
Coming Down Christmas

Written as Karen L. Abrahamson

The Cartographer Universe series:
The Warden of Power

The Cartographer's Daughter

Afterburn
Aftershock
Aftermath

Terra Incognita
Terra Infirma
Terra Nueva

Also by the Author
Mutable Things
Emberstone
Ice Dragon

TWISTED ROOT PUBLISHING IS PLEASED TO PROVIDE A SNEAK PEEK OF KAREN L. ABRAHAMSON'S
Shadow Play.

Prologue

March, Phnom Penh, Cambodia

Jeremy Blackwood shook his head, ran his hands through his thinning hair, and tried to look calm and collected in the cushioned wicker chair at the bar's outdoor, glass-covered, wicker table. He sat just off the main street of Sisowath Quay, watching the night mists off the Tonle Sap River turn yellow in the long line of haloed and pulsing streetlights along the road. They could lead you on like a young man's hopes. Or an old man's.

Beneath the lights, in the sweltering heat and next to the French colonial buildings, ran the seething mass of taxis, moto-taxis, motorcycles, and cars that belched out carbon monoxide and noise. It was the perfect bedlam for this grimy strip of real estate that housed the tourist bars and guest houses, and the dissolute expat community of Phnom Penh.

Which meant it wasn't so much mist around the streetlights as air pollution.

Time to stop looking at the world through shit-tinted glasses, old boy. After all these years, things were going to change—had changed—or would once the paperwork got signed at the Ministry of Lands.

He pulled his precious canvas satchel close beside him on the table, checking the flow of people along the boulevard. Nothing to worry about. Once the paperwork was signed, he'd be gone—at least long enough to prove to Kaitlin she'd never have to work again.

In this part of the street, upriver from the crenellated golden walls of the Royal Palace and the faded glory of the Foreign Correspondents' Club, he'd left behind the well-heeled tour groups. Here, the cheapo independent tourists filled the run-down, open-air restaurants with the rowdy sounds of drinking, surrounded by shifting halos of begging orphans, working girls, touts, and taxi drivers waiting for the tourists the drinks knocked down. It made him feel old. He'd given up drinking-for-the-sake-of-drinking a while ago. All it did was keep him from focusing on what he had to do.

But he was enjoying a drink here in the hole-in-the-wall restaurant just far enough off Sisowath that the crowds looking for entertainment rarely showed.

It was what Jeremy needed, after his years up-country. He'd spent enough time in the mountains to get used to the quiet, and Phnom Penh was anything but quiet. The city rumbled like an earthquake about to happen. It was almost too much—people—noise—entertainment.

He sipped his celebratory wine and frowned at the acrid taste—Cambodia was no place for wine. Not that Kaitlin would approve of him drinking anything. Again.

But the wine was red, rich with tannins. Not bad, given Pol Pot and his gang had destroyed pretty much everything French during their reign of terror. So civilization—if you could call it that—was just coming back to the city.

And soon he would enjoy the good life. He closed his eyes and let himself sink into the wicker chair's cushion, thinking about the new life he could finance for himself, his wife, and his daughter.

And bolted upright when the hand grasped his shoulder.

"Jerry? Jerry Blackwood? That you, mate?" Spoken with a thick Aussie accent and a little too much strength in the grip of the fingers.

It took a moment, but the lined, blue-eyed face pasted on the bald, bullet-shaped head gradually formed into someone he recognized, but bigger than he remembered. Older, too. But the years hadn't shrunken this guy's muscles any. It looked like he'd gone on steroids—or maybe it was his own paranoia talking. He swallowed.

Don't want to be tossing those shit-colored glasses just yet, big guy.

"Brian Jones. Now aren't you a sight for sore eyes. Or one to cause them."

Brian grinned, but the smile didn't reach his cold blue eyes. Without invitation, he pulled out the empty chair at Jeremy's table and sat down. His black t-shirt was pulled tight over his broad chest, and his light linen jacket wasn't loose enough to hide the bulging muscles—or the gun he wore. The waitress, a petite young thing with the usual short-shorts, midriff-baring top, and head of long black hair, hurried to the table.

"Singha, sweetie." He named an Indian beer and leaned back in his chair like a crocodile eyeing its prey.

Just how did a guy close to Jeremy's fifty-two years come off looking like he was barely forty?

Jones shook his head and studied Jeremy with those flat, reptile eyes. "How long's it been, mate?"

Jeremy shrugged. The man Jeremy had first met ten years ago when he had arrived in Phnom Penh had been one of those seemingly jobless men who knew everyone. In their brief association, Jeremy had come to think of Brian Jones as a 'fixer.'

You need drugs? He could get them.

You get arrested for drugs? He could help with that, too.

You need a new backpack? A gun? A girl? Insert here what it was you wanted—and Brian Jones was the man for you. Back then, Brian had been a hard-bitten man of indeterminate age, who'd traded on his physique and square jaw to impress the ladies. He'd also been a drinking buddy.

He definitely wasn't the person Jeremy wanted to meet tonight.

"Eight, nine years."

"Nah. Longer, I think, mate. At least ten."

Jeremy nodded. The conversation lagged, and Jeremy wished he was back on Sisowath instead of this backwater eddy of a place, because the stream of tourists would at least give him something to talk about.

And witnesses.

Brian jerked his chin at the canvas satchel. The neon reflected off his shaved head.

"You been busy, I hear," he said, the neon catching the skin around his eyes and revealing deeper lines that made him look older than the almost fifty years Jeremy had given him.

The waitress brought his beer and he met Jeremy's gaze and leaned across the table. "So you want to tell me about it? Enquiring minds and all that shit…?"

The wine soured in Jeremy's stomach, and he pulled his satchel onto the floor beside him, because no one should be hearing anything about what he'd been doing. Unless he'd seriously miscalculated.

"Who're you working for, Brian?"

Brian smiled his broad, predatory smile, exposing the gap between his teeth that, at the moment, looked like a deep cave. "Let's just say a businessman, and like any businessman, he knows a good investment when he sees it."

Brian's smile faded, and behind it lurked the ruthlessness that had helped him assume a role in Phnom Penh that had existed since the Portuguese and Dutch set up shop in the city in the 1600s. The role had reached its heyday during the Vietnam War, and had resurrected itself after Pol Pot's reign came to an end. Then, as now, men sold influence through violence, and Brian was their tool.

"No one's seen anything, Brian." Except the staff at the Ministry of Lands had seen his geological survey. His stomach sank and a bead of sweat ran out of his hair and down his temple. He swiped it away, but not before Brian saw.

Jeremy didn't want to talk about it. He didn't want to talk about it here—out in the open with the two older tourist women eating at the next table and congratulating themselves about how brave they were, eating off the main tourist strip.

He shoved his wine glass away, the tannins too sour on his tongue.

But then, maybe talking here with the women around was the safe way to go. Safety in numbers and all that.

He hauled his canvas bag onto his lap. Opened it and pulled out the least of the samples he'd taken and shoved it across the table at Brian. Brian covered it with his broad palm and then lifted his hand like he was uncovering cards.

Brown rock was what it looked like—until Brian turned it over. His eyes widened a little and he casually turned it over again, hiding the small, rough, red gems poking out of the grey-brown corundum.

He nodded. "Nice looking, mate. More where that came from?"

Jeremy gave a single shrug and hated that he did. If he were a stronger man, he'd just tell Brian Jones to get lost. Hell, if he were a stronger man, he'd never be here at all. But not being stronger, he'd find a way around Brian. He'd always found the words to talk his way through problems.

Well… most of the time.

Brian slipped the sample into his pocket without asking permission, and a chill ran down Jeremy's back, even in the sweltering heat. Brian smiled that crocodile smile again: *gonna eat you, mate.*

"Then it seems we got cause for celebration, don't we? Our new partnership."

He reached over and emptied the wine bottle into Jeremy's glass. "Drink up, mate. We got places to go, people to see. Then we're going t'get rich. *Together.*"

No choice. *But you always have a choice, Dad*, Kaitlin would say. A choice and a plan.

He picked up the glass, knowing this time his daughter was wrong.

CHAPTER 1

June 1st, Phnom Penh, Cambodia

Typical. Dad *would* drag her into miserable weather. Of course, he'd dragged her into so many other dodgy situations that monsoons were probably the least of her problems.

Probably. Knowing Dad.

Kaitlin Blackwood hunched down Sisowath Boulevard. The monsoon deluge flooded the streets, pounded the sidewalk, and sent two-inch rivers running down the pavement and over her newly-purchased street hikers. It beat on the roofs of the French Colonial buildings and storefront awnings—and her head—like a drum. It pummeled the broad, silver river beyond the road so that the air filled with the cacophony of water on water that made her ears ring.

More filthy water poured in gushing torrents off rooftops and filled the air with the stench of wet dog and garbage. Come to earth it split into tributaries as she stubbornly dragged her overnight suitcase down the sidewalk-turned-river.

Another wave of street-water sprayed her. The damned taxis, motorcycles, and odd-shaped moto-taxis—motorcycles with small, covered four-seater trailers—belched exhaust as they plied their way up the river-nee-street. Their drivers' calls beat at her, as incessant as the pounding rain, "Taxi, miss? Taxi. It rain hard."

It was hard not to scream at them, but then she'd never been a screamer.

She straightened, determined to look like she knew where she was going. Yeah, it rained hard here. It rained hard in Seattle, too. Maybe not like this, but she was used to getting wet.

Of course, she had a Gore-Tex jacket there.

She tossed her head, but her mass of rain-blackened blond hair just slapped her in the face and plastered there. *Perfect. Perfect in every friggin' way, Dad. You are sooo going to hear about this. It's a good thing I love you.*

Her clothes—light t-shirt and denim capris—plastered to her, too, so the passport carry bag she wore under her clothes from a cord hung around her neck stood out like a third breast on her chest. But she was *not* taking a taxi.

It was one of the damned taxis that had deposited her at the dive of a hotel she'd spent last night at not-sleeping. They could just take her out and shoot her before she'd trust another one. In fact, she'd break her own rule—buy a gun and do it herself—before she'd trust anyone in this stupid country again.

Locals and tourists wore cheap, see-through rain slickers and dodged around her like the rain didn't matter. She'd buy one, but she was so soaked now, what difference would it make? Besides, buying one would require energy to communicate across the language barrier. Energy she didn't have.

She waded northward on Sisowath—at least she thought it was northward. As jet-lagged as she was, she wasn't sure of much except that the darned taxi driver had pointed this way along the street last night when she'd asked him about the address.

She looked down at the soggy note in her hand. Ink pooled on the paper and ran onto her fingers. By the numbers on the restaurants and bars and tourist shops, the place she was looking for should be right around here. At least she thought so. She paused for a moment, studying the numbers and wiping rain out of her eyes.

Yes, it should be.

A petite female shopkeeper wielded a broom to keep the water out of her trinket shop and a tidal wave rolled across Kaitlin's feet right up to her ankles.

Perfect. Just perfect. Kaitlin sighed.

The shopkeeper said something that might have been an apology, but then again it probably was more like get out of the rain you stupid woman, and while you're at it, get out of my country.

More than happy to. In fact, she'd be downright ecstatic.

If she could just find the darned address. And her father. Then she'd give him a piece of her mind and be on the next plane out of this stupid country. Cambodia. *Now I ask you?*

A tug on her suitcase turned her around and she found herself facing a man. Cambodian — she thought. Oriental at least. Five foot eight?

Shorter than her five foot ten, at least, and dressed in a khaki-colored shirt and trousers that even in this deluge looked pressed.

But his hand was holding the handle of her suitcase and all her *internal* alarms went off. Another taxi tout?

His black gaze met hers. And then he smiled, exposing a mouth of blackened teeth that made her skin crawl, but in a country like this, dental hygiene couldn't be what it was in America.

"You are lost, Miss? Perhaps I can help. Perhaps you need a hotel. Or a taxi."

Kaitlin jerked her suitcase a little closer, but the darned guy didn't release it. "I'm fine. Thanks. I'm just looking for an address, but it has to be near here."

"What is the name and I will help you?"

She rolled her eyes. Couldn't these guys figure out she wanted to be left alone?

"All right. I'm looking for the Mayview Hotel."

"Ahh, yes. That one. Is good, but not as good as my place. You have a look, okay?"

That blackened smile again, and it frankly turned her stomach, but she supposed the poor guy couldn't help it.

"It is on the way to Mayfair. Come."

She hesitated—but it would be good to get there and out of the rain. Finally she nodded. "The Mayview," she corrected.

"This way, please." He caught her wrist with strong fingers and started to lead her back the way she'd come.

"I've been that way," she said.

"Mayfair sit on different road and my place this way. We go my car."

She stopped. The internal alarms jangled again. Something wasn't right. "The address I have is for Sisowath Quay. And it's the Mayview."

"No. No. No. Mayfair — it move."

The blackened smile again, but his eyes didn't match.

"No. It move."

The lack of expression reminded her of a young Disciple gangbanger she'd interviewed for a story back home. The guy had come across as a psychopath in her estimation. And the story she'd written for the *Post Intelligencer* had earned her a credible enough death threat she'd had police checking on her for six months. The gang member had turned up dead in a prison hit not long after.

And this guy's eyes were just as dead to emotion. And now that she listened to her instincts, the cut of his clothing just didn't fit a tout. Or a taxi driver. It had a military cut to it.

She tried to ease her hand free. "I don't think I need any help, thanks."

He didn't release her.

Internal air-raid sirens klaxoned through her head. She tried to twist loose, but he didn't release her.

"Dammit, let go!"

He half-dragged her toward the street corner. If he got her off the Sisowath Quay, who knew what would happen. The question was what to do? All the self-defense training seemed to disappear.

So she kicked him.

His grip only tightened.

She could stomp on his foot if she could find it under all this water. She could slam the heel of her hand into his nose. She could....

"Bloody hell, mate. The lady doesn't look like she wants to go with ya."

A booming voice that was weirdly familiar, but then she was rattled. And the voice spoke English like a native speaker, even if it held a thick Aussie accent.

She ripped loose, grabbed her suitcase, and ran.

"Hey!" The Aussie voice she hadn't even thanked, but she needed to get out of here. Some place where she understood what was going on. A place where she could figure things out.

She splashed back the way she'd come. Past the hotels. Past the bars. Past the trinket shop where the woman had drenched her shoes. A set of clean stairs in a yellow-and-white painted building came up on her left. A brass sign read *Foreign Correspondents' Club*.

Well she sure was foreign. And a journalist.

She almost ran up the two flights of stairs, her suitcase bang-bang-banging behind her, and she hated the panic pounding in her chest. Not like her. Not like her at all, dammit.

She was cool. She was Kaitlin Blackwood, crime reporter, friend of district attorneys, lawyers, gang-bangers, and mob bosses alike.

It had to be the jet lag that left her feeling as fractured as some gothic romance heroine. And the fact that she hadn't planned for things like what had happened in the street. If you could plan things, you could be prepared.

At the top of the stairs waited a large open-air space with broad ceiling fans futilely turning the rain-soggy air that came in through the room's two open sides that overlooked the streets and the Tonle Sap River. A high counter ran the perimeter of the room to allow patrons to partake of the view, and the open space was filled with low tables and well-worn, low-slung chairs. An actual bar sat against the wall next to the top of the stairs, and a door to the rear gave a view of the rain-darkened tiered roofs of a magnificent building of ancient Cambodian structure.

She sank down into an ancient leather chair that smelled of years of cigarette smoke and spilled beer and dug her fingers into the scarred armrest. She closed her eyes and regretted the people moving around her. The darned migraine that had been coming on since just before her plane landed sat like a sniper just back of her eyes. If she didn't get some rest soon, it was going to catch her right in the forehead and then she'd be down for a day at least.

Another gift from her father dragging her half way around the world. She fumbled her note pad and a pencil out of her purse to make a new list.

"May I help you?"

She looked up to a slim young Cambodian man in a pale yellow uniform standing above her. Beyond him the huge ceiling fans churned the humid air, and outside the open-sided room, the sheets of rain still fell.

"Tonic water and lemon, please." The sun wasn't over the yardarm yet, so no booze, though, frankly, a little alcohol would probably go down good now. In the face of the neatly clad waiter, she tried smoothing her sodden shirt and capris, but only succeeded in sending a new runnel of water onto the leather chair and the floor. Drowned rat wasn't the half of it. Her hands were frigging shaking! But the voices of the people behind her were like hammers on pipes in her head, and booze was never good with a headache like this coming on.

"Very good." The server wandered away and she took a deep breath.

The restaurant/bar had none of the feel of her favorite haunts back home. No photojournalist's shots on the walls. No framed newspaper tear sheets. None of the feel of dust and dirt and old smoke and crime that went with most reporters' haunts. Instead, pale yellow walls held a few photos of Angkor, and to either side of her along the rail to the street, a few young tourists and a couple of older expats sat, singly and in small groups, getting quietly drunk.

But the low tables and leather chairs must have been a pretty nice spot to wait out the Vietnam War. For some. A view of the river and none of the bombs that fell on Saigon.

She shook her head. She never had understood the call of the wild that made people become foreign correspondents when there was so much to report back home. She looked back at her note pad, trying to decide where to start.

Find hotel. And find her father. Go home. Pretty basic. What else did she need?

The young server returned and smoothly plunked the drink amid the water marks on the low wooden table, then left without even a smile. Not exactly the kind of service she was used to, but at least a twist of lemon floated amongst the ice.

She sipped, and it was a godsend of cool in the overwhelming heat and humidity. She sweated, even though her clothes still stuck to her from the rain. And her hands had barely stopped shaking.

Darn it, what was going on with her? She'd had close calls before.

But none so far from house and home.

And home was what she was going to lose if she didn't find her dad and get home. Mac could only keep the publisher happy with guest columnists for so long, before they started thinking about giving someone else her column space.

And if that happened, her dad would have put her in a worse position than he had so many times before. She'd just dug herself out of the debt he'd put her in when, unbeknownst to her, he used *her* condo as collateral for a loan on a boat he'd decided he was going to sail to South America.

Of course, he'd sunk the damn thing somewhere off the tip of Baja and she was left paying. And paying. She picked up the bill for the tonic water. Three-fifty. Three-fifty flippin' U.S. dollars for a drink in this flippin' country with none of the comforts of home.

"And I'm still flipping paying."

"Well, if that's a problem, I s'pose I could help ya out. Can't have a pretty lady drinking with the flies, now can we? Course maybe she could buy me a drink fer helpin' her out…."

The suggestion came in thick rolling round vowels that were a tad thickened with liquor, but she was pretty sure it was the same voice she'd heard in the street. The voice of her savior and she shouldn't be ungrateful, but the slow Aussie drawl sent a jab of migraine pain right into her left eyeball. She refused to turn around, because making eye contact was where the trouble always began. Strangers could move right in on you and she really just needed to recover right now.

Out of the corner of her eye, a strong arm rested on the wooden arm of another of the worn leather chairs. Sun-bleached, blond hairs curled on its tanned and freckled back. Strong fingers curled around a sweating glass of beer. They were long. Almost artistic.

The kind of hand she always found attractive.

She looked away. Mac might not be her 'type,' but they were an item. He was a great guy. Stable. Just what she needed, not that she'd let it advance beyond dating. But she might.

Besides, Aussies were trouble.

"Thanks, but no thanks. But I'll buy you that drink for the help in the street. It was appreciated." She waved at the waiter and pointed at the Aussie's table without even glancing at it. There. Duty done. He should get the message.

Another sip of the tonic and the tension started to dissolve out of her shoulders. Too bad her clothes wouldn't dry just as fast.

"Yer lookin' a mite put out. Guy scared you, did he?"

Dammit, he wasn't going to let go and it wasn't true. She was capable. She didn't need saving. But he did deserve a thank you.

"Thanks, but I don't need any company. I'd prefer to be alone." She sipped her drink—well, maybe more of a gulp. Just finish and get out of here and find the Mayview.

"Now that's a sad tale, ain't it, lovely lady wants to be alone."

That was it. Enough, even if he'd helped her out. She turned her cold-blooded glare on him for an instant, then turned away.

"I *said*, no thank you." A slick of ice had crept into her voice.

"B.J., I think the lady wants to be left alone." A clipped British accent that seemed harsh after the lazy, rolling Aussie.

Thank you, lord. She almost looked at her defender, but something stopped her. Something he'd said. And her brief glance registered.

Oh-friggin-no....

She looked over again, into a boozy set of mocking blue eyes she had thought—no, make that hoped—never, ever, to see again.

ROMANCE AND HIGH ADVENTURE FROM KAREN L. ABRAHAMSON

If you enjoyed this book, you might enjoy other
titles from
Karen L. Abrahamson in your local bookstore or
wherever e-books are sold.
www.karenlabrahamson.com